ENSNARED

The Dragon Captured, Book One

BRIDGET E. BAKER

For my darling Isadora

Not all warriors carry swords.
Some of them ride warhorses and use
their words to slay dragons instead.
They're just as fierce and just as noble.

Slay on, girl.

PROLOGUE

My dad graduated first in his class in economics at Stanford. He was the youngest person at Harvard Business School, and he irons his sheets. He's uptight, exacting, and brilliant. Meanwhile my mom's a psychic who often keeps her hair in dreads because it's more environmentally friendly not to wash it very often. She wears sarongs, and she does henna tattoos as a side gig, and she believes crystals carry energies that alter the aura of the people and the room around them.

They could not possibly be more different.

When Dad met Mom, she was reading people's futures at one of his company events. She was a curiosity. A party entertainer.

Nothing.

But Dad and Mom were drawn to one another like opposing magnets—I was conceived the night of that stupid party, apparently. Cue my retching.

From that day forward, they took things one day at a time.

No one that either of them knew or loved thought

they would work. Heck, I didn't even think they'd stay together. They regularly fight like dry lightning strikes on a hot summer night, and it's usually over something stupid, like what to do with the snake who ate one of our chicken's fake eggs. Dad, of course, wants to kill it with a hoe and be done with it. Mom insists on spending the next two days nursing it and calling every rescue from here to Waco.

But even more fiercely than they fight, they *love* passionately and with every part of their being.

Maybe that's *why*.

Maybe that's the reason that, of all the people in the universe I might love, I'm falling for the absolute worst. I'm falling for the man—a beast—sent to slay everyone I know. The prince of the dragons, the creatures who invaded our earth with no regard for our past, our present, or our future.

I should be plotting his demise, but with every moment that passes, my resolve crumbles. And all I can think is that it's my parents' fault, because it must be in my DNA. Opposites really do attract, apparently.

How can I save the world when I'm falling for the powerful, savage being capable of utterly destroying it?

Fear makes men forget, and skill that cannot fight is useless. -Brasidas of Sparta

I was a very fearful child. Sometimes people don't believe me when I tell them that, because who would believe that an up-and-coming UFC fighter could only sleep with the lights turned on when she was seven years old?

After enduring my sobbing fits for months, my parents decided to put me into martial arts. Mom hoped learning to defend myself properly might eliminate some of the fear. Dad just thought taking a few punches might toughen me up.

I started with kendo, because I wanted to hold a weapon and a sword felt like a good one. To this day, fighting with a sword in my hand has always been my favorite. It quickly became apparent that, although fear had brought me into the ring, it was the *absence* of fear I felt in the heat of a fight that allowed me to excel.

See, most people, and by most, I mean quite a bit more than ninety-nine point nine percent of people, when they're punched, experience an acute stress response—their sympathetic nervous system goes haywire, basically. This causes tunnel vision, loss of hearing, and a short-circuit of all critical body systems. It renders you unable to think at all, much less respond to the danger that's right in front of you.

But the rare one in less than ten thousand people. . .just don't.

Most people don't even know whether this might be them, because not very many people in this day and age actually get punched in the face. For most people, the only way to deal with the acute stress response is to work to condition it out with enough time and training. In such a way, when trauma or stress strikes, you can often power through.

Mostly.

But when your opponent's trash talking, threatening, and intimidating you, when the audience is jeering and shouting, and when that first blow slams into your jaw, it often takes over in spite of your best efforts.

And that's where I have a serious edge.

If you've ever seen Conor McGregor fight, you'll know how someone like me looks. Even after a fight with months and months of trash talking and lead time, he waltzes into the ring calm and relaxed. His timing remains flawless. His reflexes are consistent, because unlike a normal human, he's genuinely not stressed. His nervous system is fully functioning and ready to respond to any hits that come his way. It's the reason his timing and accuracy are consistent. It's the reason he consistently wins.

And like McGregor, in spite of my terror at night,

in spite of my bad dreams, when I'm confronted with a terrible foe, I remain calm. Actually, I usually focus better. My reflexes heighten. My senses sharpen. My brain kicks into overdrive.

My perfect track record in UFC matches, the fact that there are way more men at my gym than women, and the fact that most women can't keep up with me means that I spar with men more often than not. It's certainly true today, though this is the third time I've taken someone down in under three minutes. I release my rear naked choke, which was way too easy to get, and drop Holden on the mat.

"What's going on?" I kick his hip, not savagely, just enough to make sure he's listening. "Why aren't you going hard?" I spin around, looking at the guys who are watching. "You too, Javi. You barely even tried to avoid the armbar."

Javi looks away.

When I look back at Holden, he won't meet my eye either.

Now I'm royally ticked. "I have to fight in just under two weeks. Coach is about to cut to just training and no sparring, and now's when you girls decide to go easy on me?" I swear under my breath, getting ready to pummel the next guy within an inch of his lousy life.

"It's not our fault," Holden mutters.

"What does that mean?" My eyes narrow.

"Nothing," Holden says.

"Shut up." Javi mouths something angrily. "Idiot."

So someone's telling them to go easy on me. . .but who would dare? Everyone knows how much this next fight matters to my career. It's almost a miracle Coach even got me the fight, and it's being broadcast on prime time. My opponent, Gisele Costa, is technically way above my paygrade. I need to bring my A-game, and that means training my very hardest.

Why would anyone at my gym want me to fail?

Maybe I'm asking the wrong question. There aren't many people all these guys would listen to, other than Coach Sousa. In fact, I can only think of one.

"Gideon!"

He's sparring across the gym, but both he and his opponent freeze, so I know they heard me.

"Gideon Evans, get over here right now."

He ignores me.

Fine. I'll go to him. I hop out and jog toward the corner where he's still holding Frank's wrist. Javi, and Holden, and Isaac take my departure as their cue to leave, ducking out the back door before I've even reached Gideon's ring.

Frank wrenches his hand free and moves away as I hit the edge of the ring and swing up. He ducks out nearly as fast as the other guys did.

"What's going on?" Coach Sousa was wrapping an ankle in his office, but he must have abandoned that. He's nearly reached the edge of our octagon.

"Gideon told the guys to take it easy on me." I cross my arms. "And I want to know why."

"He's your biggest supporter," Sousa says. "He wants you to win as much as the rest of us. . ." I notice he's not saying Gideon didn't tell them to ease up.

And we can both see the set of Gideon's jaw and the flashing of his eyes.

"Tell me it's not true," I say. "Tell me you didn't."

Gideon shrugs. "So what if I did? Getting injured before your fight won't help you."

"But if I don't train well enough, I'll get injured worse later, with everyone watching."

"You're already great at holds," Gideon says. "Javi's

a boxer, and Holden's kicks are infamous. If one of them broke—"

I'm done listening. He took my decent partners, so he can take their place. I spin a kick toward him without thinking, and it lands hard on his shoulder.

"Whoa," Coach Sousa says.

But it's too late for him to stop us. I'm furious, and Gideon looks nearly as angry. We've been in school together since I started kindergarten and trained together since I was seven years old and he was eight. He has always thought he knows better than I do, and I'm heartily sick of it.

He's had a few big wins, just like I have. He has a few decent sponsors, just like I do. He's tall, just like I am, only, tall for him is four inches over six feet. Tall for me is an inch shy of six feet. Still, by the percentages, I'm more impressive than he is.

Like me, Gideon's not afraid to take a punch. When he fights, he's relaxed, calm, and focused. My holds and kicks are better than his, but his strikes are much stronger than mine. Luckily, I'm fast enough to evade the force behind most of them.

His left hook's famous, and it's coming right at me. I shift slightly, and then I elbow the inside of his wrist, throwing him off balance. His hook glances, but it still stings.

That's part of the reason we train. Even without fear, we still have to learn to deal with pain and move through it. Now that I'm inside his guard, an elbow to his gut causes him to fold inward, which gives me the opening I need to go for an armbar.

"I thought we agreed you weren't doing these." Gideon's low tone is a little too close to a whisper, maybe because it's right in my ear.

"We agreed on *nothing*," I say. "But even if we did,

that was before you started giving people orders behind my back."

"Why do you think I did that?"

I put more pressure on his arm, realizing belatedly that he's not even trying to get loose. "Hey." I knee him. "Fight."

"Fight what?" he asks. "You got me."

I'm actually angry enough that I want to break it. He's doing the same thing he ordered them to, not going full-on. Instead of doing something monumentally stupid, I throw his arm away and stand up in disgust. "Why?" I kick his side as hard as I can. "Why aren't you trying?"

"Last month, Holden broke your nose." He stretches and bounces lightly. "Last week, Javi gave you a black eye."

And I'm swearing under my breath again. "That's the game, Gideon. It's how it works. You know that better than anyone."

He drops his voice and ducks his head. "Well, maybe it's different for me."

"What dumb crap are you saying?"

"Alright, you two. My office." Coach Sousa looks ticked, and when he's that mad, we can't ignore him. He's been known to cancel fights, or worse, sub another fighter in your place.

Gideon stops in front of the office and waves me in. I kick him as I pass. Stupid jerk, acting like he's all chivalrous. Coach Sousa closes the door, which is basically a red flag to the entire gym that stuff's about to go down.

"Alright. What's going on?" I ask.

"I can't keep watching you get hurt," Gideon says. "Don't get mad at me for trying to help."

"*Help?* I'm a fighter, not some elderly lady who bought too many groceries." I slam a fist into his stomach as hard as I can. "It's not helping, you jerk. We go hard so we can win. Your idiocy might cost me the fight."

He barely grunts, and then pushes past me and sits in a chair, like nothing even happened.

Coach reams us for fighting on the floor, and tells us how we set the example for the other fighters, yada yada. It's nothing that we haven't heard before. But then, he stops.

He yelled at both of us.

Like I was the problem. "Did you *hear* what he did?" My hand's itching to punch Coach in the stomach, now. "He told the guys—"

"Liz." Coach Sousa grits his teeth.

"What?" I look from Coach to Gideon and back again. "What am I missing here? Or did the two of you suddenly break misogynist for no reason?"

Coach Sousa sighs. "I have to tell her now—that's on you."

Gideon exhales.

"His next fight, the one the week after yours, is Gideon's last." Coach Sousa's words are flat, his mouth a grim line.

"What?" My eyes fly to Gideon's face. "What's he talking about?"

Gideon shrugs. "My heart's not in it anymore."

"No way," I say. "I don't buy it."

He shrugs. "It doesn't really matter whether you do or not."

"Our finest fighter is *enlisting*." Coach Sousa spits on the floor. His voice goes up when he says, "Special ops."

Why would Gideon do that now, when he's finally on top?

My oldest friend—my self-appointed nanny—doesn't give me any kind of answer. He just stands up and heads for the door.

I'm left scrambling after him. "Hey, whoa!" I grab his shoulder just outside the office. Everyone in the gym's watching, but I can't bring myself to care.

"What?" Gideon spins around, his dark blue eyes flashing. "You gonna tell me I can't enlist? Are you my mom, now?"

"Umm," I say. "You're the one who kept telling people what they could do with me."

"Why do you think I'm quitting after all this time, Liz?"

That's what I can't fathom. He's so close to breaking through! He could be the world champion in under a year if he keeps pushing and gets lucky. Why would he throw it all away?

"Think about it." His lip curls up into a half smile, and his voice drops to a low, husky rumble that only I can hear. "Think really, really hard, you idiot."

"You said your heart's not in it," I say, "but you love fighting."

"I need a cause," he whispers. "I don't feel like I have that anymore, but there's another reason. My real reason." His eyes meet mine, and I've never seen them look quite so intense, not even in the ring.

"Is your family alright?"

He waves his hand through the air, like he's shoving that thought away. "Fine." He points at me. "But you are denser than I thought."

"I am?" Why's my heart galloping?

He steps toward me, and for some inexplicable

reason, I back up. He steps closer, and I scramble backward again. He repeats that move, again and again, until my back hits the wall.

Finally, he says, "We can't date anyone at the gym. That's always been the rule." His voice is still low—clear, strong, but low, the volume turned up just loud enough for me.

"Okay." Something inside my belly twists.

"I've hated that rule for years, Elizabeth. Tell me you haven't."

My mouth goes dry. Is he saying. . . For years there's been *something* between us, yes. It's not like I never noticed. But like he said, we can't date. We're both focused on our careers. He's been the best friend I've needed, and he's been a constant force in my life.

"I got sick of waiting," he says. "So I'm not going to do it anymore."

"But you'll be—"

"I'll be in training for six months," he says. "And after that, I'll be on one- and two-month missions. I negotiated for that. It turns out, when you have some skills, you have something called leverage, even with the federal government."

"But—"

His head drops toward mine, his eyes staring at my mouth. "Tell me you understand, Elizabeth. In three weeks, we won't be at the same gym anymore."

I swallow. "I do."

"You think it's the right call, too."

"But—"

His hand slams against the wall, inches from my head. "You agree. Say it."

I look up at him, immediately realizing my mistake. His deep blue eyes. His locked jaw. The sweat beaded on his brow. His hair, falling across his face. It's too much. "I agree," I whisper.

His smile's devilish, and his presence is intoxicating. He leans even closer, so that only a hairsbreadth separates my mouth from his. "Three weeks, Liz."

I'm not sure I can survive them.

Boo Bash.

It's actually a cute name. Every single time I've called home for the past month and change, it's been the only thing my six-year-old brother has wanted to talk about. Apparently the Boo Bash is a huge school carnival to which everyone wears costumes.

Sammy wanted me to match him, but there was no way I was showing up as Ben Ten's cousin Gwen. Luckily, he agreed I could wear my MMA attire and gloves, and come as myself, essentially. Blocking off time a week and a half before my fight was hard enough. A ready-made costume was a major plus.

I shouldn't really be here at all. Sousa will kill me if I eat so much as a handful of candy. If I hadn't promised Sammy, I wouldn't be tempting fate, but as the youngest child in a family with four children, he's let down a lot. I don't want to be the cause of any additional disappointment for the little guy.

"You're here!" Sammy's face lights up when he sees

me. With his speech delay, it sounds more like, "yow heyah!"

"I said I'd come."

When he races toward me, I hold out my arms, my hands snagging him underneath his armpits and swinging him around. I can't believe he's wearing a jacket in this weather—seventy degrees. Typical Texas fall—but Ben Ten is known by that green jacket with the stripe and number.

The second I set him down, he's jabbering again. "When I said my sister beat people up for her job, Jackson said I was lying," he says, which sounds like 'wying.'

"Where's this Jackson?" I ask. "I think he needs a punch on the nose."

"Lizzie!" Mom's familiar voice behind me has me spinning around for a hug.

Nothing can really prepare someone for the sheer force of my mother. First I hear the schlepping sound of her flip flops, and then the smell of patchouli slams into my olfactories like a fly swatter. Last but not least, her arms wrap around me and *squeeze*. For a small, slender woman, she really knows how to commit to a hug.

Most people think I take after my dad—discipline, restraint, insane dedication—but they don't see the real core of who my mother is. She's stronger than anyone I know, and she'd do anything in the world for her family. Once, my vegetarian, save-the-planet mother actually punched a guy who was harassing the girls at the outdoor eating area of a Jimmy Chang's Mexican restaurant. Her solid right cross sent him flying backward into the painted monkey on the brick wall. Dad thought the guy was gonna sue, but I guess he wasn't keen on telling people that a tiny woman had beaten him up.

"I'm so glad you could come," Mom whispers, "but don't punch any of Sammy's friends, no matter how irritating or rude they are, alright?"

As if she needs to remind me of that. "My hands are licensed as deadly weapons," I say. "I promise not to use them in any way at an elementary school carnival."

"Thank goodness." She releases me.

I finally take in what she's wearing. "Sammy said we all had to come in costume." I arch one eyebrow. "You just came as yourself?"

"I'm a fortune teller. That's a legitimate costume for most people." She shrugs. "You came in your normal workwear, too, so you're one to talk." She gestures toward what looks like an enormous, human-sized rubber band launcher. "Coral and Jade are the cutest hippies you've ever seen. They're both over there waiting in line to do the bungee jump again, or I'd show you."

Oh my word. The school carnival has a bungee jump? "I can practically see Sousa's eyes bug out right now at the whiff of a thought that I might try that."

"You should. You only get one life." Mom's mantra for as long as I've known her. "Just don't do anything I wouldn't do."

Which rules out precisely nothing. "Thanks, Mom."

Sammy's pulling on my hand pretty hard now. "Jackson's this way."

I've been his go-to bully shield for years. It's sad that a six-year-old has *needed* a bully eliminator for years, but preschoolers aren't nice to little kids with speech delays. They used to say he sounded like a monkey right in front of him, as if his speech delay meant he also couldn't hear. Or, probably more likely, as if they didn't care what he thought or felt, because he was different from them.

I usually try to remember to give kids a pass—it's their parents I should probably blame. Some adults don't bother teaching manners to their children, because they don't have any themselves. They should be ashamed of the things they say and do, but instead, they're modeling to make kids just like them. Luckily, this Jackson kid turns out to be your average loud-mouth who doesn't think, and after just a few insistent explanations, he and Sammy seem to be fine.

An hour and twelve carnival games later, a fun-size Snickers is calling my name. I'm still not sure why they call them *fun* size. There's nothing fun about one bite, but it's better than no bites. I'm seriously wondering how much sugar it would take before I'd get sluggish at tomorrow morning's stair run when I recognize Jade's cry for help.

Thanks to my training, I'm good at dealing with rushes of adrenaline. It only takes me two seconds to locate her—bouncing up and down on the bungee line. She's still shouting, but she's laughing now, too.

Coral's dying laughing beside the line, having already gone again herself. You'd think, since Jade had already gone twice just like Coral, she wouldn't shriek so much. The two of them are only a year apart, but they manage to be opposite souls in almost every way. Luckily, they're still thick as thieves, almost inseparable most days. I actually feel sorry for Sammy. There's no one in our family close to his age, which I know all about, and Coral and Jade are usually playing girly things with no interest in modifying to include him.

Mom catches my eye and shakes her head from where she's stuck, manning the bake sale goods. Luckily, I know just what she means, because less than thirty seconds later, the girls ask me for money to do the bungee just one more time. "Mom already said no," I say. "She's worried you'll get sick."

"I won't get sick," Coral says with a sigh. Then her eyes cut sideways.

"Hey, I won't either," Jade says.

Which we all know is probably not true. She's a lightweight in all senses of the word. "Regardless, the answer's no. You've gotten to fly through the air several times. Now, gather up your little bags, and let's get ready to go."

"But we haven't bobbed for donuts yet," Jade says.

"It's not over. People are still playing." Sammy sticks out his bottom lip, but I can tell it's a manipulation this time.

"I want to do the cakewalk," Coral says. "I can win for sure."

"One round of the cakewalk," I finally say. "If we don't leave early, we'll get stuck in the parking lot for half an hour."

"So?" Sammy asks.

I ruffle his hair. "Oh, shut up."

We all head for the cakewalk in a little herd. When I was younger, it used to bother me sometimes that I had so many younger siblings. But now that they're all out of diapers, and I'm not home as much to help out around the house, I'm glad Mom and Dad had so many.

"And are you cake-walking too?" The woman who's waving all three kids through looks at me expectantly.

"Oh, sure," I say. "I'll give it a go."

Coral bumps me out on round one, snaking my chair just before I can sit. She shrugs and smiles and tosses her head, indicating that I should get out of the circle.

Jade gets cut before Sammy by some exuberant older boy, but the little guy only makes it another round or two. It's down to just Coral and two very obnoxious boys who seem to be planning to work together to squish her out when I hear it.

It's a strange sound, like a helicopter that had its tail stepped on. A whirring, shrill whine. It's coming from above us, but it's a bright afternoon in Houston, so I have to shield my eyes to make out anything at all. When I finally make sense of the genesis of that strange noise, my brain rejects it.

It can't really be a massive, silver dragon.

It has a large head with a triangular face and horns that curve back from right above its huge eyes. The scales covering its body glitter in the sun, like burnished sterling. Its neck curves, long and graceful, its limbs nevertheless broad and massive, and it moves in a very serpentine way, its wings beating wildly as it lowers toward the Boo Bash.

Maybe it's an elaborate display, because *dragons aren't real*.

Only, I can feel the wind created by the beating of its wings. I can hear the crooning it's emitting as it lowers toward us. And when I blink, it doesn't disappear or distort like an illusion would. When it lands on the roof at the edge of the school, the brick structure disintegrates, chunks rolling and then striking the ground below. Its enormous claws crush metal and concrete alike, further damaging the school just to hold up its massive form. One particularly large piece of rubble strikes an older man on the head, and he crumples to the ground.

By now, I'm not the only one who's noticed the new arrival, and a few people are running, screaming, away from it. That's probably what I should be doing, honestly, but I'm too shocked to run. I'm still trying to wrap my brain around what I'm seeing.

I'm here for you, says a horrible, sepulchral voice in my head that I somehow know is the dragon. It's cold, it's high, and it's piercing. *You, who can hear me. Come to me, and I'll spare the others. Make me locate you, and I'll destroy them all for fun.*

I look around to see who else can hear it. Everyone else around me is now sprinting away or covering their ears. Sammy dives for me, wrapping his arms around my waist and staring, wide-eyed, at the silver beast. Coral's holding Jade's hand, and they're both fumbling their way back toward me. No one seems to have heard a thing.

I know you're here. I sense you. I'll count to ten, and then I'll start to destroy them, all the humans, until you yield.

When I finally find my mom, she's staring right at me. Her eyes are wide and frightened, but her head's held high. She taps her chest, tosses her head sideways at the silver dragon, and then she points at me and mouths the words, "You take the kids and keep them safe."

Keep them safe? What's she saying? Why wouldn't she—

I hear you. I'm coming. It's my mom's voice. I'd recognize it anywhere. She just answered the beast.

Mom's avoiding the fleeing crowds as she winds her way toward the edge of the school. The creature's staring right at her, its eyes gleaming, the corner of its mouth turned up into something almost like a smile. It bobs its head.

I am Ocharta, Strike Blessed. I have need of you.

Mom bows.

And then I feel a tug—a painful pull, like someone has coated me in a sticky film from the scalp of my head down to the webbing between my toes, and they're *pulling*, hard. I double down, close my eyes, set my feet, and push back against it with everything I've got.

As suddenly as it happens, the tugging stops, but when I open my eyes, Mom's standing stock still. She looks the same, except for her hair. She always had gorgeous, nearly black hair. It shone like the wing of a raven. It was long, falling in thick, unruly waves past her waist. It's still long and wavy, but now it's changed to a metallic shade of grey that sparkles in the setting sunlight. That's when I realize that it exactly matches the dragon's scales.

Mom turns around, slowly, and her eyes cut toward mine.

Go! Mom shouts again, but this time she's commanding me to leave.

The beast lets out a shriek, and then it launches into the air. Suddenly, it's swooping and diving, and as it passes, crackles of electricity shoot from its body, striking entire groups of people.

I pick up Sammy, and I grab Jade's hand, and I run.

❧ 3 ☙

It's an awful thing to think, but all the idiots who stopped to get in their cars might have been what saved us. They kept the beast busy while we escaped.

I make the kids keep their eyes trained ahead of us, but I turn back around and watch as the creature fries car after car full of people. It doesn't even stop to eat them or anything. It just keeps on flying, attacking, and killing.

In cartoons, dragons look regal. They look majestic. They look inspirationally beautiful. The cartoons have it all wrong. As we're racing for our lives, I can't help thinking about this fluffy grey stuffed animal I got as a kid. It made hippos look adorable, like they'd be your pal. The first time I saw one up close at a zoo, I realized that real hippos weren't cute or fluffy, and they would destroy me for fun. Hippos are horrifying, and by comparison to this nightmare, a hippo's a frothy beachside drink. The dragon looks almost maniacal as it massacres every man, woman, and child who took the time to unlock and climb into their car.

I wish I had a spear. I'd head back there right now and try to stop it.

Or maybe not.

I do have three siblings to protect.

The second we've put some space between us and the beast, I whip out my phone and start tapping as we move. I type in dragon attack, and then I hit search. We're still moving, but I'm exhausted, and I'm sure Coral and Jade are even worse off. It's a miracle they aren't crying or complaining. I guess fear's an exceptional motivator.

I wait, but my phone just spins and spins.

I try dialing my dad next. He's out of town—business trip to New York City this time, I think—but the call won't connect. I'm assuming that means the cell towers are down.

That probably means there's more than one dragon. Our house is about two miles from the school, and I think we've gone at least a half mile, so I'm hoping we can make it there without being discovered. It's not like it's super safe or anything, but at least we might have access to the internet. There should be some kind of directions from the government about what to do in situations like this. We have a generator, so we should have power if we have a connection, and if there's any information out there, I'm going to get it.

That's when I see something so bone-numbingly horrifying that it stops me dead in my tracks.

An enormous red dragon, much, much larger than the silver creature from the school, is flying through the clouds overhead. He roars, and the sound makes me want to curl up into a fetal position and cry. His wings beat steadily as he sweeps past, and then he swoops downward, toward the massive neighborhood right behind the school.

A river of fire pours from his mouth and engulfs the tiny, cookie-cutter homes in an ocean of flames.

Jade shrieks.

I clap a hand over her face and push them to move faster. Heading for our house still doesn't feel like much of a plan, but I'm not sure what else to do. We need to get out of Houston and quick, and our home must be the best place to get provisions. I start making plans in my head for what to pack. The girls can't carry much, and Sammy won't be able to carry anything at all. Socks. Shoes. A blanket. Maybe some photos.

I think about Mom then, and I want to sit down and cry.

What's happening? In my wildest nightmares, dragons never played a part. My breathing picks up as I think of all the people burning. All the people who were electrocuted. My mother who was taken.

There's no way to know what the next five minutes hold, let alone tomorrow, and no matter how tough a fighter I am, I can't fight something that size that creates torrents of lava. I glance upward again, but I don't see him. The massive red beast is gone for now, at least.

Although, I suppose that means he could be anywhere at all.

Fear grips me, slowing my steps and freezing my limbs. Jade starts to whimper. Sammy's crying, and even Coral has tears streaming silently down her cheeks.

I mentally slap myself.

They can't afford for me to fall apart. I have to hold it together, because I'm all they have. A strange sort of peace steals over me then. I'll either navigate a way through this, or we'll all perish. But by golly, it won't be because I didn't try my hardest. If any human on earth is going to survive this, it should be me.

I may look fluffy, but I pack a punch.

"We'll get home soon, guys," I say. "We'll pack bags, and we'll get somewhere safe."

"Where are we going?" Coral asks.

"Why can't we just stay at home?" Jade whimpers. "We can lock the doors, and I think that's where Mom will come. Right?"

I can't think about Mom. Not right now.

"Did you see that dragon?" Coral says. "It burned all those houses up."

"Ellie lives there." Jade's bawling again, loudly.

"Who's making that noise?" It's a man's voice. It doesn't sound friendly.

We're nearly to the intersection with the Shell gas station—the halfway point on our route home. I think about all the times I picked up milk here when we ran out. Or bread. There's not a soul in sight now, though. Two abandoned cars, but no drivers. One glance at the station itself tells me the attendant has already fled. I don't blame him one bit.

But who's shouting at us?

"You kids, get out of here before I feel threatened." This time, I can tell it's coming from inside the store. Only, it's not the attendant. This man has a gun, and he's looting the register.

I hold up my hands. "We're not looking for trouble."

The man scowls, but he motions with his gun for us to keep going. Normally something like this would be horrifying, but today? It doesn't even rate.

Jade grips my hand tighter, and Sammy tucks his face against the juncture of my shoulder and my neck.

He's shivering, and it fills me with even more rage-fueled resolve.

I remember how it felt to be terrified and helpless at his age. I'm not going to let them face it alone. Not ever.

I start jogging again, but as we move farther from the elementary school, I see more and more signs of life. People are packing up cars. They're arguing in the front yard. They're hiding behind closed blinds. We pass all the different people doing all the things.

None of us know what's the right move.

"Where can we even go?" Jade's voice is small, but it's a good question. It's the same thing Coral asked earlier, but I still haven't answered.

I make up my mind. Even if we can't get there, it's good to have a goal in mind. "We're heading up north, to Grandma's."

"In a car?" Coral asks.

I don't mention that my car and Mom's are both at the Boo Bash. I'm not above stealing a neighbor's, if I have the chance. "I'm not sure yet," I say. "Maybe."

"Mom dropped Dad off at the airport," Coral says. "We could take his car, and it's fast."

Brilliant. I start reworking my plan. "We'll need to be able to hop out of the car and run at a moment's notice. We need bags that are packed and handy to grab if that happens, with essentials in them." And I don't want to delay our departure. I have no idea how Dallas is doing right now, but Houston's clearly not safe.

If we have gas cans, I should put them in the trunk. Ours won't be the only gas station left unattended.

"What about Mom?" Jade asks, in the softest, saddest tone ever. "Are we just leaving her?"

A knot forms in my throat. I can't think about Mom. I can't talk about her, either.

"She's fighting too," Coral says. "Just like us. Once she wins, we'll see her again."

Now I'm spending way too much energy fighting back tears. My little warrior sister's stronger than I am. "Yes," I finally say. "She's fighting too. I'm sure of it."

I can't stop seeing Mom's silver hair. I hope I didn't just lie, because I can't think why a dragon would want Mom, and I can't bring myself to think about what it means that I could hear the dragon just like she could.

"Alright, we've been jogging, but I think we should run for a bit," I say. "We've had a break, and I don't see any sign of more dragons right here, but our tree cover's about to end." We have half a mile to go, and it's all wide open.

It's the worst part of our two-mile route home.

Jade nods. Coral inhales slowly. Sammy wriggles. "You can put me down. I'm wearing my fast shoes."

My heart contracts. "It's alright, buddy. I've got you." What else did I train for? Suddenly, my upcoming fight seems stupid. Trivial. Like another life.

Even in my crop top and lycra UFC shorts, I'm sweating like a pig by the time we reach the edge of our neighborhood. At least my heart rate has been steadier, since we haven't seen any dragons in almost ten minutes. In fact, our neighborhood looks *practically* normal. The people out here must have made their decisions and either locked down or packed up and moved out already.

Part of me wonders whether I could have had a complete mental break. Did I imagine every insane thing that I remember happening? But I look at the still-wide-eyed Coral and Jade, and I hear Sammy's heaving breathing in my ear, and I know it's more than a dream. We're jogging through the neighborhood park when a group of three men comes into view. They're jostling one another, and they're arguing in a language I've never heard.

"Let's go around the back," I mouthe.

"Why?" Sammy asks. "Our house is right over there."

I shush him, but it's too late. The three men turn toward us, their heads tilting, their eyes alight with interest. They're dressed strangely, and I can't quite figure it out at first. . .but it finally hits me. They're wearing exactly the same things as the male leads in the newest *Star Wars* movie. I saw a movie poster for it yesterday, when I drove past the theater by my house.

Are these bizarre comic book nerds, or are they on their way to a Halloween party? Do they know about the dragons? Because if they don't they're going to struggle to believe a word I say. Even though it's Halloween and they're in costumes, they look strange in a way I can't quite pinpoint. Foreign, almost.

I bob my head to acknowledge them, and then I turn sharply away.

"Hey," one of them shouts. "Where are you going?"

"She's a bright," one of the men says.

A *bright*? What does that mean? He probably meant that I *am* bright, but that doesn't make sense. How could he tell how smart I am from this distance?

"She's too young," the tallest man says.

That phrase sounds icky, and I can't think of a scenario in which it's not. They look about my age or maybe a few years older, and that makes the comment even stranger. Now that we're closer, it's obvious that they're quite handsome as well. Shockingly good look-ing, which makes me think they were headed for a Halloween party when they realized the cell towers were down. Maybe they're trying to figure out what's going on. I decide to do the decent thing.

"There are dragons attacking," I say, somewhat hesitantly. "Honest to goodness, *dragons*. I know that sounds crazy, but if you're wondering why the cell towers are down, or if you're thinking this is a good time to make trouble, don't. The world has gone insane. I recommend you get in your car, go straight home, and hide like we are."

That's when I notice there isn't a car parked anywhere that I can see. Does that mean they walked here? This gets weirder and weirder.

"What?" The tallest one has hair that's black as pitch. He has eyes as golden as the sun, and when he stares at me, his expression's downright frightening.

Not much scares me, so that's strange in and of itself. I'm probably just jittery, you know, from losing my mom, and from the dragon attack, and also from the mad rush home. I tamp down my fear and push forward, repositioning Sammy on my back. "I know it sounds crazy. Dragons." I force a laugh that sounds as brittle as my attempt to warn them. "But listen. Sadly, I'm not making a joke. There are dragons, they're here on Earth, and they're killing people. Lots of people. I recommend you get out of Dodge."

A man with a stocky build and ruddy cheeks says, "She thinks we're—"

The tallest one, the lean, black-haired devil, claps a hand over the first guy's mouth. "Shut up." He takes a step toward me.

I set Sammy down and whisper, "Go home. Now."

Coral's eyes flash. "But—"

"Do it." I shove her gently. "Take Sammy and run." My job now is to make sure the kids' movement doesn't attract the men. I slide my head to the right and then to the left like I do before every fight, and then I bounce back and forth. "What exactly do you boys want?" I point. "You're clearly not from our neighborhood."

"Why are you sending your children away?" The tall one's pretty stupid if he thinks I'm old enough to have a twelve-year-old child.

"Why are you three standing there, threatening a girl?"

The one with the ruddy complexion cocks his head. "Axel, you can't ensna—"

"I said shut up." Axel's eyes flash.

His tone sends an uneasy chill up my spine, and that makes me think. Why didn't these guys start laughing when I said there were dragons? Or if not laughter, if they saw them too, they should have looked frightened. They should *not* have stood there threateningly, talking about whether Axel can do something to me.

"Alright. Leave nicely, or I'll make you." I assume my fight posture, legs spread, hands loose, eyes scanning, and I start looking for anything that might work as a weapon. There isn't much in the way of options. The playground's bright and happy, full of primary color slides and stupid plastic-coated chains leading to rubber swings.

What happened to the good old-fashioned, broke-down playgrounds they had when I was small? How about one of those junk-pile parks that I read about in Europe where they let the kids play on piles of repurposed, recycled crap? I'd kill for a nice piece of rebar right now, or even for a glass beer bottle.

"What are you doing, exactly?" Axel starts moving closer, his eyes tracking my movements.

I lean over and pick up a rock. Then I throw it

right at him, striking him right below his eye. A small splash of red blooms on the previously pristine skin of his cheek. His eyes flash, and he scowls at me.

My hostility galvanizes his two buddies, who both come at me simultaneously.

Bring it on, losers.

The ruddy-faced one rushes first, planning to plow into me and knock me over, probably. A quick round-house throws him to the side, where he sprawls against the springy, rubber-coated pavement. The second guy, whose insane-looking blonde hair pokes up at bizarre angles all over his head, growls and bares his teeth like a feral animal right before he swings at me with his beefy arm, his knobby hand balled into a fist.

I parry his clumsy blow easily and land a sweet hook to his jaw. He's got a huge head, but he still feels it, I can tell. While he's reeling from the unexpected blow, I pummel his abdomen, and he turns away. That's when I kick him, hard, on the side of his head. He sprawls out flat, just like his pal.

The pal is, unfortunately, already back on his feet. He now looks like an angry hornet, practically frothing at the mouth. He's speaking nonsense, and I want to laugh at him for it, but I figure that would just make it worse. I really can't place what language he's trying to use, but it doesn't matter. Until I either beat them or get knocked out myself, we're locked into this.

There are some things no amount of talking can fix.

He comes at me again, a little less like a wild boar than before, and he actually manages to land a decent jab to my shoulder, but only on the edge. I spin with it, and leap to the side, where I think I saw a long stick lying on the ground. Pecan trees are plentiful in Houston, and they shed a lot of branches, thankfully.

I get lucky. This one's actually pretty sharp on one end.

The blonde lunatic's up and coming at me again, so I need to close with this guy quick. I debate for a split second about how far to take it, but since it has the potential to become a three-on-one fight, I don't have time for moral dilemmas. I plunge the stick into his body, aiming for his heart. It's a stick, so I don't expect it to go very far, but instead of snapping like I worry it might, it slides right into his body.

My stomach turns as blood leaks out around the edges of my makeshift sword. Did I miscalculate? Did I just *murder* someone? The idiot gasps and blood spatters my face. Even with the world being upside down, this feels very, very bad.

"That's enough." Axel's jogging toward us, and suddenly, I feel it again. The *pulling* feeling, like I've been dipped in tar, and now someone's yanking on a rope that's sucking every part of me toward them.

Except this time, instead of stopping abruptly, it doubles down.

I resist of course, but I'm not sure how long I can continue. My world narrows to the tiniest pinpoint, and the only thing I can see is Axel's almost inhumanly beautiful face. His high cheekbones. His wide, clear, golden eyes. A strong brow, and a straight, long nose. The set of his perfectly curved, full lips. He looks angry, like he wishes he could end me. Is he the one pulling on my soul?

Blessedly, everything goes entirely black.

My last thought is that I hope my siblings made it home. I hope Dad finds them. I hope the dragons leave them alone that long.

But then the world rebounds, like a rubber ball flattened by immense force that's now expanding again.

My vision comes back online, and Axel's face is still at the center of my line of sight. Only, now he's also glowing slightly, like a bad special effect meant to mimic an angel's halo or something. Also, my left shoulder blade's burning like someone branded it.

I shake my head a bit to try and clear the fog from my brain, and I notice that the hair framing either side of my face has changed. Instead of being black like my mother's was, it's now a deep gold, burnished, rich, and totally unfamiliar.

"Whoa, how did you do that?" the ruddy-faced man asks. "I thought Earth Blessed couldn't ensnare humans."

"That, apparently, was not correct information," Axel says. "Because I just did."

He doesn't look very happy about it, either.

❦   4   ❧

arth Blessed?

I'm not the smartest person in most rooms, but that phrase, coupled with the same pulling sensation as before. . .

"Who are you?"

There's still a stick protruding from the chest of one of Axel's lackeys. There's blood coming from it, dripping down the front of his weird cosplay tunic, and yet he's casually standing next to Axel, talking as if there's *not* a stick stuck in his body.

These are people, *not* dragons, and yet. . .

Even though they ignored my first question, continuing to talk about things I don't understand, I blurt out another. "Are you dragons?" The entire day has been surreal, but asking that still feels insane, and yet, no one laughs. No one mocks.

They're not paying attention to me at all.

I finally realize that they're arguing in that strange, guttural language again, only, somehow. . .I understand them now.

"—can't kill her. No. I heard that killing a human

once you've ensnared them will incapacitate you for days. Weeks, even."

Axel rolls his eyes as if that's the dumbest thing his friend has ever said. "Not me."

"Probably especially you," the ruddy-faced one says. "Earth Blessed aren't supposed to be able to ensnare a human. Everyone says our powers are too weak. That's why we assume this humanoid form."

"Wait. . .*humanoid?*" I can't help spluttering. "Does that mean you're dragons pretending to be human?"

Axel slowly turns toward me, his eyes narrowed. "How do you speak our tongue?"

It hits me that I was using their language just now. "I—" I have no idea.

"She's *ensnared*, Your Highness," Blondie says. "That means she's connected to you. Of course she can understand us. It's part of the connection."

Connection? To dragons? No way. Mom tasked me to keep the kids safe. I can't be connected to a dragon. Especially not a weak one who's not even supposed to be able to *ensnare* me or whatever they were just saying.

But it hits me, in that moment. They can be injured —the bleeding one is proof of that. And he just said that harming *me* will render Axel incapacitated for days. So they can be stunned at the very least. Which means. . .

They're ignoring me again, in favor of arguing about what to do with me. I sneak toward the trash can, hoping to find a glass bottle or anything sharp. People here in Texas really like their beer. Is it too much to hope that they might have tossed a bottle or two? But, no luck.

Until I notice the broken umbrella.

The end of it's pretty blunt, but with enough force behind it, maybe. I think about the stick sliding into that guy's body and have to suppress a shudder. Sometimes we can't choose to avoid conflict. Sometimes our fate's thrust upon us. No one knows that better than I do. I grab the umbrella as nonchalantly as possible, and then I use the toe of my sneaker to pry the hard plastic bumper off the end.

At least now, it's metal on the tip, even if it's not any sharper.

"What are you doing?" Axel asks.

My head snaps back toward them. "Me?" I shrug. "Just what any good ensnared human should be doing."

"And what is that?" Axel raises one eyebrow. "What exactly do you think your job will be?"

I step toward them, leaning on the umbrella like it's a walking stick. "Oh, you know, general mayhem. Attacking. Razing. Murdering. Right?"

Axel rolls his eyes.

"Or did you want me to fetch you food? What exactly do earth dragons eat?"

"We are not dragons. We're the Blessed." Axel frowns. "And your job's to communicate with and control the local population so that we can more easily and effectively accomplish our task and leave."

"Leave?" That sounds good. "What's this task?"

"To find the Heart," Axel says.

"Should we really be telling humans?" the ruddy one asks.

"Does that stick not hurt?" I can't help eyeing it. Why hasn't he pulled it out?

"It does hurt. Thanks for reminding me." He scowls and moves toward me with jerky movements.

"You can't kill her, Gordon," Blondie says. "Remember?"

"Then you come pull it out for me," the ruddy-faced one says.

"You can't claw her either," Blondie says. "Axel will be able to feel it too."

Gordon gnashes his teeth, which should look ridiculous given his brown robe and the fact that humans don't really gnash their teeth. But knowing he's a dragon helps me resist my urge to laugh. "She stabbed me."

"With a stick," Axel says. "It's barely a scratch. Stop whining." He pivots, his hand snapping toward his companion, and then he grabs the slick end of it and yanks. The stick shoots out, spraying gore all over. It looks even more grotesque because it's splattered all over the bright blue and yellow-coated pavement. "Now heal up so we can go."

"Yes, good idea," I say. "You guys should go."

Axel's eyes swing toward me, intent. "You're coming."

"I can't. I have family to care for. Sorry."

"The young ones, you mean," Axel says. "I imagine they'll be bright too, once they're old enough."

Blondie's face lights up. Gordon's hunched over, moaning, but it's clear that a 'bright' is something they like. It's what they called me earlier, too.

"What does that mean, exactly?" I doubt they'll answer, but who knows?

"You're a bright," Axel says. "It's the reason I could ensnare you."

"Not anymore," Blondie says. "Now she's taken, so she's not pulsing."

I was *pulsing* to them? As freaky as it sounds, that must be how the dragon found Mom earlier—it sensed her. "You said I'm supposed to control the local population?"

Axel sighs. "Once you've been properly taught, you can force the humans around you to listen to your will.

They'll have no ability to refuse any command you make."

Goodie. I'm basically Dr. Xavier from the X-Men, only I'm forced labor for the minions of evil. "Thanks for the offer, but I'm going to pass."

"You're going to. . ." Axel strides toward me this time, his hand clenched at his side. "You can't *pass*. You're already caught. That means I control your actions."

"So I'm just middle management?" I grimace. "I'm not really good at that kind of thing."

Axel stops less than two feet away from me, his eyes intent, his face grim. "I can force you to do anything."

"Like what?" I ask. "Like, making me pick up my right arm?" I look down at it. "Because so far, I feel totally normal."

"Sure, if I wanted to do something that stupid. . ." He frowns. "How did they say they made the humans do what they wanted?"

Gordon's finally upright again, and through the hole in his stupid, blood-stained tunic, he appears to be completely healed. How did he. . .? Ugh. This umbrella may buy me less time than I hoped. Well, at least Axel seems to know nothing about how to use the leash he supposedly placed around my neck. Or maybe he's too weak to use it as an earth dragon or whatever.

Who cares as long as I have a chance at escaping them? Any hopes I secretly harbored of staying put in our house are gone. We'll have to flee immediately. Dad's car's probably our only hope. If we can get enough distance between Axel and me, maybe he won't be able to do a thing.

I gather my resolve, and then I strike immediately and without warning, pulling on my years of kendo, and shove the end of the umbrella right into the prince's throat. I immediately collapse to my knees, my hands losing their grip on the handle. Blood gushes from the place where the umbrella punctured his throat, pouring down his neck and soaking his clothing, but otherwise he looks entirely fine.

Meanwhile, I can't breathe.

My throat isn't working either.

I can't swallow. . .or drag in a scrap of a breath.

"What—" I wheeze with the last of my air.

Axel sighs, which shouldn't even be possible with something jammed through his windpipe, and yanks the umbrella out of his own throat. The spray of gore eclipses that from Gordon and the stick, and most of it hits me. "You can't kill me," he says, blood burbling from his throat, his words emerging in the most macabre surround sound ever. "You'd die long before I would."

Because of our connection.

Unlike his friend, he doesn't hunch over or groan or even whimper. He tilts his head, coughs a few times, and his body just *repairs* itself in front of me. As it does, my throat stops hurting too. My lungs suddenly draw a much-needed breath. The spots that were swimming in front of my eyes dissipate slowly.

"It may be hard to process that your life's no longer your own," Axel says. "I don't really care. Stop fighting me before I get annoyed."

Annoyed?

An umbrella through his throat was *annoying*? I wonder how he'd feel if. . .it occurs to me that I may not be able to kill him before dying myself in the attempt, but I do have another leverage point. A sharper one. "My death would incapacitate you. That one said so." I point.

"What now?" he asks.

"I'll kill myself." I crouch down and grab the discarded, blood-soaked umbrella. "Unlike you, I can't magically heal." I tap the front of my neck, just off center. "This right here is the jugular vein. In humans, it generates enough blood flow that piercing it will kill us in a very short period of time. If I ram this umbrella into my own jugular, I'll die, and you won't be able to stop it." I hold the end of the umbrella, comfortingly sticky and disgusting, against my neck. "You might not die, but I bet being incapacitated for a few days would be a real problem for you, especially right now when some of us humans are fighting back."

Axel frowns. "It would be inconvenient."

"Can dragons be trusted?"

His brows draw together. "What does that mean?"

"When you make promises, do you have to keep them?"

He smiles. "You don't know us, so how could you trust any answer I give?"

He's right. I swear under my breath.

"But for what it's worth, when we swear oaths, they're binding."

His companions look concerned.

That's more reassurance than I expected to get. "Make me a very simple promise, and I won't try to kill myself."

"Are humans trustworthy? Are your oaths binding when you make them?" He looks skeptical.

"Many humans lie," I admit. "But I'm not one of them. If I promise you something, I'll keep my word." At least, as long as it makes sense. I don't feel honor bound to keep any promises I make to the devil himself, but hopefully he won't realize that.

"What do you want?" He arches one eyebrow.

"I have three younger siblings. You saw them. Two sisters and a brother. I also have two other family members who aren't close." I consider telling him that Mom's been ensnared, but then I worry that might change his promise. Maybe I should keep her connection to the dragons a secret until I know more.

"So?" He looks bored. Or is it annoyed? I can't tell.

"Swear you'll keep all five of them safe, and I'll promise not to harm myself."

"And if they're injured in spite of my efforts?"

I shift the umbrella closer.

"You won't always have an, er, what is that?"

"It's—it doesn't matter. If you don't think I'm creative enough to find a way to kill myself, you don't know me well enough yet."

"Humans are quite fragile, it seems," Blondie says.

Axel seems to be considering my offer. "You must also agree to do as you're told."

"You can already force her to behave," Gordon says.

Axel arches one eyebrow. "I'd rather not need to— it's problematic, trying to think of every circumstance that might arise."

He didn't disagree though, which means if I refuse, he *can* figure out how to force me, or I can do as he says of my own will. That sounds better for me anyway. "If I agree, you'll keep my brother and sisters—and two other humans if I can find them—safe?"

"Sparing five humans is negligible," he says. "But you can't leave to look for the other two. If they appear within my sphere of influence, I'll keep them safe along with the three small ones you sent scurrying to their den. Is that correct?"

Their den? Close enough. "Yes."

"You'll do whatever I say without argument, and I

keep them safe in exchange. That's our bargain. We're clear."

The idea of 'doing whatever he says' makes me want to jab the umbrella into my jugular right now, but instead, I nod, because this isn't about me. How shocked will he be when my mom appears right inside his sphere of influence? I can't help my satisfaction in outwitting him.

"Alright." He sighs. "I accept."

Just like that? What did I forget? Was that too easy?

"Did you expect me to decline?" He's smirking, his golden eyes glinting, his sharp jaw set in a confident line, and I realize that, in spite of the ridiculous outfit, in spite of his general evilness, and even though he apparently controls my life from here on out, he's probably the most beautiful man I've ever seen.

I hate him more for that. The outside should reflect the inside.

I imagine him with pock marks covering his face. I pretend his hair's thinning on top and he's been forced to comb it over. I imagine that he has a huge, saggy gut instead of a flat belly with broad shoulders and muscular arms.

The new image makes me smile.

"Well, collect them," Axel says. "It's time for us to leave."

"To where? Where were you going that even had you here, by our den?"

"We were prepping the perimeter," he says. "But something spooked the humans here."

No kidding. "We have long-range communication devices," I say. "I'm sure they sent out a warning when your dragons started popping up and massacring people."

"Also, our costumes appear to be quite poor. No one wanted to talk to us even before all the attacks and killing began," Blondie says.

Their *costumes* are poor?

"Why are you dressed like that?"

Axel sighs. "We saw lots of recent pictures being broadcast before our arrival in which humans were dressed exactly as we are now."

Movie previews. They must've seen trailers for the new Star Wars film and dressed accordingly. I'm suddenly disappointed that there's not a new Power Rangers movie coming out. That would've been even funnier than robes with brown hoods and tall, strappy boots.

"Too bad you didn't craft a light saber," I can't help saying.

"Is that a sword?" Blondie perks up. "He does have two swords he doesn't know how to extricate—"

Axel's the uncontested leader for sure. One glare from him and Blondie cuts off immediately. "Your den is?" He definitely sounds irritated.

"How about this?" I ask. "I'll report to wherever you want me every morning, and I'll train for as long as you'd like. Then my siblings can stay at our er, den, and I'll just check in on them at night."

Axel shakes his head. "I can't protect them that way. They must be near me, or anyone could come along and—"

I lift a hand. "Got it, got it. Okay, fine. They're over here." We only live three blocks from the entrance of the neighborhood, but it's the longest three blocks I've ever walked, with three dragons-dressed-as-humans trailing after me in Star Wars cloaks and matching scowls.

"Is this how we're going to go. . .where are we going

once we get them?" Would it kill them to share any information at all without being prompted?

"Back to our den," Axel says, as if that explains it.

"But are we walking there?" I ask. "Because I have a car, and it would be much faster than—"

"Are humans always this irritating?" Blondie asks. "You talk and talk and talk and all the questions you ask are stupid."

I'm standing right in front of my own door now, and I grit my teeth and say nothing. Being called stupid's barely a blip on the radar compared to the rest of today.

"I'll just grab them and be right back."

"I think not," Axel says. "I'll come in with you."

So much for grabbing Dad's decorative sword from the study or a few other weapons on the side. "Of course. Come right on in."

When I open the door, which apparently no one thought to lock, Sammy darts away as if we might not have seen him.

"What happened to your hair?" Sammy starts to cry.

"Are you alright?" Jade's blinking repeatedly.

"Are they not bad guys?" Coral asks, stepping into the entryway. She glares at Axel. "What happened?"

I'm a little bit proud of her pluck.

"We've struck a deal," I say, "and I think they'll honor it." I don't have much alternative if they renege, but I don't mention that. There's no reason for the kids to be as terrified as I am. "Mr. Axel here has agreed to keep you safe as long as I do some work for him. Part of our deal changed my hair color."

"I don't want you to work for him," Sammy says from under the dining table. "I don't like him, and

Mom's already gone." He's crying, and I don't have the time or skill to make him feel better.

"Guys, I know things are scary right now, but I need you to be tough for me, okay? Grab your bags, stick clothing in them, and put in some food." I have no idea what kind of food there will be in a dragon's den. I really hope it's not dead humans. The idea makes me want to hide with Sammy. "Grab whatever essentials you think you'll need. You have ten minutes."

Axel grunts.

"Five?"

He frowns, but he doesn't argue. I race to my room first, noticing that Axel thankfully didn't follow me. I peel off my disgusting, ruined clothes and toss them in the trash. I splash water on my face. Then I throw a few changes of clothing into my largest backpack, along with lots of underwear and some toiletries. I slide two pocketknives and a bottle of ibuprofen in there, too. I also take thirty seconds and scrawl a note, which I leave on my counter, saying that I've been ensnared by an earth dragon, just like Mom was with an electro dragon. I say I'm stuck following Axel to the dragon's main dwelling. Probably no one will ever see it, but if anyone comes looking for me, I ought to leave them all the information I have in this moment, at least.

I rush to the kitchen the second I'm done. Luckily, my siblings love granola bars and other packaged junk I can't eat while I'm training, which means we have lots of it. I toss antibiotics, more painkillers, bandages, Neosporin, and some sleeping pills in my bag too, just in case one of the kids gets injured.

With the last minute I have to spare, I grab Sammy's backpack that's covered with llamas. "Alright, dude. What did you—" But when I open it, I find that he's stuffed Legos, bags of Skittles and powdered sugar donuts, his blue blanket, and his stuffed sloth inside. That's it. No clothes. No real food of any kind. "Sam, Legos? Really?"

"I'll feed and clothe them," Axel says. "It doesn't matter what they bring. Let's go."

I have no idea what Coral and Jade packed, but they're both waiting in the family room, wearing backpacks, with their favorite sneakers all laced up. I have no idea what I've gotten us into, and I worry that they would've been better off hiding here alone, waiting for Dad to get home.

But the deal's already struck. I have to hope it's the best one.

"Hey, what're your names?" Sammy asks. "You didn't say. I'm Sammy." He smiles.

"It's best if you just don't talk to them at all," I say.

"I'm Axel," my new boss says. "That one," he points at the ruddy-faced man, "is Gordon, and that one," he points at Blondie, "is Rufus."

"Wow. Those sounds like human names."

"You're a pretty smart kid," Axel says. "Nothing like your sister." He smiles. "They're translations of our dragon names. That's the closest we could get."

"I like your name best," Sammy says. "It sounds tough."

Axel smiles as if he cares what Sammy thinks. "It's time." He nods at Gordon and Rufus. "Change."

They walk outside, and I follow. An unaccountable sorrow grips me. I've lost my mom already today. It's not like our house was anything special, but we've lived here almost all my life. I played ball with my dad in the driveway. I swam in a crappy little blow-up pool in the back yard. Our heights are marked on the wall in the kitchen. Leaving now—it feels like I'll never be back.

The world's upside down, and we're being forced out of the one safe place we had.

The kids are looking back too, and I wrap an arm around both girls' shoulders. Sammy presses his face against my stomach.

The dragons have moved away from the house a few dozen feet, and Gordon grimaces. Then there's a sound like the tearing of fabric. I can't look away as everything on his body seems to turn inside out, his back splitting open, his arms exploding. Thankfully, it all disappears in a swirl of brown smoke as a monstrous creature rises upward. It's made up of coils—so many coils. Coils full of deep, shining brown scales that are as varied in color as the backs of dead oak leaves. They even rustle as he moves. I finally realize that Gordon does have legs, but they're small. Much too small for his size, it appears. His head's shaped in almost a triangle, like a snake, and his eyes are slitted. His tongue slides in and out like he's tasting the air.

"You too," Axel says. "Let's go."

This time, the sounds of Rufus shifting fill the air, like rocks being crushed, and almost the same thing happens to him, except instead of turning into a brown, snake-like dragon the size of an ancient elm, he splits and expands into what looks an awful lot like a lizard on steroids. His scales are greenish yellow, and his legs are much larger than Gordon's.

"They're dragons," Coral says. "But they looked like humans before."

"He's one too," Jade says. "Isn't he?" She's staring at Axel. "And he's their boss."

"Correct," Axel says. "Your siblings really are brighter than you."

"We're going to follow them," I say. "And let's be quick and quiet about it, no matter how far it is."

"You'll carry the little one," Axel says, staring right at Gordon. "Be careful with him—he's very small. Rufus will take the two females."

"We have names too," Sammy says. "Remember? I'm Sammy, and this is Coral." He points. "That's Jade."

"Rufus, you take Coral and Jade."

"We can walk," I say. "Or we could also follow you in a car."

"You agreed to do as I said," Axel snaps.

I swallow.

"Who's taking Liz?" Sammy asks. "Can she ride with me?"

Axel smiles. "I don't think so."

There's no splitting or popping when he shifts. In fact, it sounds more like the purring of a stock car engine than anything else. And suddenly, from a swirl of golden smoke, rises a very large, very beautiful champagne dragon with gleaming scales. He's as big as a trash truck, but muscular in a sinewy way. Other than the fact that he doesn't have wings, he looks like the stunning dragons on most every movie I've ever seen. His head's long, his teeth sharp, and his talons terrifying in their length. His belly is slightly lighter than the rest of his body, with pronounced horizontal lines in the scales. There's a long ridge of pronounced large, upright scales that runs from the tip of his tail to the base of his head. He moves smoothly, gracefully, his muscles and scales both rippling. Unsurprisingly, the color of his scales, like shimmering moonlight on a lake at night, exactly matches my hair.

You'll be riding with me from now on. Come, Ensnared.

"My name's Elizabeth."

Get on.

I approach the golden dragon and force myself to climb up onto his back and grip the ridge of scales on his shoulders. His head's swiveled around so he can watch, and the only thing that keeps me moving forward is the fact that Sammy's climbing on that massive snake and Coral and Jade are already sitting on the back of the lizard-like dragon, all of them looking almost excited.

If they can do it, so can I.

At least, that's what I tell myself over and over as Axel starts to race through the streets we used to drive through every single day. So familiar, and now so foreign.

Like our future. Lost in a blink.

❧ 5 ❧

It took us almost an hour to get home, thanks to the interaction with the dragons. Even without that, we'd have taken half an hour to cover those two miles. But on our way to the dragon's camp, we move far, far faster than I'd have thought beasts without wings could move.

I saw the silver dragon that electrocuted things—it had wings.

As did the enormous red one that breathed fire.

Why don't these 'earth blessed' dragons have wings? Seems like I've been enslaved by the weakest caste of dragon, which isn't very inspiring. And as we approach the dragon's den, I see more and more of the awful creatures.

Any hope I'd been harboring that perhaps there weren't many of them dwindles and then dies.

Silver Strike Blessed dart and dip and wheel around above our heads. Two of them take down a fighter jet as I watch, the flames from the jet catching a home on fire. I say a silent prayer that the home was empty and that the pilot was the only fatality.

So much for thinking that perhaps the US government isn't aware of the threat and will soon arrive on the scene to save us.

"Was that a jet?" Coral shouts.

I nod.

Jade's eyes are wide, but surprisingly, she's not crying. I'm proud of her for that. She usually devolves into tears when someone complains that she's talking too much.

Sammy's clinging for dear life, his eyes tightly clenched most of the ride. The horrible Gordon actually slows down several times when it looks like Sammy's slipping and waits for him to adjust his grip. For the first fifteen minutes, as we move at a speed that must be close to fifty miles per hour, I keep thinking that we're surely close to wherever we're going. But we never seem to stop.

I was counting dragons, the silver in the air and the brown and green ones on the ground, but after I hit a hundred several times over, I stop counting. How many can there really be? Where did they come from? Why are they here?

I don't bother asking more questions they'll just ignore.

After nearly half an hour, we start seeing signs for League City—that's a place I've been. Mom has a friend there named Anna. But before we reach the road she lives off of, we veer sharply left and head for Nassau Bay. "Are we going to NASA?"

We came here because that's where most of the boats that you sent off planet originated.

NASA. They're here because of NASA. I used to think it was cool that we lived in the town that housed our government's space program. Now I hate it.

Because it brought them here.

We're nearly there.

"Good, because if Sam gets tired and falls off and breaks his ankle, I'll break mine, too. I hope that hurts you a lot."

Is he. . .shaking? I can almost hear the laughter in my head. *It won't hurt me, so don't do anything that stupid.*

"Don't tell me you care whether I'm injured." As if.

We were told Earth Blessed couldn't ensnare a human. Somehow I have, but that will make you a curiosity. While I'm the Prince of the Earth Blessed, we're the weakest of the Blessed.

Hunch confirmed. I'm the vassal of the Prince of the Rat Dragons. Great. "Will I be in danger just for existing?"

No reply. That's not very comforting.

"At least arm me, if that's the case."

You'll be given weapons and training as well. I can keep you safe, as long as you don't do anything stupid.

My idiocy puts him at risk. If I'm killed, he'll be incapacitated for days. That's what they said. For the first time today, I feel a *little bit* in control. I have the teensiest bit of leverage with him, but if I push it too hard, or if I overplay my hand, I'm done. "I won't. I'm a warrior among my people."

You did best Gordon.

That I did.

We're here.

As if they're arriving to welcome us, a trio of fighter jets fly overhead.

I need to coordinate our defense. Get out and hide in there.

We've stopped in front of a furniture store—Star Furniture. They seemed excited about going inside a human home earlier, so why did they choose a furniture store as their den?

Probably because a home wouldn't accommodate

them in their dragon form, but a store with a massive entry would. At least this place has bathrooms and plenty of beds, I assume.

"Alright, guys," I say. "We're here." I slide down from Axel's back and land pretty hard on my feet. That prompts me to jog toward Sammy and catch him just as Gordon stretches upward, dumping him straight down.

Rufus is nicer, waiting for me to reach his side before shifting to dislodge the girls. They seem shell-shocked, and they're definitely all exhausted, but they look alright otherwise.

Go inside and don't come out until I return. Axel, Rufus, and Gordon disappear as quickly as they arrived, not even waiting to see whether we listen.

"Okay, so we're in the dragon base camp," I say. "We should get inside quickly."

"Hey!" Coral's looking up at the sky and waving. "There are jets up there. Maybe they'll see us."

A split second later, a massive red dragon launches from somewhere to our left and hurtles upward, flames spewing from his mouth. A plane goes down, careening into the bay. The other two circle around and open fire.

"Get inside," I yell.

Sammy and the girls start for the store, but it's too late. Those warheads are going to hit—the red dragon whips around and *swallows* them. They just *disappear* into his body. A moment later, there's a loud *boom*, but the red dragon merely shudders.

Then he roars in fury and accelerates.

"Go, now," I say.

The kids start to run, and I'm only a step behind them. I'm too slow to miss seeing the red beast reduce the two US fighter jets to piles of slag that sink into the bay next to their fallen companion. In the space between heartbeats as I'm about to duck into the furniture store, I swear that the red dragon turns toward me.

And smiles.

It chills me to the very bone.

Can Axel really protect me from *that*?

Can anyone keep us safe when a creature who eats missiles and melts fighter jets is flying around loose? I need to figure out what they're here for if we're going to have any chance of getting rid of them. The last desperate strings of hope in my heart that the government might appear to save me are gone.

I'm all we've got.

And maybe the other Ensnared. He did say I'd be training. Surely I'll meet others, and if we work together. . .

"Liz?" Coral's trembling.

If my bravest sibling's shaking, it's time to get them somewhere safe. Warm. They'll need food, too. My stomach's rumbling, and I'm not even growing like they are. I take a good look around the furniture store to identify the exits and the closest bathroom.

"Let's head over here," I say, pointing at the bathroom near the bedroom section. "We can each pick out a bed, alright? Any one you want."

Sammy's hand slides into mine. "Can I sleep with you?"

"Me too." Jade takes my other hand.

Coral sets her jaw. I wonder what it costs her to always be the brave one. The one who has to walk alone, because both my hands are taken. "I'll take this one." She points at the king-size bed closest to the bathroom.

"That one looks amazing," I say. "I wonder if it would fit all of us." I hate sleeping in the same bed as anyone else, but if it helps them, I can do it.

"Yay." Sammy drops his backpack and scrambles up onto the bed. "Can we jump on it?"

I open my mouth to say no, but somehow, I can't do it. "Sure, why not?"

Five minutes later, the two girls have changed into pajamas—I told them to bring essentials, and they all brought not one, but *two* pairs of pajamas. Sammy's still wearing the clothes he had on—minus the Ben Ten jacket that he put in his bag with his Legos. I think that tells you something about our family. We like to be comfortable. And Sammy does not care about clothes.

They're all jumping on the bed together.

Sure, they could bump into one another and get a black eye. One of them could break an arm. It might not be good for the mattress or the box springs. But when the world's ending, you do what you can to find joy.

That's how Axel sees us when he hunches over to squeeze through the massive Star Furniture sliding doors and drops the back half of a mangled cow on the ground.

I brought food.

All four of us stare, gape-mouthed.

"Is that a cow?" Jade's lip quivers.

Blood's pooling under the cow, which is apparently quite fresh.

Coral covers her eyes.

Sammy starts to cry.

What do you eat? Another Ensnared told me that you eat cows.

Oh, good heavens. "We do," I say. "It's just usually cooked when we do." I swallow, not able to look away. "And in smaller portions."

The enormous dragon tilts his head. Then he snorts. I had no idea dragons could roll their eyes, but this one does, right before he picks up the cow haunch and drags it back out.

I'm unsure whether I should ignore the enormous pool of congealing blood on the floor of the entryway, or whether I'm supposed to clean it up. Is it *rude* to clean up the entrails from a dragon's gift? Or as the human vassal, is that my job?

"I should have gotten a manual or something," I complain. "I mean, how hard is it to give me a little more direction, really?"

Jade laughs.

"His royal scaliness probably doesn't know what you're supposed to be doing either," Coral says. "He seems pretty clueless, like a puppy or something."

He does seem a little out of his element. I suppose it's new to them too, overtaking Earth and massacring thousands. Or more. The thought makes me sick, and I can't stop thinking of the people that electro dragon fried. The pilots the red dragon roasted. The houses that were burning.

Why are they even here?

What do they want from us?

"Liz." Jade's nose is scrunched up. "There are flies."

Even though it's October, she's right. Flies are landing on the blood puddle. If I don't get it cleaned up, this store's going to get really gross, really quick.

"I can help," Jade says. She does most of the cleaning at our house. Mom doesn't usually notice the mess, and Dad's gone a lot.

"No way. You three stay here." I point at my bag. "Eat a granola bar, and then go to bed."

"What about brushing our teeth?" Sammy asks. "Mom said if we don't brush our teeth every night, they'll rot out of our heads, and I forgot my toothbrush."

How very un-hippy-like of her. She never made me brush my teeth if I didn't feel like it. Maybe my dental bills scared her straight. I'm a little sad to hear that Mom has caved to the man.

"Jade can help you," I say. "You can use my toothbrush. March into the bathroom when you're done eating and brush brush, okay?"

He nods.

I mop up most of the sticky, disgusting blood and chunks of I-don't-want-to-think-about-what with towels I find in the supply closet. I set the soiled towels just outside the door to deal with later, and I'm on my hands and knees, going over the spot with a wet paper towel and some Clorox spray, when the doors reopen.

The smell of sizzling steak floods my senses as Axel drops the same cow carcass on the spot I just cleaned. At least this time, it's not blood that's pooling. It appears to be sizzling juices. . .or grease. Ew.

I'm understanding a little more why Mom's a vegetarian.

Eat.

"Actually, we already ate," I say. "Maybe you can eat it instead." I don't point out that he just made a huge mess in the place I just cleaned. I'm proud of myself for that.

He frowns. The dragon overlord I'm bound to *frowns*.

"I really appreciate all the hard work you did," I say. "I mean, I didn't even ask you to do it," I mutter. "But we all ate granola bars, and other than me, the three kids are vegetarian."

He stares blankly.

"It means we don't eat the flesh of animals," I say. "And you know what? I'd been considering moving to that, too. I just had this competition coming up where my coach wanted me to get more protein, and—you know what? Doesn't matter. We want you to have as much as you want to eat, big guy." I pat his back leg. "Alright?"

He growls, and it's so loud that it fills the entire empty space and echoes off the walls.

"I've been meaning to try meat," Coral says. "I could have a bite."

I shake my head. "You agreed to protect them, not bully them." I point at the door. "If you're going to growl and grump, get out."

For a split second, it looks like Axel's thinking about biting my arm off, but he doesn't. He grabs the cow, again, and drags it out one last time. *I ruined it by cooking it for you, and you won't even try it.*

I hear the implied 'how rude' even though he doesn't say it.

"Are you coming back? Or can we go to sleep?" I yell.

Sleep, he says. *I'll be back when the sun rises.*

Oh, goodie.

As lullabies go, his threat to return with the sunrise isn't the best one. I toss and turn and get kicked in the nose twice, but at least we're all alive the next morning.

That's more than plenty of other people can say.

✻ 6 ✻

The next morning, I'm up by dawn. The cell towers may be down, but somehow, the grid's still up, and the water's working too. I charged my useless iPhone and brushed my teeth. Thank goodness. Even if my phone's now the most technologically advanced alarm clock I've ever had, it's a comfort that it's still alive.

Sammy, Coral, and Jade are all still sleeping, but I'm pacing by the door. I was told to stay put, but it's dawn, and there's still no sign of Axel.

An hour later, Jade's awake and using the sink as a shower like I did, and I'm about to leave in spite of the orders, just to see what's going on out there. Did Axel die? Is the government doing anything? What's going on? I walk back and forth in front of the doors just to make them open so I can get a peek outside.

Not that I've seen anything helpful.

Axel apparently picked the most remote spot of their camp for his stupid den. There aren't even any dragons milling about like there were on our trip here yesterday.

I'm about to leave and brave the consequences when the doors finally open. Gordon looks irritated, which I can tell easily, because he's in human form. "Here." He holds out several bags.

"What is all that?"

His nostrils flare. "His Highness made me go into a market and pick out things I thought you'd like to eat."

As if he has any idea what we'd eat. I tremble at the thought of what might be in the bags. "Um."

"Just take it." He drops them.

I catch most of them, barely. Which is a good thing, it turns out, because one of the bags has a jar of pickles in it that would have shattered. There's also a container of mustard, a box of Ramen noodles, a loaf of bread, a watermelon, cans of beans, which we can't open without a can opener, and several bags of candy. Also, there's a box of tampons. I wonder what he thinks those are for.

It's like a blind person waltzed up and down grabbing one thing from every aisle.

I realize that's probably exactly what he did.

"Next time, how about I go with you?"

"I have strict orders. His Highness is very, very preoccupied right now, so it's critical that you all stay inside. Once he's settled things, he'll return, and he'll see that you're trained at that time."

Settled things? As in, once all the pesky humans who fight back are dead? Oh, heck no. "How about I come with you and I can help him—"

"No."

"But—"

Gordon growl-roars, and the odd sound coming from a human-shaped throat wakes the other two kids. Sammy whimpers.

"I'll return later with more food. If you tell me what you like—"

"Milk. Cereal." There's a fridge in the break room, assuming the power's on in the store and the milk isn't spoiled yet. "More bread. Peanut butter and jelly. Eggs, if they have any." Sammy will eat those cooked in a microwave, which thankfully the break room has. I drop to a whisper. "We can tell the kids they're free range even if they aren't. At least it's protein."

"How much of this do you think I'll remember?" Gordon arches one irritated eyebrow.

"Bread. Eggs. Peanut butter. Jelly. Cereal. Milk. Granola bars, if you see any." I pause. "Can you remember that?"

He shrugs.

"And if you have time, ask his royal fanciness again if I could *please* be allowed to leave this furniture store prison to collect some food myself. I would really appreciate it."

"Request denied," Gordon says. "His Highness is in a difficult position right now, leading the shock troops as well as rounding up humans for the other Ensnared to control."

"He's *what*?"

Gordon swallows, his eyes bugging a bit. I'm guessing he wasn't supposed to share that part. "Just stay put. Got it? Or I'll eat one of your kids."

"Again, they aren't my kids. They're my siblings—my mom and dad's children."

"Whatever." Gordon leaves as quickly as he came, changing forms just outside the door and slithering away faster than I would have thought possible if I hadn't seen him racing through the streets yesterday.

"He gives me the heebie jeebies," Jade says.

"Me too," Coral says.

"I like him," Sammy says. "The way he moves is neat, and he's tough. That doesn't mean he's bad. He brought us pickles."

I forgot how much Sammy likes pickles. He proceeds to eat the entire jar. I hope it doesn't give him an upset stomach.

The next three days go exactly like the first. Gordon does a grocery drop off, with increasingly improved items, though the milk on the third day is expired, not that we needed more. He also brought mostly things like plain old rice chex, which are edible, but not very exciting for kids.

"Sugar-coated cereal," I emphasize. "Look for the boxes like this that are bright and exciting. Those are the ones they want."

He rolls his eyes, but I think Gordon likes us a little bit more each day. He brings better stuff, and he practically preens when I praise his selections.

By the fifth day, however, we have amassed a bit of a stockpile, and nothing scary has happened since that first day. The kids and I are all a little stir crazy, and I'm getting ticked that His Royal Majesty Axel can't even be bothered to show up. "Tell him, Gordon. If he's not here himself tomorrow, I'm going out for a walk."

"You will not do that," Gordon says. "You vowed to do as he said."

"Well, I haven't heard him say it. I didn't promise to do what *you* said." I fold my arms. "If he can't be bothered to come by and give me orders himself, I'm breaking free."

Gordon shakes his head and scowls. "You're dumber than I thought."

I think about what he means. I'm essentially a captured slave, and I'm currently being ignored. I could take that as a boon, of course, and just be glad that we're safe. The less time we spend around the dragons, the better, right? But we're also sitting ducks here, and without our protector even coming by, how much time do we really have? I've never been one to pull an ostrich and close my eyes to what's happening around me.

I feel pretty ostrichy right now, hiding in a furniture store with sliding doors.

When I think about Axel's smirk, it makes me want to duck out and go exploring right now. It's just not the face of a cold-hearted killer. A villain? Sure. Even a killer, maybe, but only when truly provoked. He'd hear me out first, and then he'd understand why I didn't just sit around.

Right?

Right.

I think.

My uncertainty keeps me inside another day.

But the next morning, as I'm facing down my sixth day of hiding in a furniture store in the middle of town, I can't handle any more. I make a plan.

"You're going to stay put, right?" Gordon eyes me askance.

"You convinced me yesterday," I say. "I'm sure there are hundreds of dragons out there, right now."

"In the sky, on land, and in the water," he says.

"The water?" I didn't expect that.

"You really need to be trained," Gordon says. "The Blessed returned to Earth to recapture the Heart, and we won't leave until we have it. In order to do that, His Royal Highness sent the Blessed Recovery Team."

"Wait, did you say *returned*?" I ask.

Gordon's dramatic sigh seems over the top. "We lived here with humans for several thousand years. However, we fought often, and it became ugly. We, being the greater, stronger, and smarter beings, decided to leave."

"Leave." I blink.

"Axel will explain all of this," he says. "But you should at least know that there are four categories of Blessed. Flame, of which our Recovery Leader is one."

"Flame?" That must be the huge red dragon I saw eating missiles. "Okay. And how many of those are there on earth?"

Gordon frowns. "Nice try. No tactical information. But there are also Strike Blessed. They're silver and they control electrical currents."

One of them took my mother. I grit my teeth and nod.

"They can fly, like the Flame Blessed."

"I've seen them."

"And there are Water Blessed," he says. "They keep to bodies of water whenever possible and complain absurdly when forced to walk instead of swim."

"How did you get here, then?"

"Tactical," he says.

"But—"

"His Majesty can share that if he chooses. The last kind of Blessed is the Earth Blessed, and we're the most plentiful." He beams. "I am, of course, Earth Blessed, as is His Majesty, the Prince of the Earth Blessed. That's why he was able to ensnare a human, a feat we were told wasn't possible."

"Goodie," I say.

"Now, keep your promise, and stay here. He thinks he'll be free to see you in the morning."

I've heard that before, but I don't argue. I just nod my head.

"I mean it." Gordon points at me. He's learning human movements quickly. He's also finally replaced the idiotic Jedi Knight outfit with a pair of jeans and a t-shirt with a tiny green dragon on it that says, "Fear me. I'm dragon." I didn't really take him for an ironic kind of guy, but it's funny. The one on his shirt actually resembles Rufus a little. I wonder whether that's why he chose it.

"Hey, where did you find that shirt?" I ask.

But it's too late. He's already on his way out.

I wait for more than an hour after he leaves, just to be safe.

"You'll all hide until I come back." I'm making the kiddos lock themselves into the office at the back of the store. No windows. Metal doors. Locks from the inside. If it had a vault, I'd try to force them in there. "You have enough food for several days. Don't come out for Rufus, do not come out for Axel, and definitely don't come out for Gordon, no matter what they say."

"But I like Gordon," Sammy says.

I glare.

"We'll keep him inside and quiet," Coral says.

I'm sure they'll be fine. Right? Right. I'll be back before they even get sick of playing with Sammy's Legos.

That's a lie, of course. They're already sick of them. My six-year-old brother packed the smartest thing out of all of us, and it was the thing I almost made him leave. They've been playing twenty questions and I spy so much that if I have to hear "I spy with my little eye" one more time, I might cut someone.

Before I leave, I grab a fireplace poker and an ornamental sword that I found in an Oriental-themed room. It's probably not really smelted right, but it's better than nothing at all. Or at least, I hope it is. I'd rather not find out.

I also grab my backpack. It should cover up most of

the sword that's showing, and it'll have the added benefit of providing my reason for leaving. I can say that we need food that Gordon just isn't finding, right?

But what I really want, in order, is:

A way to contact the humans.

An idea of how many dragons there are.

Ways we might escape.

Axel barely seems to remember we're here. He shouldn't care much if we leave. If he catches me leaving and gets upset, I can explain that sending Gordon once a day to bring us food is a violation of his agreement to keep us safe. That seems reasonable.

I creep out the front doors, which fly open loudly, unhelpfully announcing my departure. But there's no one to see it. The entire area's totally abandoned. I walk past an Urban Air jump park, a steakhouse, a Waffle House, and then I see what I've been looking for—a gas station. They always have map books, right?

Only, it doesn't.

Apparently, thanks to iPhones, no one needs those anymore. I swear under my breath. How am I supposed to look at where they might have their real base of operations, knowing they likely need a place on the water, without a map? I keep walking, past a seafood place and a movie theater. There are no humans anywhere to be seen—which makes me wonder whether they got out. . .or died. I don't see bodies.

But what does that mean?

The signs are mostly unfamiliar, but the NASA Bypass isn't a big surprise. Next to that are signs for Clear Creek. If there really is a creek, that could empty into the gulf, which they might like for the water drag-ons. I head back toward the furniture store in search of some kind of provisions. If one of Axel's people catches me, I need to have a plausible story, and I've been out for more than an hour now.

A dragon flies overhead, and I duck under a store awning. I hide for fifteen minutes, my heart pounding, and then I creep back out. Just past the furniture store there's a Costco—I must have been really focused on getting that gas station map book to miss it on my way out. I duck inside and find granola bars, breakfast bars, beef jerky for me, and half a dozen other things. They're all in such big packaging that I have to break things open to stuff my backpack, but in less than thirty minutes, I've loaded up with all I can carry, and I'm ready to duck back out.

A few hundred feet, and no one will realize I've even left.

That's when I hear it.

The whimpering's really pathetic. It's definitely some kind of dog.

"Come here, baby," I call softly, hoping it'll listen. I can't risk being out here too long trying to coax an unknown animal.

Not a peep.

I try again. "Hey there, cutie. Come here. I can give you a treat."

Still nothing.

Wherever it is, it's been scared or scarred enough to stay hidden. I hope my siblings are doing the same. "Alright, well, if you won't come out, I can't help you. I've got to go."

I'm walking away when it pokes its head out. It's a tiny black Pomeranian with a tan face. I glance left and then right—no signs of any dragons—and crouch down again. "Come on, sweetie. Come here." I open a granola bar and hold out a piece in my hand. "Treat?"

To my shock, it darts out and heads right for me. It

tries to snatch the food and run, but I'm faster. When I pick it up, my heart sinks. It weighs almost nothing. And that's how I wind up heading *back* to the store to grab a bag of dog food and some canned chicken. The dog food's heavy, but the dog's light enough that I don't dare leave any of it behind.

I'm two dozen feet from the store entrance when I hear it.

A scraping, crackling sound.

That can't be good.

As I spin around, I hear a grinding noise, like gears in a car seizing up. That's two weird, low sounds now, which means two shifting dragons, somewhere. I don't dare lead them to the furniture store, but I also can't greet them while holding this little fluff. "I'm going to put you down," I whisper. "You need to stay put when I do, alright?" I tear the top of the bag of dry dog food open and drop them both on the ground in a bush. I rip my backpack open next to it, exposing my makeshift weapons.

A fireplace poker and a decorative sword.

Well, it could be worse. I could be brandishing a broken umbrella and a snapped stick. Is it possible I have nothing to worry about? Could the dragons be friends? I mean, it's not Gordon or Rufus—they sound the same every time they shift. But it could be another dragon sent by Axel, right?

Only, if the dragons don't mean me harm, why would they be shifting? Only, when I turn around, it's to face two men and a woman.

I could have sworn I heard. . .do they make the same sound when they shift to a human form? They must. And maybe they're friendly. He is their prince, after all.

Part of me hates Axel even more than before for

leaving me here and teaching me nothing. Of course, if I'd stayed put like he ordered. . .

"Hey there, fellow Blessed," I say.

"You're a human." The woman sniffs. "You reek of it."

I don't smell *that* bad, and it's not my fault Axel dropped me somewhere without a proper bathroom. "I'm ensnared," I say.

"Then where's your visor?" Her smile isn't reassuring.

My *visor*? "I, uh, left it back in my den." I'm proud of my quick thinking.

"You're not supposed to be here," the woman says. "We're tasked to round up any human stragglers and bring them in to be assigned. If you really are Ensnared, you can sort it out there."

Stragglers? There are humans out here who haven't been caught yet? But that also means they've caught others, and those humans are doing their bidding. "You must be Earth Blessed," I say, "since you can shift into human form."

"You do know some things." The woman frowns. "Who have you talked to?"

"I'm bound to Axel," I say. "The Prince of the Earth Blessed."

She scowls. "We can't ensnare humans."

I cringe a little. Will the others finding out get him in trouble? Is that why he's been hiding me? If so, my little venture outside might have been far, far worse than Gordon made it sound. "Maybe I'm mistaken," I say. "Maybe he's not Earth Blessed, but I have a dragon, and he told me to wait here. I'm going to just duck inside until he comes." I point across the street at the Costco. I can't have them searching the furniture store, after all.

The doors to Star Furniture open with a whoosh. "Liz, you're back!" Jade's beaming right up until she looks past me at three very shocked faces.

"Get back inside," I shout. "Now." I lunge for the sword and the fireplace poker as if they might actually help me.

"You lied," the woman says. "You're not alone, and you're not bound to anyone." She sprints toward me.

"We should shift back," the short man says.

"We always wind up killing them when we do that, and then Axel gets mad. He said we need humans to run all the things that need doing."

The woman has reached me now, not suffering from the same sort of indecision as the men. Her lip curls back in a snarl as she reaches for me.

I've used bamboo swords since I first started with martial arts. The familiar clacking. The strikes and parries and jabs. I do them without thinking.

She's moving toward me, so I strike with the ornamental blade.

It severs her hand at the wrist.

This thing must be much sharper than I thought, which is lucky. I suppose with enough force behind it, even a blunt blade can slice. I stop worrying about the details and focus on that moment and my most urgent opponent. She's snarling, and she brings her good hand up by her face. I'm completely shocked as I watch the fingers of her remaining hand shift. The fingernails morph into claws, and then her teeth lengthen, too.

If they can change their shape from dragon to human, I suppose it makes sense that they can also alter the specifics of it, but it looks even stranger than seeing a dragon to me now. When she swipes at me, I parry smoothly, thank you years of training, and I sweep upward with the fireplace poker, gouging the left side of her body pretty badly.

That's why she stumbles.

And I take my window without pause, decapitating her.

Mostly.

I suppose a decorative blade isn't really that great at slicing through *everything*, and the neck has bone, sinew, and connective tissue galore. Her head kind of lolls forward, still partially connected. It's probably the goriest, most grotesque thing I've seen in my entire life.

That's why the two men are able to approach me while I'm distracted. They're so close they could reach out and grab me.

And then they do.

But I react quickly, at least, and I manage to dislodge the hand of the short one, freeing my left arm. Sadly it's my fireplace poker arm, but I slam it upward and into the woman's dangling head, and it finally detaches the rest of the way.

Her head, rolling away from us, distracts the short man enough that he drops down to one knee and calls out what I presume is her name. "Jakarta!"

The tall man sinks his claws into my arm, which hurts more than I expect. I drop my sword. His smile widens, and he yanks me backward. Unfortunately for him, close fighting is kind of my sweet spot. I stomp on his left foot and bring up my poker arm, smashing his nose with the handle.

He releases my arm, blessedly, though it still burns like fire, and reaches for my throat. I drop straight down onto my heels and pivot, kicking his uninjured leg. He, predictably, drops, and I drive the poker through his eye. It won't kill him, if he's anything like

Gordon and Axel, but it distracts him long enough for me to retrieve my sword.

It takes me three attempts this time to decapitate him, and the side of the sword grinds on the pavement with each stroke, further dulling the already blunt blade. It's no shock to me that the short man's waiting for me when I finish.

And not in his human form, dang it all.

I'm sure he's more than ready to kill me by now. I hope the kids are hiding, because I'm positive I can't defeat this one. He's bigger than either Gordon or Rufus, and his scales are a deep, emerald green. I only know it's him because the eyes are the same strange shade of brown as before, glinting with hatred.

I wasn't trying to hurt any of you, I say. *For what it's worth. I am ensnared.*

The bright green dragon's eyes widen with fear, which makes no sense. He can't be afraid of me, so what could be causing that? I follow his eyes—he's staring at something over my shoulder. I turn around slowly, forgetting about the threat of the green dragon when I see what has him worried.

Until now, I've only seen the terrifying, blood-red beast from afar. He descends rapidly, his wingspan greater than a Boeing 737's, banks hard and then drops right in front of me. I clench one hand on my sword. I've killed two dragons who were in their human form. That green one was about to end me, but I planned to make it feel the misery of taking down a warrior.

But now?

This one could end me with one breath. I stand no chance, but that doesn't mean I should give up. I'll die screaming in his horrible, disgusting face. I brandish my pathetic weapons and leap sideways, my sword slashing at his wing. If I can damage it, maybe he won't be able to fly. Maybe he won't be able to kill so many humans with such ease until it heals.

But my stupid, blood-soaked ornamental blade clatters off the wing, sending a painful vibration up my shredded arm. Still, I can't give up. I just can't. I set my feet and hurl my poker at his eye.

Eyes probably aren't armored, right? If I can spear it, he might go blind on one side. Except he turns his head and it hits his eye-ridge and falls to the ground harmlessly as well.

Then he snorts.

He raises one enormous claw, and I bow my head, balling my fists at my side, preparing myself for the ending I know is coming. Will Axel still protect the kids, even after I'm gone? Maybe he'll be patient enough to wait for them to grow into adults. He might want to try and ensnare one, right?

Only, he doesn't kill me.

There's a whoosh of air as the crimson monster inexplicably flays the green dragon open and shoves it dozens of feet away from us.

"Why?" I can barely force myself to breathe. Why would he kill the dragon instead of me?

I'm a friend of Axel, he says. *I'm his oldest friend, in fact.* He scowls. *He told me you were supposed to stay inside that building.* He tosses his head toward Star Furniture.

I splutter.

Get inside, and I'll clean up this mess.

The scariest creature I've ever seen just saved me? For Axel? "But—"

Now. The word's punctuated with a snort that nearly knocks me over backward.

I jog over to the bushes where the poor little Pomeranian has ducked her head under her paws and is whimpering.

What's that?

"It's a creature I found," I say. Then I realize that he didn't say whether he knew about my siblings. It's probably better if I don't mention them. "I need *something* to do while I'm trapped in that building all day."

Is the terrifying beast smiling? It almost looks like he is.

"Can you tell Axel to come back soon? Because I'm almost bored to death."

You very nearly were, yes. He watches me calmly as I grab my backpack, tuck the terrified dog under my arm—just in time for it to wet all over me—and scurry inside the furniture store. My three siblings are *not* waiting in their room. They're just inside, and the second the doors close, they rush to my side.

"You're bleeding," Jade says.

"Is that a dog?" Sammy asks.

"You smell like pee," Coral says.

"I'm going to kill all of you," I say.

But seeing them, touching them, is exactly what my trembling body needs more than anything else. At least, it's enough right up until the venom from the stupid dragon man who clawed my arm sets in.

Then I can't think about much of anything at all.

❦ 7 ❦

Once, in sixth grade, I got a stomach bug. It was so bad that I wanted to die. For days and days in a row, I couldn't eat a thing. No matter what I tried to eat or drink, I threw up.

I wound up in the ER on an IV for three days.

That felt like a day at Disneyworld compared to how I feel right now.

My skin's on fire. My vision's blurry. I can't eat or drink. I can't even stand up to go to the bathroom. For someone who makes their living fighting, someone who dreads the idea of facing danger without any strength, this is my worst nightmare.

Coral and Jade are beside themselves, which makes it even worse.

"Try one sip of water," Coral says for the fifth time. . .in the last hour.

I can barely shake my head.

"She feels really hot," Jade says. "Here's another rag."

They keep placing them on my head, but the heat from my body dries the rag out in minutes. How long can a human survive a terribly high temperature without keeping any fluids down?

"You could try taking Tylenol again," Jade says. "If she could keep it down, that might really help."

"We've given it to her three times," Coral says. "Mom says we can't take it over and over."

"But she keeps puking it all up," Jade says.

I don't have the energy or the heart to tell them that human medicine clearly can't fix me.

Their voices blur together in my brain, and I can't tell where one begins and the other ends. It would be great if it was because I was falling asleep, but I doubt that's where this is going. I haven't slept in at least a day—the sun set not long after I stumbled back inside, and it's going down again right now.

Has it been one day?

Or two?

The mixture of their voices washes over me like waves crashing over the sand, draining and disappearing as fast as it shows up. They're bickering now, but it doesn't upset me. Maybe their fighting will keep them alive and kicking. Maybe that's the key to their survival.

No! I'm the key.

I struggle to swim upward, from oblivion back to clarity. It feels important somehow, like if I let go I'll just be. . .gone. I push, but the harder I push, the more it hurts. I want to dive back down, but I can't. I have to keep pushing.

But the pain is like a wave. It rolls over me, burning, searing, and shredding. I want to disappear, because then it will all stop. I'm pushing against it now for no reason that I can recall. The more I push, the more the pain grows, and I want to quit. I'm about to let go again when I hear a voice I know.

It's Sammy, and he's crying. "Liz is dying."

"No, she's not," Jade says.

"Yes, she is." Sammy hits my body then, striking my thigh as hard as he can with his tiny fist.

I don't even so much as twitch. I'm barely conscious of the fact that he did it. And I realize that he's right.

This disconnected feeling?

It's because I'm dying.

That dragon didn't kill me—the red demon saved me before he could. But it was too late. He'd already pumped me full of whatever toxin earth dragons have on their claws, and it's ending me slowly, like a lobster being boiled alive. At least my siblings got to see me and tell me goodbye. At least my body wasn't mangled or eaten.

But I can't have them lose me like this, with no closure. Not after having their mother snatched at a party. I try to move my lips, willing my tongue to work. I need to tell them that I love them. I need to tell them to be strong. I need to tell them to try to escape, to move away from the water. To hide from all sounds.

Something fluffy's licking my face with a tiny tongue.

"I think she may already be dead," Jade whispers, her eyes wide like saucers, her skin pale. "I can't hear her breathing."

Why would I breathe? It's not necessary now, and it's so, so hard. Every breath feels like a fight.

A fight I know I can't win.

"No!" Coral shouts. And then she stabs me.

She stabs me? Why would she do that? She did it in my leg, right where Sammy hit me. Against the cottony feeling of departure, there's now a bright spot of misery. It blooms up hard and quick, and I gasp for breath.

Coral slaps me next. "No, you can't leave. We can't do anything without you. You have to do what you told us you would do, what you want us to do. You have to fight. Right now. Breathe. Sit up. Get better."

I draw in one more ragged breath, though it feels like more than I can bear. Now that I'm trying, all the misery is back and it's worse than I remember. My eyes are burning. My skin's on fire. My lungs ache and throb and they feel thick, like they're full of water. My arm feels like it's been strapped to electric wires and a current is being forced through it constantly. I force my eyes to look downward and I can see that it's streaked with dark lines. I try to swallow, but I can't even do that.

"I'm going to get Axel." Coral stands. "He promised that he'd protect us, and you're about to die, and he didn't want that to happen."

"I hope my death wipes him out. I hope he's so incapacitated that the other dragons take him down," I whisper. "That's when you should leave. Run as far and as fast as you can."

"How long has she been like this?" Axel strides into the break room like a dark angel, his hair longish, his eyes bright. When my siblings all freeze, he asks much louder, "How long has she been like this?"

"Days," Coral says. "Three days. She's dying—I had to stab her leg to revive her."

"You did?" His hands ball into fists at his side. "You did the right thing."

"You said you'd protect her," Coral says. "You suck."

His eyebrows rise. "I swore to protect *you*. She was supposed to protect herself, but I guess she didn't do that very well, did she?"

"You just stuck us in here and left." Coral's not backing down. It's cute, but it's not very smart. The little fluff we rescued barks once from where she's standing behind Coral, and then she whimpers.

"I hate that beast," Axel says.

"You've never even met her," Coral says. "She hates you too, though, just like I do."

"Can you fix her?" Sammy asks.

Axel can't understand him, so Jade clarifies. "Can you heal her?"

He sighs. "I'm going to try." He moves closer, and my siblings part like the Red Sea, seemingly trusting that he wants what's best for me. I suppose if they're going to trust any dragon on earth, he's the one. He's the only one my death would harm.

"She's been poisoned with dragon venom," he says. "How could that be?"

"The dragon your friend killed," I rasp.

Of course, he has no idea what I said.

What happened?

Right. He can speak to me in my head. I wonder whether I can talk back in the same way. I grit my teeth and think words and try to push them toward him. *Green dragon in human form clawed my arm.*

Did it work?

I pry my eyes open to try and see.

He's nodding ever so slightly, so I'm hoping that means he understood.

"I had no idea what that would do to a human," he says. "It appears to be bad. I'm not sure any other humans have attacked a dragon and lived." It may be my feverish delusion, but he almost sounds proud.

"What can you do?" Coral asks.

Axel shrugs. "Among the Blessed, we're either strong enough to heal ourselves or we aren't."

Fabulous. *I'm clearly not. Get ready to have a few bad days when I go.*

"We're bonded. I'm wondering whether I can use my energy to help her."

"Ooh," Jade says. "That sounds good. Try that."

Axel laughs. "It may not be that simple. I'm not sure quite how to do it."

"If you'd gotten her training instead of abandoning us, you might know." Coral crosses her arms.

"You're nearly as scary as your sister. Are you good with swords, too?"

"You're lucky." Coral shakes her head. "Just words."

Axel points at the door. "I need you three to leave. I won't do a thing to harm her, but I don't know what's going to happen when I try. I swore to protect you, and that means keeping you away from any kind of magical backlash."

Coral looks at me.

I can't nod, so I blink.

"Once for yes," she says. "Twice for no."

I blink once.

"Fine." She waves and the others follow her out. It takes a moment, but they finally coax the fluffy dog to follow them as well. Coral really is a little spitfire. It won't be enough to save them if I die, but it's beautiful to watch. I just need to be strong enough to give her time to grow.

Jade's just as lovely, and Sammy too, of course, but they aren't as scary. They're more light and joy and delirium. I think it's natural that I admire the child in our family who's the most like me. If we'd been closer in age, I might have hated her.

"I'm going to try to push some magic into you," Axel says. "It may hurt."

I try to snort, but it comes out like a sniff.

"I'll take that as a single wink."

He likes them. I'm not sure how I can tell, but I can. The horrible, scary, evil dragon likes my siblings. Whether that will be of any use to them, I have no idea. I doubt it. But it's strange to see it all the same.

Axel picks up his hands and stacks them, right hand on top, and then holds them over the center of my body. I'm not sure what he's doing exactly, but his hands start to glow. He slams them down against the middle of my stomach.

A lance of fire melts through to my very core.

Energy I didn't know I had surges through me, and my body bows, and I scream. I scream louder and longer than I realized I could. I scream until my throat is raw, until it's ragged, until my vocal cords feel like hamburger meat, and then I keep on screaming.

My screams should die down, but they just keep coming.

Because the pain never lets up.

Nothing is worth this. I should have faded away.

Someone's banging on a wall or a door or something, but I can't stop. The screams keep pouring out of me, because the pillar of energy keeps drilling down further and further, like it's determined to hollow me out entirely.

Finally, Axel drops his hand, and the pain stops. I collapse back to the bed, an empty husk. Whatever reserves I had left are gone now, burned to ash. Before, I felt like I was floating away. My siblings were there, missing me already, worrying about me, stabbing me. Ha. I was at least peaceful in the knowledge that they loved me, they'd miss me, and that they didn't want me to leave. But this time, I'm not drifting away.

I'm already almost gone. There's nothing to fade.

Like the last grains of sand draining through the bottom of an hourglass.

Like the last whiff of scent in an empty diffuser.

Like smoke puffing out of the last ember as it cools.

My soul's evacuating my body when Axel uses one hand's talon-like fingernail to slice the palm of the other. Then he slices my hand open and presses both of our hands together.

His blood hits me like the recoil of a twelve gauge. Like the kick of a mule to my chin. Like Gideon's left hook to my jaw. My body shrinks inward to what feels like a single atom and then explodes outward, refilling all my empty spaces, burning through everything that I once was and replenishing all the holes and tears and empty wells with pure light energy.

Ironically, my eyes are burning, my lungs are aching, my back is screaming with pain, and my arm, which hurt worse than any injury I'd ever felt before, screams with agony. But this isn't the kind of pain that made me scream. It's the pain that precedes the repair, like the scream of muscles being torn down to rebuild stronger. Like the grinding of an old scar to expose new, healthy tissue.

His blood is healing me.

But it's also changing me.

I can't tell how, and I'm not sure quite how much, but the new, rebuilt Liz is not the same as the Liz-that-was. I'm stronger. I'm brighter. I'm tougher.

I'm Liz 2.0.

I got an upgrade. I doubt that green dragon meant to improve my life, but that stupid sadist did it anyway. Thanks to his mauling, thanks to his filthy venom, I'm now even better than I was. I'm not sure what it means, but the world's sharper, the colors are brighter, and when I sit up, I move easier, faster, and different somehow.

"Oh, that worked." Axel swallows as if it's a surprise.

"You didn't think it would?"

He shrugs. "I've been looking into the ensnared humans. I know you think I abandoned you here, and I really should have made time sooner, but the earth dragons are in charge of both defense and setting things back in place. Managing all of that has been exhausting. Your ecosystem is. . .delicate."

"What?" I ask.

"So many people with so many tasks that are all interconnected or they fall apart."

I blink.

"And trying to learn about the Ensnared while also managing all of that—it was exhausting."

"But I could have helped."

"The Blessed will struggle to accept that I've bonded you."

"So? You're best friends with the big red nightmare."

"The big red. . ." He snorts. "I've never in all my life heard anyone call him anything so disrespectful."

"Of course not. You're surrounded by yes men and lackeys. That beast is terrifying and evil and just. . ." I shudder.

"He says you tried to attack him." Axel's smiling like it's a big joke.

"Tried, yes. It was like using a toothpick on a tank."

"Ah, the rolling gun boxes."

"Yes, those are tanks."

"And a toothpick is a small piece of wood you use to pick your teeth."

"How did you learn English?" I finally ask.

"When we first came, there were only a handful of us. We assumed a humanoid form and found many books. We took them back, and one of us assimilated them, and then Azar, the dragon you hate, used his magic to spread the knowledge to the rest of us."

"That sounds handy. I'd know, like, every language."

"Once you complete your training, you probably could assimilate some of the information as well, if you so choose."

That blows my mind.

"Or you can just use our language. Soon the lesser ones will no longer be necessary."

"Pass," I say. "I'm anti-colonialism."

He frowns, but he doesn't argue.

"Was Azar furious?" I ask.

His frown deepens.

"So he was mad that I attacked him?" I swallow. "Or, was he upset because he had to come save me?" I think about that. "Speaking of, how did he know to come save me?"

"I can feel you from anywhere," Axel says. "Not well, not clearly yet, but I'm learning. And I was doing something for him when I felt your distress."

"You sent *him* as your errand boy?" I whistle. "You must be really close."

"Something like that." He clears his throat. "I've known him for a very long time, and he owes me."

"Alright, well." I sigh. "I assume that now we'll finally start my training?"

"I'm regretting ensnaring you, if you must know," he says.

That stings a little bit. "I regret being ensnared," I say. "How about you let me go and we call it even?"

"You're a liability for me," he says. "I've been

researching how to free myself, but so far, I'm coming up with nothing."

"If you can get me to the edge of dragon lands, however far that is, I promise to be very safe and very healthy for as long as possible. I will cause you no distress whatsoever." I cross my heart with my fingers.

He looks very confused. "I can't do that."

"Oh, come on," I say.

"You're a troublemaker by nature," he says.

I can't argue with that, really, not after attacking him and his man, killing two other dragons, and almost dying, all in the same week. "Plus, you're a bright. So if I abandon you, even with my bond in place, another dragon could sense you. I can't even contemplate what might happen if they tried to bond an already bonded human."

I shake my head. "Okay, so you won't let me go until you've somehow dissolved the bond, so let's look into that."

"I'm not supposed to have bonded anyone at all," he says. "That's the major problem. When I went back to the camp and conferred with the others, it became clear that it wasn't an error. Earth Blessed cannot ensnare humans. They never have. They shouldn't be able to."

"But you did, right?" I scratch my head. "Are you sure you really did it? I don't *really* feel you." But of course, if he didn't, that really undercuts my bargain. How far do I want to go down this road? Will he let me go? Or just kill us all?

I think about the time I stabbed him and how I couldn't breathe. There is clearly *some* kind of bond.

"I guess what I mean is that I can't feel much, and even that, not unless you're close."

"That may be because I didn't really seal the bond," he mutters.

"What?"

He's looking down at his hands. Is he nervous? What's going on?

"We were supposed to exchange blood after I ensnared you, but I didn't do it."

Because he was regretting what he did and looking for a way out. I approve of that, actually.

But we just did share blood.

To heal me from the venom, he gave me his blood and now. . .I kick him.

And then I double over to rub the sore spot on my own shin. "Ow."

"You did that." He's frowning, but I notice that he didn't even flinch.

"Don't tell me that didn't hurt you. I know it did."

"You humans can't mask your pain at all. You show every single thing you feel."

I straighten. "I'm tough, actually."

"Tough like a human is like scary for a fluff dog."

"Fluff dog," I say. "I like it. I think we'll name her that."

"You can't keep that thing." He stands up. "I forbid it."

I stand up, too. "Well, I counter forbid it."

"That's not how it works."

"Then you'll have to make me give her up." What am I saying? We can't give up Fluff Dog. Not now that she has a name.

He glares, and then I feel it. He's focusing on me and he's *pushing* his will at me.

I bat it away.

He grunts—he felt that one.

I can't help my smug grin. Earth dragon or not, I

feel like this guy isn't humbled nearly often enough. Maybe because he's the prince earth dragon or whatever. "I'm keeping Fluff Dog."

He points at the wall. "Turn around."

"Excuse me?" I shake my head. "I refuse."

"You keep refusing everything," he says. "The more you do that, the more you incentivize me to train enough to learn how to control you by force."

"I think something about training me scares you, so I don't think it works as a threat. Sorry."

So fast that I can barely register his movements, he spins me around and tears the back of my shirt, exposing the back of my left shoulder. "Hey!" I shout. "What are you doing?"

Are shoulders, like, erotic to dragons? Ew.

I turn to look over my bare shoulder, but he's not doing anything gross. He's just staring at my shoulder with what looks an awful lot like relief. "What?"

"It's my mark." He sighs. "It's just my mark."

"What are you talking about?"

"When you're ensnared, the magic of the dragon who bonds you sears a mark into the back of your shoulder, like so." He points.

I remember the burning feeling. It disappeared so quickly, and I haven't had a proper bath, so I never noticed. Not that I would have examined the back of my shoulder in any case. I grab the top of my shoulder with my right hand and pull hard, craning my neck at the same time.

It's there—something golden. It's like a circle with some kind of flower inside of it. "What is it?"

"It's a lotus blossom," he says. "It symbolizes the cycle of life and death that the Earth Blessed facilitate."

"Your buddies were pretty intent on the death part," I say.

"Well, you managed to beat them."

I feel a little bad about that, but not guilty. I won't feel guilty when I watched that silver psychopath fry family after family for no reason at all. "I am sorry I killed them."

"They were friends," Axel says. The coldness in his voice reminds me that we're not. In fact, he's been staying away in order to search for a way to get rid of me. He may be proud that his ensnared human—his slave—is a warrior, but he's not keen on having me around.

I'm a liability at best.

An enemy at worst.

I need to remember that at all times.

"Tell your siblings to pack their bags." Axel stands. "We're joining the main camp."

"Just like that?" I ask. "I thought you didn't want people to know—or other dragons to know, I mean—that you'd bonded me."

"They'll have to find out eventually." He shrugs. "Now that you seem to be fully recovered and we're officially bonded, it may as well be today."

❋ 8 ❋

After I got tapped to join the best MMA gym in Houston, I thought everything would be smooth sailing for me. After all, only the best of the best were invited to train there.

My first day at the new gym, someone dipped my socks in some kind of glue. I was in a hurry, and I thought they were just wet, so I decided to ignore it. By the time I realized what had happened, I yanked my shoes off. That also peeled my socks off, and all the skin on my feet went with it. I was worried Mom would make me leave the gym, so I didn't tell her. At least, not until my right foot was infected. I won twenty-four hours in the hospital with that one, and even after my release, it made for some long, miserable training sessions.

After my return, I thought they'd back off.

I was wrong.

My gloves were doused in soda and covered with ants. My Gatorade was replaced with apple cider vinegar. My clothes were dusted with itching powder. My locker was decorated with graphic photos, terrible words painted across it.

Sousa's predecessor said it was just normal 'hazing,' and he told me the other fighters were jealous. In the fighting world, complaining about things like that was considered weak. I learned pretty quickly to keep my eyes open, to watch my back, and to make myself an uncomfortable target. I never stooped to doing the same things back—I let my aggression out on the mat. Soon enough, they were afraid of using such backhanded tactics.

Jealousy turned into respect.

I'm not sure what to expect from the Ensnared who have been dragon captured for maybe a week now. I'm sure their dragons have done a better job training them—how could they not? But how much could they have learned in a week? I do need instruction. Obviously Axel hasn't had much luck being taught, since he's not supposed to have been able to bond me in the first place. Even so, I'm not worried about myself. I plan to be a very, very difficult target for any hostility. I'm only worried for Coral, Jade, and Sammy.

Axel waits patiently, or at least, barely tapping his foot, while we gather up our meager belongings.

Sammy's piled up a veritable mountain of junk he's pilfered from all over the store. Most of it's random decor items, ranging from superhero paraphernalia to animal pictures. "No way. You can't take all that. Last time, you could barely hang on during the ride."

Sammy's face falls. "But—"

"Absolutely not," I say. "You can take what fits in your backpack and nothing more."

His shoulders slump as he walks away from his treasure pile.

Gordon, crouched near the entrance in his dragon

form, slithers even closer, hisses, and starts to gather up the ends of the sheet that was lying underneath Sammy's pile of junk.

"What's he doing?" I ask.

Tell him I'll take it. Gordon's voice in my head is raspy with a hiss-like undertone that suits his snake-dragon form.

"That's not necessary. He'll be fine," I say.

But Gordon's already biting down on the corners of the sheet.

"That's not going to hold," I say. "It'll tear a hundred yards from the store, and then he'll be even more upset. Trust me. He'll get over it quick."

Axel grabs a duvet off the bed next to us and flattens it on the ground. Gordon drops the hobo pile on top, and Axel helps him reposition and tie the duvet around it.

"You don't have to do that," I say again.

They ignore me.

So they'll roast humans without a thought, but for this little boy, they're knotting up a blanket full of crap? Do they think it atones for their past evils?

Hardly.

Changing dens is hard for little ones, Gordon says. *I don't mind carrying his stuff.*

So what if he's being sweet? I refuse to be swayed.

"Let's go."

Rufus is waiting outside, his shoulder height in dragon form a little too tall to easily crouch underneath even the large Star Furniture entry. The girls, their backpacks slung over their shoulders already, climb on. Coral looks delighted, and she's even holding Fluff Dog. Miracle of miracles, though the little floof is trembling, she's sitting mostly still on Rufus' back. Jade looks practically green, clearly already anticipating a long, miserable ride like the first.

But this time, we don't set out at a breakneck pace. Although Axel didn't dump us inside the dragon colony, we must not be too far away, because he stays in his human form. "Let's go."

"Where are we headed?"

"It's a ten-minute walk," he says. "Give or take."

"Okay." I don't point out that my siblings could walk that, too. Maybe he's bringing his buddies as a show of force or something.

We don't go far before we turn down a large highway that is surprisingly not entirely abandoned. It's hardly rush hour traffic, but there are cars driving back and forth. "What's going on? Who are those people?" And why didn't he let me bring *my* car?

"We're beginning to reintegrate the assimilated humans. They're able to maintain the basic human infrastructure for us, even in occupied Houston."

Occupied Houston. Assimilated humans. My brain rebels at the words. "Come again?"

"I thought a walk would be helpful, so I can explain the basics of the training you're about to undergo. Ensnared humans are chosen for their abilities—specifically, your telepathic powers."

"Telepathic, like, my mind can talk to you?"

"That and other things."

That sounds ominous.

"Once you're properly trained, you'll be able to use your mind to monitor other humans. You'll be able to set them simple, and then later more complex, tasks. Monitoring their completion is simple, and redirecting when necessary will be done with ease."

"Are you saying I'll be directing humans like they're robots?"

"Not exactly. Think of how you just told Sammy he couldn't take his belongings. At first, he was disappointed, but you know that with time he'd accept it. With the other humans, your task is to make sure they don't break any important rules, and that they are contributing members of society. You'll be able to remove any mental anomalies they suffer from, and keep them on task in whatever direction we choose."

"Remove mental anomalies?" That sounds. . .awful.

"Humans seem to suffer from any number of unnatural problems, such as a lack of a will to live, insufficient energy to complete tasks, worsened by their inactivity. You'll be able to will those things away so that they wake up on time, complete healthy exercise, eat properly, and make intelligent, safe choices."

"But they won't really have a choice," I say. "You're saying I'll make them be good."

He shrugs. "It benefits them as well, and it keeps things here comfortable for both you and us. Don't worry. You won't need to punish them—disobedience won't be possible for them once your training is complete."

And everything he's saying about what *I* can do also applies to what he can do to me. My stomach churns angrily and my mind rejects any involvement in something like that.

"You may not like it, but this is your purpose now," he says. "And think how it will make your life easier as well. Instead of huddling inside an abandoned store as you were, or hiding in basements, sheds, or caves, humans will return to their dwellings. They can go about their tasks of cooking, cleaning, and work as they did before, but instead of taking more than their fair share, or providing nothing of benefit and being a drain on the community they live in, they'll receive only what they need to be healthy and productive citizens." He pauses. "There's no waste in an Ensnared-led community."

"It's communism, enforced with mind control. That's what you're saying."

He frowns. "Communism is a form of government where the people rule things and everyone has the same, but it never works. Human greed renders it impossible to achieve, and the lack of a singular motivating factor makes it a poor leveler as well."

"Okay, but—"

"The Blessed will be directing your actions. You'll merely control the weak-minded humans so that they don't need to be killed. I think you can agree that's a win for all of us."

He's making it sound like a public service. Control the weak-minded humans so that they don't get themselves into trouble. "But it's our choices that make us who we are."

"I think drawing breath in and out, the pumping of blood in your heart, those things make you who you are. Without them, you're nothing. You're dead. We can continue debating this later, but it won't change the reality." He points the direction we were moving. "You will keep walking, and you will learn how to control the humans, because otherwise, I'll kill you and your small family members, and I'll deal with the consequences and be done with it."

I clench my hands into fists. "Fine."

"Whether you like it or not, we aren't about to let the local humans run free under our rule."

Axel's half-grin is pissing me off.

"If you refuse to help, someone else will do exactly what I tell you to make them do. Or, I'll force you. The end result is the same no matter how you handle it."

He leans a little closer. "Your resistance is, quite literally, futile."

I hate him. Was I just thinking that it was kind of cute how he and Gordon were helping Sammy? I must've temporarily lost my mind. He's the devil. The devil in jeans and a button-down shirt.

"Your style choice sucks." I shoot past him at a jog. "And I hate you."

He's laughing as he catches up. "That's more like it."

"You want me to learn to push humans around, and make them do whatever we want, and then what? Why do you even need that?"

"In addition to creating a sustainable life for us here while we're stuck here, their job will also be to aid in the search for the Heart, of course."

"And how exactly are we going to do that, without more information from you?"

"I told you I'd provide that," he says. "It's not really a secret, our search. It's just that, if the wrong people find out—"

"By the wrong people, you mean anyone with their own, liberated brain."

"Exactly." He bobs his head. "If they find out, they might try to keep us from achieving our goal."

"Humans' greatest strength is in their freedom," I say. "And in this case, telling them should only help you. I'm sure the humans outside of Houston want you gone as much as I do if not more."

"You know, some humans actually reach a point where they like their dragon."

"Liar."

"Some of them are getting along just fine right now." He shrugs. "Not all of the Ensnared are as angry and downright rude as you."

"How sad for them," I say. But in that moment, I realize that my mom will probably be wherever we're going. "Whoa." I stop again.

"What?" He sighs. "You can yell at me all you want, but please keep moving. I have a lot of things to do other than shoving my errant Ensnared and her tagalongs into closer housing."

"My mom was taken," I say. "I bet she'll be there." Unless she threw one too many fits and was already killed. That idea fills me with dread. My mother won't eat meat. She won't use any products that aren't carbon neutral. She follows the signs of the universe to determine the trajectory of her day. Sometimes, when I got home from school, she'd just be gone. She'd leave us in the care of our neighbors, because she was called to pursue a path that led her away from us for a few days. She can be a real fruitcake, and she hates nothing in the world more than unjust authority.

Her feelings on that caused almost every fight she and my dad ever had. She'd claim he was trying to make her do things she didn't want to do, and she'd utterly flip out.

"She probably will." Axel looks uncomfortable. In all the time we've spent together, which admittedly hasn't been that much yet, I've never seen him look like this. If he were human, I'd say he was uneasy.

"What?"

"Don't be surprised if she doesn't act like herself." He frowns, and I realize he's stopped badgering me to move.

"You aren't shocked that she was ensnared?"

"Brights typically run in families," he says. "I'm not shocked."

"She's one of my people," I say. "You said you'd protect five humans."

He shakes his head. "No. She's ensnared. That trumps our arrangement. I won't have any power or authority to interfere with another dragon's property."

"*Property?*" I feel the heat flood my cheeks. "Are you saying I belong to you?"

"Of course you do," he says. "And the others will judge me by how well I manage you. Please don't make me do anything awful that we'll both regret by acting characteristically stupid." Now he's moving again, as if nothing he said was really that bad.

To him, I guess it's not. He's just out for a walk with his slave and her siblings, who are just future slaves, apparently. He's entreating me to behave so he won't have to chain me up and beat me. If he did, it would be my fault, not his. He's probably planning to take care of Sam, Coral, and Jade right up until he can throw them up on an auction block and sell them to another dragon for. . .whatever dragons want in the way of payment.

I hate him so much it makes my blood boil.

But it also reminds me that I know very little about them. Being close will give me an unparalleled chance to learn more. You can't defeat an enemy you don't know. I should be asking questions to see what information I can dislodge, but I'm worried that if I open my mouth again or if he says anything else, I'll wind up trying to strangle him.

It's a beautiful, sunny day with a light breeze, and if I weren't marching to my new prison I'd probably be enjoying it. When we reach the edge of a pretty posh neighborhood, I begin to wonder what new place we're headed. "Are we going to an actual human home?" I blink. "I assumed we'd be in another store, a large space."

"All the Earth Blessed are spending at least two

hours a day in their human forms," Axel says. "We've assigned each of them a home in the surrounding neighborhoods, and this one is ours."

The posh house he chose sits right on Clear Lake, overlooking the Nassau Bay Peninsula Wildlife Park, according to the signs. The dragons may have cleared out the humans who aren't leashed, but there are still plenty of birds, including geese and ducks, and lots of fish are hopping as we walk up to the front door of the new place.

"Will you be spending at least two hours a day here, then?" I ask.

Axel turns toward me slowly. "Are you worried? Or do you want me around more?" His eyes are only half open, as if he doesn't really care how I answer.

But his friends freeze behind us, and I know that, for some reason, my answer to this question matters.

He saved me once, but he wants me to order humans around on his behalf. He abandoned us for days at a time, even knowing our bond wasn't quite right. He didn't let me go when he couldn't terminate it, and I'm not sure he wouldn't have killed me if he'd been able to negate the impact to himself. "I don't know."

He smiles. "At least you're being honest."

"Would it do me any good to lie?" I can feel it now, barely, a thread of emotion in the back of my mind that I'm pretty sure is coming from him. It's muted, and it seems to have only a handful of settings, but I'm guessing he can feel the same thing coming from me.

"Not much, no."

Coral slides down, still cradling Fluff Dog in her arms. "We're going inside, right?"

I wave. "Yes, let's go. The sooner you're inside, the safer it'll be for all of you."

They're headed for the door when a huge blue dragon bursts through the surface of the water behind the house. Fluff Dog leaps, falling to the ground and racing into a nearby bush.

I suddenly understand why all those fish were leaping out of the water as we walked up.

I wave the kids inside even more furiously. Coral won't go until she's recovered the idiotic dog, of course, and Fluff Dog is not budging. It takes a lot of coaxing and Axel circling around behind her to say *Boo!* But finally, they're all inside. I breathe a little easier after they're out of sight, even if the water dragon didn't seem to notice us at all.

"Will there always be water dragons popping out of the lake?"

"Probably."

"Wonderful."

"The mere presence of the Blessed makes you nervous?" The emotion thread feels confused.

"Let's review. One of them stole my mother. I ran, and then you caught me. Then you ditched me, and a few of them tried to kill me. Actually, one of them would have, if your buddy didn't flay him open with one giant claw. And then that interaction still would have killed me, if you hadn't shared your blood. Blood that lets me command other humans to do things they wouldn't otherwise do. Yes, I'd say that all of you make me very, very nervous."

"But you're one of us now, fully," he says.

"Not by choice. And you told me that even as one of you, I may be a target. Because you weren't supposed to have been able to ensnare me."

He sighs. "As prince, I hope they'll see me as an anomaly and accept it."

"Has it occurred to anyone that maybe the earth dragons *can* ensnare humans after all?"

"Earth Blessed."

"What?"

"I've let it slide until now, but we're not *dragons*. We're the Blessed. It's our chosen name, and I hope you'll use it. Not everyone is as understanding as I am."

Now, nothing on earth could make me use their stupid name. Blessed, my foot. "The point is that, if you can do it, maybe the others can as well."

"They've tried," he says. "While I kept you waiting, dozens of them tried without success."

I don't want to know what their failure meant for the brights they found. I really hope those humans weren't all killed. "So you're a freak, and I'm your odd Ensnared, and now I have to go out there and learn to let my freak flag fly."

"I am keeping your siblings safe, as promised."

"But not my mother."

"I can't do anything for her," he says. "As mentioned, I can't dissolve the bond once it exists. You didn't tell me she was ensnared, or I'd have explained that at the time."

"Noted."

"I chose a house that's close, but not in the center of everything," Axel says. "It's on the water, because I'm often asked to meet with Strike and Water Blessed to coordinate our movements. I'm planning to be here as often as possible, to make sure your integration with the other Ensnared is safe."

Safe. So he's expecting trouble.

This is just like how, at the doctor's office, they tell you to expect *pressure*, but really they mean it will hurt. They say *pressure*, so that if you shout, you feel like a ninny for shouting about *pressure*.

Axel really is the worst.

"Your assigned mentor should be here in the next hour or so."

"How fabulous."

"By the end of the day, you'll have some humans to monitor."

"I probably won't be ready for that for weeks and weeks."

"Get ready faster." Axel says. "How about this? Why don't you save up all your complaints, and then you can yell at me when I get back?" He starts to walk away. "I'd also recommend that you keep your siblings away from the trainer. Not many Blessed are as *understanding* as I am. If the Ensnared was to share information about your family's existence, their master might see my indulgence of your requests as more than a little strange."

Like he knows anything about humans at all.

No ensnared human would betray my siblings to their overlord.

"Or, suit yourself. You always do." He winks, and then, with no further warning, the car engine noise revs up, his scales explode outward, and his entire body dramatically expands until a gleaming golden dragon is standing in front of me.

"Did you just wink at me?"

He doesn't even grace me with a response, but I can feel what reminds me quite a bit of humor running through the thread between us. And then he disappears, running much faster than I realized he could.

I've barely been inside the house for five minutes, helping the kids pick a room—I have no idea whether Gordon and Rufus are staying here, but there are four bedrooms upstairs and one downstairs. If they each have their own room, that leaves us two. There's no chance I'll be sharing with anyone, and my room has to be right by the kids. That puts us in the Jack-n-Jill suite on the far end, overlooking the water.

Gordon and Rufus, if they're staying here too, can have the rooms overlooking the front of the house, and His Royal Blessed Pain-in-the-Rear can have the master suite downstairs.

I'm outside, preparing to bring another load of Sammy's crap into the house when a tall woman wearing knee-high leather boots and tactical gear appears, trotting down the sidewalk. She has a strange silver bar, decorative almost, that's somehow floating in front of her forehead. I'm guessing it's the visor those dragons asked about. Her hair's a light, bright color of silver that Mom's turned to. I'm guessing that means she's serving an electro dragon.

"Elizabeth?" She arches one eyebrow until it disappears behind the visor.

I nod.

"I'm Penelope. I'll be training you today."

"Oh, great."

"You don't sound very grateful." She tilts her head and twists her lips. "If you don't really want help, I'll just head back."

"No, I do," I say. "I have no idea how to do anything."

She purses her lips as if she agrees. "Where shall we work? It needs to be somewhere you won't be distracted."

Fluff Dog races through the open front door and starts barking. Helpful. Very helpful.

"Hey." I scoop her up and jog up the path to the door, abandoning Sammy's Batman lamp. I raise my voice to top volume. "Now, you stay in there, Fluff Dog. I'm going to be training, and *I can't be distracted.*"

Even if the others don't get the message, Coral will. She'll keep them inside, I'm sure.

"What was that?" Penelope looks disgusted.

"I found her a few days ago," I say. "She's a rescue."

"Things like that won't survive in this world. You should learn to let them go."

Is that what she's done? Has she let go of anything that she thinks won't survive? I'm afraid to ask. "Let's go around the back of the house."

"Were you really ensnared by an Earth Blessed?" Now Penelope really looks unimpressed. "How unfortunate."

"He's their prince at least," I say.

"Wow, the prince of the unfortunates," she says. "Which makes you the bottom of the pile."

I stretch a bit and bounce back and forth. "I can take care of myself."

Her laugh is hard and sharp. "Maybe you could in your past life, but now you take your position from your Blessed, and yours is the worst it could be, prince or not."

"And I suppose your dragon craps rainbows?"

"Mine can take down a plane," she says. "She can kill a hundred people with one lightning bolt. So yes, she's far, far superior to yours who can. . .dig holes."

"And yet, here you are, at the request of my mud dragon prince, teaching his little lackey how to mind-control humans."

"Alright." Penelope starts to walk away. "I think we're done."

I'm not sure how hard Axel had to work or how many favors he called in to get me a trainer, and now I've already scared her off. That's not going to go over well, and if what she's saying is true, I may need to be strong enough to keep my siblings safe when Axel's not around. That means I need to figure out exactly what I can do. And also, if she leaves, I'll never be able to ask her about Mom.

But how can I stop her?

I can supposedly mind control humans just like she can. . .and she's a human.

I focus on her retreating form, thinking as hard as I can about how she should *not* be leaving, and how her feet should *not* be moving away. Her body should about-face and return to stand by me.

Then I *push* that thought at her.

She freezes.

I can't help my smile. I clearly did something.

"Was that you?" She turns around slowly, a wicked smile curving her lips.

I drop my hands to my hips. "No more digs about how my dragon's crappy, alright?"

"That was, without a doubt, the most pathetic attempt to coerce that I've ever felt."

My jaw drops. It was. . .pathetic? "I stopped you, though."

"Only because I had an uncontrollable urge to laugh."

"I didn't get any training," I say. "That's why."

"You think I did? The Blessed have been here for less than two weeks, you idiot. No one trained me at all. I learned what I know from watching my master do it to me."

"Mine hasn't ever controlled me."

Her jaw drops.

"I mean, he tells me what to do a lot, but other-wise." I shrug.

A vein pops out on her forehead.

"Is that really so bad? I mean, it's not like you

should be proud of piloting other humans like they're puppets."

She stalks back toward me, her eyes flashing. "You think I want to do that? You think it's fun for me to remove people's free will?" Her voice practically snaps. "It was that or watch them *die*, you imbecile. I'm doing what I have to do, and the fact that you don't have to —" She huffs. "You're embarrassing. Do better." The time, she pivots quickly and jogs away.

"Wait." My voice is small, and I'm not even sure she'll hear it.

She stops again, but she doesn't turn around.

I have to force the words out, and they aren't very emphatic, but at least I manage to say them. "I'm sorry I wasn't more grateful. I think I really do need your help."

Her sigh is pronounced, but when she turns, she's not smirking or scowling or even frowning. "You may be the least intuitive bright I've ever met, and there are hundreds of us."

Speaking of hundreds. . . "Do you know all the other Ensnared?"

She frowns. "I didn't know any of them before, but now we're shoved into doing the same things."

"Right, but I heard that brights tend to run in families."

She's still frowning.

"Did anyone else from your family. . ."

She shakes her head. "My husband was killed by the dragon who bonded me, and I don't have children."

And now it feels like it's in poor taste to ask about Mom. I'll have to circle back around to it later. "I'm sorry about your husband."

"I don't dwell on my losses, or they overwhelm me."

I can see a little more why she'd have wanted to stab her dragon, too.

"But for what it's worth, most days, I think he got the right end of things. I can't think of anything worse to wish on a loved one than having them be ensnared, too."

I'm guessing my mom's dragon is less like Axel and more like her master, and that thought depresses me most of all. Once I learn to master the basics of my new job, then I'll start prying for more information about Mom. Until then, I'll pray that she's gotten lucky like me.

Back when Sousa took over, he made us do as many plyo push-up burpees as we could in ten minutes, every single morning.

Ten solid minutes.

I was in decent shape, so when I first heard that, I thought I'd be fine. The first few days I did them, my legs felt like lead, and my arms shook like leaves in a windstorm. I couldn't do very many, either. None of us could. About four or five minutes in, I'd slow down so much that it felt like I was barely moving.

But I didn't give up.

I started doing another ten minutes every night at my own home. By the end of the month, no one could do more than I could. So at night, I started doing fifteen minutes. Within a few months, I actually looked forward to my burpees each day, because they turned my body into a machine.

I'm familiar with the idea that pain is weakness leaving the body. I'm comfortable with pushing past my limits to improve.

Two hours with Penelope still have me wanting to cry in the corner.

"Look, witch," I shout, "I'm trying, okay?"

"I can't feel anything anymore. I should feel a distinct pressure when you push me to do something."

"I hate you."

"You've said." She's smiling. "More than once."

My head's pounding like it's been hit with a hammer repeatedly. "I can't push any harder."

"Are you sure you were ensnared?"

I yank the neck of my shirt down over my shoulder and show her the seal. "I'm sure."

She shakes her head. "I tried everything I could to resist my Blessed, but pushing commands was always easy."

"Maybe it's because you were pushing to humans, and I'm trying to force someone like me." Suddenly, an overwhelming compulsion to flip over on my hands and knees and bark like a dog grips me. I'm dropping to my knees when I realize it's from stupid Penelope. I grit my teeth and push back as hard as I can.

She stumbles backward and swears under her breath. "What was that?"

"Well, clearly you send commands to me just fine." I sit down on the grass, rubbing my temples.

"But you didn't act on mine, either." She frowns. "Maybe it is harder to command another Ensnared. I've never been given permission to try."

Ha! Maybe I'm not as pathetic as she thinks.

"I should have brought along a human or two. I suppose I could summon one now."

"I'm supposed to have my own later tonight." My stomach turns. "I hate the idea."

Penelope shrugs. "You'll get over it quick."

"Maybe you did. I don't even plan to try."

"Your Blessed will make you," she says.

"So I'll lie and say I'm deficient." I shrug. "You should get more creative."

She frowns. "I never even thought of that."

"I may suck at mind-controlling people—"

"Because your Blessed is weak, probably."

"But I'm great at ticking off my dragon."

"Wait." She swallows slowly. "You intentionally make him angry?"

"All the time," I say. "Once I stabbed him in the throat." It almost killed me, but for some reason that image still makes me smile.

All the blood has drained from Penelope's face. "You. . .did what?"

"I know it was stupid, but at the time, I didn't realize that whatever injury they sustain also hurts us."

"But you actually stabbed him? With what?"

"I found this umbrella," I say, "and he'd just ensnared me. First, I stabbed his buddy, but then after he healed—"

She drops to her butt on the grass next to me. Her eyes aren't focused on anything.

"Hey. What's wrong?"

She turns toward me slowly. "You can't resist even the slightest command of the Blessed. None of us can. Their wishes, their whims, they're all as good as unbreakable commands once we've been ensnared."

I snort. "Maybe there are some advantages to having a mud dragon prince as my Blessed."

"What did you just call me?" Axel strolls around the tree on the corner of the property.

Penelope's eyes widen, and then she bows, her head scraping the ground in front of her. "Blessed is the day."

Is she making a joke? "Get up." I push the thought at her, figuring she needs a little help.

Axel folds his arms over his chest. "Looks like the training has been a huge success."

I hop to my feet. "Did you really think she was going to turn me into a good little slave?" My hands are itching to punch him. "Think again, Your Majesty. I'll *never* be a good slave. Never ever."

Penelope sounds like she's choking.

"You may return to your household." Axel sounds tired. "I appreciate your efforts."

"Shall I come again tomorrow?"

Axel looks at me and raises his eyebrows.

"Oh, sure. It wasn't fun, but I think I'm learning stuff."

"Same time," Axel says.

She salutes as she hops to her feet, but she never picks her eyes up higher than his feet. She practically scurries away. The same woman who was so haughty I could barely stand her is now acting like Axel's the Maharajah of India.

She said she can't resist a single whim of her dragon. Not a whim. What does it mean that I barely feel Axel's emotions, and that his commands and orders do almost nothing at all?

"I think our bond may be broken," I say. "I suck at commanding humans to do things, and apparently the other Ensnared are like, boot lickers."

"Boot. . ." Axel blinks, and then he throws his head back and laughs.

I can't help watching him when he does. I've seen him smirk. I've even seen half-smiles. But I've never seen him laugh, and it's a painfully beautiful sight. His perfect, shiny, ebony hair ripples. His crystal sharp jawline is thrown into sharp relief. His dancing golden eyes look like they belong on a movie star. And his entire, sinewy, sculpted body shakes in a way that I can't help watching in awe.

I've been so full of contempt and disgust that I've never really looked at him before. I mean, I noticed he was beautiful, but if he were a human, he'd be slap-your-mom and steal-your-best-friend's-boyfriend gorgeous. He's taller even than Gideon. He's broad without being blocky. And his skin's a perfect, deep bronze color. He could be on a tanning bed print ad without being airbrushed or filtered.

And now he's smiling, and it miraculously makes him look kind.

I know he's not kind.

It's probably something excreted by my ovaries that's making me this stupid. He's a devil sent to destroy all of us, and I'm sitting here getting all heart-eyed while he laughs at a joke everyone else on planet earth has heard thirty million times. Shut up, traitorous hormones. Shut up right now.

"You're lucky," Axel has finally stopped laughing. "That I don't want my boots licked. I don't mind a little insouciance as long as you entertain me."

Great. Now I'm a court jester. "I think I'd rather lick boots."

His eyes are dancing again. "But you're better at entertaining. Your tongue's too busy talking back to do any licking."

"I don't talk back," I mutter. Which is when I realize that even now, I'm talking back.

Axel holds out his hand, and there's a small box resting on it.

"What's that?"

I think about the cow carcass, which is the only other thing he's ever brought me, and my lip curls involuntarily. "We still have some food left over from what I grabbed that time I went out. Speaking of, can I go out again soon? Or, like, where do we get food?"

"You'll no longer be in charge of food location or preparation," he says. "While I've been ignoring you, we've been working around the clock to restore some semblance of normalcy to the humans still in Houston. The supply chains for food, energy, and basic needs are nearly in place. Your first ten humans, who will see to your basic domestic needs, are arriving before sunset."

"My domestic needs. . ." I swallow. "Ten is way too many. How about we take one. Or at most, two?"

"Ten's a third of what the others have started with."

Thirty? Penelope started by managing *thirty* humans? "I have a splitting headache from practicing for two hours with Penelope," I say. "I think your Ensnared is a real dud. You should adjust your expectations."

He chuckles. "We'll see."

I try to move past him. It's been a while, and I want to make sure the kids are alright in there.

He grabs my arm, and other than the time he healed me and the time he gave me a ride—in his dragon form—it's the only time we've really touched. A thrill runs up my body, and it sets off a shiver that I can't suppress. *Quit it*, I tell my ovaries again.

"Quit what?"

"Good heavens. I can't even talk to myself anymore?"

"You talk to yourself often?" He frowns.

I yank my arm free. "What do you want?"

"You didn't take this." He shoves the box in front of me again. "It was difficult to make. I had to do it myself."

I knock the lid off, but I have no idea what he's

giving me. "You made me. . ." I squint. "A pile of gold fluff?"

He sighs, reaches into the box, and lifts out the gold filaments. Then he shakes them from the point he's holding. They're apparently all attached in that one spot.

I still have no idea what it is, but it's beautiful, at least. The sunlight glints off them, and they ripple in the light breeze. "Is it. . .a decoration?"

"It's your visor," he says. "You'll wear it on your forehead."

This time I'm the one laughing. "It's supposed to be solid," I say. "Like a crown for the front of your face, kind of."

He frowns. "I made it exactly as they told me to make it."

"Is it possible they were pranking you?" I wiggle my wrist, and the filaments ripple and twist in total abandon. "This looks like a tassel for a graduation cap." I mean, it doesn't, really, but it looks more like that than the visor Penelope was wearing. "Looks like we're both duds."

He grabs my wrist, and again, my stupid body goes haywire. My heart races. My breathing gets shallow. I should be scared of him, not panting from his touch. I steel my nerves, just as I would before a fight.

Clearly unaware of the storm raging in my traitorous body, Axel slowly guides my hand upward, until the mass of fluffy filaments, which are quite long, are centered over the center of my forehead.

"This will look ridiculous, like I'm some strange, exotic bird." I can't help my smile. Since he's standing right in front of me, it's directed right at him. "You can't want me to walk around wearing a pompom on my head, surely."

He blows on me then, bizarrely, his breath fanning out over my face, and something inside of me stirs alarmingly, like he's waking up a hidden monster that lives in my body. He waves his free hand across the front of my face, and the filaments *shift*. "Now, call to it," he whispers, his breath fanning over my face again. "Call to my magic."

His magic.

He put magic into that blob of gold thread? I swallow, and then I reach out like Penelope taught me and I *pull* on the visor tuft, and it sucks in tightly against the space between my eyebrows, all the filaments binding together into bizarre golden lines.

He smiles, then, his joy unfettered as the insane thing he gave me shapes itself with guidance from his free hand.

"Not horns," I say.

But it's too late. He's done, and apparently, so is my visor. I can't see it, but I can sense it there, hovering in front of my face like a floating helmet that makes me look like his demonic accessory. Horn lady, the court jester for the gorgeous golden devil beast.

Ugh.

"It suits you." He looks proud of himself, and I hate that it's because I'm his creation, his pet.

"If you think— "

He presses a finger to my mouth, and that beast inside of me roars. I want to bite his hand, but not in the way I should. I back up instead. "What?"

"For once, don't argue. Don't complain. Just say thank you."

Penelope's incredulity that I *can* argue with him, that I have free will around him, comes to mind. I wonder for a split second how much of my freedom is his doing. Is it because he's weak that I have more latitude? Or is it because he's not as harsh, not as controlling, and not as angry? Do I have the ability to be myself in this bizarre circumstance because he grants it to me? And if so, should I be more grateful and less angry?

The thought that I should be grateful to him for not cinching my leash tighter enrages me, and I can't do it. I can't be prudent like I should. "I hate it almost as much as I hate you."

He sighs. "You're welcome."

"I didn't thank you, you horrible dragon."

He smiles. "Mud dragon prince, to you."

A van pulls up in front of the house. Ten humans climb out, one by one. They're all wearing white shirts and dark pants. They're all wearing sneakers. They line up in a row on the sidewalk, all of them staring straight ahead, all of them utterly calm.

"I was able to recruit humans who have already been subdued and taught." He beams like he's fishing for another thank you.

He's lucky I don't have anything sharp on hand. "Goodie."

"I made sure two of them were food preparers before, so they should be adequate at preparing your meals."

He's acting like he's my white knight when he enslaved ten people to do things I could be doing for myself. "I don't want—"

"Send them to the local stores for whatever you want, and anything they don't have, tell me about. Some things are harder to obtain, but lots of things are in ready supply."

Is he kidding? "I'm sure it's hard to manage those sorts of tedious things."

"Not really," he says. "It's basic administration, like

ensuring the house next door is available for lodging your domestic help, and the homes on either side of that are reserved for Rufus and Gordon."

"Wait, you're saying we have the entire house to ourselves?"

"Other than me, yes," he says.

"You're not afraid I'll, like, stab you in your sleep?"

"Oh, I'm always a little afraid you'll stab me," he says. "But the Blessed don't sleep. Not like you humans do."

"That's weird."

"I think your sleeping is stranger, if you think about it. You lie still, or you toss and turn, while your mind churns, and you simply breathe and rest, like you're dead."

It does sound weird when he puts it like that.

"Your culture's almost obsessed with it, buying beds and decorating rooms and preparing medicines and schedules and routines, all so that you can lie around and do nothing. Meanwhile, some people brag about how much they sleep, while others boast that they barely do it."

"How do you know all this?"

"I told you, before we came, we did research. And now that we're here, that has continued. We're forced to integrate with you until we can locate the Heart."

I hate their stupid heart. "I'll be praying you find it tomorrow."

He laughs. "Unlikely. It's surely hidden well, and the humans who know about it won't want to part with it at any cost."

"I really don't think any of us care," I say. "And wouldn't I know, as a human myself?"

"We left the Heart here as a parting gift, according to Prince Azar's father, but it was a mistake. We never should have been so magnanimous."

"Well, give me any details, and I'll do my utmost to get it so you can leave. Is it a rock? I'll dig it up. Is it an animal? I'll make a net, or weld you a trap. A tree? I'll chop it down."

If they really want to leave once they find it, they should just tell all the humans that's their plan. "I really think that if you just talked to the government leaders—"

His jaw tightens. "We've attempted communication on many occasions. Each attempt was met with more attacks."

"But—"

He shakes his head. "We don't know what it's made of, and we don't know where it's located. We know it's the key to flourishing life on earth, and that the planet may suffer if we take it. Nevertheless, our people will all perish without it. If you think of something helpful, please share." He shrugs. "Otherwise, we'll keep searching."

"Fine," I say. "Get me access to the internet, and I'll see what I can do."

"The internet?"

"It's a communication portal," I say. "All the things that humans knew or thought they knew is kind of tapped into it. If you haven't attacked more areas, I'm sure it's still up and running outside of Houston."

"Ah, the interface of ideas we were monitoring." He nods. "We did search there for records that might lead us to the Heart. Unfortunately, we deemed it too dangerous to allow access to that inside of Houston. If you can study them, they can also communicate with you."

That was kind of the point, yeah.

"Don't worry that you'll be bored, though. Your first contingent of fresh humans for assimilation will arrive in a few more days."

I splutter. "Assimilation?"

"You should practice as much as possible with these, sending them on routine errands, increasing the distance they are allowed to move away from you incrementally until you have an idea of how far you can still make contact and maintain control."

"No way."

Axel smiles. "Alright. If you refuse entirely, I'll have no choice."

I stare straight ahead like those poor humans. "Fine. You can kill me."

He laughs. "Not you. I've become invested in you." He tosses his head. "I'm talking about them. If you refuse to take care of them, I'll have to kill them."

Every single time I start to think he's a little bit human, a little bit less awful than the devil himself, he reminds me how naive I am.

"Fine," I say. "But you're going to hate how I manage them."

"Oh, I'm quite sure that I will."

But he's smiling as he shifts back into his dragon form and heads back down the road to wherever the dragons are doing whatever the stupid dragons do.

❧ 10 ❧

I'm not sure whether it's the visor, or whether it's like it was with the burpees and practice makes you stronger, but controlling the humans is much, much easier than it was trying to force Penelope to do things. Once I establish that I can get them to move by sending them all inside the house, I start trying my hardest to undo all their training.

"I'm Elizabeth," I say. "Welcome."

They stare straight ahead, like their brains don't work.

"I'm not like the last, uh, person who told you what to do. You know, whoever sent you over here."

They don't move.

"You can kind of do what you want with me."

Several of them frown.

"Like, I have to 'keep you in line,' or whatever, but I'm not going to control you."

A woman on the end with long hair and pronounced crow's feet asks, "Are you freeing us?"

I cough. "I mean, I'd like to free you, but if I do,

they'll just kill you or round you up and bring you back to another Ensnared."

"So you aren't freeing us."

I shake my head. "Look, I'm an underling. I'd love to free you. I'd love to free myself, and believe me, I've tried."

The woman frowns. "How is this any different than the last assignment, then?"

I sigh. "It's not really, I guess. Except I would prefer to just list the things we need to get done, and once they're done, you can just do whatever you want to do with your free time."

"I want to be with my family," a bald man says.

"I want to play Minecraft," a chubby guy says.

"I was only here on a business trip," a skinny woman with dark hair says. "My boyfriend didn't even want me to come."

I close my eyes, hating Axel a little bit more for making me do this. When I open them, they're all still standing there, but instead of the homogenously impassive expressions, they're frowning, irritated, or confused. "I was in the wrong place at the wrong time, just like all of you. I went to my brother's Halloween party for his school, and an electro dragon ensnared my mom."

They're all watching me now, at least.

"I took my siblings, my brother Sammy and my sisters Coral and Jade, and we ran." I sigh. "Only, we got caught right in front of our house, and after I tried my best to fight my way free, I was ensnared as well."

"I hear it's an Earth Blessed who ensnared you."

"The prince of the others, if that helps," I say. "But yes, it was. His name's Axel, and he's horrible like they all are, but he puts up with a lot from me. And." I pause to make sure they're all really listening. "He let me keep my siblings here with me. He's vowed to keep them safe."

They're all murmuring now, and I can't keep up with the directions their conversations are all going.

"You're saying we can do whatever we want?" the chubby guy asks. "Because I hated scrubbing floors all day."

"Is that what they had you doing?" I shake my head. "I'm pretty sure that you'll need to keep this house and the one next door clean, but I don't think that will take too long."

"I can scrub the floors once a week in both," the chubby guy says.

"What's your name?" I ask.

"Joseph," he says. And then he smiles. "No one's asked me that in a while."

"We weren't allowed to talk unless necessary," the dark-haired woman says. "My name's Rachel. I'm from New York City, and to be honest, I hate Texas."

I laugh.

They all do.

We introduce ourselves. We make a plan and assign tasks.

"So you're not planning to, like, fight them," Rachel says. "But we're going to try and live as normally as we can?"

I make eye contact with each of them in turn. "I can force you to do things, just like all the other Ensnared can." I think about all of them folding their arms, and I push the thought.

They all do it at exactly the same time.

"I can be just as awful as the last ensnared human you worked for—"

"They call themselves Master," Joseph says. "Like

they think that being called that makes them less slaves themselves."

"The whole thing's messed up," I say.

"Can you still take away my anxiety?" Joseph asks. "I kinda liked that the other guy did that."

"Wait, you want me to take your anxiety away?"

Joseph grimaces. "It's always been bad, but since I was picked up and brought here. . .nothing." He shrugs. "Way better."

"Um, sure, if you want me to."

"And my depression too," the woman with the crow's feet asks.

"Sure," I say. "I guess. But until we can figure out how to escape or how to get them to leave—"

"Or how to kill them," a tall guy named Kevin says. He's a college basketball player, and he's definitely the angriest person in the room.

I don't even disagree with him, but I can't have them walking around talking treason. There are too many of them. "We can't talk like that," I say.

"Not while anyone else might hear, anyway," Rachel says.

She's smart. I like her.

"But my sister already killed two of them," Sammy says from the stairwell.

"Is that your brother?" the woman with the crow's feet asks.

"You did?" Kevin's eyes are wider than I realized they could be.

I shake my head. "No, I stabbed two." I glare at Sammy. "It's not the same."

"He makes up stories sometimes." Coral grabs him and whispers in his ear. She's a lot quicker to pick up on things. We can't go around telling people that I've murdered dragons, or Axel could get in trouble. He might even decide that I'm too much work.

"They healed almost immediately," I say. "Trust me when I tell you that we're not going to be killing any dragons."

"That's good," Axel says as he opens the door. "If you were, we'd need to have a talk."

I hate how often he comes and goes, like he thinks he owns the house.

Although, I suppose he does.

"Welcome to Elizabeth's home," he says. "I'm her bonded, Prince of the Earth Blessed. I know she harbors some radical views, and I'm trying to work with her on them. I hope you understand that's between Elizabeth and me, and you are to behave as proper workers should." He scans them all in turn, but they're all on their knees, like Penelope was, staring at the ground. "If I hear that any of you are speaking trai-torous thoughts, or that you're not doing as she commands?" He exhales slowly. "I'm not sentimental like her. I'll just kill you. You're very replaceable. Don't forget that."

And with one little speech, he undoes all the work I'd put in to try and help them be less stressed and abused. Even several days later, they're still keeping their heads down, not using names around me, and acting like rabbits hiding in holes.

But at least Sammy, Coral, and Jade are doing well. They almost seem happy. Sammy's spending half the day building things with Legos—Kevin fetches and delivers things, and he found loads of Legos for Sammy the first day. Coral and Jade play with Fluff Dog a lot, who is calming down a great deal. They also take turns writing plays and then performing them, though Sammy's tired of playing all the male roles. It's almost like they've forgotten that we're captives, biding our time until we can somehow escape or defeat our captors.

They're kids. They probably have forgotten.

But I haven't. I never will.

I spend an hour or two each day training with Penelope, who no longer thinks I'm an idiot. Apparently the visor aids in focus quite a lot. But also, it's nearly impossible to command another dragon's ensnared human. Once I have my visor on, she's as bad at pushing me around as I was. For our session today, I test how far I can sense the humans—several miles, at least—and how hard I need to push a command to make it stick—not hard at all—and how much resistance they can exert against any of my orders.

Not much, sadly.

Since our control over them seems to mirror the dragons' control over us, that's disheartening. Penelope was right about the most important part. Our job's painfully easy. Commanding my ten humans became almost effortless by the third day, and I can see how easy it would be to settle into complacency with a task once it becomes routine.

After Sammy nearly revealed how I'd killed those two dragons, I realized that I couldn't treat a bunch of humans I don't know as family. If it was only me, I could risk that kind of familiarity. But Axel did me a favor that day, reminding me that both he and I have a role to play. He's the Prince of the Earth Blessed. I'm his Ensnared. I can't let them wander around, and I can't really free them from the leash, either. One rebellious human might be comical to the right dragon.

Lots of them running around will get us all killed.

I struck a deal, and I have to uphold my end, however distasteful. If I don't, then Sammy, Jade, and

Coral will die. I can't risk that, no matter how unsavory I find my new job. Even when I have to start asking more and more of my humans—they work for me primarily, but Penelope brings me an increasing number of tasks they're supposed to handle locally.

Without a government in place, without utilities and management teams, no one is at the helm on food production, water sanitation, keeping the grid running. The dragons stepped in, but they're using humans to keep those things going.

I think it would be easier for them to simply dump us all outside the barricade, drag in a lot of cows or whatever they like to eat most, and live a human-free existence.

If they didn't need to figure out what this Heart thing was and recover it, they might have done just that, because most of what the humans are doing is keeping the area livable for the humans.

"I'm the leader of the Earth Blessed," Axel explains on the morning he brings my first fifty workers. "I'm in charge of many things, but due to her past experience, we're putting Liz in charge of building a defensive human force."

"I thought the Strike Blessed handled most of the defense," I say.

He shrugs. "There are a few hundred of them. There are thousands of us, and they consider us expendable."

"But why do you need humans at all?"

His smile is predatory. "We've found that the humans outside our perimeter hesitate to fire on other humans."

Great. I'm training shields for his dragons—human meat shields. This gets better and better.

"Why do you do it?" I ask.

"Do what?"

"Your own people don't value you, so why do you keep working so hard for them?" If I could flip thousands of earth dragons to our side. . .

He meets my eyes. "It's fine. Don't feel sorry for us. It's the way the world works."

"We can change the world when it's wrong," I say. "In fact, it's our duty to change it."

His eyes dance. "Your naiveté is showing."

"Maybe it is," I say. "Or maybe I'm right, and you're too afraid to admit it."

"Your job is to prepare these humans to defend against an attack on the ground."

"You want me to teach them to fight against other humans who might come and try to free them?"

Axel nods. "Exactly."

"Is this a test?"

"You're a fighter, Elizabeth. You're being asked to prepare them to fight. Is that really so hard?"

I shrug. "It's what I do," I say. "I fight things, like stupid orders and stupid dragons."

He rolls his eyes, but he looks tired. Actually, now that I've noticed it, he looks *really* tired, and when I search out the thread in my head, it feels. . .thin. Like it's strained.

"Hey, are you okay?"

His brows draw together. "What do you mean?"

"I know you said dragons don't sleep."

"The Blessed don't sleep, that's correct."

"But you must need something, because it looks like you're not getting it."

He frowns. "You should be prepping your new soldiers."

My fifty shiny, new humans are standing stock still in front of my house in lines of ten, staring at their feet, because that's the order I gave them. But this feels like a conversation we should have. I can't just have them stand around while I talk to Axel for an hour.

Since I'm supposed to make them into fighters. . .I glance at them, and they all look reasonably fit. I push a command to make them all do fifty pushups, fifty sit-ups, and fifty squats. Three times. Talk about a great workout regimen. They all have to do exactly as I push —their bodies won't let them opt out.

I'm the best personal trainer ever created.

Unless, like, their hearts give out. I slide in a little caveat that if they feel ill, they can take a break. But *then*, my attention goes back to my mud dragon prince. "Alright, they're all hard at work. Now tell me what's wrong with you. You can't defend my family if you're on the verge of a breakdown."

"I'm fine." I mean, technically that's true, but the signs of strain are also clear. I can't really identify any of them specifically. He *looks* the same, but also, he doesn't quite.

"You look tired," I say. "If you were human, I'd say you need a nap."

He tilts his head. "Are you worried about me?"

"As if," I say. "I hope you're tired. I hope you're drained, and that all of you are really fraying here on earth."

His half-smile's back. "You do."

"For sure," I say. "But also, you don't really look like you're ready to protect anyone. I just want to make sure you're fighting fit."

"You going to make me do pushups and sit-ups?"

Unbidden, my mind cuts to an image of Axel without his shirt on—which I've never seen—doing sit-ups on the ground. His chest and arms are gleaming with sweat. His abs are contracting and his breathing's heavy.

That sets my stupid heart racing. Ugh.

"You do want me to do sit-ups?" Axel's lips twist.

Oh, no. Could he see that?

"It's much easier when we're close like this." He smiles. "You still don't get it. Any clear thought you have, if I'm focusing on it, I can see."

I want to die. No, I want to die and be buried and never face him again.

"Do you find my human form attractive, Liz?" He steps closer, his eyes studying my face.

I swallow. "I just said you look tired, and then I was imagining you doing sit-ups, because that's what I do when I need to prepare for something."

"Maybe you should be doing them too," he says. "You have things to prepare for as well."

I drop immediately—anything for a distraction—and start doing sit-ups. He's probably right, though. I've been slacking off, and that won't do, not when I'm living among the enemy.

Only, instead of walking away like he usually does, Axel drops down next to me. "Like this?" The insane dragon starts doing sit-ups. "Oh, right." He whips his shirt over his head and tosses it next to me.

"Where do your clothes go when you shift?" I'm still doing sit-ups, but barely. I'm too distracted to do them very fast.

He shrugs. "Clothes are almost insubstantial. I can make any that I want. Where do they go?" He shakes his head. "I'm not sure."

Do they even exist? I stare at his shirt for a moment, glad to look at something other than the half-naked Adonis next to me. His body looks even *better* than it did in my mind's eye, which is so unfair. It's not like he's worked to earn that body in any way.

I suppress a groan.

"Are they tiring for you?"

When I look back in his direction, Axel's staring right at me. It's clear that his mind is full of curiosity, not lust, and that's pretty embarrassing. "Not at all." I huff. "I'm fine."

He keeps doing sit-ups, but he's still staring at me, like I'm a puzzle he can't quite work out. "We don't sleep."

"Yes," I choke out. No matter how much I lie, it's obvious that doing all these sit-ups is a little bit tiring. Meanwhile, Axel appears to be totally fine. "You said."

"But every week or so, we do need to decompress."

"What does that mean?"

"Your human bodies intake oxygen." He's still doing sit-ups, perfect ones, like he's a robot and his body's just performing its stated task. "Then they expel the unwanted carbon compound afterward."

"Okay." I am *not* going to quit doing sit-ups before he does, but I swear, my abs are burning. He has to quit soon, right?

"We need nitrogen and argon, both of which exist in your atmosphere, but unlike your breathing, which I only mimic in this form, we need a few moments of down time to process and properly synthesize what we intake. Our bodies are much more efficient and economical than yours, but we do have to essentially shut down for a short time."

He needs a time out. "Then you should do that."

"It's been busy lately," he says.

"Right, but I have to make time to breathe or I'll die." I'm really puffing right now. Maybe he'll think I'm making my point.

Meanwhile, he's not winded at all. He's *still* doing sit-ups, perfectly, his beautifully sculpted abs contracting and releasing like poetry in motion. My fingers itch to reach out and touch them.

Which is idiotic. What's wrong with me?

Other than the fact that my abs are about to set fire and burn down the entire block.

"It's not like breathing," he says. "I already said—"

"Yeah, yeah."

He stops doing sit-ups then and leans toward me, grabbing my arms. "You need to stop. Your body's overheated and your heart's beating too fast."

Thanks a lot for pointing that out, jerk. "I was making a point." Yes, Liz. Spin this so you don't look idiotic. "You're being like me right now." I wheeze. "You need to take a break."

He looks down at his bare chest and abdomen, and I can't help following his gaze. Gah, he's beautiful. This is not helping my heartbeat drop back to a normal range. Even without sweating properly, he looks *good*. "Unlike you, I'm perfectly fine."

"You know what I mean."

He sighs. "I do, yes."

"But?" I ask. "What's stopping you?"

He blinks. "You really don't know?"

I shake my head.

"You," he says.

"Me?" I must've heard him wrong. "How could I be stopping you?"

"You're at the center of everything I do now. If I shut down, what might you do? Or what might happen to you?"

"I'm not a child," I say.

"All evidence to the contrary."

That stings a bit.

"The last time I left you alone, you were nearly killed, and you murdered two of my people."

I wince, because all of that's true. "But you abandoned me," I say. "You said you'd protect us, and then you disappeared. Surely you can trust me for a few hours. You leave all the time."

He taps the side of my forehead. "I'm always monitoring you, though."

"So, you knew that day?"

"Of course," he says. "That's why I—" He coughs. "That's why I sent Azar to help you."

I can't help shuddering when he mentions the terrifying beast who flayed that green dragon open like he was a butterfly shrimp. "Right."

"But now that we've fully bonded, it's even easier."

"And if you take an hour or two off, you think I'll, what? Arm my people and come try to murder you?"

He shakes his head. "You'd be killed in an instant."

Because whatever happens to him. . . Ugh. I'd almost forgotten that little gem. "So, then go decompress or whatever."

He stares at me for a moment. "I'll have Gordon and Rufus keep an eye out."

"Sure, yes. They can make sure I don't do anything stupid while you're taking your nap." I try not to be annoyed—I walked outside one time. It wasn't that bad.

"It's not just that I worry about your judgment," he says. "I have enemies."

"Among the other dragons, you mean?"

He grunts.

"But you're best friends with the commander, right?"

"That's the reason a lot of them hate me." He flops back on the ground and closes his eyes. "None of them understand why Azar likes me. They're constantly looking for ways to get rid of me or convince him to like them better."

"How does Azar feel about that?"

He opens his eyes, and the look he gives me. . .I can't interpret it, even with the benefit of the bond. "He doesn't like it any more than I do, but what can he do? If he tells them to leave me alone, they hate me more. If he acts like he dislikes me, they'll attack me openly."

"But you're a prince."

"Which means all the Earth Blessed answer to me. The expendable ones. The ones without wings, whom all the others of my kind despise."

"The water dragons don't have wings," I say.

"They can essentially fly when they're in the water, and they can walk just like we can on land. Looked at from a strictly objective perspective, we are the least valuable and the most populous."

"Which is probably why they hate you."

"How so?"

I push the workers a message to go to their assigned rooms in the houses across the street and take a break. "You command the largest force on earth, do you not?"

"Azar does."

"Okay, but among the subordinates, no one leads a force as big as yours."

"Undeniably."

"And the head commander likes you best."

He grunts again.

"They're jealous."

"The Blessed don't have emotions in the way you humans do."

I'm not sure I really believe that, at least, not as a blanket statement. They may not have always had the same range of emotions, and they may not understand them. But I've seen him laugh, smirk, scowl, and regret, at the very least.

"We desire things. We know anger and hatred. We also yearn to possess. But I've read about the range of emotions humans feel, and. . ." He snorts.

"Sorrow?" I turn to face him, my face pressed against the grass.

"Nope. Nor hope, joy, or fear, at least, not in the sense that you feel it. That may be why I find you so refreshing. Most humans quiver and cry and beg. You didn't do any of that. You reacted much more like an Earth Blessed would."

"By stabbing you?"

"Exactly." He props himself up on one elbow. "My rivals watch me. They know when it's been a while, like now, and that makes them even more attentive. When I decompress, you'll be at the highest risk of dealing with a Strike Blessed or Water Blessed attack."

"Surely Azar would punish them."

"It wouldn't be official."

"A small force at least," I say. "Got it."

"Liz." His tone carries a warning. "Literally any Blessed could kill you, so it's not like I expect you to defend me."

"Gee," I say. "Thanks for the pep talk."

"It's the truth." His eyes are as serious as I've seen them.

I rise to my knees and twist sideways to grab his discarded shirt, leaning over him, but careful not to touch him in any way. I'm planning to throw it in his face and tell him to go already.

Before I can fully straighten, he says, "What're you doing?" Because of the way he turns toward me, his shoulder bumps my side, and I collapse on top of him. Our faces are suddenly less than two inches apart, and my body's pressed against his from my toes almost to my nose. All those abdominal muscles, *I can feel them.* The muscles of his arms bunch as they wrap around me.

"Elizabeth." His breath on my face reminds me of the moment he activated my visor. That makes me think about how deeply we're connected. No matter what I do, I can feel him. He can feel me, too.

I swallow slowly, my eyes dropping to meet his. My

heart's hammering, and my entire body feels like one long run of raw nerves. What's wrong with me? Why am I acting like this?

Is this Stockholm Syndrome?

"Are you injured?" Axel's voice breaks the spell that fell over me. "Why are you still lying here?"

I scramble off him quickly, working doggedly to blank my mind. The last thing I need is to send him some kind of stupid, inadvertent message. His cluelessness about human minds has been my salvation. I really mustn't be so horribly obvious that he figures it out in spite of that. "I'm fine. Go do your little thing. Right now. Don't wait." I turn away so he doesn't see the color rise in my cheeks.

"I don't understand—"

"Just go," I say.

Luckily, after a moment of indecision, he listens, retreating to the house. I almost follow him inside. I mean, on top of promising to stay out of trouble while he did his little nap, I also just dismissed my fifty worker-humans less than an hour after they arrived. I feel like standing around outside like a dope after essentially shirking my first official Ensnared task is probably not copacetic, but I'm not walking inside until I'm positive that he's not going to see me.

So instead, I pace in front of the house, until Fluff Dog sees me and starts freaking out.

It takes about two minutes. When I do finally go inside, Sammy's holding a jump rope around Jade's waist, clicking, and saying "Heyah, heyah!"

"Do I want to know?" I ask Coral.

"She's his horse." She shrugs. "It keeps him busy since we're still stuck staying inside."

I may never really understand the six-year-old

brain, but Coral's right. He's staying inside like I asked. Jade's foot kicks the edge of the coffee table as they pass, and it hits a stupid decorative bowl, which topples over, spraying weird glass bead things all over the floor.

I groan, but the kids didn't even notice, so I shuffle over to pick them up myself.

"Why don't you guys head upstairs," I say. "Axel's doing something in his room, and he shouldn't be disturbed."

"Then someone should tell that to the silver dragon," Sammy says.

"What?" My heart leaps into my throat.

"The one that's by his window." He points.

I swear.

Sammy repeats my exclamation.

"No," I say. "Not that word. Never that word."

Then I say it again. Because, if I try to save him, I'll die. If I let them kill him? I'll die. If any situation warrants the use of that word, it's this one.

Sammy's gaping at me.

"Oh, just go upstairs, rugrat."

If I'm dying either way, I may as well be front and center when it happens. Besides. If my death delays them enough to buy him the time he needs to survive, he might honor his promise to care for my siblings, right? Maybe?

I hop the coffee table, and then the sofa, and I hang a right around the office and shove the master bedroom door open. Axel's nowhere to be found—certainly not on the bed like I assumed he'd be for his nap thing.

I have no idea what *processing* means, but maybe it's more of a bathroom type of situation. Ew. Wherever he is, I doubt he's ready to be attacked by a silver dragon. Not that I'll ever be ready for it.

But ready or not, it's coming. It's peering through the window on the door that opens onto the porch, clearly trying to figure out where to enter. The silver dragons are the smallest ones, other than a few of the earth dragons that look pretty young, and I think it'll be able to shove its way through the back door with minimal damage to the wall, sadly. The solid brick might have slowed it down otherwise.

I glance at my watch. We're, what? Fifteen minutes into this nap thing? Why didn't I press him for a time estimate?

It's okay, Liz. You don't have to kill it.

I just have to keep it from killing him long enough for him to wake up. Didn't he say Gordon and Rufus would be around? If I start shrieking, would they hear me? Or would that just alert more villains to the fact that Axel's out of commission?

I start digging around for a weapon. Any kind of weapon will do. Axel's room looks like he's never used it. The bed's pristine. The desk has zero papers on it, and why would it? The Blessed have no hands, and they communicate with mental messages. They suck.

The nightstand's bare. Why'd he even claim this room? And where is he, anyway?

Both the closet and the bathroom doors are closed.

But the stupid silver dragon's done waiting, and it's noticed me. It shakes the door. Bumps against the door. And then it whams repeatedly into the door.

I dive for the closet, wondering whether I can wake Axel up. But the closet actually has something weird inside it. There's a giant rock, like, bigger than Sammy, with two identical swords sunk into it. I'm getting major *Sword in the Stone* vibes, only there are two long blades. Carved into the base of the stone are some letters I wouldn't have known before I was ensnared, but now I can miraculously read, just like how I now speak dragon.

To carve the Heart and save the Blessed.

They must be some kind of holy swords. It makes sense the prince of the Earth Blessed would have them, I guess. They're the only ones who might have hands to hold them. It's not like any of the other dragons could use swords.

A huge crash outside tells me that the silver dragon has broken through.

I swear under my breath, and then I leap toward the stone, pulling with all my might on the swords. They both slide right out—so much for Arthurian legends. I guess this stone's more of, like, a display stand for the dragons.

Electro dragon outside's huffing and sniffing and muscling its way around, and my adrenaline spikes. Time to see what I can do with these things. They've got to be better than a fire poker and a decorative blade. They're much heavier than the shinai, the bamboo swords we used for kendo, but I did sometimes use two. Maybe I won't cut my own arm off at the wrist when I go out there.

"Did someone say traitorous murderer?" I burst out of the closet.

I'm left staring at a huge silver dragon butt.

Not exactly the scene I had in my mind, but I'm less likely to be electrocuted from this side. I lunge forward and jab with my right hand—my dominant hand—straight into its nicely rounded hind end.

The sword, unlike the stupid one I jabbed at Azar,

slides right into the dragon's derriere, and boy does it roar. If a bear got caught in a trap, and an elephant lost a toenail, and a whale's fin was severed, the three together couldn't wail as loudly as this whiner.

"Oh, please," I say. "I barely poked you."

But when it spins around, I'm regretting every-thing. *Where's the prince?*

"Why would I tell you that."

I have urgent news from our leader about human troop movements.

Whoops.

"So. . .you're not trying to kill him?"

Today, I did not expect to learn that dragons can glare.

"The thing is, you kind of broke into his house, and that seemed a little hostile to me. So, I know that I stabbed your butt, and you could get angry about that, but I—"

The dragon doesn't warn me in any way before opening its mouth and zapping me.

Once, as a kid, I touched an electric fence. I wanted to know how it felt. Yes, I was that idiotic as a child. Anyway, it didn't feel great. I shot back about a foot and a half and landed hard on my bony rear end.

That was *nothing* to this.

The electric charge that channels into me rattles me down to my genetic code, probably jumbling my DNA beyond repair. My pain sensors are shaking, they've been so overloaded. I can't breathe, I can't see, and my brain shuts down. I can't even recall my own name.

But then the world sort of bows outward and then shifts back in, and the weight of my poor choices slams into me like a freight train. It feels like someone's inverted all my cells and is playing a song with them.

All of that misery pisses me off.

Royally.

"I think you lied to me," I hiss. "You aren't here to convey a message at all, are you?"

The dragon hisses, but this time, I don't aim for its butt. I stab that nightmare right next to its front leg, hitting who knows what, and it howls even louder than it did the first time.

And it bleeds black.

It's throwing its head back, ready to zap me again, probably ratcheting the power knob all the way up to demolish, when the bathroom door opens.

"Axel, really?" I can't believe it. "Shift, already, would you?"

"Are you using my swords?" He sighs. "You didn't even ask."

"I'm about to die, here."

"I know," he says. "I heard."

"You were awake?"

He shrugs. "I told you we don't sleep. Of course I was awake."

The stupid silver dragon zaps me *again* while he's chatting, and it hurts even *worse* this time. But by the time I regain consciousness, lying sideways on the plush carpet of Axel's master suite, I can see the carcass of the awful silver monster that tried to kill me.

"You still alive?" Axel doesn't even look worried.

I can't feel my toes. I'm drooling. My tongue feels too big for my mouth. My hair has probably fallen out. I'm positive my teeth are loose. But I manage to moan, "I hate you."

He chuckles. "I feel it, too. I wasn't the idiot who got shot."

I find the thread of the bond and I lean on it, hard,

projecting all my misery, all my anger, and all my frustration at him like a right hook.

"Yeah, got it." He drops next to me on one knee and holds up both his hands, channeling magic into my visor, I think. All I know for sure is that it creates a burst of power that finally stops all the pain.

That's when I let go and float in a sea of relief and sunshine.

When I wake up again, I'm in a bed, and nothing hurts. In fact, I'm warm, calm, and surrounded by fluff. "Fluff Dog?" I croak.

"You really like to milk your injuries, huh?"

I know that voice. I force myself upright. "Are Sammy, Coral, and Jade alright?"

Axel nods. "Fine. All the damage was localized in here." He points at the hole in his wall where his back door used to be. "Stupid Strike Blessed thought she was smaller than she was."

"Women. Always overly optimistic. I think it's those stupid mirrors they sell that make us look slimmer than we really are."

I think his lip curls a little—maybe he's starting to really get me.

"Did you kill her?"

"Of course," he says.

"I thought they were stronger than you," I say. "Wasn't that what you found so upsetting?"

"Not me," he says. "They're stronger than most of my people. I'm a prince." He's frowning now. I've clearly hit a nerve.

"Don't get me wrong. I'm glad you were stronger."

"Actually, my hot-headed human had nearly killed her when I finally intervened. I finished her off without ever changing out of my human form." He sits on the edge of the bed. "You shouldn't have been able to use those swords at all."

"Well, no one told them that—or me."

"I'd never actually used them before today," he grumbles.

"Why not? You never fight as a human, I guess."

"Well, that," he says. "But also, no one's ever been able to get them out of that rock."

I straighten up. "You're kidding. I'm the only *worthy* one?"

"Huh?"

"It's in all the movies and stuff," I say. "When there are swords stuck in rocks, or like special, magical hammers, only one worthy person can use them."

"I doubt that's—"

"Trust me," I say. "That's what it means."

"Well, thanks for pulling them out, because I used them just fine tonight, and not many blades can penetrate Blessed hide."

"That's so unfair." I swing my legs out of the bed, alarmed at my lack of pants.

"Your clothes were covered in blood," he says.

I fling my legs back under the covers and look down. I'm wearing a huge button-down shirt.

It's definitely not my shirt.

"Who dressed me?"

"Me," he says. "Who else would be strong enough to do it? Sammy?"

Did he just make a joke?

"Listen. I feel a little bad about keeping the swords."

"Great, then give them to me."

"Nice try," he says, "but those are a Blessed relic. There's no way I'm giving them to you, Miss Stabby."

"I saved you," I say. "Or did you forget?"

"You were trying to save me so you didn't also die," he says, "but I was awake and would have come out to stop that misguided attacker no matter what you did."

"Potato, pohtahto."

"What?"

"I think I earned a sword. Let's go halfsies." I hold out my hand. "And I'm definitely going to need a pair of pants."

"My pants kept falling off," he says.

My jaw drops. "You tried putting them on me?" I can't even let my mind think about what that would've been like.

He frowns. "First you're upset you're not wearing any, and now you're upset I tried to put them on you?" His brow furrows. "You make no sense, Liz."

"That's all human women. Get used to it."

"In any case, I came up with another way to reward your efforts."

A reward? "What is it?" I point at him. "If you say pants, I'm going to stab you with the sword that's mine."

He stands and crosses his room, and then he rummages around in the bottom of the nightstand. If I'd had a little more time, I'd have checked there myself. When he comes back, he's carrying a belt with three small daggers in a custom scabbard.

"Those are a little small," I say. "Have you seen all the dragons? You guys are huge."

"These aren't normal daggers."

I lean closer and narrow my eyes, searching for large, magical gems or ancient glyphs. No luck. I look up at him slowly. "Axel, did you pull them out of a rock?"

"They've been dipped in Azar's venom," he says. "If you use them on any dragon in this camp, they'll be immediately incapacitated. And unless Azar himself decides to spare them, within an hour, they'll die."

Any dragon here, which implies that it would even stun him. Right? That must mean he trusts me now.

He's an idiot.

I hold out my hand. "I still maintain that one of those swords should be mine, but I accept your gift."

"I thought you might."

❧ 12 ❧

After giving me that amazing gift, Axel practically disappears. At least, it feels that way. He's gone all day, and most every night, too. Either Gordon or Rufus, sometimes both, are tasked to watch over us, typically in human form so they're less scary to Fluff Dog.

She's not very smart, but she really brightens everyone's mood.

Yesterday, I caught Rufus feeding her half a sandwich. He was grinning. So no matter how much they grumble and malign her, I know at least some of it's a show.

Working with the humans that have been assigned to me is depressing, but even that becomes a bit routine. I'm pretty sure that hand-to-hand combat will be useless for them, but it's almost the only thing I know, so that's what I teach them as well. Being able to compel them to do things makes my job much easier. No one can tell me they don't have the coordination to do something—I just override their inner Eeyore and make them.

But at the end of our training sessions each day, when I assign them their post-training tasks—usually a few hours of work at some kind of distribution center—I'm beat. The best thing about every day is when I come home and bask in the afternoon and evening with the rugrats.

"Come on," Sammy says as I walk in the door. "You said that when Liz came back in, you'd think about it."

I should have no idea what they're talking about, but Sammy's like a Pomeranian with a flip-flop. Even when he has no hope of actually shredding it, he just keeps his teeth in there, trying his best.

"He doesn't want to play Reign of Dragoness," I say. "Real dragons don't play silly games like that."

"That's not true," Rufus says. "We play, but we hate to lose."

Sammy leans closer. "I promise I'll let you win. . .the first time."

Jade shakes her head. "You are so getting eaten."

Sammy scowls. "Nuh-huh. Rufus would never eat me." Rufus sounds like Wufus, but Sammy's faith in the dragon conveys just fine.

"Only because you never take a bath, so you'd taste nasty," Coral says.

"He'd eat you so you'd stop crabbing at everyone," Sammy says.

Rufus arches one eyebrow. "I wouldn't eat any of you."

For a split second, it warms my heart. My rugrats are so cute that even dragons like them.

"You're all too small for me to bother with." His grin is toothy.

Sammy huffs. "If you have to eat one of us, I'd be the best one."

This conversation has taken some very strange turns.

"Dad would be the best one," Jade says. "He's the biggest in our family."

Ah, Dad. When I sigh, I realize that Coral and Jade sighed at exactly the same time. We're all hoping he's alright. It stinks not knowing.

"My dad could probably beat you up in a fight." Sammy clearly has no idea what's appropriate to say yet. "But he wouldn't, because he's really polite."

"Did your dad teach Liz to fight?" Rufus asks.

"Nah," Sammy says. "She used to have nightmares, so they took her to lots of fighting champions. That's why she's so good. Scary stuff makes you way scarier, so when I'm all grown, no one will be able to beat me."

"I hope Dad's alright," Coral says, absently shuffling cards.

"I'm praying for him," Jade says.

"You should save your prayers for us," Sammy says. "We're the ones living with the bad dragons."

Rufus ruffles his hair. "I won't let any of them kill you, big guy."

"Me either." Gordon drops into a chair next to Sammy. "Now tell me how I can beat you at this game so I won't get angry and eat you as revenge."

I didn't think they'd really play, but both dragons listen patiently as a six-year-old explains the rules of a basic ladder-style card game. They proceed to both lose to that same little boy, which makes him beam.

Maybe it's all in my head, because out loud, they both protest vehemently about the pain of their tragic loss, but I think they're both smiling when they head back outside for their patrols.

Over the next few weeks, I complete training on my first fifty, settling them into small part-time jobs each afternoon as well. They add fifty more, which figures, and once I have them ready, they bring another hundred. You'd think that having two hundred and ten humans under my command would be hard, but after you figure out how to set up rules and push them out, it's pretty simple to manage.

Actually, it's far, far too easy.

Penelope still comes by sometimes, but usually only when she's figured out something new.

"The visor's an important tool," she says when she comes by this time, "but you might be surprised by how much you can do now without it. I think the bond with the Blessed actually makes us stronger in a lot of ways."

"Ways that help us betray our people more and more."

She hisses. "Stop saying things like that. Static is always listening."

Yes, her dragon's name is *Static*. I don't laugh, but only because she says her stupid master's always monitoring her. The last thing I need is another electric shock therapy session. I'm still twitching occasionally from the last two hits I took.

I'm a lot less nervous about moving around the camp now that I'm wearing the three daggers Axel gave me. Maybe he's less nervous about me now that I have them, too. Maybe that's why he's gone so much.

I almost fall into a pretty low-stress routine, staying in my little corner of camp, forcing my two hundred humans through their daily exercises, and playing games with the kids. Yes, we're prisoners of war, but we're comfortable enough, and I start to feel pretty safe. Sometimes I even forget that we don't want to be here.

And I can't admit this to *anyone*, not even to myself

for fear that he'll sense it, but I almost *miss* Axel when he's gone, which is most of the time.

It's a stupid thing to think. Traitorous, even.

I have no idea what he's doing, and that should really be my lamentation. If we do escape, which I think about less and less, what will I be able to tell the humans about the dragons? Not much. A pathetic amount, given that I'm bonded to one.

In a rare moment of guilt, I actually sneak away from the house and take a look around. If I manage to stumble on something valuable, maybe I can use it in some way. Maybe I could discover something about the Heart that could help me track it back to its hiding place. Maybe I could observe something about the dragons' plans that could benefit the humans if we're ever rescued or if we escape. Or maybe, I don't know.

Sitting at the house and running through the motions with a massive group of mind-controlled humans is not enough. It feels wrong to have become so complacent in my lot.

Am I kicking a hornet's nest?

Yes.

But I'm scared of who I'm becoming. Even though Axel's rarely around, his two men always are, so we can't sneak out without being seen. Even if we did, there are roving patrols of earth dragons all over the area. We're in the epicenter of the earth dragon quarters.

On top of that, there are literally thousands upon thousands of humans now, crawling all over the place. On boats. In cars. On bikes. Walking around. They're going to jobs. They're running the power plant. They're staffing grocery stores, but as distribution centers. The dragons don't make us use money. They simply ask that people take what they need, and they require everyone to work a fair amount in return.

Where the food is coming from, I'm not really sure. You'd think that the supply chain from anywhere outside of dragon headquarters would have run dry, but I guess when you have an army of flying nightmares, you can pretty much hijack whatever trucks and trains you want, or raid any supply warehouses you need.

If he would ever come by, maybe I could pry some information out of Axel. As a prince, surely he's connected. But he spends all his time doing only dragons know what, leaving me to train and retrain humans that will probably never need to do a single bit of fighting.

I'm wandering aimlessly toward the edge of the earth dragon territory, my hand caressing the tiny hilts of my three venom-dipped daggers, when I hear a disturbance.

It's gunfire.

I haven't heard that in quite some time.

Guns are kind of a waste with dragons. The bullets can't pierce their scales, and even if they did, they'd heal from such small punctures almost immediately. In order to kill a dragon, you'd better blow it to smithereens or decapitate it, and both are pretty hard to do. You'd think the humans would have figured that out by now.

I jog in the direction of the sound, fully aware that I might be the only one anywhere near who would be injured by a stray bullet. That's why I sneak very slowly, and I try to stay behind things while I check out the new area. I'm peering around the corner when a dozen men burst through the back door of a building, several of them clearly speaking into earpieces.

These are my people.

Warriors, here to slay some dragons.

Maybe more than anything else, this is why I'm wandering around. It feels like I've forgotten who I am. Like, somehow the bond and the magic and the time I've spent with the enemy has fundamentally changed me. That thought might be the most terrifying—without even using his bond to force me, has Axel already tunneled out what makes me *me*?

Being out here is the first time I've felt alive in weeks—since the silver dragon attack, really. That's also, coincidentally, the last time I spent more than five minutes around Axel. I'm sure that's not it, though. I wouldn't come all the way out here just to try and get myself into trouble so I could grab his attention.

That would be idiotic.

No, I'm here to try and find the old Liz. And it worked. Human rebels, right in front of me. Before I can say a word, before I can even think about greeting them, a water dragon rushes through a gap between a shoe store and a burger place, and a dozen earth dragons flank the troops on the other side.

"Surrender," a man says from the back of the blue dragon.

Ensnared.

"If you don't surrender, we'll be forced to kill you."

"We're here to warn you," the man at the front says. "In three days' time, we're going to bomb this entire area off the face of the earth. We're using nukes. Nothing will survive."

Are they serious? Will the United States really nuke its own people just to take out the dragons?

Actually, now that I've thought that question, I realize that it's ridiculously naive. I'm a little surprised they've waited this long. Now that the man has delivered his message, the man opens fire on the blue dragon. His troops follow suit, all except one. The guy on the farthest side peels away from the others and sneaks around the corner. He appears to be hiding, which is good. Because moments later, the dragons have—ignoring the gunfire—killed all eleven of the other men.

No one else appears to have noticed that one man snuck off. Or if they did, they must not find him to be much of a threat. After all, his gun can't do much, and if he fires and kills some of their slave humans, oh well. Plenty more where they came from.

It occurs to me for the first time that if I enslaved him, I could just march him into my pods and no one would notice or care.

I could save his life.

Once the dragons are distracted with talking to one another, I dart after the escapee. Saving someone who would otherwise be killed is admirable, right? I'd have finally done something good. I could save someone who might have died if I hadn't been here.

It takes me a few minutes of searching to figure out where he went. He's moving away from me quickly, but finally I'm close enough to an unfamiliar mind to reach for his consciousness.

I tug, and he slows.

I doubt he even realizes he's doing it. He probably thinks he's tired, but I slow him enough that I can catch him. Bizarrely, he's headed in the general direction of where we're staying, which will make my job easier. I won't have nearly as much time in which I could be discovered and punished after I take hold of his mind.

A little closer, and I'll do it.

Only, when I do get close enough, he feels familiar somehow. Like he's a movie I've already seen, or a pair of shoes I've broken in some time in the past. Instead of taking over his brain, I wait, creeping closer still. Close enough to see his face, if only he'd remove the helmet. Thanks to that bizarre feeling of familiarity, I feel worse than ever about forcing him to pull his helmet off, but I do it anyway.

And then I gasp, because he's Gideon. *My* Gideon. Special forces Gideon.

He turns toward the sound of my exhale and our eyes lock.

"Liz!" Gideon shouts.

Then Axel, in his golden dragon form, crashes around the corner, snarling. Before I can even think about stopping him, Gideon raises his weapon and opens fire.

Axel roars even louder, and I realize he's here to protect me. He probably felt my adrenaline rush, sensed my movements, and raced over to keep me safe.

From my, well, from my *almost* boyfriend.

"Wait!" I shout. "Don't kill him."

Both Axel and Gideon freeze and turn toward me slowly.

"Why not?"

He's attacking me.

Great. They both think I'm talking to them. But then I remember the promise Axel made to me. "You promised me five humans," I say. "Remember?"

The golden dragon frowns, the corners of his mouth turning pointedly down.

"I have three living with me, but my mother you claim you can't help. I haven't even seen her."

He snorts.

"This is my friend, my *dear* friend, Gideon. He's come to try and rescue me, not knowing that you were already keeping me safe." I hold up a hand, trying to make a soothing gesture. "He's number four."

Axel blinks.

"We aren't using all the rooms in the house. He can have one." I pause and check whether he's calmed down at all. "Yes?"

The golden dragon sniffs.

Gideon hasn't lowered his gun yet.

"Put that down," I hiss. "It won't do anything anyway."

"These are armor-piercing rounds," he says. "They'll shoot through—"

"Put it down, you idiot."

"He's your friend?" Axel asks. Somehow, while I was focused on Gideon, he shifted. "Or he's your *boy*friend?"

I didn't realize he knew there was a distinction. "He's my friend," I say.

At the same time Gideon says, "I'm her boyfriend."

Axel frowns.

"He's been my friend since I was a child," I say. "We had just talked about maybe dating when. . ." I gesture around. "All this."

"I'm here to save her," Gideon says.

"She doesn't need saving," Axel says. "And you can't have her. She belongs to me." He arches one eyebrow. "If you want to stay with us as her friend, you're welcome." His lip curls. "You can't stay as her boyfriend."

"That's not what you said," I argue. "You promised me five humans."

His head snaps toward me. "I promised you five *family members*. I'm willing to extend that courtesy to this man, this man who came in with a weapon and threatened to try and kill me, but only if he's not romantically involved with you."

"You can't possibly think she might like you." Gideon's disgust is clear and apparent.

Axel steps closer, a muscle in his jaw working. His voice comes out as a snarl as he towers over Gideon, which is not an easy thing to do. "She belongs to me, and when humans think they love someone, they act even dumber than usual. She's already made some questionable decisions. I'd rather not invite someone under my wing unless I'm sure they won't make that propensity worse."

"You don't have wings." For someone who couldn't have known that was a sore spot, Gideon sure did manage to needle it.

"What will it be, little man," Axel asks. "Will you stay or will you die?"

The lyrics to that stupid song start to run through my head, which is absurd. The last thing I should be doing right now is humming a Clash song from the 80s, but with 'die' in place of 'go,' but this is how my brain works, apparently.

"I'll stay." Gideon drops his gun and lifts his hands. "Message received. I won't do anything stupid, I swear."

"See that he doesn't," Axel says, ignoring him. "I'd hate for him to endanger Sammy, Coral, and Jade."

I expect Axel to go back to whatever I yanked him away from now, but he doesn't. He walks with me, slowly, staying by my side the entire way back to the house. Then he stands next to me, awkwardly, while I show Gideon to a room.

And then he still doesn't leave.

"Are you alright?" I finally ask, once Gideon's showering.

"Are you?" Axel's staring at me. "That man likely came here to find you."

I think about the letter I left at my house and cringe. "You might be right."

"He wants to take you away from here."

"I won't go," I say without thinking. But I realize Gideon won't be easy to dissuade.

"You *can't* go," Axel says. "I haven't done it, but I can force you to do things, just as you force those humans."

I had all but forgotten that, in the weeks I've been bonded to him. "Why haven't you forced me before?" I've certainly given him plenty of cause. He could order me to stay in the house or within a hundred yards of it, for instance.

"I never wanted to," he says. "I think rules and orders limit your ability to stay safe, to flex with situations as they arrive. But after today, I'm afraid I might not have a choice."

I shake my head. "I never even considered leaving with him."

"Yet."

I roll my eyes.

"Do you want him here? Or were you just trying to keep him safe?"

"Does it matter? It's done."

"Do you love him?" The word love, coming from Axel, sounds bizarre.

"Do you even know what love is?" My words are soft, because I hope that Coral, Jade, and Sammy won't hear. But also, because I'm not sure that I want to know the answer.

"I've read about it," he says. "I've watched human movies that talk about it a lot."

"So that's a no."

"What does it mean to you?"

He likes to ask the really impossible questions. "It's. . ."

"Also, you didn't answer. You deflected."

"I'm trying to answer," I say. "It's a complicated question."

"Not that one—my first one. Do you love that man?"

"Oh."

He really does ask hard questions.

"I don't know," I finally say. He can feel my emotions, so I can't just lie. "I don't want him to get hurt. I don't want him to be in danger. Does that count as love?"

Axel shrugs. "I'm the wrong one to ask."

Clearly.

"I don't want you to be hurt," Axel says. "I don't want you to be in danger. Does that mean I love you?"

Gideon's out of the shower and standing in the hallway behind Axel, and he looks ready to try and murder him. "Don't you have humans to terrorize?"

Axel's wry smile is bitter, but only I can see it. "Make sure you don't get confused. I'd hate to be forced to kill him."

But that's clearly a lie. He wouldn't hate it at all.

❧ 13 ❧

After giving me the daggers, Axel all but disappeared, but now that Gideon's here, I can't shake him for anything. Whatever was keeping him busy must have either resolved itself, or it wasn't that pressing after all.

Usually I'm actually almost happy to see him, but right now, he's just making me uncomfortable. Gideon's reunion with the rugrats should be exciting. Sammy shrieks and races toward him to give him a huge hug. Coral and Jade beam and wrap their arms around him, too.

But Axel's glaring so openly that it sets my teeth on edge.

"How did you even get here?" Jade asks.

"He's alive because I didn't kill him," Axel volunteers.

"Thanks," Sammy says. "I'm glad." It sounds like gwad, but Axel understands him pretty much all the time now.

Sammy's non-sarcastic gratitude makes Axel smile, so that's a relief.

"Gideon's the best. I'm glad he's not dead," Sammy continues.

Apparently, hearing Gideon's the best does *not* make Axel happy, but his pronounced frown on the heels of his smile makes me laugh.

Luckily it's already pretty late in the day, so after eating—which is uber awkward when the servants show up to bring us our meal—I'm able to muddle through a bit of interaction here and there and then I shepherd everyone toward their rooms.

"You can have the room downstairs," Axel says, upending all my plans.

"But that's the master," I say. "It's the biggest room in the house."

"Right," Axel says. "I'm being polite."

"It's clearly yours, when you're here."

"I don't sleep, remember?" Axel looks at the stair-well. "I'd rather he not be upstairs with you and the kids."

"I think they'd be safer with me there." Gideon leans against the wall. "Don't you?" He's looking at me.

Axel answers before I can. "If someone's going to keep them safe, it's not going to be you. Liz already has hundreds of soldiers just like you at her command, and she keeps them all across the street where they belong."

"I'm not like any of them," Gideon says. "Actually, I'm unlike any other human you've met."

"I don't know. You seem just as stupid as all the others to me," Axel says.

"It's fine," I say. "We've been safe all this time without anyone here. If Axel wants you to sleep down-stairs, just sleep there. The bedroom's bigger and it has its own bathroom, and if any bad guys show up, they'll have to get through you first."

"If you're worried," Axel says, "I can work upstairs, right outside your room."

Has he gone insane? "I'm not worried. It's fine. Go do what you always do wherever you always do it."

"What's that?" Gideon asks. "Slaying humans along the border?"

"The border?"

Gideon frowns. "Houston's been overrun. Dragons and enslaved humans are all that's left inside their earthen walls. Everything inside 99 is under their command."

"You put up walls?"

"You don't even know that? They fly over them easily, of course, but the wall—mounds of earth tightly compacted—is at least twelve feet tall."

"I made that," Axel says. "Or at least, my troops did."

Earth dragons. Makes sense.

"They've got the gulf locked down too," Gideon says. "And even the humans we've found refuse to be rescued. They voluntarily head back to the interior."

"They're being controlled by the ensnared humans," I say.

"Like Liz," Axel says.

"She doesn't seem to be ensnared to me," Gideon says.

Axel sits on the sofa and kicks up his feet. "I let her do as she pleases, because she does better work that way."

"How many of your Earth Blessed treat their humans as well?"

"My troops don't ensnare humans," he says. "That's the Strike Blessed and the Water Blessed."

"What about that red monster?" Gideon asks.

Axel stands up, his face stormy. "What about him?"

"Let's maybe not call him a monster," I say. "Azar saved my life."

Gideon's head swings my way. "Excuse me?"

"He's Axel's best friend, and once, when Axel was busy, he sent Azar to save me."

"Liz had just killed two of my dragons," Axel says. "But I didn't punish her. I sent him to save her."

"Twice, actually," I say.

"Why?" Gideon asks.

"Apparently if I die, it means a bad few days for Axel here," I say.

Axel grabs my arm. "You can't share that kind of information."

"So you're his weakness?" Gideon's eyes narrow. "Interesting. Is that true for all the ensnared humans?"

"She's much more powerful and much stronger than she was, thanks to our bond." Axel drags me next to him. "I wouldn't call her a weakness."

"Compared to a dragon?" Gideon scoffs. "I would."

"Alright," I say. "I think we've made some good progress, but I'm tired." I fake a yawn. "Let's go to bed. Alright?"

Gideon's glaring at Axel.

Axel looks ready to flay him wide open.

I shake loose from Axel's grip on my arm and shove Gideon toward his door. "You, there." Gideon looks back over his shoulder, but he goes.

I grab Axel's arm. "And you." I try shoving him toward the front door, but he's so solid, it doesn't work right.

"Yes?" His eyes stare into mine. They're so bright. So intense.

"You don't have to stay. You can go, like you always do." Why do I sound so bitter?

"The humans have pulled back," he says simply.

"Wait, so all those times you were gone. . .you were, what? Fighting?"

He frowns. "What did you think I was doing?"

My shoulders droop. "Looking for the Heart." It never occurred to me that he might be in danger. Or, you know, doing horrible things to other people. That's the bigger issue. Obviously.

"We are searching," he says. "The Water Blessed have explored the entire floor of the Gulf of Mexico and they're working their way outward. Meanwhile, my Earth Blessed have already checked as far north as Pilot Knob, and we've scoured all eighty-six of the active surface faults in the area."

"You think it's hidden inside the earth?" Is it a rock? Is that why they think that?

"We're keeping our options open, but yes. We believe that it must be hidden or buried somewhere. Otherwise, surely the humans like you would already know about it."

"Huh."

"Now that we've explored most of the areas around our settlement, we'll need to expand our search."

"But that's not why you've been gone." I don't really want to, but I have to circle back to the whole humans attacking thing.

"I'm the Prince of the Earth Blessed. My primary job in the Return is to secure our settlements to keep the Blessed safe while we're here, and to search any earthen locations for the Heart. Of course that's what I've been doing."

"And you've been killing humans."

"Only when they attack us."

"And are they?" I ask. "Attacking you, I mean."

"Almost constantly," he says. "What shocks me is that they keep using the same methods, more or less, over and over. You'd think that they'd have realized that they won't work by the third or fourth failure."

"What do you mean?"

"They can't tunnel under us. Earth Blessed feel that. They can't prevail by attacking on water. The Water Blessed sense them and they dominate. And the Strike Blessed make sure they can't defeat us in the sky."

"How many humans have you killed?"

He shrugs.

Shrugs.

"You don't even care?"

"I keep track of our dead, and I'm assuming the humans do the same." He sighs. "Liz, you're angry about this, but you shouldn't be. We haven't been the aggressors."

"You invaded us."

"Only because we had no choice. We had to start somewhere. When we made landing here, they immediately tried to eliminate us."

"So, now what? You just roll over the whole earth like a steam roller, enslaving humans to do things for you and searching every nook and cranny until you find this thing, whatever or wherever it is, no matter how many of us you kill?"

Axel looks baffled. "Of course."

"I'm going to bed." I head for the stairs.

"See you tomorrow."

I freeze on the second step. "Why? You're not leaving to slay more humans?"

"I told you, they pulled back."

"For now." Then I remember what the men said.

"Gideon came with a group tasked to deliver a message. The humans are going to hit this area with a nuclear weapon in less than three days."

"Nuclear?" His eyebrows rise. "The bombs they make from either a decaying atomic reaction or a hydrogen bomb? Is that what you mean?"

I nod slowly. "It'll kill everyone who's living here."

Axel laughs.

"It's not funny," I say. "They may not kill you, I don't know, but you're forcing them to play their last card. The humans who are living here will all die, including me. I imagine all of you will be having some very bad days, then."

"Not the Earth Blessed," Axel says. "And that's most of us."

"Lovely," I say.

"But Liz, don't worry. Azar can swallow that bomb and metabolize it just like all the other missiles he's rendered ineffective. This is what I mean. They keep doing the same things and expecting a different outcome. It's madness."

"He can't swallow an atom bomb," I say. "Trust me."

"Oh, I think he can," Axel says. "What mechanism do you think powers his fire?"

"I wouldn't have the slightest idea."

"Think. Hydrogen's the most basic element in the entire universe. Your hydrogen bomb is elemental science for us."

Part of me hopes he's right, because I really don't want us to die. But part of me's desperate for him to be wrong, because if our most powerful weapon does nothing to them. . .

Humanity is doomed.

When I wake up in the morning, Axel's still here.

"I had your people make a few extra things for breakfast." He points. "You look like you've lost some weight."

I blink.

"And I've arranged for some other people to come in and fix the door and wall that were destroyed when you killed that Strike Blessed."

"Gideon's the one who'll be freezing with that wall being exposed," I say. "So why do you care?"

"You said he's one of your five," he says. "I have to keep him safe." I can't tell whether I'm imagining it or not, but he sounds almost like he's being sarcastic.

Is it possible that he's doing it specifically to torment Gideon? Gideon will hate having people in his room banging and whamming and cutting and sawing, enslaved humans who won't even talk to him or acknowledge his presence. He'd vastly prefer to keep the makeshift wall I made with sheets of plastic and duct tape, even if it means he's a little chilly.

"That's a lot of food," Gideon says as he walks into the family room. "It smells good."

"It is good," Axel says.

"You don't eat," I say.

"I do eat," Axel argues. "I just don't usually eat around you."

"Don't let us distract you," Gideon says. "You can go eat wherever you usually do. Liz and I have a lot to catch up on." His smile's dismissive and self-assured.

Axel's smile's almost as bad, so smug that I wonder how he can bear it. "Don't let me stop you from 'catching up.'" He sits at the head of the table, his plate loaded up with bacon, eggs, and fruit. "Please." He tosses his head. "Eat as much of our food as you want."

Our. It's literally the first time Axel has ever

referred to anything as ours. He's clearly doing it for show, but it works.

Gideon grits his teeth.

The two of them are like a pile of gasoline-soaked firewood, just waiting for a spark.

"Alright," I say. "Well, I'd better get across the street and start working with the humans."

"Humans?" Gideon perks up. "I can help."

"Sure." Axel's smile widens. "You should join them." He looks positively devilish. "Actually, now that I think about it, he'd make an excellent soldier—he said it himself. You should put him on the front lines to defend us."

Gideon's about to do something even dumber than the humans leading the attack on Houston and pick a fight with a dragon in his lair. If I leave, maybe Gideon can follow me. We need to escape this pressure cooker before it blows.

I hop up and head for the door.

"You haven't eaten anything, Liz. Sit." Axel's words are light, but he's not asking. If I ignore him, I might find out how good he is at ordering me to do things.

I make a U-turn and head for the kitchen, tossing things onto my plate without thinking. I lope over to the table and drag out the chair right next to Axel. Maybe that will mollify him. Hopefully Gideon will follow my lead and sit far on the other side of the table.

Fluff Dog, utterly unaware of what's going on, is sitting where she always does, right at my feet, her eyes following my every movement like her tiny life depends on it.

Gideon's right on my heels with an equally laden plate, but instead of sitting on the opposite end of the table, he sits right next to me. Then he makes it all worse by dropping an arm around the back of my chair.

Axel opens his mouth, probably to argue more, but he's interrupted.

Glory be.

Sammy's clomping down the stairs, "Hey, Fluff. Where are you, Fluff?"

She turns toward him, but doesn't move an inch.

"You need to take her out," I say.

"I'll do it," Jade says. "She won't go with him, not when there's food to beg for."

"We can just open the back door," Coral says, her voice full of irritation. "You guys always make everything so much harder than it needs to be."

"And who keeps cooking bacon?" Jade asks. "Every single time you eat that, a pig has to die."

I stuff mine in my mouth as quickly as I can, just like Dad always did at home. Gideon's doing the same thing. We both smile as innocently as possible.

"What's wrong with pigs dying?" Axel asks, eyeing his huge pile of bacon. "That's their purpose in life—to feed us."

"Their purpose is to *die?*" Jade pauses, three steps from the ground floor. "So you think that all animals are born just so we can eat them?"

I shake my head at him and mouth the words, *don't bother*.

"Animals eat other animals," Axel says. "Lions and dogs and other predators all consume the flesh of other animals. It's the way of life."

"It's the way of *death*," Jade says.

"But if the predators didn't eat them," Axel says, "the deer and squirrels and rabbits would overrun the earth."

"So?" Jade puts one hand on her hip.

"Then they'd slowly starve," he says, "and so would the rest of you. Isn't it better that they're born, they grow up and live nice lives, and then die so that the population is balanced?"

"Murderers always have some justification for murder that makes them sound better." She huffs. "I don't buy it."

"Your sister ate bacon, too," Axel says. "Why isn't she getting a lecture?"

"Elizabeth! Did you really?" Jade spins around to face me. "Mom would be horrified."

"Mom's been here for weeks and hasn't even looked for us," I say without thinking. I snap my mouth shut, but it's too late. I can't snatch the words back.

"She's ensnared," Jade says.

"So is Liz," Sammy's voice is tiny. "But she's here."

"She got ensnared by a nice dragon, though," Coral says. "Maybe Mom didn't."

Nice.

Coral just called Axel nice.

Axel doesn't even look upset by it. The Prince of the Earth Blessed who has been heading their defense operations, commanding his dragon troops to throw up earthen walls and slay any humans who attack, was just described as *nice* because he's taken in four pet humans and a yappy dog.

I shovel eggs into my mouth until they're gone, and then I stand up. "Well, I've eaten. Dead pig carcass and everything. May I be excused now?" If Gideon can't manage to stay alive while I'm gone, well, that's his own fault.

"I'll come." Gideon stands too. Somehow, he managed to clear his entire plate in the same amount of time it took me to eat my one large spoonful of eggs.

"Be back by dinner," Axel says. "I need to hear a report on how the humans are doing. You're currently managing one tenth the number of any other Ensnared."

I snag my visor off the mantel and drop it into place. "Fine."

Gideon's trotting to keep up with me, and I realize that I'm practically running across the street. Somehow, having him here reminds me how far I am right now from where I ought to be.

"You seem upset," he says.

I spin around. "I'm training an attack force."

"Okay."

"Of humans, so that they can attack other humans on behalf of *dragons*."

Gideon blinks. "Is this news?"

My eyes well with tears. "How is this my life?" I haven't cried often, but in this moment, it feels like I'm drowning in sorrow for what my life has become.

"Oh, hey." Gideon hugs me.

I've spent a lot of time comforting my siblings. I regularly have to pet and calm Fluff Dog. But since Mom looked at me and ordered me to keep the rugrats safe, no one has comforted *me*.

Until now.

Gideon's arms are strong, and they're steady, and they're utterly useless against the massive beasts who might kill us all. But it's just what I need in this moment anyway, to help me remember what team I'm on.

"I have a plan," he whispers. "I need to get you out of here before the nuke hits."

"What?"

He doesn't release me. "I know you have to be careful what you say and think, because of your bond with that guy." He clears his throat. "But I'm getting you and your siblings out of here."

I pull away. "You would have been killed with your friends if it hadn't been for my intervention."

"That was a gamble," he says. "But I knew you were bound to an earth dragon, thanks to your note."

"You did get it," I say.

He nods. "Before they expanded the perimeter, we snuck in several times. I prayed every day that I'd find you, but even though we evacuated thousands, you weren't among them."

I'm suddenly acutely aware that we're just standing still in the middle of the street. "Let's get the training started."

He follows me to the field behind the neighborhood that used to be a park full of soccer fields. "This is where we're supposed to train."

"What about weapons?" he asks.

"We have plenty." I point at the storage buildings. "The dragons don't care what we use—none of them work on them. They're only effective against other humans. We're loaded up with guns, knives, and plenty of bullets."

"They really trust you with all this?"

"I think you dramatically underestimate what I can do." I tap the front of my visor to give him some context, and then I push the humans in my group a command to come out for training.

Like good little automatons, they all march out and form into perfectly straight lines in front of me.

"That's creepy," he says. "So you just magically lobotomize them?"

I shake my head, and I push the command to rest at ease, but not to leave the field. The men and women's posture immediately changes. They're chatting and talking and moving around freely.

"What just happened?"

"I released them," I say. "It's really that simple. It might be scarier than the dragons. Something about my brain and that bond has made me some kind of horrible puppet master. I can tell them what to do. What not to do. How high to jump. Whatever I order, they just do it. Or I can release them, and they revert to their non-controlled states."

"But surely they can refuse some of your commands."

I shrug. "If some of them can, none of mine have been among them."

"But when you're not ordering them to do something, they just." He gestures. "They're normal?"

I nod.

"And they don't try to attack you, or run around screaming?"

I tap my visor again. "I told them to always remain calm, and always be ready for my new commands. I told them not to fight. I give them rules, and they follow them."

"That's. . ." Gideon swallows. "Unsettling."

"What's more unsettling to me is how *okay* they are with it. Actually, quite a few of them have come and asked me to help them manage their mental health. In the same way that I order them around, I can simply eliminate their anxiety, eradicate their depression, or manage their bipolar symptoms."

"I wonder whether the numbers we guesstimated are correct," he says. "Maybe there are more people still alive in here than they think. It's not like they can send drones."

I take a few moments to set my trainees some basic tasks and general physical fitness training, and then I circle back. "What are the numbers?"

"What do you mean?"

"I was stuck in here, remember? I have no idea how many humans have died."

"They think about three and a half million," he says. "Houston area had close to eight million, and a lot of them evacuated. The ones who stayed were probably either killed or." He points at my would-be-troops who are doing pushups and burpees.

"So maybe it's less than three and a half million."

"Is this really better than being dead?" Gideon shakes his head.

"Still," I say. "If we can get rid of them, all these people could go back to normal."

I hope.

"We've also sent a lot of troops against them." His expression's pretty grim.

"None of those attacks succeeded."

"We've killed less than two dozen dragons, at least, as far as we know."

Two dozen.

"I've killed three," I say.

His jaw drops. "How?"

"Well, four if you give me credit for one that I got killed but that I didn't stab myself."

"You—really?"

"Earth dragons, mostly," I say.

"Axel just. . .let that go?"

I shrug. "I'm not sure how he'd feel exactly if I died, but I gather pretty bad. He's been much more tolerant than I expected him to be since I threatened to kill myself on the first day."

"You did what?" Gideon shakes his head. "I should've known."

"It worked," I say. "And he's not so awful."

"I think he likes you." Gideon's lips are compressed into a thin line.

I punch his shoulder. "Stop."

He turns toward me slowly, his eyes capturing mine. "I mean it, Liz."

"No way." I sigh. "Listen, dragons don't even feel emotions like we do. They don't love or desire or long for things. They don't have compassion or disappointment, either. He told me that himself."

"You think they can't learn?"

I shrug. "I think emotion's something you may learn about, but I don't think you can really grow into emotions. You just feel them or you don't."

"You're saying they're all indestructible, maniacal sociopaths."

"Maybe." I'd never thought of it like that. "I don't think they form connections in the same way that we do. He watches me with Sammy and Coral and Jade sometimes, and he looks genuinely surprised that we show affection to one another."

"They have families, though, right?"

I shrug. "He hasn't said much about it. I think Prince Azar has a father. I definitely heard that somewhere, so yeah, I guess they must. But I don't think they resemble ours very much."

"We need to get you out of Houston ASAP," Gideon says. "You have so much to teach our commanders."

I'd actually been lamenting the opposite, that I felt like I'd learned nothing. I suppose I hadn't compared it to what I'd know if I'd only been battering myself against the dragons in military applications.

But the idea of telling some general everything I've learned about Axel feels. . .wrong. "I do think they really just want to find this thing they need and leave. Why do we keep attacking them over and over?"

"They dropped in and just *took* Houston," Gideon says. "Do you hear yourself?"

"Yes, but most of the deaths have been caused by us attacking them, right? I'm just saying, maybe if we helped them find what they came for, they could leave without turning every city into Houston."

"That red dragon is the problem," Gideon says. "It's *eating* warheads, apparently, and it flies faster than our jets." He drops to a whisper. "But we've discovered that there's only that one. If we take him out. . ." He shrugs. "We think we can take the others down."

"Azar is Axel's best friend," I say.

Gideon's brow furrows. "You met him."

"And?"

"And you said your death would incapacitate Axel for days," he mutters. He frowns. "When we get back, you can't tell anyone that fact."

"They'll hear that I'm ensnared," I say. "Obviously they have to—"

He shakes his head. "You can't tell them, Liz. Promise me."

"Why not?"

"They're desperate," he says. "They're running scared. If you tell them your dragon's connection to Azar, if you say you've met him, if you mention that Axel values you, they might kill you to wound him. Or they might send you back with some kind of crazy plan to kill Azar yourself."

Why didn't I think of that already? If Azar's the key to their dominance, I should already have considered whether I could take him out.

"You've already killed three times the number of dragons any other individual has ever killed."

"Actually, Azar might have one weakness they could use." I'm so stupid for not thinking of this before. "The dragons have this downtime they have to take once a week."

Gideon's eyes light up.

"They have to, I don't know, process the gases they breathe or something. They're vulnerable during that brief few moments."

"We have to escape in the next day or two," Gideon says. "Not just to escape the nuclear attack, but also so you can tell them about this."

"There's no way to know when it'll happen," I say.

"They'll want to send you back," he says. "They'll want you to come back, find out when his downtime will be, and get a message back to us."

"Or you could take them that message," I say. "If you could escape, you could tell them what I've told you."

"No." He shakes his head. "We all go together."

"What's your plan to escape?" I ask. "Just run as far as we can, hopefully get over their wall, and then hope the humans on the other side see you?"

He shrugs. "I'll go back the same way I came."

"Which is?"

"I can't tell you," he says.

"Because?"

"You're ensnared. If he forces you to share information, it's better if you don't know."

I can't even argue with him about that, but it worries me. Is there any chance Axel might be listening in on us right now? I feel for my emotion thread. He's focused on something.

Could it be me?

No, he's also bored. That's a color I associate with grey—a dark, smoky grey. He has work he does when I'm not with him, and I don't know quite what it is at any point, but he finds a lot of it tedious and frustrating.

Once I'm reasonably certain Axel's distracted and not listening in, I finish our conversation. "I've got to start doing some actual fighting with these people momentarily. But I've thought about it. Take the kids and get out of here. I have to stay—bomb or not."

"You can't," Gideon says. "I can't lose you."

"If Axel's right," I say, "that bomb won't kill them, and if that happens, taking me with you will lead him right to you, thanks to my bond. I won't take that risk with my siblings' lives."

I can tell Gideon's not done arguing, but I force him to help me drill the humans on some basic combat maneuvers. Weapons training is next. Gideon knows much more than I do about firing guns, loading, and unloading, so I let him teach them, reinforcing the things he says with commands.

With his help, I actually do more today than I ever have before in terms of making these humans into weapons that could be used against the rest of the world. Goodie.

"Alright, well, I think that's it for today." I've just released my people, and I'm nearly back to the house when I spot Penelope walking down the street. She doesn't come much, but it's usually a welcome break in my routine.

Only, this time, she's not alone.

She has two other Ensnared with her, judging from their fancy headgear.

"You've been summoned," she says.

"Summoned?" I can't help my smile. "As far as I know, the only Prince around here is already bonded to me."

"The Strike Blessed have a princess, and her Ensnared wants to meet you."

Ah, shoot. That doesn't sound good. I lower my voice, but I keep my face calm. "Hey, Gideon. Why don't you go back to the house and if you see Axel, tell him where I'm going. Okay?"

At first, Gideon looks like he might argue, but thankfully, he doesn't. The last thing I need is for them to drag him along, too.

❧ 14 ❧

Admittedly, I was a little naive when I was first bonded. It quickly became clear that any kind of insurrection I wanted to organize would have to be handled with more skill than I possessed. Training for MMA may have left me suited to deal with surprise dragon attacks while using a broken umbrella or a fire poker.

It did not prepare me to lead troops or create spy-like networks.

But perhaps meeting the other Ensnared will be a good thing. Surely one of them, an older and wiser human than I am, will be planning a way to send the dragons home while mitigating the human death toll. One of them must be doing *something*, and if so, they can teach me. I could finally be of some help.

Also, I feel like I ought to warn them all about the nuclear attack.

As I follow Penelope, I actually feel a sense of purpose. I may not be able to escape with Coral, Jade, Sammy, and Gideon, and I may be stuck here all alone, but perhaps I can still contribute.

Plus, I'm a little excited. I've been scared and nervous at the prospect of meeting my mother since we arrived, but then it never happened. She's bonded to an electro dragon, and that's where we're going, so. . . Surely I'll meet her today, right?

I sort of thought she'd come by to visit me. I'm not sure why I expected that. It's not like Axel and I have advertised about the kids being here, so she'd have no way of knowing that his Ensnared was anyone special. To her, I'm just another human girl among many. But she did know I could hear the message that day, surely, since I listened to it and escaped with the kids. She might have been *somewhat* curious about the other Ensnared in case one might be her oldest daughter.

Right?

Only, as we walk and walk and walk—I thought Axel said we were finally living inside the main area—I start to get nervous.

What if Mom's not Mom? What if she's evil or something? What if she doesn't remember me? Or, worse, what if she *does*, but she blames me for not getting the kids free?

"What's wrong with you?" Penelope's a dozen feet ahead by now, and the other Ensnared who came with her are another two or three feet ahead of her. "Hurry up."

I inhale sharply and pick up the pace. "Sorry. I was thinking."

"Less daydreaming and more focus," she says. "Get your head in the game." When I catch up, she hisses. "I vouched for you, idiot. I told them you weren't so bad. Don't make me regret it."

Penelope vouched for me? Really? "Uh, thanks."

"I didn't like you at first you, know." Her voice is low.

"I had no idea," I lie.

"Really? I called your Blessed weak."

I shrug. "He's an earth dragon, and I know all the others think they're better."

"They are better," she says, "but that doesn't mean you should be punished."

I'm not sure I agree with her statement that Axel's not as good as the other dragons, but I don't get hung up on it. "I should hope not."

"The world's different than it was," she says. "You need to catch up." She snaps. "We're almost there."

Turns out, *there* is a car. "We're driving?" I blink. "Then why didn't you just drive to where I was?"

"We didn't want to spook you," the heavy lady says. "Penelope said you're a little different."

"I'm human, just like the rest of you. Axel's an earth dragon, but really, I think they worry too much about that. They're all dragons."

Her look of disgust has me lowering my opinion of her. "I heard he doesn't even have wings. Were you really bonded by an *Earth Blessed?*"

"Yep," I say. "No wings at all, which isn't really that big of a deal."

"Don't worry. It's not a long drive," Penelope says. "At least there's no traffic anymore."

Because all the people with ideas of their own aren't around to cause it. That's a sad thought.

"I thought the dragons all settled around here." I point back the way we came, toward Clear Lake.

Penelope arches that eyebrow, the one she always arches around me. "Oh, hon."

"What?"

"The Water Blessed and the Earth Blessed have chosen Clear Lake as their headquarters, since they need to be close to the ground and the water." The

Ensnared who answers has silver hair, so I'm guessing he's yet another Strike Blessed Ensnared. He's small and effeminate, which is quite a contrast to the larger woman who was just denigrating Axel's affinity.

"Oh," I say. "I didn't realize the dragons didn't all live in the same place."

They *all* stare at me, then.

"Where are we going, exactly?"

"The George R. Brown Convention Center," the male Ensnared says. "I think you'll be impressed with how well the Blessed fit there."

I really doubt anything about the Blessed is going to impress me, but I don't say that. "I think I went there once before all this happened, maybe?" I vaguely recall being dragged to some kind of gymnastics competition there for Coral. "It's a big building, right?"

"The Strike Blessed are quite large," Penelope says. "They find most of our buildings too small. They also prefer places that are easily accessible by air."

"I suppose that wouldn't matter to those who can't fly." The larger woman smirks.

"The earth dragons can also shift into a smaller form, so living in a variety of places is easy for them. They're very adaptable." I can't help bragging a little.

"Like cockroaches," the other woman says.

I hate this lady. "It seems you already know a lot about me, but you didn't even tell me your names."

"I'm Dovie," she says.

"Dove, like the bird?"

"No, Dove-ee," she says, clearly annoyed.

"And I'm Seth," the man says. "Bonded to Heaston, Strike Blessed."

"I guessed you were all bonded to electro dragons," I say.

"The hair's a dead giveaway." Seth's smile this time looks genuine.

When we finally reach the Convention Center, both Seth and Dovie have relaxed. I'm a little proud of how I won them over, but my triumph's short-lived.

I've barely stepped out of the SUV when a massive Strike Blessed lands in front of us.

"So this is the bizarre human that Earth Blessed Prince bonded."

The dragon's shimmering scales are distracting enough that I don't even see the human who spoke at first. When I slide my eyes all the way up, I finally make eye contact with the woman I assume is her Ensnared.

She's my mother.

❧ 15 ❧

fter our eyes meet, Mom's widen. "Oh."

"That's me. The loser dragon's vassal, at your service."

Mom swallows, and then she exhales gustily.

What are you waiting for? Her dragon's just as horrible today as she was when she ensnared Mom. *Destroy the abomination.*

But did she really summon me here. . .just so she could kill me? "I feel like I keep having to say this over and over. I'm just an average human. No mutations or growths of any kind."

Your Master has overstepped. He should never have ensnared you.

I think I hate Mom's dragon more than I've ever hated anything on earth, including that red nightmare. "Sounds like you're attacking the wrong person," I say. "Your problem's with him, not me."

The silver dragon tilts her head. *But killing you is easy, and it'll weaken him.*

Her logic's not wrong, sadly. "Yes, but at what cost? I hear the guilt from something like this can be really bad. Do you want wrinkles before your time?" I'm not sure whether dragons can even get wrinkles, but if I kill enough time, maybe Axel will get his crap together and realize I'm gone. I send the brightest red feelings of panic that I can muster down the bond.

Clearly, your Master's unable to control you. Killing you is a service.

But why isn't Mom defending me? She's just sitting there on the dragon's neck, not even moving.

"I think Axel may have things right," I say. "I follow his rules, but I'm not a robot. You might want to learn from him."

"Don't be rude," Mom says.

Those are her first words to me? Really?

Before I can respond, six more Strike Blessed circle and land on all sides of me. The courtyard in front of the conference center is massive, but with them closing in, it's feeling much smaller.

How shall we kill her, Your Majesty? asks the largest one. He sounds male, but who knows? I'm not sure how I can even tell which one is speaking, but somehow, I just know.

If we strike her, Azar will be angry, says the smallest one. She's standing a solid dragon's distance away from the others. Nervous Nelly. That's what I call her in my head.

"Yikes." I cringe dramatically. "You're right. Azar won't want you doing this. He and Axel are close, and if I were you, that big red dragon would scare me. Badly."

Mom's dragon laughs.

"Look, Princess Petunia, if I know one thing, it's this. You do *not* want to upset Prince Azar."

I don't plan to, she says, her head tilting toward the other Strike Blessed. *Fly her high up, and then drop her.*

Her gaze is crafty. *I won't have anything to do with your death or know a thing about it.*

I can't believe I thought Mom or Penelope or any of the other Ensnared might speak up for me. No one says a single word in my defense. Good thing I know how to defend myself. "As I'm dying, I'm going to think about all the ways Azar might torture you before he kills you. I had one of my humans tell Axel where I was coming and at whose orders before I left. Azar will find out, and you'll pay the price, no matter how you try to disguise it."

She smiles. *No one trusts the word of humans.*

"That's where you're wrong. Axel actually listens to me, and you may think it's a weakness, but I think you'll find it has its perks. You know, when you're dying horribly."

Either way, you'll already be dead.

She may be right, since it's currently seven dragons to one paltry human. But what she doesn't know is that Axel armed his useless human. A sword would have been better, but at least I have three daggers dipped in Azar's venom.

Fly her up and drop her. Now!

Nervous Nelly steps back, but two other electro dragons aren't as nervous, and they both advance. I grab one dagger for each hand. "Let's play, drag-queens." I'm actually smiling at my stupid joke they won't even get. I must have lost my mind.

But now that they're actually trying to kill me, I sink into the calm place. The spot where I hang out during a fight. I might die, but that means I have nothing to lose by fighting my hardest. That makes my decisions terribly simple.

The biggest silver dragon is one of those advancing on me, and he opens his mouth and whips his head toward me preternaturally fast, but I'm not a normal human anymore, either. I leap sideways and slash with my right hand.

The blade catches him on the side of his triangular head, and unlike every other blade I've tried to use with them, it slides through his hide like a hot knife through butter, even sizzling.

His scream of pain is a beautiful thing.

Which is good, because while I was distracted with him, the other beast snapped its horrible maw around my left leg. The pain tries to incapacitate me, but I step away from it.

I trained for this—well, not exactly *this*, but to ignore pain.

With great determination, I block it out, and focus, bending at the waist, twisting like a rat in a trap, and plunge the other dagger in the psychopath's eye. It roars, widening its jaw, which releases me. I stumble away, tripping over the massive body of the first dragon. It's utterly motionless in the center of the courtyard, and I'm not the only one who's shocked by that. The other gathered dragons are backing away.

Axel wasn't lying. These daggers are, hands down, the best gift I've ever received.

"Alright, who's next?" I'm smiling maniacally.

It might have been nice if Axel mentioned whether they're multi-use, or like a one-dragon takedown type of thing. Either way, one's stuck in a dragon's eye, and the other's been used. I have one sure-thing left. I hold it in my right hand, my dominant hand.

What magic is that? Princess Petunia's not backing down, and she looks ticked.

"I told you Axel and Azar are tight, idiot. Did you think I was just going to stand here and let you splatter me on the pavement?" I look over my shoulder at the second dragon, also now lying unmoving on the ground.

Did I kill them? Or are they just unconscious? I definitely don't know enough about dragon anatomy to be able to tell.

Disarm her!

At first, I'm not sure who she's commanding, because no one moves.

But then my mom slides off the princess's back and walks toward me, her brow furrowed. She isn't a warrior. She knows nothing about fighting. I could incapacitate her easily.

And I should.

But my hand trembles as she approaches.

"Mom?"

No reply.

She's not even meeting my eyes.

"Mom." It's not a question now, but a plea. Why are my eyes welling with tears? "Mom!"

She finally looks at me, and I realize that she's in there, but she's not in control. She lifts her sword arm. A *sword*. My mother's holding a sword.

And all I have is a poisoned dagger.

When she swings it at me, I barely duck in time, my wounded leg a misery with every movement. I make the mistake of looking down at it, and blood's steadily flowing from my thigh downward, pooling in my shoe. My entire calf's bright red. Even if I can ignore it, losing that much blood's going to slow me down soon enough.

While she's distracted, take her. Fly her up and drop her. Now. Go! Great. Princess Petunia's ordering more dragons toward me.

Mom's not slowing down either, and her movements definitely aren't hers. Mom's graceful, but she's gentle and kind. She cares for everything, from the smallest bird to the largest beast. The woman hacking at me isn't my mother. It's a puppet piloted by Princess Petunia.

But if I kill the puppet, Mom dies.

It's an impossible puzzle that I can't solve, not even with a magical, venom-infused dagger. It feels like, with every dodge and stumble, I'm stumbling closer and closer to a total loss.

Mom's sword clips my right shoulder. Now I'm limping on the left and slow at using my right arm. I flip my dagger around and spin into Mom's guard, slamming the hilt into her nose.

She stumbles back, spraying blood on my chest.

I hop back out, limping as quickly as I can on my bad leg before she can hit me back. But that move cost me.

Nervous Nelly was not who I expected would dart in and grab my left arm, but she does. I almost hate stabbing her, but not enough to let her gnaw on my arm. I drag my slow right arm across my body and stab her on the nose.

She's resigned as she releases me—I can see it. She snorts before her eyes close and her body goes slack.

Mom's sword swings toward me again, a hairsbreadth behind Nelly's collapsing body, and I leap backward. Only, my left leg can't support my landing, leaving me to tumble over Nelly's unconscious body in the process of evading it.

And. . .Princess Petunia had *six* helpers, and I've only dispatched three, which means there are three more dragons and the princess herself.

When another confounded silver dragon grabs my already wounded left leg, I bite off a swear word, wrenching my arm into motion. I fight back a wave of terrible, cutting, burning pain, but this time, when I scratch the dagger across the stupid dragon's mouth, it merely clamps down harder.

I drop the dagger with an agonized shout as the dragon bunches up and then vaults into the air. I've never been in a helicopter, and I've never been bungee jumping or skydiving, and if I survive this, which seems unlikely, I don't plan to ever do any of those things.

The trip into the stratosphere while dangling from a dragon's mouth has ruined air travel for me permanently. At least it won't be my own mother that kills me.

When the wretched son of a worm drops me, my heart quits working a little early. The ground may be very, very far below me, but no one gave me a handy pocket-parachute, so clearly this is the end of the line.

Surprisingly, as I plummet toward the earth, my thoughts turn to Axel. He's so despised by his own people that they'd hunt down his bonded human and murder her, and yet, he's just earnestly doing his job most days. He was kinder to me than any of the other dragons seem to have been. I might not have been very fair to him.

And my death is about to be very bad news.

I'm pretty sure the second I die, they're moving on to him. "I'm sorry," I say, my eyes welling with tears. "I'm sorry that I couldn't get out of this. I'm sorry you're about to be attacked when you're already weak, and my last wish is that you will be able to kill all those silver devils." I'm smiling one last time at that prospect as the earth races to meet me.

Because, surprisingly, I really want him to be fine.

But instead of splattering on the pavement below, a huge, blood-red dragon slides in underneath me just in time, his massive wings pumping furiously, and suddenly I'm moving upward again instead.

Azar.

Somehow, when I was about to die, Azar found me again.

Axel may not be very well liked, and certainly the Prince of the Return has his flaws, but I can't fault Axel's faith in his friend. He comes through in a crunch in a big way.

❧ 16 ❧

I thought, when that insane electro dragon yanked me up into the sky, that was the highest I would ever fly. I thought it was the highest I'd ever *want* to go. But now, riding Azar, the city below's barely visible. Some of that is thanks to cloud cover, of course, but a lot of it is that we're higher than I thought humans *could* fly. I can't help wondering how much farther I can go before I won't be able to breathe.

I must be clutching him pretty tightly, and maybe dramatically gasping for breath a bit, because he addresses my concern before I've even voiced it. *I'm able to generate enough oxygen for you. Don't worry.*

"You can generate. . ." Asking him about science right now is probably pretty stupid. Instead, I squeeze his neck a little tighter, and then I inhale deeply. Fall in Houston can be pretty hit or miss, but it's usually still fairly warm.

On the ground.

Up here, I'm freezing half to death. It's totally worth it, though. This is definitely a once in a lifetime kind of view. It might be nicer if I hadn't just been bitten on both my thigh and arm by dragons with dagger-sized teeth, and then grazed on the shoulder and side with a sword. Even so, I'm lucky Azar showed up when he did.

I can probably heal from this with Axel's help.

There's no healing possible after becoming pavement jam.

"Thank you," I say. "You saved my life again."

But that makes me wonder *why* he's the one saving me. The earth dragons may not be as powerful as the electro dragons, but he is a prince. Surely Axel could have marshaled his army and brought hordes of dragons over to save me. . .or something like that. "Is Axel okay?"

Aren't you really just worried about your siblings?

"I'm worried about Axel, too," I say. "Those stupid electro dragons—" I catch myself too late. "Er, I mean, the Strike Blessed who took me were trying to harm him."

Axel can defend himself.

"Maybe, but why are they so angry?"

They're jealous.

"That's kind of your fault."

If I hate him, they attack. If I like him, they attack. It's a problem with our society, which is proving difficult to repair.

"Aren't you the only one who can fix it?"

It's treason to criticize the established power structure. The Strike Blessed are more powerful than the Earth Blessed. There's nothing I can do to change that.

"But the way the powerful behave models behavior for the lesser creatures. As adults, it's our job to teach our children good manners and ethical behavior."

His head curves just a bit so his massive eye can see me. *You have some insight, but you don't understand the Blessed enough to be helpful.*

"Well, that's not my fault." I've been trying not to show how cold I am, but it's getting harder and harder. My fingers are numb, and my grip's getting weaker. An involuntary shiver runs through my body.

You're cold.

"Aren't you?"

His snort is definitely half-laugh. *I'm fire and flame. I'm never cold.*

"That must suck," I say. "Being hot is the worst."

He snorts, and flames burst from his nostrils. The air around us warms up.

My goosebumps finally go away.

But instead of blowing past the warmth immediately, the air around us stays warm. "Why's it still not cold?"

I can regulate the temperature. I would've done it sooner had I known to.

"While I'm lodging complaints, what can you do about my leg wound?" I joke. "Because I think I've probably got another five minutes until I pass out from it. That's an estimate, though, so it's probably give or take four minutes either way."

His head really does crane around this time. *You're bleeding. Quite a lot.*

"I just fought three dragons," I say, a little proud of myself. "But two of them chomped on me."

I'm sorry I came too late.

"I think Axel can help."

There's nothing Axel can do that I can't.

"Okay, maybe that's true, but he's my bonded." I don't say that I feel safer with the guy who doesn't incinerate small towns, but I'm hoping he'll intuit that last part.

I'm his best friend. You can trust me.

"Human factoid. When someone's trustworthy,

they generally don't have to go around telling people they are."

Now that the eminent danger's past, my right arm's throbbing so badly I want to cut it off, and my left leg both aches and stabs with every pulse of Azar's monstrous wings. "Maybe make that a minute. I'm feeling pretty lightheaded."

I'll land now.

I want to be grateful, but I'm too busy hanging on for dear life. Apparently *land now* means plunge straight toward the top of a skyscraper at Mach ten. He whips his wings out at the last minute, and once again, I'm spared from becoming a Liz pancake. At least it got the small amount of blood I had left pumping.

Wait. Maybe that's bad. It *is* kind of pumping *out*.

I'm at least aware enough to recognize that a skyscraper is *not* the house I was expecting. "Where are we?"

It's safe.

"Where's Axel?" I may sound like a petulant child, but I'm hurting, and I'm scared, and I want the person who healed me last time.

I wouldn't have guessed that dragons could sound so annoyed through their thoughts, but Azar keeps teaching me new things about them. *He's coming.*

I practically collapse against his neck. "Oh, good."

He walks several steps across the helipad inside what looks like a keyhole-shaped cutout in the top of a skyscraper. With my eyes closed, I realize that his neck's surprisingly smooth and soft for something that's covered in impenetrable scales.

"Where are we?" My voice sounds faint, even to me. I'm not sure whether he can hear me.

The signs call this place the JP Morgan Chase Tower. Now, it's mine.

Ah, yes. Dragons like to possess things. Why am I not surprised he claimed one of the tallest towers in Houston? "But no one lived here. How can you. . ."

No human residence would accommodate me. The top floors are two stories tall, and below that, there are two levels of living space.

Probably for the important executives or something. Or, who knows? Maybe there's a Mister Chase, or a Mister Morgan? I don't really know much about rich people or posh penthouses, clearly.

Azar's walking off the helipad when spots begin dancing across my eyes. "I think I'm about to pass out," I whisper. "Humans do that when they lose a lot of blood."

Elizabeth.

The way he says my name, it feels like a caress. "Again," I whisper.

Elizabeth, stay with me. Axel will be here very soon.

But I can't. No matter what I do, the darkness beckons. Finally, I can't fight it any longer and it pulls me down, down, down.

When I finally wake up, I'm still tired. I'm so weary, so bone-deep exhausted that I wipe my eyes before opening them, but they still burn. Whatever room I'm in is bright, painfully bright. I cover my burning eyes with my hands.

I'm in a van with several people, but I don't know them.

None of them is my mom *or* my dad. That makes me cry. "I want my mom." I'm sucking my thumb. I know I'm not supposed to, but Mom's not here to yell at me, so I can do what I want.

Only, when she doesn't show up to yell, I'm sad. I thought she might.

The people in the van keep speaking words I can't

understand, and it's cold. So, so cold. I shiver. I wrap my hands around my arms, but it doesn't help much.

The man who's driving looks back at me and says something I don't understand. Then the woman next to me and the man in the front passenger seat both laugh. I don't think what he said was nice. That means he shouldn't have said it at all.

"Who are you?" I ask.

No one answers me.

"Where are we going?" I ask.

Still nothing, but the woman next to me looks a little uncomfortable. She won't meet my eye and keeps looking out the window instead.

"I'm scared," I say. "I want my mom."

"Your mother not here," she snaps. "Quiet."

She does speak some English. "Can you call her? I want to talk to her."

"Quiet." The man in the front passenger seat is wearing a large, wool cap. He scowls.

"No." I glare at him. "I won't be quiet. I want to see my mom."

He throws his can at me, which happens to be full of beer, and it hits the side of my head. It hurts, and it also spills beer all over me. Now I'm colder, I smell, and my head aches. "I want my mom." The tears return, but this time they're mixed with something new.

Anger.

I clench my hands, but I'm too afraid to do anything.

Yet.

The ride goes on and on. No matter how many times I ask, no one tells me who they are or where we're going. The ground's covered with snow. The car's freezing. Wherever we are, it's nowhere near Houston.

Finally, the woman says something, and the men snap to attention. When I look ahead, I realize we've reached something. Something huge. A very tall, very scary looking snow-covered mountain. The van stops, and they force me to get out.

"I'm c-c-cold," I say, my teeth chattering. "I don't want to get out."

"Here." The woman hands me a coat that's far too large, but I pull it on gratefully. It's not easy to button, and it's so big that I can't seem to keep both shoulders in place, but it's better than just my Hello Kitty hoodie, which is clearly not even close to warm enough.

She hasn't been kind, but the woman has been a great deal better than either man, so when we start walking, I make sure to keep close to her. At first, the walk's not so bad. It's cold, but the more I move, the warmer I feel. They pass out sandwiches, but no one gives one to me, even when I ask.

We must've gone a very long way—more than the mile they sometimes make us walk at school—when I finally give up. "I can't go any more." I sit down on the rocky ground and fold my arms. "My legs hurt. I'm cold. I'm hungry. I'm not moving."

The man who chucked the beer can at me tosses a rope around my neck and drags me until I fall forward on my hands and face. He barely gives me five seconds to get up before he's pulling again. Blood's dripping down the right side of my face, but no one else seems to care.

I cry, but the tears make my cheek hurt more. I clench my fists, but the hamburger-like parts of my palms sting too badly to do it long. Finally, I start to think about all the ways I'll inflict pain on the bad people who are dragging me along like one of those bobbing duck-on-a-string toys I used to pull.

"When I get home, I promise I'll cut that string and free you," I mutter. "No one should make you move when you want to sit still."

But no one else even notices that I'm talking.

I start to sing *Mary Had a Little Lamb*. No one cares about that either, but it makes me feel a little better. I launch into *Twinkle Twinkle* next, but I never paid much attention in music class so I'm rapidly exhausting my repertoire. A few songs later, I'm forced to start tapping into Christmas songs, like *Jingle Bells* and *Rudolph*.

My horrible captors don't seem to notice that I'm singing, much less care what I'm saying or why. As long as I keep moving, they're indifferent. If I stumble, fall, or stop, they start shouting and yanking.

The sun sets, but we keep right on stumbling along. That's when I realize that, even though the sun has set, the sky's still bright.

Not a normal bright. It's red.

It's unnaturally red. "Why is the sky like that?" I ask.

"Eyjafjallajökull," the woman says.

"Why's the sky red?" I ask again. "I can't understand you."

She points at the brightest part. "Lava. Hot."

The place she's pointing? That's where we're climbing. That can't be good. If that's a volcano—it must be. The sky's red, she said lava, and then she pointed. . . If it is a volcano, I do not want anything to do with it. These crazy people can go there without me.

I stop and sit down.

Beer Can laughs. He mutters something. He yanks on my rope. The fibers of the rope hurt my neck. I'm pretty sure it's bleeding, but that's better than letting them walk me right up to a volcano.

"Come." The man yanks again, this time loosening the tension and then whipping the rope as hard as he can.

It collapses my throat, or that's how it feels. I can't breathe at all, and then I can't stop coughing. "No," I wheeze. "I will not go." That makes me cough again, but the man's done caring.

"Up. Move." He yanks, and yanks, and yanks. Not as hard, but more persistently, and finally, another hard pull. Bleeding skin, I can ignore. Chafing burns. But a snapped neck can't be fixed. I stumble back to my feet and start walking.

The higher we get, the hotter the ground gets.

"Why are we going there?" I ask, my voice raspy.

No one answers me, of course, and no matter how many times I repeat my question, they still say nothing back. I try grabbing rocks and throwing them. I wrap my hands around the rope and yank when it looks like Beer Can isn't paying attention. Once, I even manage to pull the rope free from his hands, but a half dozen steps away, Beer Can steps on the rope and knocks me back on my rear.

I stop trying to escape after that.

But I keep watching them, and I keep my eyes open. By the time we reach the top, there's a group waiting, and I have a few ideas. The men seem to be the stronger ones, but I think the woman's in charge.

"Why am I here?" I ask. "Why me?"

I know they'll ignore me, but I can't seem to keep from asking.

"Tattoo," the woman says.

Her response surprises me, and I just blink at first. "Tattoo?" I ask. "I don't understand."

She points at the spot just above her breast on her left side. "Tattoo."

"Do you mean my birthmark? It's not a tattoo. I've always had it." I frown. "What does that have to do with—"

But Beer Can's as impatient as ever. "Go in." He yanks again, and this time, it's from the side. I fall to my left, hitting the woman on her left side.

She stumbles, muttering loudly, and I notice something. Her right leg isn't quite right. When I look closer, I realize that it's a prosthetic. I've been so preoccupied with where we were going and with trying to escape that I didn't pay enough attention to my captors. My teacher had a fake leg, so I know what it is. Something happened to her real leg, and they had to replace it, probably.

If she wasn't so horrible, I might feel bad for her.

Beer Can and his driver clap and shout and point, dragging me little by little to a massive stone doorway. It's dark inside, and I don't want to go, but nothing we've done has been my idea, so what's new? Once we pass through the doors, I hear something strange.

A lot of people are there already, and they're chanting the word *hjartanu*.

Beer Can's smiling now, and he drags me along, tugging, tugging, tugging, until I see where he's taking me. It's a long, narrow ledge that overlooks the volcano's crater.

It looks like a scene out of a cartoon or something. Only the blasts of hot air that smell like ash and coal convince me that this is really happening. You can't dream that kind of heat up.

"No." This time, I'm more forceful. This time, I'm not going to let them drag me. I claw at the rope around my neck.

Beer Can's driver gets tired of waiting, I guess. He leans over, knees me in the stomach, and then throws me over his shoulder like I'm a sack of potatoes. A few dozen paces away, he drops me on the ground.

The woman pulls a knife from her pouch and brandishes it. She starts to yell, and the chanting falls silent. Then she leans over, and thrusts toward me with the knife. I try to scramble out of the way, but the driver won't let me move.

Her blade slices through the thick fabric of my new coat, and she shoves it off my body. With as warm as this area is, I don't mind that much. But she's not done. With Driver's help, she slices through my Hello Kitty hoodie and my My Little Pony nightshirt. She drops the knife on the ground to her left, and then she grabs both sides of my nightshirt and pulls them back. She shouts something else, and then she exposes the front of my body.

It looks nothing like my mom's, but I'm still horribly embarrassed that the dozens of people gathered have all seen most of the front of me—naked.

Until I realize what they're looking at. It's not my flat chest.

It's the bright red birthmark above my left chest that's shaped in the form of a perfect heart. Mom always told me it made me special. The hospital actually did an article on it, because I was born on Valentine's Day so no one could believe I had a perfect heart-shaped birthmark. Mom wanted to name me Valentine, but Dad got first pick.

Thank goodness he did.

The people watching us start chanting again, and it gets louder and louder. My actual heart's racing, and I start thinking about what these people could be planning to do. It doesn't seem like it'll be anything good, but I'm starting to worry they're planning to throw me into the volcano.

No one could really be that crazy, right?

Only, the woman grabs my arm and starts to drag me that way. "No," I shout. "No, you can't do this. I don't want to go. Stop!"

No one's listening to me. The woman's looking at the bubbling, popping lava, beaming. She's clearly insane.

"Stop," I shout again, my throat so shredded that it emerges as a faint rasp.

But we're nearly to the edge.

By the time we're just a step away, I'm out of options. I lean away from her, and then as hard and as fast as I can, I jump and kick with the force of my whole body behind it, aiming for her bad leg.

She goes down like a battered piñata, and then, before she can regain her footing, I shove her as hard as I can. I wasn't sure it would work, but it does. She slides off the ledge and goes right into the volcano below. I watch her screaming, her arms flailing, and then I hear the explosion as she hits the lava.

It's as awful as I thought it would be.

Maybe worse.

But it's not me. It's the lady who deserves it.

Driver and Beer Can clearly don't agree, and now they're coming toward me. I pretend to run toward Beer Can, but at the last minute, I dart right beneath Driver's legs. He tries closing his legs around me, which slows me down, but I squeeze past as fast as I can.

Right as someone grabs my leg, my fingers close around the woman's discarded dagger. I don't even think. I pull in close and then spring outward, stabbing with the dagger for all I'm worth.

It stabs Driver in the hand, and he screams.

For a moment that seems to stretch forever, I stare at him. I drop my eyes to look at his hand, where the dagger slid between two of the bones of his palm. Then I pull it out, and I use even more force to stab him in the chest.

I think about leaving it there, but I can't. There's Beer Can and all those people. I yank the dagger out, ignoring the fountain of blood that follows, and run away as fast as I can.

Oddly, at that moment, I can almost hear my mother's voice.

You should never run with a pencil, darling. You could poke your eye out.

I can't stop laughing the whole way down the mountain. Somewhere along the way, I fall and drop the dagger. I don't stop to look for it. I just keep running. One of my shoes gets caught between rocks and I can't pry it loose. I leave it and run the rest of the way with just one shoe.

By the time I reach the bottom and I'm looking around for the car, I realize that my sock gave out long ago. Every step behind me is marked by a bloody footprint. The strange thing is that my foot doesn't even hurt. By the time I finally find the van, other vehicles are pulling up next to it. They're white, and they have a blue stripe. The word Lögrelan is written on them, but I have no idea what it means.

When someone spots me, they turn on flashing lights.

It should scare me, but it makes me feel better. Police have flashing lights, right? Police, firefighters, and ambulances. But it's not a police officer who climbs out of the car. It's my mom. Her hair's a mess, tumbling down her back. Her mascara has smeared and made raccoon circles under her eyes. Her floral caftan's skewed so badly that I can see her hot pink bra.

I run on my bloody foot until I can leap into her arms.

"Oh, my darling Liz. Are you alright?"

I lie and nod.

"Your father and I were so worried," she says.

I see Dad then, too, standing right behind her. "You're going to be alright, darling. We're here."

But just when I should feel better, I hear the chanting again.

Hjartanu. Hjartanu. Hjartanu.

I open my eyes with a whimper and realize that I'm not back in Iceland. I'm not seven years old. No one's chanting. I'm warm, and I'm not in pain. That's when something clicks for me—I should be in pain. I was mauled by not one, not even two, but *three* different electro dragons.

Or was it four?

My brain is definitely still fuzzy.

But one of the reasons I'm warm is that I'm lying on a bed. And the other reason. . .someone's arms are wrapped around me tightly. Someone strong. Someone large.

I lean back enough to see a familiar face.

Axel's looking down at me with concern. "Are you alright? You sounded scared."

I close my eyes again and collapse against him. "You're alright."

"Of course I am." His breath warms my face, and my eyes finally stop burning.

"I'm still tired."

His left arm releases me and his hand moves up to stroke my hair. "Go back to sleep. Your brother and sisters are fine. You're safe. I healed you, and no one can hurt you with me right here."

I know the world's full of monsters—even before the dragons came, that was true. I know that no one can really ever keep me safe. But in this moment, I gladly believe his lie. My heart seems to buy it, too.

And this time, when the darkness beckons, I embrace it and let it drag me back under. After all, why should darkness scare me when I'm under the protection of my dragon prince?

17

I've always been a light sleeper. Most of my life, I didn't even need an alarm clock. If I knew what time I needed to wake up, I'd usually wake up a few minutes before my alarm was set to go off.

After spending quite a few tournaments in the same hotel, Gideon surely knows that.

When he taps on the door, the noise startles me and I open my eyes. He doesn't wait before coming inside, which is why he finds me with my head on Axel's chest. His *bare* chest. My cheek's pressed against it, all smooth, golden-brown skin and nearly rock-hard muscle. I try to sit up, but Axel's arm wraps more tightly around me, his bicep bunching to hold me in place.

"So you just barge into people's rooms?" Axel asks.

Gideon's eyes widen. "This isn't *your* room."

Axel shifts and eases the rest of my body back down against him. "I was here all night with Liz, helping her to recover. I think that makes it mine." He's smiling a lazy, possessive smile that I've never seen before. At least, not on him.

"She looks fine," Gideon says. "You should get out."

"She was nearly dead yesterday when I reached her," Axel says.

"From what?" Gideon's scanning the room now, as if the threat might still be lurking here.

"Nothing you could have helped her with."

"If she was almost dead, you didn't do much either."

"So much for stretching, yawning, and getting up peacefully." I shove away from Axel, who doesn't try to stop me this time. "Both of you should get out."

"It's good you're awake." Axel looks utterly unconcerned that he's lying back in the middle of my bed, naked other than his black pants. "Azar called a convocation today. I'll need to get going pretty soon."

That drags my attention away from his bare belly. "A convocation? Is he graduating?"

Axel frowns. "He's summoned all the Blessed. He has an announcement to make."

That sounds ominous. I touch Axel's hand. "Will you be alright? Is it something bad?"

He glances down at our hands and smiles, and I can't tell whether it's to reassure me that he's going to be fine, or whether he's pleased that I touched him. The bond shows that he's happy—it's a light green. "I'll be perfectly fine."

"I want to come," I whisper. "Can I?"

He shakes his head. "It won't be a safe place for humans."

"What's this convocation about?" Gideon asks.

Axel's nostrils flare like he'd forgotten Gideon was at the door. "None of your business."

"If it's Elizabeth's business, then it's mine too."

Axel purses his lips as his gaze shifts to Gideon. "Nothing in Houston is your business, human. And nothing that concerns Liz is your business, either."

"He's just trying to help," I say. "But what's it for? Do you know?"

Axel shrugs. "No one ever really knows what to expect with Azar—he's a bit unpredictable, like most Flame Blessed—but I suspect he's going to kill Ocharta."

Kill Ocharta? That name sounds familiar to me. I rack my brain to try and figure out why, and it finally hits me.

I am Ocharta, Strike Blessed. I have need of you. That's what she said, when she called my mother to her side and changed her hair to silver. I had been calling her Princess Petunia in my head, but I already knew her name.

I bolt upright in the bed, the covers sliding down around my waist. "Axel, he can't kill her."

He frowns. "But she tried to kill you. I thought you'd want her dead."

"What happens if she dies?"

Axel shrugs. "Not much, I should think. The Strike Blessed will choose another to lead their group here. When Azar returns, if he hasn't found the heart, her family could retaliate, but it's risky, retaliating against a Prince of the Flame. They probably won't dare to do anything."

"No." I shake my head. "I mean, what happens to a dragon's Ensnared if the dragon dies?"

"Oh." Axel frowns. "They die, too."

"That's awful." Gideon looks even more distressed than I am.

Axel shrugs.

"Of course he doesn't care about the humans," Gideon says.

"I've been caring for my human," Axel says, "*and* her annoying friend." He frowns. "I think I've been more than patient and understanding." He narrows his eyes and climbs off the bed, the muscles in his stomach rippling as he does it. Apparently dragons don't really store body fat in either form.

"I thought you didn't sleep," I say. "But you were in here all night?"

His half-smile's pretty lethal. "The best way to heal my human," Axel says, speaking slowly and drawing out every word, "was to spend some time with her." He pauses again. "Skin to skin."

"Okay," I say. "Well, I appreciate that." I flex my leg and move both arms back and forth. "A lot, actually. I can't believe you fixed everything. I thought I'd lost enough blood that—"

"You lost blood?" Gideon sounds frantic. "What happened?"

"It's a long story," I say.

"You should have plenty of time to tell me, since he has to leave, right?" Gideon glares pointedly at Axel. "He has a convocation to go to alone."

Axel frowns.

"I need to talk to him for a moment," I say. "Can you give us a bit?"

Gideon nods. But he doesn't leave.

"Now?"

Gideon blinks. "Wait, did you mean me?"

"Yes," I say. "I need to talk to Axel."

Axel's watching us with a broad smirk.

"Oh." Gideon bumps the doorframe with his toe. "Sure. I'll go make some breakfast."

"You do that," Axel says.

"Stop," I say.

Gideon's hand squeezes the door so tightly that it turns white, but then he releases it and stomps down the stairs.

"He's a real hothead."

"You're not helping." I spin on Axel. "Can you just stop?"

"Stop?" He raises both eyebrows.

"Never mind," I say. "I need a bigger favor."

"A favor?" He takes a step toward me.

I swallow. "I know this is a big ask, and I know she was going to hurt you through me, and I know Azar's mad too, but can you beg him not to kill her?"

Axel exhales.

"My mom—"

"The woman who was hacking at you with a sword?" His brow furrows.

"How do you know?"

For a split second, Axel looks nervous. But then he shrugs. "Azar took complete reports from people who were there, of course," he says. "And they said that Ocharta's Ensnared was attacking you."

"Well, she was, because Ocharta ordered it," I say. "But she's still my mom. I know she wouldn't have done that if she had a choice."

Axel steps closer still, his eyes on mine. "You humans—your emotions are complicated. If someone was trying to kill me, I wouldn't step in to protect them."

"She spent the past twenty years protecting me," I say. "And now, because of circumstances outside of her control, she's being forced to harm me. You'd do the same."

He inhales slowly and then exhales again. "I'd still focus on the situation at hand. How she treated you before is admirable, but if she's your enemy now. . ." He throws his hands up in the air. "You can't keep yourself safe by ignoring those who would harm you."

"You won't do it?" My heart feels like it's splitting in two.

Axel's jaw tightens, and he looks at the doorway. "I didn't say that."

I reach for his face to smooth away the frown lines without thinking, but when his eyes cut back toward me, my hand freezes, inches from his face.

"I can ask Azar, but I don't know what he'll say."

"You're his best friend, right?"

Axel's eyes flash. "He was very upset yesterday." He turns away from me and begins to pace. "You were injured—badly—because of your connection to me. They resent me for my connection to him. Azar, rightfully, feels like this was all his fault. He wants to fix it." His head, from across the room, snaps toward mine. "He wants to keep you safe." He swallows. "I agree with him."

"Are you saying that if someone touches me, you want them dead?" I can't keep my lip from twitching. "That's pretty corny."

He crosses the room in three steps. "It's not corny, Liz. It's the world I live in. You eliminate threats, or they eliminate you."

"You didn't kill me when we met, and I stabbed you."

He's right in front of me, shirtless, breathing heavily, his chest rising and falling, and I think about that first moment we met. I wanted to kill him. I tried. But instead of killing me, he agreed to help my siblings.

"You didn't kill me, even when I was threatening you and your friends."

"You were never a threat to me." His hand lifts, his index finger brushing against my temple. "At least, nothing to the risk you pose now."

I can't breathe. What's he saying? "I'm not a risk," I whisper.

He drags his finger down the side of my face, and then runs it slowly down the side of my neck. It stops on the spot where my shoulder joins my neck. His eyes are staring at that point like they could bore through it. "When I thought—when I realized who took you." He shakes his head, his hand dropping back to his side. "I've never been more full of rage."

Anger's a masking emotion. That's what my mother always said. "You were angry because you were scared."

He doesn't nod, or say yes, or agree in any way, but he doesn't disagree or call me a liar either. He doesn't shake his head. He just stares into my eyes. His burnished gold eyes, eyes that don't feel like a human's do, eyes that don't connect to a human soul, stare into mine with what looks and feels a lot like longing.

"Maybe you do feel some emotion after all." I shrug. "Or maybe you were just worried about how you'd feel if I died."

"Ocharta." He chokes. "I can't spare her life, Liz."

"Please," I say. "I'm begging you. If you have any regard for me at all—" My voice breaks. I'm his property. I'm nothing to him—a liability. Ocharta's death helps mitigate the risk I pose to his life. Nothing I say is going to change what he does. "If I matter to you *at all*, please ask Azar to spare her." I've just set myself up to be disappointed. I know I don't matter to him, not in that way, but now I'm hoping that I do.

Axel nods, and then he heads down the stairs and disappears without another word. That's not the action of someone who's going to modify his behavior for me.

"What's this convocation?" Gideon asks.

"It's a big dragon meeting," I say. "I guess they're all gathering so Azar can yell at them."

"Where?" Gideon's eyes light up.

I shrug. "Probably the George R. Brown Convention Center. That's where the electro dragons have taken up residence, anyway."

Gideon glances left, and then he glances right. Sammy, Coral, and Jade are all playing some kind of card game in the family room. He drops his voice. "There were flares just before dawn," he says. "They're going to deploy the nukes at noon today."

"But you said—"

"That's the signal, and if I can tell them where to send them, they could get them all with the first strike."

He's right. It's their best shot. "It's got to be at the convention center," I say.

"How do you know?"

"The only other place I've seen any of them go is the—" I was about to say the Chase Tower, but really only Azar lives there as far as I can tell. For some reason, I'm hesitant to tell him that. The only reason I know at all is that he was saving my life.

"Downtown Houston should be close enough in any case. We need to leave in the next hour," he says. "And to get out, I need you to set us a task that gets us close to the perimeter. Maybe send a few of your automaton humans as well."

That's not a bad idea. Maybe they could even get out, too. "Let me jot a letter down for my dad."

"I can probably get it to him," he says. "But hurry."

I don't spend a long time on the letter, and I pass it to Gideon on my way out the door.

"Where are you going?" Jade asks. "Training?"

I shrug. "Sure, and I've got to ask Gordon some questions."

"He's digging for grubs," Sammy says.

I freeze. "He's *what?*"

Sammy turns around, smiling. "He loves them. Those nasty, crawly things that wriggle in the earth?" He nods. "He said they're his favorite thing about earth."

I can't even imagine—is he serious? "Where does he do that?"

"He usually goes to that park across the water." Sammy points. "He said lots of 'em live in the ground there, like under the grass." The gwound. My heart twists hearing it. I'm going to miss him so much. But I don't have time to get all weepy.

I follow the line of his arm, but I see nothing. Until, suddenly, a sinuous brown snake-creature pops up and curls over. . .and then disappears again. "He must be wrecking that entire park, digging around like that."

Sammy shrugs. "He said they're always at the top of the soil, but he can spew through a lot of soil because he's an earth dragon."

Good heavens. "I can't reach him without a boat."

"I can call him over," Sammy says. "He told me he'll always listen for me."

Gordon's dragon form is nasty. He looks like the biggest snake to ever terrorize the world. Or a huge, scaly earthworm. I shudder.

But he's been surprisingly kind to Sammy, and he keeps watch over us often. I'll be sad if he dies today.

That surprises me.

I don't have enough time to wallow in regret or sorrow. I have too much to do. "Hey, guys." I wave the kids over. "I need some help with something." Just the thought of sending them away makes my eyes threaten to fill with tears.

"What?" Coral looks ready.

"Are you alright?" Jade asks.

"I'm fine," I say. "But I think it's important that we all have some basic first aid supplies." That feels like a decent cover story. "I'm sending Gideon out to find them, and I thought you could help."

Sammy blinks. "Like band-aids?"

"Exactly." I nod. "You should be in charge of band-aids, actually. And your sisters are supposed to get Tylenol and ibuprofen. We've been running low."

"What's Gideon getting?" Sammy asks.

He must've walked up while I was distracted, because his voice comes from right behind me. "Antibiotics, suture kits, casting supplies, and anything else we can find."

"I'll send a few of my men with you," I say.

"Or your women," Coral says. "They can be tough, too."

This time, my eyes do well with tears. "They sure can."

"What's wrong?" Jade steps closer. "Are you okay?"

"I'm fine." I fight my hardest to restrain myself from crying. "I'm really good, actually. But I might need a big hug this morning, okay?"

I love these little guys so much. They don't pry with questions—they just pile on and hug me. One of the best things about small children is their acceptance. It's the reason they have to be protected so vigilantly, but it also makes them adaptable.

After I finally release them, I say, "I love you guys. You know that, right?"

Jade frowns. "You're being weird."

"Mom loves you, too."

"Jade's right," Coral says. "What's going on?"

"I saw Mom yesterday." Now I'm full-on crying.

"She's—her dragon isn't very nice, and she's forcing Mom to be really mean, too."

"Oh, no," Jade says. "That must be horrible for her."

I hadn't even thought about that, how Mom must be feeling right now after trying to kill her own daughter. "Yes, I think you're right."

It must be pretty hard on Jade too, being an empath in the world we're living in. I squeeze her hand. "You're such a sweetheart. Try your hardest to let go of other people's pain. Okay?"

"Are you about to do something?" Coral asks. "Because you're still saying weird stuff."

"No, she's just having trouble with seeing your mom," Gideon says. "Here. Stand up." He taps my shoulder.

It's the reminder I need. They can't know what's going on. I wish they could just stay here, but we have very little time before that nuke hits. "Alright, I'm going to run and talk to Gordon, so you guys grab bags and get ready to go with Gideon. Okay?"

"Bags?" Coral frowns. "Why?"

"To carry the medicine, duh." Gideon smiles. "Actually, I'll go grab your bags. You go make sure that you fed Fluff Dog."

My head whips toward his, and I shake my head. They can't take her. It would be too obvious.

He nods slowly. He already knows.

Once the kids are out of earshot, he says, "Please reconsider coming. If Axel's busy with the convocation, he won't come after you right away. We could get away before the bomb hits."

"If it kills them, I'll die in front of the kids. And if it doesn't kill them, Axel will come after me, and we'll *all* die." I shake my head. "No. I have to stay either way."

Gideon steps closer, so close that his mouth is bare inches away from mine. "Liz, if I don't see you again—you need to hear it."

I shake my head. "I can't."

"I love you." His eyes are intent on mine. "I've loved you for years, and I always thought we had time. I wish I'd quit before. Way before." His finger touches my lips. "I wish so many things. Maybe you wouldn't have been at that carnival."

"My siblings would have died without me there," I say.

"Maybe—I don't know anything, except that this is all wrong." He closes his eyes and sighs. "I want the world to go back to the time when I was the scariest thing out there. I want all this to go away."

"Maybe it will in a few hours."

His eyes look so pained, so conflicted. "But if that happens, then. . .I don't know which is worse."

"I hope it works," I say. "And I hope the world is free of the ravages of the *Blessed* soon."

"I'd let them stay if it meant you were free," he says. "I know that sounds awful, but the rest of the world can die, as long as you live."

I can't help smiling at his sentiment, misguided though it is. He might say it, but I know full well that neither of us would ever act on something like that. "Take the kids to safety. Tell your superiors to hit the convention center. Give the world its best chance at a return to normal. That's what I want more than anything else."

Gideon balls his hands into fists. "Maybe I tell them to wait. I could ask them to delay until tomorrow—"

"When we won't have any idea where all the dragons will be." I shake my head. "You're a warrior, and a warrior listens to his companions. I'm telling you to take the shot."

"I know you can't come with us—you won't endanger your siblings' chance at escape. But you have to promise me that the second we leave, you'll get away from here. I don't care which direction you go as long as it's away from the convention center."

"I can take one of the cars and drive," I say. "At least to the edge of their occupation. All the Blessed will be answering to Azar, so no one can stop me."

"Yes." Gideon nods. "Do that." He breathes a huge sigh of relief. "Then once it's done, you can circle up north and look for any military personnel. Tell them you need to talk to me."

"Don't worry about me. I can't go with you, but I can get clear."

I can't even watch as they drive away. I'm forced to call Gordon over and distract him while they depart, so he won't notice that all three of my siblings and Gideon are leaving. "I need a favor," I say.

Gordon always changes into his human form to talk to me, even though we can communicate telepathically. I used to think it was to practice, but now I think he might be attempting courtesy. "What is it?" He looks nervous. "I have to leave soon."

There's a grub on his neck. I can't focus on anything with that thing wriggling on him, all white and disgusting. "Um. There's. . ." I point. "I think you missed one."

"Oh." He plucks it carefully from his shoulder and pops it in his mouth.

I choke.

"They taste better in my other form," he says. "But

they're not bad like this. I can bring you some if you want to try them. They get better every time."

"Ah, an acquired taste." I can't get that image of him popping that squirmy, dirty whitish thing in his mouth. "That's a hard pass from me, but thanks."

"Oh good," he says. "I didn't really want to share, but Sammy says I'm supposed to."

Sammy says. *Do not cry, you stupid idiot.*

"Are you alright?" Gordon asks. "You look. . .not well."

"Yesterday was a rough day," I say.

"I heard." He frowns. "But I really don't have long to chat. I don't have wings, so it takes me a little longer to get places."

"That's what it's about," I say. "Axel was worried about what may happen today, and after he left, I realized that he might need his swords."

"His swords?" Gordon frowns. "Why would he—"

"If Azar doesn't kill Ocharta, she could challenge him." I have no idea whether this could happen, but I need some kind of excuse. "He can't beat her in his dragon form." Is that true? I'm not even sure.

"But—"

"I proved yesterday that Strike Blessed aren't good at dealing with blades."

"I heard you did well against them with the daggers."

"I can't let him face her alone," I say. "He needs our support."

Gordon looks torn.

"If you let me ride over with you, I promise I'll keep quiet and not make a peep."

"I'm not sure Axel would want you to ride into the middle of the gathering with swords that can penetrate the scales of the Blessed."

They can? That's good to know. . . "But it's not like *I* could do any damage with all those Blessed there."

Gordon looks like he's about to throw up. I'd normally blame the grub, but I think it's his way of dealing with indecision.

"Axel won't blame you," I say, "even if he's annoyed that I went. I'll tell him that I made you do it."

He cocks his head sideways. "As if you could make me do anything."

"Maybe not, but Axel knows how annoying I can be. He'll understand."

Finally, Gordon nods.

"I'll just run grab the swords."

I race toward the master bedroom closet, a bit nervous they won't still be there since Gideon's been using the room, but when I open the door, they're in the massive stone. I pause for a moment, struck by the strangeness of it. Why would dragons need swords when only the lowest caste—earth dragons—are able to shift?

Swords that apparently no one can even remove.

Except for me.

I feel stupidly special as I grip both hilts. Only, no light shows up and no choirs sing when I pull them free. Actually, my grand gesture doesn't work. That's a little concerning, and a bit anticlimactic. I let go of the left one, put both hands on the hilt of the sword on the right, and tug. This time, it slides slowly free. I'm panting when I finally set it down. I have to repeat the whole thing—tugging, shifting, and yanking—with the second sword as well.

I don't have a scabbard, so I'm stuck using shirts from the closet, which really don't look like Gideon or Axel's style, so they probably came from this house's prior owner, to create a makeshift sword sling. I really hope the blades won't slice it to ribbons as we move. I have no idea how I'm supposed to ride Gordon while carrying them.

Once I get outside, the snake dragon takes one look at me and starts laughing. A dragon's laughter isn't an easy sound—it's like a hissing bark.

"Listen, it's not like I have the tools I need to make a scabbard, alright? Since I'm trying to help *your* friend, you'd think—"

Then there's that awful sound, and Gordon shifts again. But this time when he coalesces into his human form, his ruddy face even redder than usual thanks to the laughing, he's holding something in his hand. "Try this instead."

"What is it?"

"It's a baldric," he says. "Or rather, it's two baldrics. You can adjust them. I doubt Axel would thank me if you got sliced to ribbons on the way."

It takes me a minute, and it's a little embarrassing, but I finally get the sword holders all strapped on and slide the wickedly long blades into place. "How did you make that?"

He shrugs. "It's easy to craft clothing or boots when we shift."

"How about a saddle?" I think about his slippery smooth back. "Could you shift so that there's something for me to hold onto?"

He's laughing as he changes into his snake-dragon shape, but I notice that he listened. There's a dark brown saddle thing secured tightly around his midsection.

"Gordon, you're brilliant, and I love you."

He ducks his head then, almost as if he's embarrassed, but he's very still as I climb on and grab the straps of his shiny saddle.

"Thanks for this. The ride and the saddle."

I promised Gideon that I'd get as far away as possible, and I'm breaking that promise, but if Axel has any thoughts of not asking Azar to spare Ocharta's life, I mean to be there to remind him. And failing that, I'll beg Azar to spare her myself. I'm not losing anyone else if I can help it.

Although, if all goes well, everything I do in the next ninety minutes will be pointless. I really hope that two hours from now, we're all dead from a nuclear bomb.

You know your life's messed up when you're hoping that soon you'll be dead.

18

It's a long way from Clear Lake to the George R. Brown Convention Center on the back of a dragon that slithers like a snake, even when he's really booking. Actually, it feels *scarier* when he's moving quickly. Even with the saddle, I nearly slide off a few times. It gives me more appreciation for Sammy, but that thought makes me sad.

I may never see him again.

And that's my best-case scenario.

It's immediately obvious when we're getting close by the sheer number of dragons heading to the same place. They're on all sides of us now—blue, teal, green, yellow, brown, and reddish-brown. They're running, loping, and slithering down the streets of downtown Houston, leaving one another space, but not nervous about their proximity, either. When I turn my head, silver flashes dip in and out of the clouds above.

More than a few of the dragons, brown, blue, green, and silver, have eyed me strangely, possibly due to the saddle, or more probably because they know that earth dragons can't bond humans, so my presence on his back is bizarre at a baseline.

Watching these dragons moving through the city streets has to be the strangest—and possibly coolest—sight I've ever beheld.

"How many dragons are coming?"

A little more than ten thousand Blessed came to your earth. We've all been summoned.

"And how many have died since your arrival?" I cringe a little asking that, because I'm secretly hoping the number's high.

Less than twenty, last I heard.

Well, that's disappointing. "I'm sorry."

Only three were friends of mine, and you're the one who killed them.

Awkward.

We may have trouble getting closer. Can you call Axel from here?

Oh, boy. How do I say no without cluing Gordon in that I don't actually want Axel to know that I'm here? I push tentatively toward the connection in my brain, which I usually leave alone, because it scares me.

He's close.

Very close, actually, but I don't see him anywhere.

"I can definitely call him over—he's really close right now. In fact, if you want to drop me off right here—"

Gordon's head whips around, his eyes wide. *Leave you? I would* never *do that. You're surrounded by. . .* His eyes narrow. *You want me to leave you here? Why?*

"I just don't want to cause any problems." I shrug. "I saw how those other dragons were looking at me. I only wanted to be close enough that if Axel has problems, I can help."

Gordon snorts. *Then stay put and keep quiet. If you're*

too nervous to summon Axel, you shouldn't have come at all. He sighs heartily. *I shouldn't have brought you. Now I'm stuck babysitting.*

Before he can say anything else, Azar rockets over our heads and flies straight up into the air. Just when I think he's going to disappear into the atmosphere, he freezes in the sky.

And then he plummets down again.

For a moment, I'm terrified he's not going to stop —what would happen if he hit the Convention Center? At the last second, his wings whip outward, and he practically stops mid-air again. A wall of air from his full stop practically knocks me off Gordon's back.

He drops like a rock then, and nearly crash lands on the center of the front of the convention center, over-looking the park where most of the dragons are gathered.

I've been lenient since our arrival, because I was grateful that all of you chose to join me in our search for the Heart.

The force of the words is very different than any other telepathic communications I've experienced. It's almost aggressive with its projection, as if he's unabashedly displaying the magnitude of his anger by the strength of his words.

Yesterday, a group of Blessed gathered without my permission to take action against the Ensnared of my dear friend, Axel.

I didn't realize there could be telepathic murmurs, but it turns out, there can be. It's strange to hear snatches of the communications of the dragons nearby.

Water dragon voices sound like the murmuring of brooks or the crashing of waves. Earth dragons are more rasping, like leaves crackling under boots in the fall. The electro dragons' voices are clear, like the ringing of a bell, even when they're keeping things quiet.

I know that most of you had nothing to do with this attack, but many of you knew about it and did nothing to stop it. His head whips around, his massive golden eyes flashing as he glares at different groups of dragons. *Axel's the Prince of the Earth Blessed. That alone should be enough to grant him a measure of respect from all of you, regardless of your affinity. But he's also my trusted ally. I've gathered you here today to ensure that we are united in our efforts to locate the Heart. Fragmenting into groups and fighting amongst ourselves is absolutely prohibited, as I said before we came.*

The murmurs die down. Apparently the affinities, as he calls them, have fought amongst themselves for quite some time. That sounds like what Axel was saying before—but at least Azar's trying to fix it, at least a little bit.

Ocharta, Princess of the Strike Blessed, present yourself.

Did Axel ask him to spare her? Will Azar listen? I can't help scanning the gathering. There are lots of blues, plenty of silvers, and an ocean of green and brown dragons, but I don't see a single golden dragon, not anywhere. I can sense that he's near, somewhere in the gathered group, but why can't I spot him? He's such a unique color that it should be simple.

Did he ask Azar to go easy on Ocharta, and did that make Azar mad? Did they fight?

What's wrong? Gordon asks. *You're shifting like a grub.*

"I'm not," I say. "I'm nothing like those nasty white worms."

You're agitated.

"Where's Axel?" I ask. "I don't see him."

Gordon tosses his head in a move very reminiscent

of a shrug, which is hard to do without shoulders, but apparently not impossible.

"Aren't you worried that he's not out front?"

They don't appear together often, Gordon says. *The Earth Blessed adore their prince, and they tend to focus on him when he's around. Axel usually hangs back when Azar's making declarations so they'll focus on Azar.*

"That's weird," I say.

The murmurs increase, because apparently Ocharta's missing too.

This time, the only way to describe Azar's tone is thunderous. *Ocharta, Strike Blessed, you will appear before me, now.*

Even I shake at the force of his fury, but the dragons have all flattened themselves against the ground, including Gordon.

Up above, a silver dragon circles.

She's powerful, Gordon says. *I couldn't resist his summons for a single moment.*

"Are you saying that Azar can force the dragons to come to him?"

Gorden grunts.

"Why can he do that?"

Any prince or princess can do it, but he can summon all affinities, because flame rules us all.

As she slowly circles downward, I can't help but notice the sun. It's nearly at the top of the sky—noon is when the nuclear strike's supposedly coming. We're all gathered perfectly. The thought of that makes me tremble even more.

Azar roars, and she plummets to the ground. Silver dragons crawl toward her, attempting to protect her, it appears.

I didn't raise a claw against the human, Ocharta says. *Though had I, I would not apologize for it.*

Attacking his bonded is the same as attacking Axel himself. Having her in front of him seems to have calmed Azar, or at least, he's not bellowing as loudly.

His human's not right, she says. *She's rebellious and not well controlled. He shouldn't have bonded one in the first place. Even an Earth Blessed Prince can't manage them.*

Azar raises his wings and shoots a column of flame straight up into the air. His nostrils are flared when he drops his head. *You're neither Princess of the Earth Blessed, nor the Prince of the Flame. It's not up to you to determine how to handle Prince Axel or his Ensnared.*

Ocharta tilts her head. *Yet, the Prince of the Flame wasn't doing anything about it, perhaps because it was his friend. I did what needed to be done, and I'm willing to pay for my decision.*

Azar's back to bellowing at full volume. *What would you tell me to do to a subordinate who challenges my authority? Should I let her rebellion pass with a mere singe, or should I annihilate her?*

Ocharta rocks back and spreads her wings halfway. *You have yet to choose a mate. It's been said that you want an equal. Someone who's willing to do whatever it takes for the good of the Blessed. Someone who thinks for herself.*

Azar hops down, his wings half-spread as well. I'm not the only person who's on the edge of my seat—all the dragons around me have leaned forward, craning their necks for a better view.

I wouldn't choose you if you were the last Blessed on earth, Azar says. *I'm looking for any reason why I shouldn't kill you, and you haven't given me one yet.*

Ocharta's wings drop to her back. *Kill me?* She hisses. *You wouldn't dare.*

This is not going well. I don't see my mom anywhere, but her life is dangling by a thread. I wonder whether she knows it? Why can't Ocharta just back down?

"Hey," I whisper. "Gordon."

He cocks his head back. *Hush.*

"What would happen if another dragon challenged Ocharta? Do they ever do that?"

Why would they? She's about to die.

"But if someone did, do you guys have, like, rules?"

Gordon sighs. *Usually, if another Blessed issues a challenge, they'd be allowed to fight her. She's pretty irritating, so she's been challenged several times.*

"What happened to the dragons who challenged her?"

They're all dead. She's irritating, but she's powerful.

Awesome. "What if you defeat her, but you don't want to kill her?"

You would kill her.

"But what if you didn't want her dead?"

Gordon rolls his eyes like I don't even deserve a response.

Axel must've asked Azar to spare her, because he looks irate, but she's still alive. *You must issue an apology and promise never to do something similar again. Without both, you leave me no choice.*

Ocharta's eyes are flashing and her tail's whipping back and forth. *I'll apologize to you, Lord, for insubordination, of course. But I won't apologize to Axel, to whom I owe no respect, and I certainly won't promise never to challenge him again. He's beneath us, and I despise him.*

Azar's practically shaking. Flames are literally bursting from his nose intermittently. Ocharta's just desperate to get herself killed.

Which would be fine, except for my mother.

But the US Government chooses this moment to make all of this moot. Two fighters roar overhead, firing on the gathered dragons. If the regular fighting falcons and raptors are here, the larger jets carrying the nuclear warheads won't be far behind. The military may not have had much success so far, but they'll send in the distractions first, and once the huge red dragon's busy, they'll drop the big guns.

Nukes.

That means time's up.

19

Chaos would be a mild term for what breaks out among the gathered dragons. The first round of missiles hits in four places, and dragon bodies are flung in every direction. Luckily, none of them struck near Gordon and me. Rufus has bounded up next to us, and he's already itching to leave, gesturing at Gordon and shouting.

We've been ordered to the perimeter.

Gordon wheels around and begins to run, which doesn't feel very brave when his leader is under attack, but then again, he doesn't have wings and it's an air battle so far. Since I'm just a passenger on his back, I don't get much input on where we go. I watch as a much larger jet approaches. The dragons were warned, but whether they listened. . .

I'm sure that one's carrying the nukes. Even though the fighter jets have already wheeled away, Azar's not moving. He's watching the bigger aircraft, and he looks totally calm—way less upset than when he was shouting at Ocharta moments before. In fact, he almost looks bored.

Doors open beneath the jet up ahead, and it drops a projectile, a much, much larger one. I'm sure it's a nuclear warhead.

And it's headed right for Azar.

I know he's the devil, and I know that he's the reason the humans haven't stood a chance against the dragons. I even saw him roasting an entire neighborhood. I should be giddy. I should be relieved. This should be a patriotic moment, full of glee and joy.

But he's also saved me.

Twice.

Axel says they're only here to recover something they left, and he says that their attempts to communicate have all been met with attacks. Maybe that's why a tiny part of me is sad at the thought that Azar's about to be destroyed. Even so, I know it needs to happen. I know that the world must be safe again, and that means the dragons have to go. Blowing them to kingdom come is the right move, even if it destroys me and all the other humans still captured within Houston.

But Azar doesn't run. He doesn't move even a hair.

He waits, unconcerned, until the warhead's about to hit, and then he spreads his wings, opens his giant maw. . .

And he swallows it.

Gordon's bounding away as quickly as possible, and I'm turned all the way around in the saddle, grasping the top of it with both hands, but I'm quite sure I see it correctly.

Azar just swallowed the nuclear bomb that the humans sent to kill him. He doesn't even shudder. A moment later, his entire body shakes and he lights up, like a phosphorescent jellyfish, or a lantern that's just been lit with a candle. Then he squats back on his haunches and launches into the air.

He looks ready to unleash hell.

Gordon stops running then, and we both look up at the sky.

The next few moments are some of the saddest of my life—the grimmest, too. Azar's far faster than I realized, pivoting seemingly on a dime to completely roast jets anytime they come anywhere near.

Go, go, go, I want to cry out. *Escape while you can.*

Two more warheads are deployed, judging by their size, and two more are swallowed. Each time, he lights up a little brighter than the last, like they're powering him up or something. Each time, my heart sinks just a bit lower.

In spite of their massive failure, the humans don't pull back. I suppose if this is their big push, the generals won't call them back easily.

I'm stuck counting, my heart sinking a little more with each, as Azar melts at least a dozen jets into slag. Others he bats down or redirects into the top of a building, but they all go the same place. Into another section of the skeleton of Houston.

My city.

My people.

Life as we knew it.

And now it's all just gone.

He's not alone, of course. All the dragons who were gathered for his little meeting surge into the fray. The earth dragons, all except Gordon, have rushed to the perimeter, ready to take out surface troops and crush tanks. Water dragons hit the rivers, creeks, and lakes, running, diving, and surging toward the gulf. The electro dragons join Azar, diving and striking everything that moves in the air above, ensuring that the humans can't do anything but fall back. . .or just fall.

I can't help worrying about Sammy, Coral, Jade, and Gideon. He seemed so sure that they'd make it out, but did they? Was there enough time? Or will the earth dragons rushing to the perimeter catch them? It'll be obvious, with the direction they're traveling, that they're not ensnared.

Actually, if I hadn't convinced Gordon to bring me here, I'd be back home right now, probably marching with my poor, half-trained humans toward the earthen barricade, bracing myself to force them to attack their own kind to secure the dragon's city.

"Why did you stop following Rufus?" I ask.

Axel wouldn't want you to be put at risk.

Or is he more worried that, if he got close to the edge of their territory, I might unsheathe my swords and try to escape? "I can't leave while Sammy, Coral, and Jade aren't with me."

Gordon grunts.

But it's a matter of minutes before it's all over.

Azar bugles once, then twice, and finally a third time overhead, and Gordon finally relaxes. *It appears the humans have fallen back again.*

I say a silent prayer that Sammy and the girls are alright. Gideon, too, though that seems greedy.

"Can you take me back home?" We're in the center of the street at an intersection I've never seen before. There's a high rise on one side and a medical plaza on the other. "Or do we have to—"

But a large silver dragon that just passed overhead wheels around and drops to the ground in front of us.

Ocharta.

How convenient that you're here.

"You look pretty when you smile," I say. "I wonder

why Azar wanted nothing to do with you. I guess personality *does* matter, even to dragons."

Ocharta steps closer, her head angling a bit sideways. *Today wasn't going my way, but the humans have given me a gift.*

"You're a fan of nuclear candy as well?"

Gordon's still beneath me, but his muscles are tight. I can tell he's very, very nervous.

All the Earth Blessed are supposed to be near the perimeter. Imagine my surprise when I notice that one of them isn't, and that he's carrying a human.

"Axel's close," I lie. Although, when I feel for the bond, I realize he is heading this direction. "I'll call him over. I'm sure he can explain." Actually, I'm not at all sure he can explain why I'm here when I was told to stay put. He'll be furious, but I'm hoping he'll reserve his anger for after I'm not about to be electrocuted. I find the bond between us, and I give it a good *tug*. I'm not sure whether that'll keep him coming, but I hope it will.

Oh, do call him. That would allow me to rid myself of both of you at once, without any accountability.

He's still moving closer, so he must have gotten the message. "Are you positive you could destroy him? He is a prince, after all. And he may not have wings, but he's got thousands of dragons who answer to him."

He can't even force his human to use respectful words. Ocharta scoffs. *Azar has always been blind when Axel was around. Once he's gone, he'll realize that I've been helping him. Things that hold us back should be eliminated.*

I just need to keep her talking a little longer. Axel's moving closer and closer, and surely he'll have some other earth dragons with him. We were just under attack, after all.

"What's your plan?" I ask. "You're going to fry me,

and then if you can manage it, you'll kill him. Then Azar, who despises you, will suddenly find you irresistible?"

If Azar wanted me dead, he'd already have killed me. This is a dance you don't understand, human.

"Actually, the only reason he didn't kill you is that I begged him to spare your life."

Ocharta straightens and her eyes blaze. *Liar.*

"You're actually delusional. I didn't realize there were mentally ill dragons."

There's no warning before she strikes, lightning bolts shooting toward Gordon and me and striking us dead center.

We used to have a bug zapper at our house, on our back porch. I used to cheer when bugs died—if you've ever been bitten by a mosquito, you probably understand the sentiment. But now? I actually feel a little bad about that. See, our bug zapper had different settings. If you were killing, say, small mosquitos, the lowest would work. If you were plagued by horseflies, you might need the highest setting.

What that electro dragon hit me with in the house was for tiny critters. It hurt, but I recovered. Maybe it was because it was smaller. Maybe their place in the pecking order determines the strength of their attack. I don't know.

What I do know is that Ocharta's zap is quite a bit stronger than anything I ever imagined, and that old me would have died immediately. My bond with Axel has made me stronger, strong enough to withstand a lot more pain, a lot more damage, and a lot more misery. But in this case, I'm not sure how grateful I really am.

Dying by electrocution is not a good way to go.

After I bob in a sea of misery for a while, when I come to, I'm dangling from Gordon's saddle by one leg, foam spewing out of my mouth, and my brains feel well and truly scrambled.

If he's not already on his way, at least it should bring Axel running.

My legs are jelly. My arms feel like rubber bands that have been overstretched and snapped. My head's pounding. But I've never been someone who just rolls over and gives up, no matter the punishment doled out.

Gordon's spasming underneath me, and the twitches from his body knock some sense into me. My hand's trembling, but I force myself to sit up and grab the top of the saddle. I pull my leg—wrenched badly, but not broken—loose from the saddle strap. I clench my hands into fists to try and restore feeling in them.

What are you doing? Hold still, bait.

This time, I'm expecting her strike. "Sorry, Gordon." I whip one sword free and slice the saddle strap, dropping to the ground in time to miss her next volley.

Poor Gordon takes the whole hit. Judging by his twitching, he's still alive. I hate that I couldn't deflect it entirely, but I can't waste time on guilt. I'm sprinting, my speed dampened significantly by my exhaustion and misery, across the space that separates us, both swords now drawn.

Ocharta laughs. *You're a funny one.* She bats me, like a cat would a lizard.

I roll sideways, barely retaining both of my swords. I land on my stomach, and I want to collapse, face first. She won't kill me until Axel shows up, or at least, I don't think she will. But hiding and avoiding her isn't who I am. I shove myself back up to my feet, and I head after her again.

You're supremely annoying. I haven't even eaten today. Did you know that? She steps forward, eliminating the space between us, and opens her mouth, presumably to eat me.

My arm's not working right, but I swipe anyway.

And though I'm weakened, I manage to cut off her tongue.

Judging by the shrieking sound she makes, it's not pleasant. She snatches at me with one enormous talon. I can't evade her, not in my current shape, and she easily lifts me off the ground.

I can't help smiling at the gobs of bloody drool dripping out of her mouth, but that ticks her off more. She shakes me like a dog with a snake, and I finally lose my grip on the swords. They fall, point first, and sink into the earth below. She hoists me even higher, and then she opens her mangled mouth again.

Unfortunately, her teeth are all intact. Why couldn't I have taken out a few of those? Before she can snap off my arm like a particularly juicy pretzel stick, Azar crashes onto the side street, slamming into the medical center, shearing one side of the building off, and turns toward us.

Ocharta shudders, and I start to wriggle, sensing this may be my only window. Before I can pull free, a narrow ribbon of flame shoots out of Azar's mouth and slams into Ocharta's tail, incinerating it immediately.

Release her.

Ocharta drops me, too busy writhing on the ground to do much else.

Boy, do I know that feeling.

Azar's walking toward us—stomping—and I realize that he's angry. His eyes are flashing, his tail's whipping back and forth, and his nostrils are smoking.

"Wait," I shout, "please don't kill her!"

Azar screams in her face, his talons wrapping around her neck and squeezing. Blood pours from her throat, and at first I'm a little proud of causing her injury, but then I realize it's coming from where his claws have pierced the shimmery silver scales. All that gore's coalescing into a nasty pool on the street below. His head turns toward me, and he roars.

And in that moment, for the first time, like a dunce, I realize something. Something very, very strange.

Something I really should have noticed before. My one excuse is that all our interactions have been fraught, and they've all taken place when I was majorly stressed. The only reason I notice this time is that I've been yanking on my bond to Axel like it was a dinner bell in the hopes he might save me.

That very bond tells me. . .that Axel's finally by my side.

But he's not.

Only Azar's nearby, saving me for a *third* time.

20

"**D**idn't Axel tell you?" I glare. "My mother's bonded to her." I toss my head. "Step away from the burned, broken, and bleeding electro dragon."

Azar's talons tighten.

Ocharta's whining is now an incoherent, high-pitched plea.

Please, I beg. *I'll get down on my knees if I have to. Please, Azar.*

Azar disembowels her with one swipe.

Watch her, he growls, addressing Gordon, I think.

Then he drops the electro dragon like she's a hot potato. Judging by his command, she's not going to die from losing half her insides onto the pavement below. Or at least, he doesn't seem to think so. But the great stuff is short lived.

He snatches me next, rocketing off the ground in an insane burst, his wings beating the air around us into a tornado-like frenzy as we shoot up, up, up into the sky. We're getting high enough that the ground below's obscured and I'm struggling to breathe when I finally cry uncle.

Stop, I beg. *Please, stop. I can't survive up here.*

Azar's wings straighten like the sail of a ship, snapping open, and we coast, slowly descending back toward the ground.

"Are you mad I know you're Axel?" I ask, once there's enough oxygen I can breathe again.

I'm not Axel, he says.

"Nice try." I tap my head. "But the bond don't lie, big man."

You've been around me before, he says. *You never thought anything was amiss.*

"I wasn't really monitoring Axel's location in those instances," I say. "But this time, I was calling for you."

He's not looking at me, and I'm beginning to think it's intentional.

"Why are you carrying me this time, instead of letting me ride?"

You weren't being rational. I didn't think you were safe to ride.

I pat his leg. "I'm fine, now. I can ride."

He drops me.

My stomach does fifteen or so flips as I freefall through the air before he glides beneath me, his hard, shiny, red scales sliding past me smoothly until my fingers reach the juncture of his shoulder. There's a pronounced ridge there I grab, just like the last time. "That's better," I whisper.

You're mistaken, he says, still doggedly trying.

"You want me to pretend that I don't know you and Axel are the same person?" I ask. "I mean, I can do that, but I don't see the point. Wouldn't you prefer me to be honest with you?" I think over the other times he showed up to save me, and how I inexplicably felt comfortable with the most terrifying of all the beasts who invaded earth.

Axel is Earth Blessed.

"And you're the Prince of Flame, yes, I know. I've heard." I lean down closer, wrapping my arms around the top of his muscular shoulders. "I was there, you know, when you defended Axel to all the gathered dragons. You know who coincidentally *wasn't* there?"

He remains silent, only the movement of his wings showing that he's not entirely frozen.

"I'm so glad you asked. It was Axel. Your best friend, your alter ego, the Prince of the Earth Blessed. Yep, the very dragon you were there to defend? He wasn't there. I wonder why that was."

Still, silence.

"You know, the earth dragon who wasn't supposed to be able to bond a human, but somehow did? Yep, that one. The one who's always gone—night, day, whenever. That one."

I can't believe he's not admitting it yet.

"What I can't figure out is why he thought that he could fool the human he bonded, *forever*. I mean, sure, at first, the whole bond is new and exciting. You could make sure that while I train some, I don't really learn everything. You could stay away a lot, so that I don't get to strengthen our connection." I realize something. "That's why you wanted to get rid of our bond so badly. Bonding me as Axel was really bad news, because Axel shouldn't be able to bond anything. What I can't figure out, because I'm not a dragon, is. . .why is it a secret?"

That sets him off. Azar plunges toward the ground, and I'm genuinely worried he's about to bank and whip me right off, finishing off Ocharta's original plan of creating a Liz jelly spot on the ground. But when he finally does flip out his wings and slow, I'm still safely on his back. And then he lands, his tree-trunk legs thunderously walking, and I realize that intentional or not, we're standing in the very park where he bonded me.

The last time we were here, I stabbed him in the throat.

"You could just leave me here," I say. "Or better yet, you could release me just over the barricade. I promise not to, like, die stupidly. You won't need to worry about your secret anymore, because I won't be able to tell any other dragons about it."

Elizabeth. Azar's staring at me intently. *No one can know.*

"No one, like only Gordon and Rufus?" I ask.

I can't help noticing that Azar's sort of dripping lava-like fluid from his mouth, as if he's angry enough that it's just spilling over. It's searing its way through the pavement and into the ground below.

"Maybe you should shift for a little bit," I say. "Just an idea. I mean, you can do what you want, obviously, but like, we could talk better if you weren't likely to accidentally broil me for saying the wrong thing."

Azar stares at me for a moment, and then I hear the same engine-revving sound I'm used to hearing, and there's a dark cloud of reddish smoke, and then his human form emerges, wearing a black suit, a charcoal shirt, and a deep, blood-red tie.

"This look really works for you."

Axel blinks and glances down at his suit. He snorts. "Stupid magic just takes over whenever I'm not thinking."

I slow clap. "Bravo, magic. Nicely played."

"I mean it, Liz. No one can know."

"Why's it such a big secret?" I walk toward him slowly, wondering how much of him is really the same as the person I've been around the past few weeks. Is he the guy who has saved me, who has kept my siblings safe, and who has put up with Gideon? Or is the real Azar the massive red beast who melts dragons' tails off and. . .oh, heavens. Eats nuclear bombs. "Are you really fine?" I step toward him again, my hands lifting to touch his arm and run down it lightly. "You *ate* a nuclear warhead."

"Three," he says. "I actually really liked them. It was like getting some kind of. . .I don't know. A jolt of energy unlike any I've had. It was delightful."

He really doesn't seem any worse for the wear. "But you aren't answering. Why can't anyone know about the Axel-Azar axis of evil?"

Axel turns away from me, leaning against the side of the playset. It's a really funny image. The dragon-man who just foiled all the humans' efforts to destroy him is leaning against a fire-engine red and royal blue kids' slide.

"I'm not exactly on your side," I admit. "But I'm not really your enemy, either." I realize as I say it that I mean it. Mostly. Sure, if I could destroy him, I might do it. But since I can't, at least, not without dying before I can complete any attempt, I'd rather try to convince him to do the minimum damage while he's here looking for this heart thing.

"You keep forcing me to spare the creature who wants to kill you," he says.

"She's bonded to my mother," I say. "Would you want your mother to die?"

"I never knew my mother." He shrugs. "Sure, you can kill her if she's attacking me."

He never knew his mother? That's depressing. Or maybe not. Maybe that's normal for dragons. "Hey." Something occurs to me, as I review our recent interactions. "You told me you'd talk to Azar, but you didn't know what he'd say." I whack him on the shoulder. "You liar."

Axel frowns. "I couldn't very well tell you that he already knew and would take it under advisement."

"You almost killed her."

"Your mother isn't my top priority," he says.

"What is, then? This heart thing?"

He steps inside of my guard, his face hovering over mine. "I find that you distract my focus. When you're around, I can't always prioritize our real goal."

Mr. Dragon Baddie almost just said that *I'm* his priority. I mean, he didn't. He said I'm a distraction, but his answer was dangerously close to that. "I'm sorry for causing you distress," I say, "but my entire world is at stake right now, so I may not be making measured decisions, either."

He's still standing right next to me, almost unnaturally still. His eyes slowly slide down my face, finally stopping on my mouth. "You stole my swords."

That is not what I thought he'd say.

My entire body's trembling—he may be a terrible, awful dragon prince, but he *feels* like a terrible, awful *man* in this moment. A man I've seen shirtless. A man whose rippling abs have made my mouth go dry. A man whose breath has the capacity to fog my brain. A man whose undivided attention makes me forget my priorities.

My brain really needs to focus around him. He's accusing me of stealing his property right now.

"I think, if you want to be technical," I say, "they're really more *my* swords."

"How so?" His eyes shift back up to mine, and I breathe an embarrassingly audible sigh of relief.

"*You* can't remove them from the stone." I duck

underneath his arm and hop up on the slide. Then I scamper up it and stand at the top. "But *I* can."

"I gave you daggers," he says.

"After I used them, you never replaced them."

"I was busy punishing the person you had to use them to fight." He steps up on the bottom of the slide, and then he begins to stalk his way toward me.

I squeak and run.

And now he's chasing me, the most alpha predator I've ever seen—and the deadliest. I hop off the far end, grabbing the monkey bars and moving across them, arm over arm. I hear him behind me, still moving forward. I wonder whether he's even capable of breaking off a chase once it's begun. Most predators aren't.

What have I gotten myself into?

I speed up, hopping off the end of the ladder and racing away, ducking under the weird rock wall and then sprinting—because I can hear by the crunch of his feet on the gravel that he's gaining on me—to the much larger, wavy slide. I race up it, my shoes squeaking on the hard plastic. I finally reach the top, but it's slippery, and I lose my footing and fall backward.

The back of my body crashes into the front of his, and his arms close around my waist, his face pressed against my hair and the side of my face. The weight of my fall should have bowled us both over, but the laws of physics don't appear to apply to him.

He's a force of nature.

Instead of falling over backward, he simply stops at the top of the slide, my body curved into his from his shoulder down to our feet. His words are soft against the shell of my ear. "You can run from me, but you'll never escape, Elizabeth. I only let you run because it entertains me."

"You wanted to be rid of me," I whisper. "You spent days searching for a way to dissolve the bond."

"Even then, I couldn't bring myself to harm you," he says. "And now, I don't even want to let you go."

The words send shivers through my entire body, and what's worse is that we're so close that I know he feels them.

"Are you cold?" he asks.

Ha! Again, my saving grace is that he's a dragon, not a man, so he has no idea what my body's reactions really mean. "Uh, yes."

His arms tighten around me. "Then you're with the right person." The air around us heats up, and I realize he's using his magic to do it.

"You can do that in human form?"

I can feel his smile against my cheek. "Prince of Flame."

"That's pretty cool."

"No, it's hot," he says.

I turn toward him just as he's finally trying to flip me, only we're working at cross purposes, and my elbow hits his arm and our legs shift, and my feet slip, and this time, we do fall. He hits the slide first, with me landing on his lap, and we slip all the way to the bottom.

"This thing is interesting," he says. "Is it for mating rituals?"

Mating. That word sends another shiver up my spine, but it also makes me laugh. "It's made for children."

He's smiling, too. "You humans are very odd."

I turn around to see him better, and with our

height difference, while I'm sitting on his lap, our faces are even. "We have our charms."

His eyes drop to my mouth again. "You do."

"You do realize that this is where we first met."

He blinks. "It is?"

"I thought that's why you brought me here."

He shakes his head slowly. "I was just flying—I was upset."

"Why can't anyone know?" My voice is soft this time, barely audible.

"No Blessed have two affinities," he says. "The Blessed who raised me made me promise never to share my abilities with anyone. She said it was a great gift, but that no one would understand it. She made me guard the secret with my life—and she's been right. Father chose me as his successor, even though I'm his youngest child. He never would have done that if he knew I was. . .strange."

"Maybe she was wrong," I say. "Maybe everyone will see it as the miracle it is."

His smile's sad. "You're a human. You don't understand. Our affinities define us in every single way. We can't accept something that defies expectations."

"So your entire life is a lie," I say.

"Except when I'm with Euphrasia, and now with you," he says. "But you have to swear to keep the secret from everyone. Your siblings can't know. No one can."

My siblings. I can't help my cringe.

"What?" He stiffens. "Are they in danger?"

I'm a terrible sister. I'm sitting here on Axel's lap while they could be anywhere. "I'm not sure."

He blinks. "Even if you left, Rufus would have gone back as soon as the—"

"Gideon left with them," I confess. "They were planning to escape when the attack happened."

Axel's eyes are hurt, and I feel the pain of betrayal through the bond.

"I'm sorry," I say, "but I told you about the nuclear warheads, and you didn't plan to do a thing about it."

"Because," he says, "I told you it would be fine."

That's technically true, but. . . "Warheads less powerful than those leveled two cities full of humans many years ago. Every man, woman, and child who was anywhere near the blasts died. The ones who survived the explosion sickened from the exposure and died soon after. It was horrific."

"None of that will happen," he says. "I took care of it."

"I didn't know you could," I say. "You weren't very forthcoming about a lot of things." I arch an eyebrow.

"There's been a lot I couldn't tell you," he admits.

"But not anymore?"

He sighs. "I'm not sure. Do you still want to stab me while I'm sleeping?"

I shrug. "Depends on my mood."

To my surprise, he laughs. "I'd expect nothing less."

"You're ruining my world." I'm sort of kidding, and I think he knows it.

"You lost my swords," he says. "Let's go retrieve them before someone else does. We can talk about what to do with Ocharta on the way."

"And can Rufus and Gordon check to make sure Sammy, Coral, and Jade escaped?"

"Do you really hope that they did?" Axel sounds curious.

"I'm not sure what I hope anymore," I say.

That may be the scariest part.

My first kiss was a disaster.

I liked a guy named Nat. No, not Nate. That's short for Nathan. The guy I liked was a skater, and his parents were California, through and through. He was way too cool for me. He knew it, I knew it—everyone knew it.

He had long hair.

He did dozens of impressive tricks on his skateboard.

He vaped behind the school sometimes. I knew it was unhealthy and gross, but I was also a little bit in awe of his diffidence to authority and rules.

He was also really, really hot.

I told my best friend that I liked him. She told her best friend. Isn't it funny how the person who's closest to us sometimes is closer to someone else?

Funny. Or is it sad?

Potato, tomato.

After Nat found out I liked him, he became absolutely insufferable. He'd walk by and make rude comments. He'd say things like, 'Hey, you.'

I'd spin around and smile. 'Me?'

But he'd look past me, and make it clear he was talking to someone else. When my face would fall, he'd look back and laugh.

Nat was cool. He was good-looking.

And he was a jerk.

Gideon was my best friend already, and he hated him. The third or fourth time Nat pulled a stunt like that, Gideon dragged him across the hall by his collar, shoved him against the wall, and broke his nose. Nat never looked my way again. No one else laughed at me after that, either. Everyone in the school was terrified of Gideon. Except for me, of course.

But while he was in detention for breaking Nat's nose, I joined the chess club. It was a big mistake. I've always been a bit of a blunt instrument, mentally. Trying to see patterns and work out things that will happen several moves ahead was never my strong suit. The smartest kid in our school also happened to be the chess club president, and Jacob Wong spent a lot of time that week trying to teach me the basics.

On the day before Gideon was due to return, after school, I lost a chess game in six moves. Six. "I quit," I said.

"You don't really seem to be getting better." Jacob pushed his glasses up his nose. "Maybe it's not your thing."

I sighed. "I'm just a dumb jock, I guess."

"Some of us would love to be jocks," Jacob said. "I tried to do soccer last year, and after I broke two pairs of glasses, my mom made me quit."

That made me laugh. "But you're so smart. I think that's better."

"Only because I study all the time." He started putting the pieces away. He'd stuck around after the normal chess club practice to try and help me every single day this week, but clearly it was a waste of time. I hadn't improved. If anything, I'd worsened.

"Sorry for wasting your time." I reached for the same piece as he did, and our hands touched.

My heart sped up, and my breath caught in my throat. "Oh, sorry."

He bit his lip, shoved the chessboard over, and moved his chair closer to mine. "It's fine." His eyes, through the large round lenses of his glasses, were open wider than usual.

I licked my lips, and I watched as his eyes dropped to my mouth.

"Um, would you—I mean." He cleared his throat.

"Yes," I said. "You can."

He blinked several times, and then he scooted even closer. He tilted his head and leaned toward me, but then he decided it was the wrong angle and tilted the other way, his hands kind of floating at his side. "Um, I've never."

"Me either." I took pity on him then, grabbed his jaw, and pulled it against my face, our lips smashing together.

"What the heck!"

When Jacob and I leapt apart, Gideon was standing in the doorway. His scowl was deep and angry. Jacob jumped up from the chair so fast that he knocked the chessboard over, scattering pieces everywhere. He ran around the room twice before darting out and disappearing down the hall.

Gideon's hand was clenched at his side. "Really, Chadwick?"

I shrugged. "I wanted to see what it felt like."

My best friend smashed that chessboard on the floor, and we left it broken in pieces. We never talked about my first kiss again, but Jacob Wong never met my eye again after that.

Even for humans, kissing someone is hard. It's complicated. It's confusing.

And it can be a real mess.

So when Axel shifts back into his Big Bad Red form and he's waiting for me to climb onto his back, the question he asks takes me by surprise. *Why do humans kiss?*

I freeze.

How am I supposed to answer that?

"Um. Well."

I know it's something they do when they're happy.

I can't help my laugh. "I'm not sure I'd say *happy* is how they're feeling when they kiss." Though that's not exactly wrong. "It's more complicated than that."

He's waiting for me, both physically to climb into place, but also I can tell he's really curious about what a kiss means. His question makes me feel strange about climbing onto his back too, for some reason. *Do you kiss Gideon?*

Oh, man. He's asking all the questions today. Heat rises in my cheeks. "I never have, no," I say.

Good. I don't want you to.

Oh, heavens. "Why not?" I wish I could clap my hand over my mouth.

When he's around, I want to incinerate him. Then I want to bury his pile of ash so I never have to see it again.

"He's just a human," I say. "You don't hate all of them."

Only him.

That makes me laugh.

What's funny? His eyes are narrowed. *It makes me angry that you trusted him with your siblings. I promised to keep them safe. That's not his job.*

Was he always this cute? As I think the words, I wonder when I stopped being afraid of the massive red dragon who was melting the entire world not too long ago. That helps me think of an analogy. "Stoves are hot," I say. "We cook on them. Without them, we couldn't cook our food, but if a human touches the stovetop with their fingers, it'll burn."

Azar frowns.

"You're like the stove. You may not intend harm to my siblings, but being who you are puts them in danger."

But humans are all safe? One eyebrow arches.

"You may not like him, but Gideon's a pretty scary human. He'd have done anything he could to make sure none of the less-scary humans would hurt them, if they escaped."

Azar lowers his head until it's on eye level with me. *I don't like this, but if you want them to leave here, I will fly them all out.*

My heart explodes. My big red dragon just offered to free my siblings—even though he hates the idea.

I think it's a mistake. He snorts. *I could keep them safe better than that tiny, feeble human.* He spins around again, shifting so his left shoulder's lower.

I try not to think about the human version of Azar when I scramble over his scaly red back to reach his shoulder. "Is our bond the reason why I wasn't terrified of flying with you before?"

Probably.

I should've known. I'm remarkably obtuse sometimes.

Azar's powerful muscles shift and bunch, and then he launches into the air, his wings beating regularly as we lift up, up, up and into the sky. He wheels around sharply, and we're headed back to Clear Lake.

"Won't people think it's strange that you're drop-ping me off?"

Azar's wings skip a beat and we dip.

"Maybe you should shift and drop me off a mile away."

I need to deal with Ocharta first. I'd do it without you, but it seems like you get into too much trouble whenever I leave you alone.

He's not wrong about that. "What are you going to do?" I bite my lip.

He blows air out of his nostrils. *I should just kill her.*

I do feel a little bad for making his life harder, but it's not like our bond has been a walk in the park for me.

I'll demote her.

"Can you do that?"

I'm guessing not really. His wings beat harder and we gain speed, and then he dives downward, bringing his wings in tightly so we're rocketing. In that moment, for the first time ever on his back, I relax and fully enjoy what I'm doing.

I'm riding a freaking dragon.

A fire-breathing *dragon*.

When he drops onto the ground with a bone-jarring thunk that rattles my teeth, I rethink my prior elation.

Sorry. I'm not used to having a rider.

"It's fine," I say.

You're back. Gordon bows. *I kept her here, Your Majesty.*

Ocharta.

She's curled up into a dried-and-sticky-blood mess. I almost can't recognize her in this state, her silvery scales dull and coated in places with black and brown goo. Her tail looks like it's about half regrown.

It's nasty. I slide off Azar's back and retrieve the swords I dropped when I was last here. Luckily, I'm still wearing the scabbard Gordon made me. Once I've sheathed them, I walk a few steps farther away, standing near Gordon. It feels like something I should do, to move away from the big scary dragon to stand near my bonded dragon's worker.

You're back to kill me? Ocharta struggles to stand. *Do it.*

"Release my mom," I say.

Azar glares at me.

I can't release her, human. No one can release their Ensnared. She'll die with me. She's smiling. It's not in my head. I've never wanted someone to die and also wanted to keep someone safe as much, at the same time.

Your people will choose a new leader.

It doesn't work that way. Ocharta's smile broadens. *If you let me live, I'm their leader.*

Azar roars in her face.

She looks shockingly unconcerned.

It works however I say it works.

Your pet is weakening you. Ocharta leans closer. *He'll prove your demise if you don't put him down.*

I thought she meant me, but I realize she's talking about Axel.

Azar's lip curls, and he begins to glow.

"What's going on?"

No one answers my question.

The reddish golden haze around Azar glows brighter and brighter, becoming so bright that I'm forced to look away. And then there's a low humming noise, like an engine that's stuck in one gear, followed by a shattering sound, like a million glass panes being hit with a baseball bat at the same time.

When I open my eyes slowly, it's not nearly as bright as it was.

What have you done? Ocharta's looking around herself—she's trapped in a large red glass-like bubble. *Release me.*

"What's that?" I whisper, hoping maybe Gordon will know.

He, helpfully, shrugs.

Rule from here. Or waste away. Maybe your Ensnared can free herself when you're at the lowest ebb. Azar tosses his head at me.

"Meet me at home?" I whisper.

Gordon frowns. *You're traveling with Azar?*

I can't believe his two lieutenants don't even know his secret, but Azar seemingly has no plans to change that. *Axel wants you and Rufus to redirect the Earth Blessed. They're to search any humans along the perimeter for Sammy, Coral, Jade, and the other one.* Azar tosses his head again, clearly impatient with me holding him up.

I finally walk away from the red-bubble-caught electro dragon. "You're sure she can't get out of that?"

Azar's laughing when I climb up on his shoulders. He doesn't wait for me to get a good hold before launching into the sky. I lose my grip and have to scrabble forward, one tightly gripped handhold at a time.

Once I pry my heart out of my throat, I'm pretty annoyed. "You know, Gordon made me a saddle."

Azar's laughter is deep and full as he redoubles his speed.

"Ash brain."

It takes me a moment to realize what we're doing, but once I realize we're rocketing past the earthen walls the dragons created, I settle in and try to enjoy the ride. I keep my eyes open, of course, searching for sweet little Sammy, darling Jade, and tough Coral.

The wind beats my hair into tangles I'll likely never undo, but I become a little more accustomed to the dips, drops, and direction changes, only nearly falling off once. Eventually, though, the terrain starts to look a little familiar. "I think we've flown over this already," I say. "I remember that weird purple trailer."

Azar ignores me.

But eventually, he decides it's a waste of time, and he flies me home. When we get closer, I can sense the humans—my humans—who live across from me. When Azar lands, it's almost a mile away, behind an uninhabited section of smaller homes.

Instead of changing into his human form after I slide off his back, he changes into his earth dragon shape. It's interesting, looking at the two of them, one immediately after the other. They're clearly the same dragon. They have the same elegant, intelligent head shape, the same curvature to the brow, and the same toothline.

And the same golden eyes.

Once I know, it's obvious.

It's funny how many things we blindly miss because the world tells us a lie.

Climb back on.

"Still no saddle?" I ask. "Really?"

Axel rolls his eyes.

It doesn't stop me from grumbling as I scramble up, my hands now scraped, sore, and straining.

You're injured?

"Hardly," I say. "But your scales are hard, and holding on isn't easy for a puny human like me."

I'm sorry.

I didn't expect to hear that from a dragon in my

lifetime. It's a little gratifying. "Don't worry. It's no big deal. Thanks for spending so long looking for them."

We're nearly back when Rufus shouts a message. *Found them in a boat. Nearly drowned.*

I can barely breathe while we wait for Rufus. "Maybe we should go to them," I say for the third time.

"They're almost back," Axel says.

I'm pacing in the kitchen and have been for nearly twenty minutes now.

"Rufus says they're alright."

"That doesn't mean the same thing to him as it does to me," I mutter.

"It's strange that you care so deeply for your siblings." Axel looks as if he's studying me.

I stop and pivot to face him. "Is it? I think most people do."

"We don't," he says simply, as if that makes sense.

"Dragons, you mean?"

"Why do you persist in calling us dragons?" He frowns. "It's rude."

"Maybe I want it to be," I say. "You did take over our world. The least we can do is call you what we want."

Axel stands up and walks toward me. "I would not risk my life for any of my siblings."

"No?" I sit on the edge of the table. This way, even though I'm markedly lower than he is, it's for a reason. When we're both standing up straight, I'm so much shorter that I feel. . .small. I don't like it.

Axel stops a step away from me. He sighs. "I'd kill most of them if given the chance."

"Really?" That I can't understand.

"They've all tried to kill me, and they will again."

That thought is a horrifying one. "Your brothers and sisters tried to kill you?"

He shrugs. "Only one of us can replace my father. It's natural."

"But you don't *need* to rule, right? So why do you need to kill each other over it? Just live your life." I think about how upset Ocharta was that he didn't just kill her. I clearly do not understand the dragons at all.

"I find it fascinating, the affection you share." He's studying my face as if it's a Sanskrit scroll when I hear Rufus arrive outside.

I shove my way around Axel and sprint for the door. Somehow he gets there the same time as me. He waits while I exit.

The sun has set, but I can still see outlines well enough. Sammy's asleep in Gideon's arms. He's clearly just dismounted from Rufus' back. Jade and Coral are huddled together on the ground by Rufus' leg.

"Everyone's alright?" My eyes scan them all frantically.

Gideon's expression is tight, but he nods.

I hover, but I don't take Sammy from him, nervous it'll wake him up. Jade and Coral both look too tired to stand, so I offer my arms to Jade, who lets me lift her.

To my shock, Axel leans toward Coral.

She stares at him for a moment, unsure of his intentions, but as he stays steady, she nods. Axel, secretly Azar the Prince of Flame, picks up my ten-year-old sister Coral and carries her inside the house and up the stairs. I drop Jade on the thick mattress next to her sister, and I tuck Sammy in, and then I back out of the room.

"What happened?" I practically round on Gideon the second the door closes.

"The hovercraft should have worked," he says. "In the past, the water dragons didn't notice them. The land dragons don't worry about the water. The water dragons don't pay attention to the air above the water."

I close my eyes. It was a strange day. Any other day, he might have been right. When I reopen them, Gideon's right in front of me. "You're alright too?" His eyes search my body for signs of injury.

"The bombs didn't detonate," I whisper.

Has it really only been fourteen hours since Gideon and I parted paths? I'm bone-weary. Gideon must feel just as drained, but he also looks desperate. "You're really alright?"

"Axel was right," I say. "Azar handled it." It's strange, talking about Axel. . .Azar. I don't know what to call him, even in my head. I know it's one person, but I can't let anyone else know. It's a heavy secret, and that's taking a toll on me, too. "I'm just so glad you're alright." If something had happened to Sammy or Coral or Jade, I'd have died.

His fingers brush the side of my face. "Liz." The intensity of that one word shocks me. I've been sinking deep into equal parts relief and exhaustion, but his touch is like an electric wire.

"Gideon, I—"

Do not kiss him. Axel doesn't usually speak to me telepathically when he's in human form, and he's only a few feet away, waiting at the top of the stairs.

I look past Gideon's intense face at Axel. His eyes are stormy and bright, like a fire burning in spite of a rainstorm.

I'm caught between a hammer and an anvil, doomed to shatter.

"Liz, all I could think about the whole way back was how happy I was not to leave you." He swears. "I know that's horrible. I tried to escape, I really did, but if it meant losing you." He swears again. "I can't do it again. Please don't ask me to do it ever again. I'm not strong enough."

"Actually." Axel's voice is steady. "Just today Azar offered to escort Sammy, Coral, and Jade to the barricade, safely freeing the four of you, if you swear to care for them."

Gideon freezes. "Why would he do that?"

"As a favor to me, of course," Axel says.

When my oldest friend turns around, he's stiff. He's angry. He's like a gasoline-soaked woodpile, ready to explode in a shower of sparks. "Why would *you* ask him to do that?"

"For Liz," Axel says. "Why else?"

Gideon grinds his teeth.

"Did you think you were the only one who could do anything for her?" Axel arches his eyebrow. "I feel like her loved ones would be safer with me, but for some reason, she trusts you."

The muscles in Gideon's arm, an arm that has knocked out countless numbers of America's top fighters, are bunched and ready. "Stop talking."

"Gideon," I say. "He's trying to help."

"He's one of them, Liz. He may look human, but he's not. Don't forget that."

Gideon doesn't know the half of it. "Will you do it?" I ask softly.

His nostrils flare. "What if I say no?"

"We'll all live here," Axel says. "Like one big, happy family." He lifts one hand and beckons me with two fingers. "Come, Liz. We have some things to discuss."

"Like what? What's going on?" Gideon's brows furrow as he glances from Axel to me and back again. "What would you have to talk about?"

Axel shrugs. "We're bonded, or didn't you hear that?"

There's a vein in the side of Gideon's jaw that always pops when he's angry. It's beating a staccato rhythm on the side of his face right now.

"He saved my life today," I say, "in more ways than one. We do have things to discuss." I hate breaking Gideon's heart, but I'm not sure what else to do.

I watch as he walks down the stairs, one agonizing step at a time. He stops at the landing and looks back, and I almost jog down to him. But I have too many people to protect and too many secrets.

Once Gideon's gone, I round on Axel. "What do you want?"

"I require your assistance," he says.

"Fine." I drop my hands on my hips. "With what?"

"I want you to teach me how to kiss."

❧ 22 ☙

Once, when I was eighteen, I had this co-worker I'd known for a few months. His dad owned the restaurant we were working in, so he was almost immediately promoted to assistant manager, even though he wasn't very good at, well, at anything.

He wasn't a jerk; he just wasn't very competent.

At the end of a long shift, I was carrying an entire order out to a table of six when he walked out right in front of me. I stopped quick, but the food tray didn't react as fast. I dumped the entire order onto the ground, food splattering, dishes shattering, and silverware clattering.

It was a disaster.

Several people stepped in to help, including the guy who caused it, Jack. By the time we finally got the mess taken care of, I was done for the night. I was leaning against the counter in the back of the kitchen when he came over to chat.

Out of the blue, with no lead in, he said, "Hey, you

know, you're really good to have around when things go wrong."

I didn't remind him that he was the thing that went wrong.

He continued. "I'd love to have you around all the time. Would you marry me?"

I thought he was kidding, or maybe I was just really uncomfortable, but either way, I started laughing.

He got angry. . .and fired me.

I could probably have made it into a big thing, but it wasn't the best job in the world anyway. Losing it wasn't a big travesty or whatever. I just walked away.

When Axel says, "I want you to teach me how to kiss," my first inclination is the same as it was that night.

To laugh.

I've learned a little since then, at least.

"Are you making a joke?" I keep my face utterly serious.

He shakes his head. "Nothing you humans do surprises me when it comes to tactical maneuvers. You're pretty amateurish in your military strategy, to be honest."

Maybe I misunderstood him. He's talking about battle strategy now. Maybe he's confused about what a kiss is. I frown.

"But in your personal relationships, I'm constantly confused. You shelter and care for your siblings. Your companion Gideon risked his life by coming into enemy territory to look for you. Then, when you asked, he left you here to protect your family." He frowns. "He doesn't want to leave your side, but he does it anyway when you ask." He shakes his head. "I can't understand it."

"I told you. I haven't kissed him."

Axel steps closer. "I don't experience emotions the way you do, but I'd like to try to understand your actions in spite of that."

He's only a foot and a half away from me now, standing in the center of the game room at the top of the stairs. My back isn't against my bedroom door, but it's not far from it. I've backed away quickly from Axel before, and I know what happens when I do.

Prey drive kicks in, so backing away from him is out. Instead, I step closer, my eyes meeting his. I stare into his eyes for a moment. "Humans experience a lot of emotions, but we don't always know what we're feeling or why. It's a little like our bond in that way. I know it's there. I know it connects me to you." My voice is low, but I drop it lower still. "But I don't know all the things I can do with it, or exactly what it's telling me a lot of the time."

"Okay." Axel picks up his hand and runs his fingers down the side of my face.

My heart reacts instantly, picking up the pace. I lick my lips.

Axel smiles. "Your heart did that when he touched you, and I didn't like it."

"That's close to an emotion we feel too. It's called jealousy."

"Jealousy." He drops his hand. "Our studies tell us that's wishing you had what someone else has." He frowns. "I don't want what Gideon has."

"Maybe not," I say, "but you might want my attention." As I say it, I realize how presumptuous I sound, like I think he's pining for me or something. I already know he doesn't have feelings like ours.

"You're mine," Axel says. "I don't share what's mine."

Maybe it's that simple. "You clearly feel possessive

about things, and maybe that's why you slide into something close to what we know as jealousy. You don't share, and jealousy is when you feel like someone else is taking what's yours."

"He can't have you." He lifts his hand again, this time absently, like he's not really aware of what he's doing, his fingers brushing the hair back from my face. "I don't want him to touch your face. I don't want anyone touching your face."

"Humans don't like the idea of belonging to anyone else." I push his hand away. "We've fought wars over it, and we don't relinquish our independence easily."

"All of life is about hierarchy and power structures," Axel says. "Pretending otherwise is foolish."

"Perhaps." I lift my hand this time. "But think about this. You may own me, but I make demands on you, and you listen and honor them." I touch his brow, my hand far above my own shoulder, and then I drag it down slowly until my finger's next to his mouth. "I can't teach you to kiss, because no one can do that. Kissing's an extension of an emotion you don't possess."

"What emotion?" His lips move as he speaks, pressing gently against my finger. As if he likes it, he leans closer, turning his face toward my hand.

I'm not ready to teach a lesson on love. I'm not even sure I understand it.

"Lust," I whisper. "When two people want to touch one another, when two people can't think about anything but touching that other person. . ." I drag my finger downward, pulling his top lip toward his bottom, and then stopping, my finger pressing harder against his mouth. I swallow slowly. "You want to press your bodies closer, too." Why's my voice so breathy?

"So it's like a mating ritual," he says. "But why the

mouths?" He's looking at my mouth, still speaking against the pressure of my finger.

I pull back, but he stops me—by biting the tip of my finger. He releases me quickly, but he still looks confused.

"Why not hands?" His voice is as low as mine was, like he's mimicking me in everything I do.

I drop my hand. "People usually hold hands first."

"Like this?" He reaches for my hand, covering the back of my hand with his, sliding his fingers between mine, his fingers easily sliding past the one he just bit.

It's been a really, really long day, and I'm one of the only beings who knows about his secret. That's probably what's going on—the excitement of a shared secret—but every nerve ending on my body is awake and alert, almost in overdrive. My hand, where he's touching it, feels like the only place on earth that matters.

It's the only thing I can think about.

"Can you feel this?" His words almost sound like a rhetorical question, but the bond's a bright gold color I've never noticed before. It's almost shining.

This doesn't feel smart. I try to slide my hand free. "We probably ought to—"

"No." Axel tightens his hand around mine. "This is different from anything I've ever done." He lifts his eyes to mine, and his are glowing softly. "I like it."

He likes it.

For some reason those three words shift something inside of me, something strange. It's like I'm a boat that's come unmoored. I'm floating in the middle of the ocean, no anchor, no dock, no course set. I'm free, but also so very lost.

"Axel," I say, "I think—"

His free hand whips up, his finger pressing against my mouth this time. "Shh."

"Axel."

He smiles and moves his finger. "You can say my name. I don't mind that."

"Today has been really long."

He freezes. "You're tired." He closes his eyes. "I forget that about humans. Of course you are."

"Yes," I say.

He releases my hand, looking down a little longingly. "Go right ahead."

But when I turn, he follows me, just a step behind. "What are you—" I frown.

"You were injured today," he says. "It was a long, exhausting day."

I nod.

"The last time you were injured, you slept better with me present."

A shiver runs through me at that memory. "Yes, well, I'm not sure—"

"You'll sleep better this time, too."

"I need to shower," I say. "I'm filthy."

He nods, as if that's just fine and he sees no reason to duck out or leave me alone.

"Humans don't shower together," I say, blushing furiously.

"They don't?" He frowns. "I'm sure that in some of the video transmissions we saw—"

Movies. He means movies. "Not unless they're. . ." I close my eyes. "*Together.*"

"We're together." When I open my eyes, he's simply staring at me in confusion.

"We're not together like that," I say. "That's for people who are in love."

"Show me," he says.

"Axel."

He smiles. "I still like it."

He's like a golden retriever right now, impossible to shake. Maybe I'm handling it wrong. I grab his wrist and drag him into the room and close the door, pressing him up against it.

His eyes widen and he stiffens, but he doesn't stop me or say a word.

"If we were together," I say, "this would have a lot of meaning."

"Meaning?"

"I'd be pressing you against the door because you were invited to spend the night with me."

He blinks.

"Then I'd peel this off." I unsheathe the swords one at a time, and I unbuckle the straps holding them on. Then I unbutton my shirt, peeling it off, leaving only a camisole covering my bra.

His eyes widen and his head dips. "What is that?"

I can't help my smile. He's staring at the outline of my bra. "It's—" I can't help laughing.

"What?" His eyes come back up to mine.

This is totally *not* working. "I'm going to shower. You better be gone when I'm done."

He frowns.

As I shower, I can sense him. He's still in my room. When I step out of the shower and dry off, I can feel that he's still out there, waiting. I put lotion on myself, giving him time to make the right decision, and then I dress. Still, he hasn't moved an inch.

When I open the door in my pajama shorts and t-shirt, he's sitting on the edge of my bed.

"*Axel*," I say. "You were not supposed to wait."

"You never do as you're told." He's smirking. "I thought it was a human thing."

"I'm going to sleep alone. Having you in here means something to humans, and it's not something that reflects what we are."

"But you never did what I asked," he says, standing.

I sigh. "What's that?"

"You were supposed to teach me to kiss." His eyes drop to my mouth again.

"I already told you—that's not something I can teach. When you feel a certain way about someone, it's just something that happens."

"When I think about it, about you feeling that way about someone, it makes me angry." He steps closer. "Isn't that meaningful in some way?"

I shove him. "Not at all. You already told me you feel possessive, like you own me."

"We're connected," he says. "You can't deny that."

"I'm connected to Gideon by choice," I snap. "He's been by my side, protecting me, since we were children."

Axel grabs the edge of my dresser and squeezes.

It shatters.

Wood shards drift to the ground.

"Look what you did," I say. "You really need to go while I have a room left to stay in."

"You said you'd do anything I asked." Axel doesn't look like he cares about the dresser at all. "That was part of our deal."

"So, what? Now part of that deal is teaching you how to kiss?"

He shrugs.

"Alright." I pick up my hand and turn the back of my hand toward my mouth. "Take your hand like this." I pucker up my lips and press my mouth against it. I make smoochy sounds. "There. Now you know."

Axel grabs my wrist, circles it lightly, and drags the back of my hand toward his mouth.

"No," I say. "Not like that."

But it's too late. He's pressing his mouth against the back of my hand. Every part of my body lights up, and I practically squirm out of my own skin. It's like someone connected live wires to my entire musculature, and now they're zapping me.

I've never, not once, not ever before felt like *this*.

"How was that?" He doesn't release my hand, but he does look right into my eyes. "Am I getting it?"

I drag in a breath. "I mean, it's fine. I think it's a good first lesson."

"So you think I'm ready for this?" He grabs my hip and pulls me closer slowly.

I could pull away.

I should pull away.

I ought to dead sprint out of the circle of his arms. This isn't Axel the tolerant earth dragon. This isn't the playful shifter I made a deal with.

This is Azar, Prince of Flame.

His hands are almost unbearably confident as he drags my body closer, pressed against him from thigh to waist. His hand shifts, curving around my side and squeezing.

His other hand fans across my jaw, wrapping around my cheek and cupping under my chin, tilting my face upward. His eyes are on my mouth, and he inhales quickly, and then his head dips until it's just above mine. "Is it supposed to feel this natural?" His words sound almost like a prayer. "Maybe it's the bond." His head lowers so slowly that it feels like he's slowly killing me.

Not a heart attack.

A form of dragon torture.

He's deconstructing me from the inside out.

With the way my heart's racing, it could give out any moment. His mouth stops when his lips are just a hair away from mine. "How long do you usually wait?" His breath feathers over my face, and I can't help it.

I whimper.

"Oh, I like that. Do it again." His mouth's curving upward, now. "Please."

I can barely breathe, and my hands curl around his arms right where his elbow bends, gently scraping the muscle of his bicep. "Axel."

"Azar," he says. "Call me Azar now."

"Azar," I whimper, like he's pulling his name from the depths of my broken, shattered soul.

"Yes." He closes the distance, his mouth finally pressing against mine.

My heart flips and spins. My hands squeeze tighter, wanting more, my fingernails digging into the muscle of his arms.

"Oh," he says against my mouth. "Yes." This time, he's the one groaning.

I move my mouth against his, hungry for more. My tongue brushes against his lip, and he growls, lifting me up in the air like I weigh nothing at all. A strange vibration starts then, but I'm not sure where it's coming from. It's nice, like someone tickling my back, but stronger and soul-deep. I realize it's coming from the bond.

Azar grazes my bottom lip with his teeth, both his hands now circling my waist, and he murmurs, "I should have done this earlier. Much, much earlier." And then he kisses me harder, like he's a starving man, and I'm his only sustenance.

"Azar, I think something," I whisper between kisses, "is happening."

He drops his mouth to my chin, and then he trails kisses down my neck slowly, his lips practically branding me with their heat. "Yes, something I never knew existed." The vibrations deepen, and then shift, and this time, Azar freezes, finally feeling it too.

"What is that?" I murmur.

"It's. . ." And then his body arches and mine does, too, his hands still holding my waist. "It's the bond."

It twists, and then like our fingers intertwining, the bond shifts and clicks into place. What once was rope that bound me to him is now more like interlocked fingers. What before was a thread of connection, a way to get a sense of his direction, a feel for his temperament, is now a conduit of energy, flowing from him to me and back again.

"What's happening?" I cry out, not in pain, but not entirely in pleasure, either.

The thrumming gets stronger and harder, too. Azar pulls me closer and presses my body against his. "Our records say that sometimes, but it's very, very rare, Ensnared can become Entwined."

"Entwined?" I don't understand. "What's that?" A burning pain begins in my other shoulder, just like the first time. Only, this time I squirm back and peel the fabric of my shirt down to look.

A large, metallic red brand appears on the back of my right shoulder blade. It's a flame surrounded by a dragon, and its mouth is consuming the flame.

Or is it creating it?

It's hard to tell.

I check my other shoulder, and the first mark's still there.

"Now I have two?"

"I have two affinities," Azar says. "It makes sense."

As he says that, my back bows out and there's a

flash of pain in my head I don't remember happening the last time. "Ahh," I cry out.

"Your hair," he says. "It's. . ."

I can see it myself. It had become a deep golden, but now it's bright red. The color of a burnished flame.

Azar sighs. "There's no way around it."

"What?"

"You're clearly bonded to a Flame Blessed, now."

23

Kissing someone is always a bad idea for me. I should have known that kissing a dragon prince would end like this.

"What are we going to tell people?" I sit, but somehow I miss the bed and land on the floor.

"Are you alright?" Axel crouches next to me.

I hold out my hand, palm out. "Do not get too close."

He's smirking.

I snap my head up. "No, none of that, mister. The last time I let you come close, you entwined me or whatever, and now my hair's fire-engine red, and everyone in the world is going to know about your secret."

His expression sobers. "We'll tell them that you passed your bond from Axel to Azar."

I straighten. "I'm not that kind of girl. I don't just go passing my bond around."

He arches one eyebrow. "What?"

"Never mind."

"Or we tell them you're bonded to both of us."

I stand up, holding one hand out to keep him at arm's length. "That's worse."

He sighs. "It's worse for me than for you."

"How so?"

"You get upgraded," he says. "You can all move to the tower, and no one will pick on you anymore."

"Wait, how's that bad for you?" I scowl. "Are you saying that having me around more is bad?"

He sighs. "Is there a right answer to this?"

"Can we undo it?"

"Definitely not."

I flop back on the bed and shove a pillow over my face. Axel and his stupid demands—learning to kiss. I groan into the pillow.

"It really will be better for you. Ensnared take their position from their Blessed, and as Axel's, I had no choice but to keep you out here. I had to make sure you'd be as safe as possible."

"That went well." I can't help thinking about Ocharta's first attempt to kill me. And the time I wandered out. And also, her second attempt. Ugh.

"She's caged now," he says. "And only because you won't let me kill her."

"Wait, can bonds really be passed?"

He shrugs. "Does it matter?"

"If they can, maybe we could pass my mom's bond to someone else."

He frowns. "I can't really ask around. Not since we'll have to say we've already done it."

I guess not. "Maybe you could say that you're wondering if we're the only ones."

"Liz." Azar's eyeing me with that patronizing expression again. "We'll have to announce this, tomorrow morning."

"Every day, it's something new."

"And for now—"

I point at the door. "Out. I'm going to sleep. I'm exhausted."

"I'm staying." He folds his arms.

"You can't stay." I'm not budging on this. "I need to sleep alone."

"We're entwined," he says. "That means I need you close."

"Nice try," I say.

He shrugs and heads for the door. He's walking toward the stairs, and suddenly, I'm out the door and padding after him.

"What's happening?" I hiss.

"I told you."

"You said we're entwined."

"I've only heard of it from my father, and even then, there were only one or two mentions," he says. "But he said that once a dragon and human are entwined, it's painful to be separated by any significant distance."

"Painful?" My shoulders droop. "Did he say how to undo it?"

Axel's lip twitches. "It can't be undone. I told you that."

"We're doomed."

"There are benefits," he says.

"Like?" I could use some benefits.

"It increases my power," he says. "And yours, too."

"Explain," I say.

"Essentially, I'll be faster, stronger, and heal faster, and you will as well. If it used to take you weeks to heal without my help, you'll be able to do it in hours."

I yawn.

"You're tired," he says. "We can talk about details tomorrow."

"What do you suggest we do about this?" I point back and forth between us.

He shrugs. "I already proposed my solution. You vetoed it."

I huff.

Axel's being entirely too reasonable.

"Fine." I point at my door. "But you're sleeping on the floor."

He puts up not a single protest. I don't even give him a pillow, expecting him to complain about that, but he doesn't. He simply lies on his back, closes his eyes, and sighs.

"Wait," I say. "You don't sleep."

"I'm going to take my weekly downtime," he says. "Seems like a good time. No one's coming after us right now. Everyone who wanted to already has."

Solid logic. He defeated the humans today. He caged Ocharta. Good enough time for him to process his gas or whatever it is. Dragons are weird.

I watch him as he powers down. His features go slack. His muscles relax.

"Are you worried that I'm here?" I ask.

His eyes open and focus on me, but nothing else shifts. "Should I be?"

I shake my head.

He closes his eyes.

Not long after he powers down, I drift off, too.

When I wake up the next morning, I'm warm. I'm relaxed too. I slept better than I have in a long time. Warm arms are wrapped around me, and they tighten, pulling me closer. "Morning."

His breath on my ear startles me, and I scoot away, almost falling off the bed.

"Easy, there." He drags me close again.

"You were supposed to sleep on the floor." I sit up,

clutching the blankets against me as if that somehow makes things better.

Axel sits up. "I don't sleep, remember?"

I point. "The floor."

He's smiling now. "You're cute in the morning."

I slap his chest, and he snags my hand, his fingers wrapping around mine. "I like being entwined. It's. . .bright."

The door bursts open, and Sammy runs through. "Hey, Liz, can I—" He stops, his mouth dangling open. "Why's *he* in here?" His left eyebrow arches.

"We're together," Axel says.

Now my mouth's dangling open. "No," I say. "No way."

"Why's your hair bright red?" Sammy asks. "Did you dye it?"

"My—no, he's not—"

"What's going on?" Gideon's standing in the doorway now, with Coral and Jade's heads peering around his body.

"I'm Liz's boyfriend now," Axel says. "Because her bond has passed to Azar. We're not ensnared anymore, but we're still connected."

He really should have run this past me.

I can't help my hiss. "He's not—"

Axel takes my hand in his. "That's why we'll be spending so much time together, even though she's bonded to Azar." *This is the perfect solution. I'll be your boyfriend and your Entwined.*

I close my eyes. I can't even argue with him, because how else can I explain him being around me all the time in his human form?

This is getting so complicated.

Gideon always seems to be the collateral damage.

"I think we'll all be safer here with you instead of

leaving Houston." Gideon's tone is flat. "You've shown that the humans can't best you."

"Let's all go down and have some breakfast," I say.

"We should." Axel stands up. "Because Azar's going to be here soon to pick you all up and take you to his tower."

"What about Gordon?" Sammy asks. "I'll miss him."

Axel's expression softens. "He can come if you'd like. He can be your personal bodyguard."

"Really?" Sammy's face lights up. "Can he be my friend, too? My best friend used to be Danny, but now I'm not sure if I'll ever see him again, and Gordon's really good at Uno."

"What about us?" Jade asks. "We want Rufus."

"Do you really?" Axel asks.

Jade nods.

"No one likes Rufus," Gordon says from downstairs. "He bugs everyone."

"I like him," Jade says. "I do."

"He's okay," Coral says.

"He can come as well," Axel says.

"What about you?" Gideon asks. "Will you be staying here?"

Axel walks toward the door, but he stops right in front of Gideon. "You'd like that, and that's almost reason enough for me to go."

Poor Gideon looks like he's about to punch Axel. That brave move would be his last, so I practically race to step between them. "Hey, I'm going to change clothes and throw my stuff in a bag. You guys should do the same thing."

"I can help you pack," Axel says. "I don't have to do it myself." He grabs the top of the door, ushers the kids back through, and then slams it in Gideon's face.

"You should stop doing that," I say.

Axel leans against the wall, his eyes roaming slowly from my legs upward.

"And that, too."

"You might want to make me a list. There seem to be a lot of things I'm not supposed to do."

"And you'll stop doing them?" I grab my backpack. "Because I'll start with the fact that you should stand outside so I can change."

Axel takes my backpack and holds it open. "I don't plan to pay any attention to what you tell me I can't do." He smiles. "But you seem to like telling me, and maybe making a list would be cathartic."

I snatch the backpack out of his hands. "You're pissing me off. If I've leveled up, maybe making me mad's a bad idea."

He grins. "No matter how much you level up, you can't hurt me." He taps the center of his chest. "Entwined, remember?"

I huff. "Then it's all useless. You've always been the one I wanted to defend against." If he won't leave, I'll escape. I grab my clothes and duck into the bathroom to change.

I hate that I can hear him chuckling outside the door. "Go away," I shout.

"You don't really want me to." His voice is so soft that I shouldn't be able to hear it, but I can. Clearly.

When I come out, my backpack full of toiletries, I scowl at him. "Why can I hear you crystal clear now, no matter how softly you speak?"

He presses his hand to my clavicle. "Entwined."

"Stop saying that." I bat his hand away. "And humans don't touch women there." Technically, it's a little above where he shouldn't be touching, but close enough.

"Why not?" He looks genuinely curious, his hand slowly reaching toward me again.

"No reason." I turn to stuff my clothes into my bag. "And listen."

"I'm always listening, as you pointed out."

"It can't stay like this forever, right? I mean, at some point we won't need to be so close all the time, right? Please say that's true."

He chuckles. "It gets better, yes. The closer we get, the more we can stand some separation."

"That makes no sense."

"Our bond will force us to stay in close proximity until the bond in our lives mirrors the bond that now exists in our hearts."

"Hearts?" I roll my eyes. "More like chests."

"Sure," he says. "Call it what you want."

"I will." I'm scowling as I walk out.

Gideon's already holding his bag, standing at the top of the stairs when we emerge. Now it's time for Axel to leave and shift into Azar. No one else can see that, clearly.

"I'll check and make sure the kids have what they need," I say. "You go see if Azar's around yet."

"Can't you sense him?" Gideon asks. "How did you pass the bond, anyway?"

"It was an accident," I say. "And I can sense him, so I know he's closer, but it's more art than science."

"I'll say." Gideon crosses his arms.

"I'll see the rest of you at the tower." Axel leans closer, his head dipping by my ear. "Be safe, sweetheart."

I know it's just a bizarre cover, but it still makes my heart flutter a little, so I swat his shoulder. It physically makes me uncomfortable when he walks away, and I have to plant my feet on the ground to keep from following him.

"Liz," Gideon whispers.

Once Axel ducks out the front door, my discomfort grows to actual pain. My body's tingling, and an ache starts at the base of my skull. It's a concerted effort not to start moving outside to follow him.

"How could you possibly be interested in a dragon? Especially one who passed your bond to that monster?" Gideon shakes his head. "I mean, they're all monsters, but none of them compare to that red one." His mouth twists in disgust.

"It's not like that." My arms and legs are trembling. I try to still them, but I can't. Not quite.

"Are you alright?" Gideon steps back, watching me closely. "You look sick."

I bite my tongue to give me something else to focus on and force a smile. "Fine."

"Oh." He closes his eyes and exhales dramatically. "That makes so much more sense." He looks both directions, noticing that the kids are dragging their bags out the front door. He waves at them. Then he drops his voice to a whisper. "He's forcing you."

"No," I say.

"Of course you can't say, not if he's making you act like this. He's sicker than I thought—he forces you to pretend to like him, and then he makes you act like it's your decision." He swears. "I hated him before, but this is disgusting." He frowns. "Or is it Azar that's forcing you now? Either way."

"Gideon—"

He covers my mouth and looks over the balcony. "Shh."

"It's really not—" But mumbling against his hand

isn't getting intelligible words out, much less anything that might convince him.

"I swear to you, Elizabeth, by all humanity, by everything we hold dear, by everything I ever fought for, I will slay Azar, and Axel too. I'll kill them both, and I'll free you, and one day, we'll both heal from this." He releases me and ducks down close. "I love you, Liz. I always have. You and I, we're meant to be. This isn't the end. Don't give up hope."

I just sigh and nod.

Gideon leans toward me then, and I realize he's about to kiss me. If he does that. . .

An image of a pile of ashes that used to be Gideon flashes before my eyes. Azar'll do it—I have no doubt. And he'll know he kissed me, thanks to the new and improved mega-bond. I shove him backward, but that sends Gideon flying over the edge of the stairs.

I reach for him, desperate to stop him from falling, and he freezes mid-air.

Gideon's floating, his legs up over his head, his head a half dozen inches away from striking the wooden stairs below.

"Whoa," Sammy says. "You can make people fly now?"

I freak out, dropping my hands, and Gideon falls with a thunk, his head striking the stairs after all. Thankfully, it's only a drop of about six inches, so he rolls over once and manages to struggle back to his feet.

"What was that?" Gideon asks.

"I'm bonded to Azar now," I say. "I guess it comes with some perks."

Judging from the roar outside, it also comes with a tighter leash.

"We should go."

By the time I get outside, Coral and Jade are already on Rufus' back, and Sammy's scrambling up on Gordon like they're old friends.

Gideon rides with Sammy, Azar says.

"We're all headed for Azar's home," I say. "It's the J.P. Morgan Chase tower."

"We're going to live in a business building?" Jade asks.

"It has a really nice penthouse," I say.

"But how are we going to get up there?" Jade asks.

"Elevators," I say. "I assume."

Not you. You'll be flying, Azar says, smug through and through.

"That sounds cool," Sammy says. "But what about your humans?"

They'll be brought, Azar says. *New lodgings will be assigned. Don't worry.*

"Can you hear him when he speaks?" I've wondered that for a while.

They can hear me when I want them to, Azar says.

"I heard that just then," Sammy says. "That's pretty cool. Maybe I can learn one day."

"It's not that great," I mutter.

All Blessed will meet at my tower in three hours. Azar's voice felt like it was set to *blast* on that last message.

"You don't need to be that loud," I say. "We're all right here."

He just summoned all the Blessed, Gordon says. *We should get you all settled first.*

"Why'd you do that?" I'm not that keen on seeing all the dragons in the same place again.

It's time we tell them about your promotion. Before I can complain, he launches into the sky, leaving the others to struggle their way to the new digs on the ground.

24

When I was twelve years old, I waited in line for over four hours to do the Avatar ride at Disney World. My dad complained nonstop, mostly about how much he could have made if he had been at work. He had his phone, and I know he was working, even in line. Even my mom grumbled about how silly it was to spend so long on something that wasn't really going to enrich my life. Jade was a baby, and playing with her while we waited was not fun. I recall that part vividly.

Even so, those four hours were well worth it.

That ride mimicked flying, and it was the closest I thought I'd ever get to really being up in the air. Water sprays in your face, air puffs against you, and the machine you're sitting on bumps up and down. With a little imagination, you really feel like you're flying.

It was a highlight in my childhood for sure.

Flying on Azar was fun before. I mean, it was a pee-your-pants-in-horror kind of fun, but fun nonetheless. But now? With this new, improved bond?

It's bananas.

My fear of falling's utterly gone, and unlike before, I intuitively know when he's going to shoot upward, when he's going to bank, and when he's going to dive. The world practically races past down below us, the wind whipping through my hair completely unlike the little bursts of air I liked so much on that ride. The upswings and drops feel unlike anything I ever could have imagined—they blow that Avatar ride out of the air, literally.

I thought we were headed to the tower, I say, switching to telepathic communication thanks to the insane air interference.

The bond's bright green—pleasure, I'm recognizing—when Azar replies. *We have time. They're slow.*

He's playing.

No, not quite.

He's showing off, I realize.

For me.

I lean lower over his neck and ask, "How fast can you go?"

I'm not sure whether I've ever checked.

I already know we're about to find out. He coasts for a single beat, and then he inhales deeply and shoots forward, the propulsion from his wings clearly not the only thing moving us forward.

Magic, he answers my unasked question. *The Blessed are magical creatures in our core, after all.*

And then I can't speak or even form thoughts, we're moving so fast. I have no idea how far we go, but it's far enough that jets fall in behind us, so we're definitely out of Houston's airspace.

"Oh, shoot," I shout.

Don't worry. We'll head back soon. They won't be able to keep up.

And he's right. We leave them behind almost

immediately. My heart's going to burst if I keep living like this. From having Azar around all the time to flying through the air at Mach ten, humans weren't made for this stuff.

You're not human anymore.

Is that true?

The bond has changed all the Ensnared, but you're entwined. You're entirely different, and it may just be starting. My magic will continue to alter you as our bond deepens.

That idea scares me, but it's not as shocking as I thought it would be. When Azar flies through the gap in the large stylized T-shape in the center of the top of the Chase Tower and lands on the helipad, I'm still thinking about what exactly it means.

I'm not only Flame Blessed. I'm a Prince of the Flame.

"What does that mean, though? It feels like everyone's a prince or a princess." I can't help teasing him.

Each affinity has a ruler. Their children are princes and princesses, but only one is slated to rule. I'm the Prince for all my people. The Flame Blessed rule all the other Blessed.

Oh, shoot. He's the whole enchilada.

What's an enchilada?

"You have so much to learn."

At least I have a teacher.

He's not what I expected, not at all.

Your family's arriving shortly.

Which means I need to see the tower myself. "So how do I get in here again?" I was pretty wiped out last time we came.

He climbs through an opening in a side wall leading into the penthouse that he made, judging by the red glasslike dome that's patching the ripped part in the wall. Luckily, we can walk through it. It's eerily similar to the magical dome he put over Ocharta.

"Why can we walk through that, but she was stuck?"

It's magic, he says.

As if that just explains everything.

Did you want me to go into the magical theory of the flame and its connection to the Blessed of each affinity?

I shake my head. "Nope. Sorry for thinking irritating thoughts."

Almost between one step and the next, there's an engine growling sound, and Axel in a black suit and red tie steps through next to me.

"I may never get used to that."

He shrugs. "You will."

"So what's the layout in here?"

"The top few floors are a massive living space, which is why I chose this tower over that other one, the one that says Exxon on the side."

"I wasn't sure whether you realized this wasn't really the tallest tower in town," I say.

"More like I don't care. Men who are worried about whether their tower is the tallest aren't very confident."

"Says the man who's currently living in the second largest tower in Houston."

"It's easier for me—I'm always up high. Plus, others find it hard to come after me up here."

"Will my siblings be safe?" I arch an eyebrow. "And will they be comfortable?"

"I may need to recruit some Strike Blessed—"

"Absolutely not," I say.

"Not all of them are like Ocharta." He chuckles. "I quite like some of them."

"They are beautiful," I say. "But I'd rather stick with Gordon and Rufus. Can't we just give them wings?"

This time, instead of chuckling, he laughs. "You really have no idea what's possible."

"Your problem is that you think you already know."

He's frowning as I start to prowl around his living area. As expected, he's destroyed a lot of it with his massive frame, clearly breaking and piling up a lot of the formerly wonderful furniture to make room for a dragon to rummage around.

"This entire floor is more than two stories tall," I say. "So clearly this must be where Azar stays."

"Clearly," he says.

"But what about Axel and me?" I arch an eyebrow. "And the others?"

"The floor two levels below this one has several separate apartments. Rufus and Gordon can share the first apartment on the seventieth floor, and your siblings can have the other."

"And Gideon?"

He frowns. "With your siblings, I assume."

"While we will be. . ."

"On the seventy-first floor, one above."

"Nice try," I say. "I need to be closer to them."

He walks toward the elevator and presses a button. "Don't forget that you can't be too far from me, either."

This is going to be a really weird situation. I hope we can survive it without anyone dying. I'm relatively sure that Gideon's the one at risk, and that's not acceptable. He's done too much for me, and he's really only trying to help.

"What has he done for you, exactly, other than pick fights he can't win?"

"You need to stop reading my thoughts," I say. "I'm not reading yours."

"I'm just better at shielding them." The elevator doors ding, and he steps in.

I can't help wondering how he knows about elevators as I step in beside him.

"We did extensive research on your earth before coming, or did you forget? I've assimilated several languages, and hundreds of thousands of humans are still living here, repairing things, maintaining the energy grid, and ensuring our supplies are not running low."

We only go down one floor, and when the doors ding, he gestures. "If you don't want to be separated, this level might be large enough for everyone."

I can't help my gape-mouthed expression as I look around. The entire floor was apparently owned by the same person, and they were not poor. The floors are marble. The furniture's lavish. Without a dragon wandering around, smashing things into piles to get them out of the way, this place is *posh*.

A huge wooden slab table rests in the center of the entry hall, a marvelous jade vase resting in the center. The flowers are dead, but it still manages to look pretty impressive.

I follow Axel past it and into the dining room. It has a massive dining room table made from another raw-edge wood slab and the most gorgeous, luxe-leather chairs I've ever seen. If someone told me they were crafting furniture meant for a dragon lord, this is what I'd imagine.

"Did you have this made for you?"

"Apparently your captains of industry have similar taste to the Blessed."

Overinflated egos, too much wealth, and no connection with reality. Sounds about right.

He rolls his eyes as he walks me through the kitchen—all gleaming stainless appliances, including a catering kitchen behind it—and the family room, complete with a monstrously large television. Then he points. "There are at least six bedrooms."

"So we'll all stay here on this floor. That's a good plan." Or, even if it's not a good plan, it's the best one we've got.

"It is just one level down from where Azar lands. It seems the safest bet. There are also emergency stairs if the power ever cuts out." He grins. "Not that you'd ever need that."

The front elevator dings, and it's time to wave the urchins in. Although I give them their choice, all three kids want to stay in the same room, just like before. I suppose fear does that to you. Gordon and Rufus would rather sleep upstairs in Azar's lair in their dragon shapes, but they agree to take turns having one of them down below in human form for safety's sake.

"I don't really see why we need them," Axel grumbles. "Not when I'm here."

"It's always a good idea to have more than one dragon on call," Rufus says.

"You can sleep up with us too, when you want," Gordon says.

"Yes, I agree. Sleeping upstairs is a great plan for you." Gideon claimed the room on the far side of the kids. He's not keen on any of the dragons being on our level, even though I explained that it's for safety.

I said I'd take the master. Mostly I picked that because it has an antechamber. Axel can sleep there, and I'll hide in the bedroom. The bed looks amazing, and the door has a lock.

Before there's time for an argument, Axel says, "It's almost time for Liz to go upstairs. The Blessed are gathering below."

"How can you tell?" Sammy asks.

It's a good question. He's a smart kid.

"I feel them," Axel says. "The Earth Blessed ones, anyway."

"Can Azar feel them all?" I ask.

Axel frowns. "I've never asked him, but probably."

When it's time, we take the elevator up, leaving Gordon and Rufus with Gideon and the kids. Gideon wanted to come, but I convinced him to keep an eye on Coral, Jade, and Sammy in the new place. Eventually, he's going to get sick of me asking him to do that. I'm not sure what I'll do then.

Azar shifts the second we emerge from the elevator. I can't tell whether the engine growling sound is actually smaller, or whether I'm just growing accustomed to it. Either way, his shifts seem less and less disruptive. Less shocking. He swirls his way, in a cloud of red smoke, into a dragon that can destroy the world.

My dragon who can destroy the world.

It's a subtle shift, but when I think the words, they feel right. It may be scary, but I think he might have been right when he said we were inextricably connected. Instead of looking for ways out, I'm now contemplating a future that will always have him in it.

That alone is horrifying.

You need to change.

Lying on the ground next to Azar, right by where he just shifted, there's a pile of clothing. It's all red and brown and gold, and an even larger visor's resting on top of it. "What's that?"

You're the Entwined for the Prince of Flame. You have to look the part. Underneath the clothes are the two swords I pulled from the heart stone. Next to them, there's another belt with three small daggers on it.

I duck into the bathroom and do my best not to struggle with all the strange and stiff clips and clasps. At first, I assume the entire thing is made of leather—it's bright red and dark brown, made of a skin of some kind. It's supple and it's strong. But as I do the last round of buckles, I realize something.

I'm wearing dragon skin.

It must be.

The red isn't dyed.

The brown and gold sections aren't either. The golden part of the skin exactly matches the gold visor and the golden shoulder shield that both lock into place without any external mechanism.

"Where did you get this?" I ask, as I leave the bathroom. "Is it really dragon skin?"

Of course, he says. *It's my skin. What else would you wear?*

"But you need your skin, surely."

I saved it when I shed. Now it's yours.

"You saved it? Where?"

He sighs.

"Magic?"

He snorts, smoke wafting upward from his huge nostrils.

"Alright, alright. Let the slow kid in the class through. We have some dragons to greet."

Climb on, he says.

It's easier than it was, and I notice I'm developing calluses on my hands where I've been gripping his shoulder ridges. So much for magic. Some things I'm figuring out the human way—painful and slow, but much more familiar.

If you really want a saddle, he says, *I can make you one.*

"We can talk about this later, when I'm not about to meet a thousand of your closest friends."

Try ten thousand.

I really did not have the best view the last time, but this time, when Azar walks out, there are dragons arrayed around his tower as far as my eyes can see. In case I wasn't yet sufficiently in awe, Azar steps off the platform and plummets nearly to the ground before spreading his wings and coasting in a slow, lazy circle.

This is Elizabeth Chadwick, he says. *She was Axel's bonded. I took her from him, and now she's mine. She isn't merely ensnared. We're entwined, so if you lay so much as a finger on her, I will reduce you to ash. And then, I'll utterly destroy anyone who ever cared for you.*

Okay.

Bow.

They all do—like an ocean of shining, shimmering scales, all the dragons beneath us drop down, their heads lowering to the ground and staying low.

"How long are you going to—"

As long as I want.

I've never really seen absolute power in my life. After all, even the President of the United States has to be elected, and his term is limited.

But now, I guess I have. Azar commands ten thousand dragons. He swallows nukes and converts their power into a nightlight. He magics boundaries and dragon skin suits, and he fears nothing.

And now he's protecting me.

I'm not going to lie. It's a heady feeling. I give myself a moment to revel in it before I start to think about what that means. In thirty seconds, I went from a human who was fighting against the devil to save all humankind to a minion of the destroyer.

Oh, crap.

Good feelings definitely all gone.

Azar roars, then.

The dragons all throw their heads up—blue, green, silver, brown, and every shade in between—and bugle into the air.

All hail Elizabeth Chadwick, Entwined of the Prince of Flame.

That was strange. All those dragons, thinking the same thing at the same time, with my name thrown in there.

"Maybe we should have, like, I don't know, used a new name or something."

You don't like your name?

"It's just, listen to it. Azar, Prince of the Flame, and. . .Elizabeth Chadwick. They sound. . .strange together."

I'll think on it.

"Alright." We make a few more loops, and right as I'm wondering how much longer this is going to last, Azar flies up to the tower and the dragons start to disperse.

I'll say this for dragon meetings. They're not long and overblown.

We're still upstairs in Azar's lair—I decide that's a better place to shower and get changed. The new outfit's pretty awesome, but it's also a bit pro-dragon for my family. I've changed out of it and I'm sliding back into my *Pink* t-shirt and ratty jeans when Azar calls for me. *Liz.*

What now? I zip up my pants and burst out of the bathroom. "What? I was barely in there for—"

You have visitors.

"I thought we were going to keep the kids downstairs."

He tosses his head toward the entry area near the elevator bay, and I realize it's not the kids who are already here, waiting to see me.

Dozens and dozens of Ensnared—no, make that at least a hundred of them—are crowded into the center of the vast space that makes up Azar's urban lair. It's a good thing he shoved all the furniture out of the way to clear more space, because they look like they could give a mob of Swifties a run for their money. They're wearing outfits not dissimilar to what I was wearing, with fewer scales of course, and their hair's all varying shades of blue and silver.

Which is really strange.

"Uh, hello," I say. "I'm Elizabeth—"

Before I can even finish saying my name, they bow.

All of them.

"Whoa, guys. What's going on?" They don't move a single hair. They're all just lying there, utterly still, face-down, just like the dragons earlier. "Seriously, stand up. What are you doing?"

They don't move.

"Okay, for real," I say. "Stand up."

They all jerk forward and finally rise, like they're half robot or something. That's when I realize I put a little too much force behind my command.

I made them stand.

Aw, geez. This is seriously bizarre.

"So, not that I'm not happy to meet you all, but is there a reason you're here? Right now?"

"Help me." The woman closest to me has royal blue hair. She drops to her knees again. "My Blessed spends all his time underwater, and he doesn't make me stay there, but the only thing he wants to eat is fish, and—"

"Please." The man next to her shoves her. His hair's silver. "Do you have any idea what it's like to be electrocuted half a dozen times a day? My Blessed thinks it's funny to zap me. It doesn't cause permanent damage, thanks to the bond, but it's painful. I wake up every half hour at night now in a panic, worried I'm about to be electrocuted."

They're all here. . .to complain? Is this for real?

You're now the leader of the Ensnared.

"But I'm not ensnared," I say. "I'm entwined, and—"

"How did you do it?" the woman who was complaining about being underwater too much asks. "If I could do that, I might not mind the fish. I heard that being entwined's totally different. Your Blessed is —" She cuts off with a squeak and bows again. "But he seems to adore you."

Clearly she's scared of him, but she's also jealous.

This is all very, very strange.

Liz is too tired to talk to you today. You'll have to come again, in groups of no more than five. Azar sighs. *Talk to Rufus one floor down. He'll group you into batches and set up a few meetings a day.*

"But we need guidance," the man says. "We need a leader."

And she needs time to understand her role. The whiplash in his voice that time shocks even me.

The Ensnared all flatten themselves to the floor again.

I glare. "That's hardly helpful," I mutter. "Alright, alright, on your feet."

They slowly rise with a lot of backward glances and trembling, and then they exit through the stairwell. I'm hoping they'll find an elevator on another floor and not try to walk all the way down. Trotting down seventy-five levels would destroy me, and I'm in decent shape.

But one of them hasn't left, one with silver hair. When I finally notice her face, I realize why.

It's my mother.

"I know it's presumptuous of me to ask this of you, Your Highness." She drops to her knees. "But please, can you hear me out today?"

My mother doesn't look good. Her formerly vibrant silver hair's tangled and dull. Her skin's dirty and sallow. Her eyes have hollows underneath them.

"What's wrong?" I ask, and then I realize.

Her dragon's half-dead and stuck in a magic red bubble. Did I think she'd be fine? I'm such a selfish jerk.

"It has been such a long day and a half," I say, realizing that's all it's been. "I'm so sorry, Mom." I drop to one knee and reach for her.

She skitters away, her head bowed again, her eyes trained on the ground. "I'm sorry for my impertinence, but I have an urgent request."

"Anything, Mom. Say the word."

She turns her face up slowly, her lips trembling. "Can you transfer my bond to another Blessed?" She inhales sharply. "I'll still serve, just with another Blessed. Any one you choose." She bows her head.

Oh, no. We did tell everyone that my bond was transferred. I want to tell her that's not what happened, but I can't. It's not my secret. "Mom, I can't do that."

Her eyes are haunted when she pleads with me. "Can't? Or won't? Because I'll do anything. I'll *be* anything—"

I grab her hand and wrap mine around it. "Mom, I would do it if there was any way I could. What happened with me, it can't be repeated. It was. . .not something I can help you with."

"Then, if you can't transfer my bond. . ." A tear rolls down her face.

In that moment, all the moments in my life that Mom held me, that she wiped my face, that she brushed my hair, that she helped me dress, that she laughed with me about something silly, all those tiny moments roll together in my mind, and they're all painful.

Because the one time she's asking for my help, I can't give it.

"If you can't, then will you—or your master—" She pauses. She breathes in and out, and then she grunts. The rest of her question pours out in a rush. "Will you please kill my Blessed?" She begins to shake uncontrollably.

I wait for it to abate, but it seems to only be getting worse. "What's going on?" Clearly Mom's not going to be able to answer me, so I'm looking to Azar for answers.

She must've been commanded not to think any harmful thoughts about her Blessed, he says. *Breaking those rules is impossible for most Ensnared. You should be proud. Your mother's quite strong.*

And Ocharta really is the devil's bride.

"Mom, it's okay." I want to reassure her, send energy her way, but I'm worried that if I do, my command and Ocharta's will fight, and then what?

Azar shrugs.

Mom's still convulsing, so I decide to risk it, keeping it as simple as possible. *You did nothing wrong. You're healthy and strong and fine.* I push the thought at her and hold my breath.

She bows upward, and then she collapses, no longer trembling. I rush to her side, hoping she's still breathing. . .and she is. I exhale slowly and sit next to her. "Mom."

Her frame still rocks gently, but I realize it's

because she's crying. "Please," she whispers. "Please kill her."

"I can't," I say. "Mom, I can't do that. It might kill you, too."

"It will." She turns toward me. "And I still want you to do it."

25

I thought, when I saw my mother again, I could bring Jade and Coral and Sammy up to see her. She'd see that they're alright. They could hug her. She could kiss their cheeks.

It never occurred to me that I'd have to carry her like a wounded animal to a bed and nurse her back to standing upright.

"I can't stay," she whispers. "I have to go soon."

"Why?" I ask. "Why can't you stay here? I'll bring you food. It's warm inside."

She shakes her head. "Even now, she's calling me. I have to bring her food, or she'll die." Her lips twist angrily. "I wish I could resist her."

I hate this.

I hate it more than anything I've ever hated in my entire life. In the end, we load her up with food. I funnel as much energy into her as I can, and then we send her back to the abuser, her captor, to be tormented another day.

"Maybe you should let her die," Axel says.

My head snaps around toward him.

He holds both hands up. "I'm not trying to pick a fight, but she is in bad shape."

"You're the Prince of the Flame," I say. "You have to be able to do something."

He shrugs. "There are some things that can't be changed."

I think about his secret, how he has two affinities, how he's led a double life for. . .I have no idea how long. "How old are you?"

"We don't reckon time in the same way you do." He shrugs.

"That's useless."

"I'm very, very old compared to you," he says.

Great. Now I feel even more pathetic. "Look." I start pacing. "I may be young. I may be human. I may be stupid, but I will not just stand here while my mom's out there, being mistreated and wishing she could die!" I fling my hand at the opening in the side of the building, and a three-foot-wide fireball blasts from my hand into the air, sailing outward.

My jaw drops. "What in the world was that?"

"You were saying," Axel says, "that you're young and you're human and you're stupid." His mouth curves into a half grin. "Was your next line going to be that you're powerless?"

"How did I just make a fireball? Or was that you?"

He shakes his head. "All you."

I jog to the edge of the building and peer over the side. I don't see anything on fire down there.

"I snuffed it out," Azar says. "One of the flip sides to making fire is the ability to control it. If not for that, I could destroy everything around me unintentionally."

Which means that when he burned that neighborhood, he meant to do it. Ugh. I quickly shove my thoughts along, hoping he didn't hear that one.

"Soon, I'll teach you how to harness that power." Axel's still on the fireball. Thank goodness. "You've been entwined for, what? A day?"

It feels way longer than that. "You chose the wrong human for this."

"I think I found exactly the right one." He looks serious.

Uh oh. Time to bail before he starts asking for more kissing lessons. "I should get some sleep." I back up. "I barely slept last night, we were out so late looking for the kiddos. How about you stay here, since you don't need to sleep? Tomorrow, when I wake up, the very first thing I'm doing is learning whatever I can about the bond, about the Ensnared, and about what I can do with them. Maybe I can, I don't know, learn to transfer a bond."

I hate how sad that suggestion makes Axel look.

"You didn't know I could throw a fireball until I did. Clearly we don't know what I can do, and I've learned that lots of things people think girls can't do, we can. Lots of things people think fighters can't do, we figure out. No matter how many times I get knocked down, I always climb back up."

And I'm monologuing. . . A pep talk for myself.

"Liz."

My shoulders droop. My heart wilts. Moments ago, I was soaring on the back of a dragon who could destroy the world, thinking how much my life had changed. Now I'm right back to square one.

I can't do anything.

The world sucks.

Strong arms suddenly sweep me up, one under my knees, one behind my shoulders, and Axel's carrying me toward the elevator bay. "You're right. It's time for bed."

Bed.

Something about the way that word sounds in his mouth has me all strung out. "I really need to sleep," I say.

"I know you do," he says. "You will sleep."

"I'll sleep better if you stay up here."

"Patently untrue," he says. "Do you really need to go downstairs alone to realize that?"

I think about the discomfort I felt earlier, just when he went outside. I grit my teeth. "You know, we have a word for this. It's called co-dependent."

"What does it mean?"

"It's when people can't function alone, and they need the other person to feel complete."

"I like it," he says.

I shake my head. "No, you shouldn't like it. It's bad. It's a kind of human dysfunction."

He shrugs. "Maybe dysfunction for humans is high function for dragons."

It's like arguing with a lamppost.

"I'm smarter than a lamppost," he says.

"It's not fair for you to argue with my *thoughts*," I say.

"Fair is irrelevant. I'm stronger than a post that holds lights on the street. And I can defend you much better than any inanimate object ever could."

He's absolutely absurd. "The point is that we need to work toward finding our independence again."

"You'll never be independent again." He narrows his eyes. "Why would you want to? Are you looking into transferring your mother's bond so you can figure out how to dissolve ours?"

I wasn't, but I should've been. "No."

"Liar."

I really am so very tired. As he's stepping into the

elevator, I finally give up on arguing for the night and rest my head against his chest. That makes the bond pulse bright green. I want to be annoyed, but for some reason, I can't manage it. It's hard to be mad at a man who's carrying you downstairs when you're bone tired.

Maybe a stronger woman could manage it, but not me.

In fact, the only thing I do manage to do when Axel carries me to my room is shoo Gideon back to his room, overriding his concerns that Axel's staying with me again, and check on the kiddos to make sure they're alright. They must be as tired as I am, because they're all completely passed out.

Their innocent, sweet faces heal part of the broken shards in my chest from the interaction with Mom.

Not all of them, but some.

I brush my teeth, and then I flop onto the biggest bed I've ever seen. It makes king-size beds look like a twin, which is good, because even in his human form, Axel's massive.

For a moment, I'm ultra conscious that Axel's beside me, his chest rising and falling as he breathes my air. "Do you use oxygen in this form?" I *am* exhausted, but sometimes the more tired I am, the more my brain spins round and round.

"Do you really care?"

I ball up my pillow and flip on my side. "I guess not."

"I do," he says. "In this form, my body's closer to yours than in my other form. It's why we're not as strong like this. Before we fight, Earth Blessed always shift."

"So why did you have those swords?" I yawn.

Axel's less intimidating when I'm not staring right at him. All that beauty, all that savage grace, it's a little off-putting to a normal human like me. But just the sound of his voice behind me kind of rolls over me, like a familiar lullaby.

"I thought they were for me, to use once I had mastered this form," he says. "But now I wonder. The only Blessed yet alive who remembers the time we inhabited this planet, sharing it with your ancestors, is my father. The other elders have reunited with the Blessed Kin, their mortal bodies dissipating."

"Your dad used to live on earth?"

"He was like me, the Prince of Flame, when we decided to leave Earth for good."

Wow, that's crazy. I yawn again, and this time it's so big that I hear my jaw crack.

"You should sleep. We have plenty of time to discuss things while we search for the Heart."

"Do you have any leads?" I ask.

"You jump around like a foundling," he says. "You asked about the swords first, and I never finished. I now believe that I was given them for you."

A strange sense of destiny washes over me.

What are the odds that I would meet the Prince of Flames in his weak, human form, just outside my neighborhood? What are the chances that I'd be a bright, and that he'd inadvertently bond me? What does it mean, if it's not a coincidence?

Fate is stupid. It's worse than co-dependence.

If I buy into fate, it means I don't have choices at all. It means all the things I'm doing, all the things that have happened to me, they've all been predestined. I was meant to hurt Gideon. I was meant to discover Axel's secret. I was meant to bond to him and betray my own people by Entwining.

He's saying that the swords that he brought back to earth, the swords buried in a massive boulder that no one could remove, like the stupid Arthurian legend, were always meant to be mine. And I was always meant to be his.

If it's true, that's insane.

If it's true, everything feels futile.

So I choose not to believe it. I choose to believe that my decisions matter. I can change the course of my future, and I can make things better. I can fix my errors and do better tomorrow.

Maybe I'm a stupid human, but I need to believe that, at least.

"You can choose to do good things, and they can also be foreordained," Axel says.

"Oh, shut up."

He doesn't make a sound, but I know just what face he's making.

"You know, I've never seen you eat as a dragon." I close my eyes.

"Go to sleep, Liz. We can talk about what we eat tomorrow."

Please, let it not be grubs.

Axel's laughing as I finally drift off.

But the dream that grips me is not a good one, and it's not new, either. It starts out like it always does.

I'm just waking up, and I'm exhausted. So tired that I wipe my eyes, but they're still burning. It's bright outside the vehicle I'm in. The light is so caustic that I cover my burning eyes with my hands. I'm in a big van with several other people, none of whom I know.

I cry for my mother.

The people in the van are cruel, especially the two men in the front. One of them hits me with a can, covering me with a smelly liquid. Beer. The woman isn't nice, but she's not as awful as the men.

It's cold. Painfully cold, and then we reach the base of a snow-capped mountain.

Somehow, I already know it's a volcano.

We climb, and we climb, and we climb more. My feet are bloody. My hands are scraped. I'm dragged by a rope around my neck when I don't want to go any farther. And then, finally, we reach the top of the volcano.

An active volcano.

I'm dragged toward it. I ask why. I ask them why I'm here. They rip my shirt, exposing my birthmark, the heart-shaped reddish mark that lives just above my left breast. I'm horrified that I'm uncovered, but I soon stop worrying about that.

Lots of people are gathered there, far more than the three who dragged me here.

They're all chanting.

They keep saying the same strange word over and over. It sounds like shartanu. I have no idea what it means, but then they try to drag me toward the volcano.

They want to throw me inside.

But the woman who brought me here has a prosthetic leg. I noticed it's not quite right, and when she tries to shove me in, I fight her. Even then, even though I'm quite small, I manage to kick her back leg, and then shove her into the volcano.

She takes my place, burning to ash.

I run, then, and after I'm caught, I manage to use the woman's dagger to stab my captor. And then I'm free once more, running as fast and as far as I can.

Before I see the bizarre police cars, I wake up, in a cold sweat, like always. Tears are streaming down my face, and my breathing's coming in great, gulping gasps.

Like that night, the worst night of my life before

the dragons came, my throat feels raw, as if I really have been inhaling ash and screaming again.

You're okay, now. Axel's holding me against his chest. *You will never be terrified like that again.*

"I murdered that woman," I say, my breaths slowing. "When I was a child. That dream—it really happened. I might have killed the man, too. I'm not sure."

Axel clears his throat. "They deserved to die for treating a child like that. I would have tortured them first, for a very long time." His eyes are dark, and I realize that he's angry.

Very, very angry.

The bond is dark.

"But Liz."

"It was a long time ago. I still get nightmares sometimes, but I'm fine. Really." I blink some of the sleep away, realizing that it's still dark outside. It must still be the middle of the night. "I should go back to sleep. Humans sleep longer than this."

"The people in that dream who were chanting."

"Wait, you saw those people?" I shake my head to make sense of his words. "Did you actually see what was happening in my mind?"

"Our bond makes that part simple."

It should feel invasive, but somehow, it doesn't. "Huh. I don't hate that. It's like, for the first time, I wasn't alone that night." I can't help a little grin. "If you'd been there, things would have gone very differently."

"Yes," he says. "They would have."

"But that woman still would have died."

"True."

"What were you going to say about the weird chanting people?" I never remember much about them.

Just that one word, over and over. "I still have no idea what shartanu means."

"It's the Icelandic word *hjartanu*," Axel says. "And it means 'the Heart.'"

No way. "Are you serious?"

"It's one of the few words we learned in every language that humans speak, for obvious reasons." His face is solemn, his eyes intent.

"Axel."

"I know you're not keen on the idea that this was all preordained." He brushes the hair back from my face gently. "But it can't be coincidence that your worst nightmare contains the key to our locating the Heart. Can it?"

"How do you know the dream had anything to do with your heart?"

Axel's eyes drop to my shoulder, and then he swallows.

"Do you mean, because of my birthmark?"

I drag my shirt down, exposing a little more skin than I really feel comfortable with, even though most girls I know would show this much with half their bikinis, but on the top of my left breast, there it is.

A perfectly shaped red heart.

"Those insane people took you because of that, and they were going to throw you into an active volcano." Axel's eyes are intense. "It must be related somehow, don't you think?"

I pull my shirt back into place. "I think that those people were crazy, and now I'm worried that you are, too."

"It's the best lead I've found in all the time we've been here."

Would it really be so bad to go to Iceland? At least it would get the dragons out of Texas, right?

✺ 26 ✺

The day of the Boo Bash, Gideon called me. "You trained early today?"

"I promised Sammy that I'd come to his Halloween carnival," I said.

"But you promised me you'd train here every day so I'd be able to see you."

That made my breaths come a little faster. "I did no such thing."

His voice dropped. "In my head, you did."

Oh. "I guess I should've told you I'd be coming in earlier."

"I could skip out early—go with you to the carnival."

"But you're still at my gym." I was nervous, even then, at the prospect of Gideon, whom I had known for my entire life almost, flirting.

"Does that mean we can't go anywhere together?" His voice was light, but I could tell he was really, really serious. "And if two friends held hands, who would know?"

My breath caught.

"And if I were to bob for apples with you, and wipe the water from your face, or if I smashed the base of the strongman game with a hammer and rang the bell. . .or if I shot the most balloons with the dart gun and won you a stuffed animal. . ."

"It's not a real carnival," I said. "It's a fundraiser for the school."

"Is that a no? You don't want me to crash this party?"

I did. I really, really did. But I was also going for Sammy, not to spend time with a boyfriend I wasn't supposed to have yet. "I need my little brother to be my actual focus," I said, regretting the words as they emerged. "But at the next carnival. . ."

"Maybe I'll propose at the next one, with a ring in one of those dumb balloons."

My heart stops.

"Or would that be too corny?"

"You're thinking about proposing?" I can't even swallow.

"I've been thinking about proposing for years, Liz. I'm finally *talking* about it."

When I hung up the phone that day, I spent the next few hours floating around on a cloud. And then on the day of the carnival, that cloud burst and released a torrent of rain, drowning the world.

I have a track record now, of feeling joyful, of feeling *hopeful*, and then the world beneath my feet just collapses. After Axel heard about my dream, he started making plans to leave Houston. On the one hand, I was giddy. On the other. . .it felt ominous for some reason. All the dragons just arrived in a flurry, and then after one horrible memory from my brain was dislodged, they're just magically pulling up the anchor?

"It's not only you," Axel says. "We've thoroughly

searched this area. It felt like as good a place as any to start, but we've found no evidence of the Heart, so it's past time to move on."

But that leaves us dealing with some tricky loose ends.

"She has to come with us," I say. "We can't leave Ocharta here, stuck in a red bubble."

"She's regenerated," Axel says. "If we take her, she'll be able to do whatever she wants."

"But if you leave her, the humans will kill her, and my mom will die." Which is the whole reason we didn't kill her in the first place.

"We'd have to free her for her to follow us, and the risk to you will continue, unresolved."

"I'm not bonded to an earth dragon she despises anymore," I say. "Now I'm Azar's Entwined. Do you really think she'll do anything to me?"

He fumes. "I don't like the idea of letting someone who defied me free."

I hate the idea of her being free as well. My own mother begged me to let her die, but I can't live with that being my last memory of my mother. Hard things always seem the worst in the middle—we just haven't figured out a solution yet. I'm working on it, though, learning about the bonds and trying to figure out how to transfer or dissolve hers. Without more time, I'm doomed. But with a little more study, I'm confident there will be *something* we can do.

I drop one hand on his arm. "Can you let it go anyway? For me?"

Axel pauses, and then he exhales slowly. "Fine. *Fine.*"

It may not always have been easy, but since that strange night when our bond shifted, things have steadily improved with Axel. Er, Azar. Whoever he is.

Deciding which name to use is complicated. If I stick to just one in my head, I'm more likely to spill his secret, so I call him Axel when he's in earth dragon or human form, and Azar when he's red. It's. . .bizarre, and I'm still wrapping my head around it.

It's been almost a week since my dream, and the dragons are wrapping things up in Houston. Azar wanted to just fly to Iceland straight away, but I convinced him that we should pull up stakes and move along.

I may have partially defected, but I'm still a Houstonian. If I can clear the dragons out of my town and let people move back in, I'm going to do it.

"The Blessed are still insisting that we should take some of the humans with us," he says. "Even the Ensnared agreed that starting over with all new humans—"

"But we agreed that *I'm* in charge of the humans and that includes the Ensnared," I say. "Taking humans from Houston who speak English and understand how the world works in Houston to Iceland is a bad plan. We can subjugate new humans there." That phrase doesn't sit well with me, but what choice do I have? It's either snatch thousands of humans from their homes here and take them with us, or have the Ensnared free them and find new recruits in Iceland. That felt like the better way to go.

If we could have left the Ensnared here, I'd have pushed for that, too.

"The humans who aren't ensnared all stay," I insist. "And about the government in Iceland—"

"How we handle interactions with the local government falls to me. I've attempted to talk things through dozens of times now." Axel shakes his head. "It always leads to more jets and bombs, and then more humans will die, and I can't have you all agitated."

"I don't get agitated," I say. "That makes me sound like a Karen, complaining about my cheesecake being too dry."

"A Karen?" He frowns. "I don't understand."

I roll my eyes. "Never mind. It's a stupid name anyway, and some of the nicest people I know are named Karen."

"But you said—"

"Forget it."

Sammy pokes his head through the crack in my door. "Are you guys fighting about cheesecake?"

"We aren't fighting," I say.

Axel says, "What's cheesecake?"

Sammy's eyes widen. "We have to eat cheesecake before we leave."

"I'm sure they have cheesecake in Iceland," I say. "And I told you that we have to leave today."

"But what if their cheesecake is gross?" Sammy's bottom lip juts out. "What if all the cheesecake factories get blowed up when they try to attack us?"

Good heavens. "Sammy, I told you already—"

"And I don't want to ride underwater to get there. Jade says Iceland's an island, and that it's so cold that you turn into ice the second you land."

"Jade said that?" It really feels more like a Coral thing to say. "But I told you that—"

"She said Coral saw it in her school book, and they have huge fish underwater, with teeth that have rows and rows and never stop growing."

"I have teeth in rows and rows," Axel says. "And so does Azar. How'd you like to ride with him?"

Sammy's eyes light up, but then he frowns. "But

what about Gordon? He might be sad if I ride with you. I usually ride with him."

I throw my hands up in the air. "Are you at least done packing?"

"Actually, I didn't pack at all." Sammy leans closer, putting one hand by my ear, and cupping it. His whisper's so loud that I doubt it would do any good if there was someone we didn't want to hear. "Did you know that Gordon can make me clothes? He uses magic to do it, just like he makes his clothes when he changes shape."

"Have you asked him for a light saber yet?" Axel asks. "You should tell him that you need one, and then when he's not paying attention, hit him with it as hard as you can."

"Axel Earth Blessed, how dare you?" I slap his shoulder. "Are you trying to get my little brother eaten?"

"Gordon wouldn't dare."

"So I shouldn't ask for a light saber?" Sammy looks disappointed.

"You can ask for whatever you want, as long as you don't get upset if he can't make you one," I say. "And do not, under any circumstance, hit Gordon with anything."

"He says you stabbed him," Sammy says.

"She did," Coral says, skipping through the door. "With an umbrella."

"No," I say. "With a stick." I poke Axel in the chest. "I stabbed *him* with an umbrella."

"But not here." He catches my hand and drags it up, pressing my fingers against his throat.

That makes my heart race. I drag my fingers down, but they slide across the ridge of his chest in the process, the pronounced muscles a stark contrast to the soft skin of his throat.

I swallow and force my eyes upward toward his.

His eyes are light, almost dancing. "Today, we're all moving to Iceland, and once we get settled there, your sister and I have some *training* to do." Axel's grin is practically evil.

"About what?" Coral asks.

"The nature of our bond and how it works," he says, his eyes still not leaving mine.

"But you're not bonded anymore," Coral says. "Actually, we've been talking and we aren't sure why you still come around all the time."

Axel's eyes whip toward mine with mild concern.

"It's because we *were* bonded," I say. "And now we're not, and so he's the perfect person to study it with." Please, please buy that super lame explanation.

"But what could Liz teach you?" Coral asks, her tone a little terse. "No offense, Liz, but you aren't really good at anything but fighting, and I think he's better than you at that."

"As a sister, I feel like I should teach you this. If you have to say 'no offense,' then you're probably saying something offensive. You'd be better off keeping your mouth shut," I say. "And as a matter of fact, I did teach him something already." But then I realize what it was —kissing—and I clam up.

"What was it you taught me again?" Axel asks. "I must have forgotten." He taps his mouth with his finger. "Why don't you remind me?"

Before I can say a single word, the bright sunlight streaming through the window dims, like something has moved in front of the sun. Then there's a crack of something that sounds almost like lightning, if lightning struck a thousand times in the same place. It feels like the entire world shrinks down, and then expands back out.

My brain feels battered, and I drop my face in my hands. "What was that?"

Axel's already leapt from my bed and he's running out the door.

"What's wrong?" I shout.

Stay put, and keep the kids with you.

How can he still not know me at all? I spring from the bed, pointing inside my room as I race to follow Axel.

"I know," Coral says. "Find Gideon and stay put."

I'm sprinting faster than I ever have, and I'm still falling behind. I'm not wearing my outfit, and I don't have my blades, but I know Azar's already shifting. I can sense it. I sprint up the stairs, not even slowing down to breathe. I'm just bursting through the doorway to Azar's level when I see him, poised to launch.

"Wait," I shout. "We can't be apart, remember?"

Other than the day he introduced me to all the dragons, Azar has never cared a fig for what I'm wearing. He's never even seemed to notice it. But in this moment, he scans me from head to toe, and he droops.

I'm wearing a pair of jeans and a Metallica shirt. Is that so embarrassing?

You should stay.

But I can sense that he's unsure. He probably has some indication, however dim, of what's happening, but I have no clue. I don't want to hear a story, or worse, be stuck here while he's in danger.

Get your swords.

In the weeks I've known him, one thing I've never felt from Azar is even a single iota of uncertainty. That command, terse though it was, terrifies me.

What exactly is going on?

I don't argue. I turn and hit the elevator button, and when it opens and the doors part, Jade's standing there, her enormous blue eyes wide. "You forgot these." She lugged my swords, my daggers, and the holsters for each up here.

"Thank you." And I really mean it. I was genuinely worried that Azar wouldn't be here when I got back. Could he have told me to get them as an excuse, to get me away so he could leave?

I'm not sure.

"Head back down," I say. "And—"

"Stay put. I know. Gordon and Gideon and Rufus are all there, pacing and shouting."

That's not very promising, but I don't have time to deal with it. At least I feel like Rufus and Gordon have some genuine affection for them. I know Gideon does.

None of them are power players, but if I've shown anything, it's that sometimes weak people can do amazing things in the right circumstances and with enough bravery. And that's what I'm going to try to channel today, too.

While Jade travels back down, I buckle my steel to my body. "I'm ready."

Azar, miracle of miracles, hasn't left yet.

"What's going on? What happened?"

That crack, that inversion you felt, that means more Blessed have come.

Wait. More *Blessed?* More dragons are here? From where? "More dragons are here. . .from your home?"

I've missed the last two scheduled meetings with my father, and it appears he's become impatient. He grunts. *And only the Flame Blessed can portal.*

Oh, shoot.

The Flame Blessed.

Until now, Azar has been the only Flame Blessed. He's been the uncontested superpower on earth. Nothing could touch him. Nothing could harm me. But if another Flame Blessed is here. . .

And if Azar's nervous, what does that mean?

There's only one way to find out who was sent.

I don't allow myself to fret. I don't allow myself to freak out, either. I may be weak, and I may be more of a liability than anything else, but one thing I don't do is freeze during a fight. What skill I have, I won't forget out of fear. "Let's go see who showed up on our door."

They wouldn't have come through a door. Your doors are much too small.

If Azar can make a joke, things will be alright. Surely.

But when I climb onto his back, he's stiffer than usual. His movements are blocky, almost, and I realize that this is what Azar looks like when he's nervous. I mentally downshift into the place I go before a fight, the place I go when I need my mind to be clear, and then I push that serene sense of calm outward, trying to share the tiny thing I can do with him.

Thank you.

As we launch into the sky, I notice that blue and green and brown dragons are teeming on the ground below, and electro dragons are darting and spinning around in the air outside.

"Are these ours? Or are they from elsewhere?"

Ours.

That's a relief, at least. "Where do we think the new arrivals are?"

Azar heads, unerringly, toward the George R. Brown Convention Center. *They'll be where they felt the most Blessed.*

"It seemed like a lot were near us," I say.

They're moving, he says. *But I don't want to bring them to me. I prefer to meet them.*

Smart. Basic psychology with predators: don't let them stalk you.

Exactly.

We don't bolt over there, but we don't take a circuitous route either, and within moments, we're drawing near. Like the Chase Tower, dragons are winging through the air, gathering in the courtyard below, and bellowing to one another.

But unlike at the tower, there's a bright red dragon down below. I didn't think anyone could be more beautiful than Azar—maybe he's not. But this new red dragon is substantially larger.

If Azar's the size of a whale, this new dragon's a battleship.

And he looks built for destruction.

He has twice as many horns, and when he opens his mouth to bellow at us, his teeth look bigger, sharper, and more plentiful.

We rarely kill with our teeth, Liz.

I know he's right. "You're stunning," I say. "I didn't mean anything."

Hyperion's my older brother.

Oh, geez. Family reunions are always pretty awful, but it could be worse, right?

Remember I told you that only one Blessed knows my real identity?

"The female who raised you, right?" There's a slender silver dragon right next to Hyperion, and she's all graceful lines and moonlit scales. Compared to Ocharta, she looks like a graceful ballerina. That must be her, and I can't wait to meet her.

Not only because of how Azar's spoken about her, but also because she's the only person from his past whom he doesn't seem to hate or fear. If anyone else needed to come, I can't imagine anyone better.

When we finally land, it's not next to the silver dragon or his brother. It's on the ground, near the tiny lake in front of the convention center. Kinder Lake, I think it's called.

Euphrasia. Azar's tone is so affectionate, there's no doubt in my mind that the smallish blue dragon at the edge of the lake is the Blessed who raised him. I didn't expect a water dragon, though I'm not sure why. Maybe because I've spent the least amount of time with them.

Azar. She smiles, and her already nicely shaped face lights up. *I was so delighted when your dad asked me to come.*

Earth is different than I expected, he says. *But it has some beauty, too.*

The massive red dragon hops down, hitting the ground with tremendous force and walking toward us with ponderous steps.

I see Hyperion also came. Azar sounds grim.

Your father was hoping to have heard from you by now.

I sent him two messages.

Euphrasia smirks. *The first said you were safe, and the next said you hadn't found it yet.*

With absolutely no direction or explanation other than 'retrieve the Heart,' is he really shocked it's taking time?

He had high hopes, Euphrasia says. *You know he's always boasting about you.*

Brother! Hyperion's close enough to see clearly now, and his features are fine, just like Azar's, but he's not quite as sharp somehow, like his edges were buffed or smoothed. *Father sends his regards.*

Azar sighs. *And what other orders does he send?*

Who is this? Hyperion's gaze shifts, focusing on me. *You do not look like I expected. I was told humans were small, ugly, and easily breakable.* He crouches, turning his head to the left, and then to the right, studying me from all angles. *I actually think you're kind of cute.*

Mine. Azar blows flame at his brother, a long, steady stream of it.

I crouch down low against his neck, ready for the fight. Heat doesn't bother me like it once did, but I'm not entirely immune to its effects, either.

Only, instead of rearing back or striking back, Hyperion laughs. *You haven't changed a bit.*

Azar snorts. *Neither have you. Coveting from the very second you arrive.*

Now Hyperion's really laughing, almost doubled over. I've never seen a dragon laugh quite so much. It makes me like him quite a bit more than I was prepared to, based on Azar's initial trepidation.

"Looks like things are alright?" I whisper.

You asked about Father's orders, Hyperion says. *But don't worry. It's nothing major. Asteria came with me, and Father insists you marry her and mate within the next month. He wants to see whether proximity to the Heart has fixed the problem.*

Azar just nods.

Not that you need to hear this, but it's the usual threat if you refuse. He'll call you home, strip you, and name a new heir.

Asteria.

Mate.

Marry.

The words are coming so fast that I'm having trouble keeping up. "You have to—in a month. Mate?"

Your cute little human is having trouble, Hyperion says. *Maybe they really are as delicate as they say.*

The silver dragon practically floats down, landing next to Hyperion and tilting her exceptionally beautiful head. *Where's Ocharta? Mother wanted me to pass along a message.*

Oh, no. "Who's Ocharta to you?" I know I should keep my mouth shut, but I can't help myself.

Asteria's slender head shifts toward me. Without missing a beat, she answers. *She's my older sister, and she's awful, isn't she?*

I want to hate her. I'm primed to hate her with every iota of my entire body, but how can I hate someone who's so beautiful, and who's so honest? "She really is," I say. "She ensnared my mother, or I'd already have killed her."

Hyperion's head rocks back and he absolutely roars. If I thought he was laughing hard before, I was wrong. It takes him a full minute to calm down enough to talk.

I love this human. He's talking to Azar, but he's looking at me like I'm a rare, first edition copy of *The Canterbury Tales* or something. *What do you want for her? I'll give it to you.*

Azar's nostrils flare.

Oh, calm down. No need to roast me again. I get the message. You're not ready to share. He winks at me. *Yet.*

Ever. Azar still seems unconcerned, other than about his brother's obviously intentional ribbing.

Find a tower you like, Azar says. *Since you just arrived, we'll delay our departure by a day or two, but we're about to move on a recent lead. In two days' time, we're leaving Houston and going to an island called Iceland. We believe the Heart may be hidden there in a mountain full of flame.*

Without waiting for any questions or providing any further explanation, Azar launches into the sky, flying straight back to the Chase Tower.

"That could have been worse," I say.

Much, much worse.

I breathe a sigh of relief. "And how about that weird stuff about the marriage and the mating?"

Azar shrugs. "Hardly unexpected."

I nearly fall off. "Excuse me?"

We're already landing on his floor, so I scramble off his back as quickly as possible.

"You're—it's hardly unexpected? That you have to get married and *mate* in the next month?"

Azar's head tilts, and then he melts back into Axel. "Why are you so upset?"

"Why am I upset?" I'm practically shrieking. I force myself to lower my voice. The last thing I need is for Jade and Coral and Sammy to come running up here. Or worse, Gideon.

Oh, Gideon. Right.

The bond is messing with my head. "I'm not upset." I fold my arms. "This is the best news I've ever heard." I shake my head. "Actually, better than the best. It's epic."

"Why?" Axel steps toward me like a lion tamer might sidle toward an irritable cub.

"I—because. If you're getting married, you'll hardly need to be *entwined* with me, so we can both work double hard to dissolve this stupid bond. Once we do, we can do the same thing with Mom's, and then I'll finally be free."

"Why would I do that?" Axel frowns.

"Why would you—you don't mean to—in a month —" I cough. "I can't even, I just." I jog toward the stairwell. I have to get away from him. Even though separating from him still hurts me, I have to do it.

The pain reminds me of how it feels to hear him saying he's about to *marry* someone. *My* dragon is about to *mate* with some ballerina dragon.

Ugh.

What's wrong with me? Why do I care? He's a *dragon*, for heaven's sake. I want them to leave and never return. I want our world back. Why am I doubled over in the stairwell, hyperventilating?

I block off my mind, which I've only just learned to do, unwilling to share the thoughts I'm having right now. Unwilling to allow the stupid, idiotic, block-headed dragon to feel what a loser I am.

Because the only reason I'd be this upset is if I'm in love with that horrible, earth-destroying plague of a beast. And that can't be. Not only because he's supposed to be my enemy, but also because. . .

He's going to marry some gorgeous dragon who's just like him in a month. And that thought makes me feel like my heart's being ripped out.

I can't have that.

I may be many things. A dragon rider. A dragon slayer. An MMA fighter. An older sister. A daughter. A friend. But one thing I am not. One thing I will never be: a pathetic idiot running after a man, begging him to love me.

I'd rather die.

With the way my life has been going the last few weeks, that may be my most likely option. Either that, or I may kill the greatest threat humanity has ever seen. Because I am not about to stand by and watch him marry that ballerina dragon. I'm not okay with it.

Not even one tiny bit.

Alright, I really hope you enjoyed Ensnared. It was so much fun to write, and the next book in the series is, predictably, titled Entwined. I hope you're looking forward to reading it as much as I am to writing it. It's up for preorder now, so go snag your copy so you don't forget. It's set to release in JUNE of next year, and I know that feels SO FAR AWAY!

Don't worry! It won't take that long!

I always put my preorder dates way out and then move them up. (I have five kids, two of whom I homeschool, and we have a lot of animals. Between the kids, the hubby who works out of town, the chickens, the dogs (who occasionally have puppies!), and the horses, sometimes things come up. I never want to have to bump a release back, so even though I'm aiming for January, I want to give myself time in case that turns out to be too hard.

This series will have a total of FOUR books, and I'm hoping to have them all out by the end of 2024 or shortly thereafter. You won't need to wait a long time, I promise. I'm indie, and I'm super fast.

Also, if you want to talk about the book, come join my Facebook Reader group called Bridget E Baker's Binge Readers. We have a lot of fun over there.

While you're waiting on Entwined, I've dropped in a sample chapter for another book of mine you might like. It's called My Queendom for a Horse, and it's a STALLION SHIFTER ROMANCE. Yes, you read that right. It's about a woman who buys a horse and then discovers he's actually a mage who was trapped in his horse form.

Sadly, she just made him collateral on her farm loan, so to save him will cost her family their farm... Whoops! If you like zany situations (like a horse that's crashing her dates), and a lot of great banter, you might just love it. Read on to check out the first chapter right now. (That series has several books out, so you won't be stuck waiting!) And PSST. Like all my books, it's CLEAN of language and adult content.

SAMPLE CHAPTER OF MY
QUEENDOM FOR A HORSE

I have a history of making rash decisions. You know, the kind of move that saves the day in fairy tales. Only, when I climb the beanstalk, the giant smashes me into jelly. When I ride to a ball in a carriage made of pumpkin, my gown that was sewn by rats splits up the back, and I wind up covered with pumpkin innards.

Big, bold decisions just don't end well in real life. At least, not for me.

I know this.

Which is why I ought to turn around and walk away, but I don't have much choice. It's all or nothing today, thanks to my dad and his idiot rivalry with an old university nemesis.

Well, that and his lifelong gambling problem.

And yes, it's a little hypocritical that I'm planning to fix his mistake. . .by placing a risky bet and hoping it pays out.

But I worked hard and I have faith in myself. Today's race may be a Hail Mary, in American football terms, but there are only seven horses, and Five Times

Fast is the best one. I know it. Plus, the only person my gamble might hurt is me.

If this works, I'll save the family farm we've had for ten generations. I can't even think about what happens if I lose today. If I take time to think about it, I'll start crying again. That won't help anyone.

I squeeze the wad of fifty-euro bills in my fist and force myself to take a step forward. Every step feels harder than the last. I've saved for *forever* for the down payment on my own horse hospital, but losing our farm would be even worse than delaying my dream yet again.

Finally, I reach the front of the line, but before I can say anything, someone grabs my arm and spins me around. It's the very last person in the entire world that I ever thought I'd see standing in front of me.

Sean bloody McDermott.

I haven't seen his face in person in more than ten years. It feels surreal to have his hand on my arm. He's wearing an impeccably tailored suit, like he was the day we broke up. His blonde hair looks exactly the same as it did. It's like time hasn't touched Sean. His face is unlined. His eyes are just as bright as ever. And his shoulders might even be broader.

Why am I even surprised? The aristocracy never changes. Eventually he'll gain a few grey hairs that make him look dignified, but everything else is a constant.

I hate that his appearance affects me this much, even after ten years. He dumped me, but that doesn't mean I'm still the pathetic girl I was back then. I'm a confident, capable business owner now. I need to remember that.

I wrench away and back up with so much force that I run into the window. The employee inside clears her throat.

"We have some business to handle first," Sean says smoothly, with a practiced smile on his face. "She'll come back."

He turns and starts to walk, just assuming that I'll follow after him like a good little baby duck.

Too bad, Sean. I'm not a baby duck anymore. I'm in my mid-thirties, and no one tows me around behind them.

I turn back to face the Totes employee. "I'd like to put fifty thousand euros on Five Times Fast. To win."

The Totes employee blinks. "There's a €250,000 winning limit per day in Ireland."

I shrug. "With the odds on Five, that'll be just about right."

"Kristiana." Sean's tone is terse. I wonder how far he went before he realized I wasn't following him and circled back.

"I don't have much time before I need to report for the race," I snap. "Go away and leave me alone." I start to hand the money through the window.

Sean snatches it from my hand.

"This is new," I say. "Is work not going well? You're stealing now?"

He grits his teeth, his gorgeous blue eyes flashing. "I'm trying to help you."

"Kris." My dad's voice floats toward me from several paces away.

Something in my stomach twists. "Dad?" I turn around.

"Miss, if you aren't betting. . ."

I step aside. If my dad's here with Sean, and he's not jumping in to defend me. . . Suddenly my blood runs cold. We *are* in Ireland, which is much closer to where Sean lives than I usually am, but what are the chances we'd run into him by accident?

He's a banker, not a jockey. His family still races,

but I imagine his work keeps him from trolling the racetracks every so often.

"Dad." I don't even have to ask.

I can tell he's guilty from the look on his face.

"You're in silks." My dad steps out from behind the awning that was blocking him from my view. "You fired our jockey and you're planning to ride. Aren't you?"

He's got me there. "I had to let him go. He was drinking again. His carelessness was ruining Five." And also, we couldn't afford to pay him, anyway.

Dad inhales slowly. "I know I'm the one who called him, but like you, I had no choice." He glances sideways at Sean.

"Your dad made the right call. The terms for the balloon note he showed me are just awful, and—"

My head pivots. "Go away. This doesn't concern you. It's between my dad and me."

"Kris," Sean says, "be reasonable. Your farm has been in the family for more than a hundred years, and—"

I snatch the money he just took back. "After the way you dumped me? I wouldn't dump my soda on you if you were on fire." I shake my head. "Go away, Sean. We don't need your help."

He flinches, but he nods and pivots on his heel. One thing rich Brits are excellent at is walking away without a fuss. The only thing worse for them than talking about money in public is making a scene.

"And as for you." I spin around to face my dad again. "You're the reason we're in this mess, so you don't get to question the way that I fix it. How could you call him without even asking me first?"

Dad inhales shakily. "But Kris—"

"But nothing. Go away and let me place my bet."

If he wasn't torn between chasing after Sean and

yelling at me, he might have ignored me. But as it is, Dad's already struggling with the fact that his meal ticket is practically jogging away.

The odds against Five Times Fast aren't terrible, but they aren't great either. He's not a favorite, for sure. Which means with a bet of fifty thousand, I'll make enough to pay the first balloon payment that's due next week.

Only, when I try to place the bet a second time, the woman narrows her eyes at me. "You're wearing silks."

It's her job to ask. My bright yellow silks mark me as a jockey, and jockeys can't bet against their own horse. Most jockeys don't bet at all. It's poor form, really. You run the risk of pissing off the boss, or making future employers nervous, or both.

I hand her Five Times Fast's registration papers and my passport. "I am a jockey, but I'm also the owner."

She glances at my paperwork. "You're the crazy rider-owner." She slaps her hand over her mouth.

It's not common to ride a horse you own. Usually you're a terrible rider, or you've got a terrible horse. I'm hoping to disprove that particular stereotype today. "That's me."

Owners can bet on their own horses, as long as it's to win or at least to place, so she accepts my money. "You're optimistic."

Desperate is probably the more accurate word, but saying 'optimistic' is more diplomatic. I extend my hand and she hands the papers back. She runs my money through a counting machine, shakes her head, and hands me my ticket. "Don't lose that, now. It might be worth a lot."

I really, really hope it is.

I push past dozens of people waiting to place bets. The constant noise at the racetrack is comforting in its familiarity. I try to pretend this is like any other race, but my stomach isn't buying it—it's twisting into knots. The fourth race at Down Royal, the Ladbrokes Champion Chase is the first Grade One race of the Irish steeplechase season, and it starts in thirty minutes. Ladies' day is always packed, but the beautiful weather today probably contributed to the mass of bodies.

I navigate briskly through the throng of people, jumping to the side to avoid impalement on a ridiculously long peacock feather. The best-dressed contest this year is offering a trip to Rio de Janeiro, and the women have stepped up their game accordingly. It's all part of the fun of racing, but I don't have time to look around. I need to do my final check-in and then get Five ready. It always passes in a blur, the final moments before a race. It's been seven years since I rode as a professional jockey, and I'm a little nervous to be doing it again.

At least my tall bay pony is perfect.

Five Times Fast is sleek and shiny and his feet practically float as I lead him toward the racetrack. I think he's the prettiest bay here, and he's easy to recognize with just the one small dollop of white over his front right hoof. His coat gleams and has very faint dapples. His ribs don't show, but they almost do. That's what you want with a racer, really. As fit as he can be without looking half-starved. He isn't sweating at all in spite of the workout we just finished, the warmth of the sunshine, and the anxious energy that always precedes a race in a strange place.

Five loves to race, and it shows. His ears swing right and left, but his eyes are calm. I lean my head against his, and he exhales loudly, as if to tell me he's ready. I hope he really is.

I've always felt like I understood what my horses

felt and what they wanted. I don't ask them to do anything they aren't ready for, and I never jump a horse that doesn't love it. Five Times Fast pulls eagerly toward every fence I point him at. I've been riding since before I could walk, thanks to my mom, and I've never been thrown, not once. Even when I was a professional jockey for two years, I never came out of my saddle. It earned me a rather irritating nickname.

I glance around at our competitors. There are only six horses in the race with us, for a total of seven, but they're some of the very best horses in Europe. The excitement is nearly palpable as the race with the biggest purse of the entire weekend approaches. It's not National Hunt money, but still, 125,000 euros attracts some attention.

Earl Grey, a clever name for the grey gelding next to me, is favored heavily to win. He's larger than Five Times Fast, but he looks nervous. He didn't travel far enough to look that nervous—fifty kilometers to our three thousand. His rider's also a grade A jerk. Jackson Buley doesn't even make eye contact with me. If I lose today, I really really hope it's not to him.

Persnickety, a bay gelding to my right, shifts from one hoof to the other repeatedly and his ribs are a little too prominent. They're working him too hard. I bob my head at his jockey, Natalie Coolie. There aren't many female jockeys, and it makes me smile that there's another in the Ladbrokes Chase. I don't really know her, though. She started a few years after I retired officially to focus on my veterinary practice.

In It To Win It is a nut-brown gelding who was favored to win last year. He's back this year, and his owner, a twenty-year-old IT millionaire from America, has been emailing me. Odds are against him, but that's what makes chasing fun. The odds don't always mean very much. In It

To Win It's sweating a little more than I'd like if he was my mount, but sometimes the nervous sweaters win. I don't know his jockey, a young man who looks quite dashing in his red silks. I raise my hand and he salutes back.

"Hey Sticky," a familiar voice behind me says.

I turn to see Finn McGee, resplendent even in his traitorous green and blue silks, walking toward the starting line. He doesn't like Rickets much more than I do, but he can't afford to snub the owner of the wealthiest barn in Europe. Finn's the most successful jockey in Ireland, maybe in the entire UK, but he still has to make a living. I've known him for years now, so he doesn't intimidate me like he used to. I should've properly greeted him—I should pay attention to my old friend. But he can't possibly blame me. I can barely squeak out any words at all.

"Hey, Finn," I manage to say.

Given the beast he's leading, he'll understand my distraction.

His horse is entirely ebony, a stallion I notice, not the typical steeplechase gelding retired from a career on the flat. His coat and mane shine like a reflection on water. His eyes flash. His hooves strike the ground sharply with cracks, like flint on steel.

I don't think I've ever seen a more beautiful horse.

He's also monstrously tall, a good hand taller than Five Times Fast, and Five's just above sixteen hands. "What the devil are you riding?"

"Aptly worded question." He grins. "His papered name is Obsidian Devil. It'll be our first real ride together. Forrest hates him, and I guess we'll find out why Rickets is willing to defy the best trainer in the country. He picked him up in Russia, of all places."

Forrest Smithers is arguably the best trainer in

England. If he hates this black beauty, he must have a reason. But he has managed Rickets' stable for a decade or so, and I know Rickets trusts his opinion—he'd be a fool not to—so it's strange to hear that they don't agree on something.

"I always heard vodka was the only good thing to come out of Russia."

Finn winks at me. "It may still be."

Obsidian paws the ground and snorts heavily. His mane shimmers, and I want to touch it so badly that my hands practically itch. As though he's similarly affected, Finn reaches over to pat his neck, but Obsidian snaps at him.

Finn snatches his hand back and shakes his head at me. "I've never seen a more ill-mannered horse," he says, "and that's saying something. The good news is, I negotiated a bonus that's actually more like a small fortune in exchange for riding him."

On impulse, I lean forward and place my free hand on Obsidian Devil's magnificent muzzle. Even with my riding gloves on, a zing runs through my entire body. Obsidian calms immediately and presses his face gently into my palm.

"He likes you?" Finn rolls his eyes. "Of course he does. Every horse on the planet loves you. It's so unfair."

Five tosses his head jealously, and I step back from Finn's magnificent creature. As soon as I move my hand, Obsidian snaps at Finn again. I can't help laughing.

"Forrest should be paying you two small fortunes," I say. "I don't envy your ride today." But that's a complete lie. I want to ride him so badly I could cry.

Five tosses his head again, which is unlike him. If

horses could scowl, he'd be scowling at Obsidian. As it is, he's stuck flaring his nostrils and stamping.

"It's okay, boy," I whisper. "He may be beautiful, but you're gorgeous too, and you're much better behaved. I still love you the most. Now, make sure you run your heart out today. Mom put all her money on you. I'm utterly *doomed* if we lose, and that Obsidian is making me very nervous."

Obsidian's ears flick my direction while I'm speaking to Five, and I have the most uncomfortable feeling that he's listening to me. I shake it off. Horses are intuitive, yes, and I believe they understand far more than we give them credit for, but there's no way he could even hear me whispering from here, much less understand the words I'm using. I scratch underneath Five's forelock, and he leans his head against me and sighs.

"It's you and me, Five. We can do this. We *have* to do this, or I'll lose the farm." I snort. "No pressure."

I've just mounted when Sean shows up again.

"You aren't supposed to be over here," I hiss. "We're about to be called up."

"A win here is temporary," Sean says. "I can loan you whatever you need and give you real time to repay it."

"Please go," I say. "Now."

But he isn't giving up as easily this time. He sets his jaw, like he's determined to be some kind of superhero, coming boldly to my rescue. He drops his voice even lower. "I know racing still scares you. It's not worth the risk."

"You're a little late to start caring about me." I roll my eyes. "It's been a decade. Or were you stuck in some kind of stasis all this time?"

I swear, at that exact moment, Obsidian Devil snorts. The timing is so perfect, that I almost believe for a moment that he's paying attention to our inter-change and that he understands it. He's also dancing around a lot less than he was—and maybe it's because Finn's finally on his back, but it feels like it's because he's listening in.

I'm going crazy.

Sean's brow furrows. "I know I screwed up, but I'm here now."

"I don't need you here," I say. "Not anymore." I urge Five forward.

Sean starts after me, clearly not dropping anything.

Obsidian lunges forward at the same time, nearly running Sean over.

Then they call for us to enter the track. Sean finally grits his teeth and walks away. A moment later, when they call us to approach the tape, Five prances up perfectly, prettily even. Obsidian's chomping at the bit and dancing left and then right like a drunk bumble-bee. It's even worse than it was before, on the ground, and I can't help laughing.

"It's not funny, Sticky. Knock it off." Finn's smile belies his gruff words. We circle up and move toward the tape in an inconsistent bunch, the horses shying and head-tossing as they move forward. As always, my jittery nerves fade away when they finally release us. I know what Five Times Fast is capable of, and I'm ready to help him win.

We pull ahead quickly at the beginning. Five did quite well with flat racing. If he didn't jump quite so beautifully, I might have kept him there, but as we approach the first jump, his timing's perfect.

He's ready to win this.

He sails effortlessly over the first fence and heads into the bend in perfect position, a full length ahead of the other horses. The cool November air streams past my face as we clear the next fence and round the bend to the ditch. From the corner of my eye, Earl Grey's bearing down hard on the inside. When we reach the ditch, he's only half a length behind me, so I push Five toward the inside and Earl Grey falters on the ditch.

We pull ahead again.

Five and I sail over the fourth and fifth fences and into the downhill jump on the sixth, just as I planned. We're rounding the turn toward the stands when a pounding sound has me glancing to the outside, just in time to see Finn's salute as he and his monster fly past me.

I could scream with frustration.

Five can't pick up that much speed, not going into the seventh and eighth fences, which are brutal. I hope maybe, just maybe, Obsidian will botch things, going so fast over the fences, but he doesn't. He clears them with nearly a foot to spare. I've never seen anything like it. The crowd's going wild. Finn's always been an attention monger, but this is shaping up to look very, very bad for me. I try not to think about the fifty thousand pounds I'm about to lose, not to mention the purse money.

I lean down near Five's neck. I don't use a whip on him—never have. "Come on boy, I know you're really flying, but I need a little more. We've gotta beat that big bully or we lose the farm. You can do it. I know you can. Let's stay as close as we can, and at the end we'll really push, okay?" I pat his neck, and I swear Five bobs his head. Horses understand me, and I under-stand them. If Five can possibly win this for me today, he will.

We gain on Obsidian on the long stretch between eight and nine, and pull up until we're almost neck and neck.

I look Finn in the eye and he winks. That jerk winks at me. Like he knew Obsidian would eat Five for breakfast. He whips Obsidian once as we approach the ninth fence, and Obsidian's ears flatten. The black stallion clearly hates the crop.

Some horses don't mind a tap now and again—it encourages them, letting them know when to move. I've rarely used it, because my horses understand me. I only race horses that love to run. But for most jockeys, it's an invaluable communication tool.

Finn should already have known that Obsidian hated it, but clearly he didn't. After we clear the ninth fence, he uses it again. Obsidian actually slows down, and we pull even with them. I smile broadly at Finn.

He scowls back at me. He has the faster horse. He should beat me. But he doesn't know his horse like he should.

We both clear the first ditch on the second loop, Five and I on the inside, and Obsidian giving us a wide enough berth that it almost feels like he's being polite.

After the second ditch, with only five fences to go, I lean down and croon in Five's ear. "You can do it, boy. You can pull ahead. I know you can beat that evil, black beast." My sweet pony hunkers down and runs, putting everything he has into it.

He's tired, though.

He clips the fence on fifteen and nearly stumbles. Obsidian pulls ahead.

An entire length ahead.

Five's giving me everything he has. . .but it isn't enough.

I don't want him hurt—I can't stand the thought of that—so I pat Five's neck. "It's okay. You're magnificent, but if he beats you, it's okay."

Nothing's okay.

If we lose, I lose everything. My life savings, my family farm.

Maybe even Five.

Tears stupidly well up in my eyes. As we clear the sixteenth fence on a downhill incline, Obsidian's three full horse lengths ahead. Even if Finn screws up, we can't catch him.

I've lost.

Everything.

Then inexplicably, with one fence to go, Obsidian slows. Finn's whipping him, but it doesn't seem to matter. Five and I race alongside him. Five pulls around on the outside, clears the last jump, and puts on every bit of speed he has. We fly past Obsidian, and I swear he bobs his head at me when we pass him to win by a nose.

Obsidian pulled back and let us win.

I'm sure of it.

A *horse* let me win. A *horse* just granted us a stay of execution.

I can hardly hear myself think for all the cheering, the loudest of which is coming from my father. The world feels crazy and confusing, but when I see his smile, I know everything's okay.

**I f you liked that, you can grab it now on any platform, in audio, in ebook, or in paperback! My Queendom for a Horse

ACKNOWLEDGMENTS

Thank you to my readers for their excitement and support, especially those of you in the Bridget E Baker Binge Reader Facebook Group. I love you all!

Thank you to my husband and my kids, who let me write this book in seven days. YOU are AMAZING. Thanks for being so supportive.

And thanks to my editor Carrie, who helped clean up the mess of a book that was written in a week. HA!

Thanks to my ARC team for their excitement and their help spotting pernicious typos.

Big thanks to Axel, because he would not SHUT UP and so this book finally, after more than seven years, jumped the line and got told.

And thanks to Kat B. and my other fans who never gave up on me, even though I kept putting off the dragon story I first had back in 2016.

ABOUT THE AUTHOR

I have animals coming out of my ears. Seven horses. Three dogs, three cats, thirty-ish chickens. I'm always doctoring or playing with an animal… and I wouldn't want it any other way. But Leo (my palomino) is still my very favorite.

When I'm not with animals, or even if I am, I'm likely to have at least one of my five kids in tow, two of which I'm currently homeschooling.

My hubby is the reason all this glorious madness is possible. He's the best parts of all the amazing men I write (although he's bald and his six pack sometimes goes into hiding because of cookies.)

I also love to bake, like to cook, and feel amazing when I find time to kickbox, lift weights, or rollerblade. Oh yeah, and I'm a lawyer, but I try to forget that whenever I can.

I adore my husband, and I love my God.

The rest is just details.

Capsized (4)

The Sins of Our Ancestors Series:

Marked (1)

Suppressed (2)

Redeemed (3)

Renounced (4)

Reclaimed (5) a novella!

A stand alone YA romantic suspense:

Already Gone

I also write women's fiction and contemporary romance under B. E. Baker.

The Scarsdale Fosters Series:

Seed Money

Nouveau Riche

The Finding Home Series:

Finding Grace (1)

Finding Faith (2)

Finding Cupid (3)

Finding Spring (4)

Finding Liberty (5)

Finding Holly (6)

Finding Home (7)

Finding Balance (8)

Finding Peace (9)

The Finding Home Series Boxset Books 1-3

The Finding Home Series Boxset Books 4-6

The Birch Creek Ranch Series:

The Bequest

The Vow

The Ranch

The Retreat

The Reboot

The Surprise

The Setback

The Lookback

Children's Picture Book

Yuck! What's for Dinner?

9 781949 655742